Kimberley Freeman was born in London in 1970. She worked as a musician for a number of years, both as a classical singer and in pop bands, before turning her hand to writing. She has published numerous books under the name Kim Wilkins. Her novel *Duet* was published in 2007. Kimberley lives in Brisbane with her husband and two young children.

Also by Kimberley Freeman

Duet
Wildflower Hill

GOLD DUST

KIMBERLEY FREEMAN

Dedicated to K, D, M & K
for a decade of wisdom, and a lifetime to come

hachette
AUSTRALIA

First published in Australia and New Zealand in 2008
by Hachette Australia
(an imprint of Hachette Australia Pty Limited)
Level 17, 207 Kent Street, Sydney NSW 2000
www.hachette.com.au

This edition published in 2011

10 9 8 7 6 5 4 3 2 1

Copyright © Kimberley Freeman 2008

This book is copyright. Apart from any fair dealing for the purposes of private study, research, criticism or review permitted under the *Copyright Act 1968*, no part may be stored or reproduced by any process without prior written permission. Enquiries should be made to the publisher.

National Library of Australia
Cataloguing-in-Publication data

Freeman, Kimberley.
  Gold dust / Kimberley Freeman.
  2nd ed.

  978 0 7336 2384 4 (pbk.).

A823.4

Cover design by Christabella Designs
Cover photograph courtesy of Getty Images
Text design by Bookhouse, Sydney
Typeset in 12.4/16.2 pt Adobe Garamond

He who remembers old wrongs may lose an eye; he who forgets them will surely lose both.

Poverty is cunning.

Russian proverbs

PROLOGUE
Winter, 2005

Of course she was anxious. She had never planned a murder before.

It had taken a long time for the whirr of blackbird wings in her head to settle enough that she could think straight. But now she had arrived at this moment, it was time to work out how she was going to do it.

She had fought her battles against guilt, fear, anger and a white-hot sense of injustice. Now she had to be cool-headed. No turning back, only going forwards.

The morning sun strained her sleepless eyes. It skimmed across the back of the armchair, highlighted dust on the TV unit. Her gaze was drawn to the photograph of the three women. Her own face. Her victim's face. Smiling. Their companion looked more serious; what had she been thinking? A glimpse of the future perhaps? In the photograph, the snow and the sunshine had bleached away shadows. The three of them had their arms slung around each other. *Nothing will ever come between us.* They had said that to each other so often. She called to mind just how many things *had* come between them. Cruel betrayals, seething anger, painful jealousies, and the ordinary variety of carelessness that can lead anyone, unwitting, to devastating consequences.

She sat on the arm of the chair, dropping her face into her hands. Steeling herself. She hadn't the stomach for violence, nor the focus for mixing poisons. If an accident could be arranged . . .

The answer was remarkably simple when it came. Winter Gathering was in Briggsby this year. The cliff path was a favourite route for all of them. Twenty-five metres below were rocks, the sea. She experienced a giddy rush of vertigo, as though the ground were slipping away from the arches of her own feet. She pushed her toes firmly into her shoes to combat the feeling.

A fall, a tragic accident. Then it would be over, and she would remain standing, alone.

Alone. The word was like a bell tolling on a distant hilltop. She felt her own sense of loneliness, the empty despair that had lately imbued her life. There was no way she could back out of the murder now. It was the only thing that could right these wrongs.

And so, despite their shared blood, their shared dreams and their shared sins, she turned her thoughts towards the unthinkable.

I

CHAPTER ONE
Leningrad, 1976

'You are not beautiful.'

Sofi Chernova leaned her seven-year-old face close to the corroded bathroom mirror. Her mother had not intended for her words to be cruel, only matter-of-fact.

'You are not beautiful, Sofi. Not like your cousins,' Mama had said as she cleared away the breakfast dishes in the communal kitchen that morning. 'But you have a good brain, and that counts for something. When they get themselves into trouble, they will need you to help them out.'

But now, studying herself in the gloomy bathroom, the compliment about her cleverness was forgotten. Instead, she counted freckles, studied large flared nostrils, traced a finger along lips that seemed determined to turn down at the corners even if she smiled. No, she wasn't beautiful. She wondered what benefits beautiful people acquired in life that she wouldn't. She'd never given much thought to it, but beauty was arriving this afternoon in the form of her two cousins, Natalya and Lena.

A thunderous knock at the door. 'Will you be in there forever?'

This was Papa, who had been tense for a week. Ever since the letter came from his brother asking if he could take care of the two girls for three months. Mama and Papa wouldn't speak about his tension in front of her, but she had picked up shreds of ideas and – thanks to her clever brain – formed a clear picture of what was going on. Uncle Viktor and Papa didn't get along. Natalya and Lena's mother had died giving birth to Lena nearly six years ago. Since then, Viktor had off-loaded his daughters to relatives and friends all over the Soviet Union. Now it was Sofi's family's turn.

Sofi didn't mind so much. She had met her cousins twice before, at their grandmother's house in Izhevsk, at family gatherings so large that everybody and nobody supervised their wild games. Marching in circles around the lightning-struck birch whistling the Soviet national anthem, scrambling over the rocks behind the garden pretending to be cosmonauts on the moon, nursing their grandmother's fat ginger cat as though it were a baby, and threading the stalks of dandelion clocks through the chain-link fence so that the wind could carry away the seeds, while they wished and wished so hard that their chests hurt afterwards.

Papa knocked again, and Sofi climbed down from the stool she used to reach the enamelled basin and opened the door. 'Sorry, Papa.'

She emerged into the dim sitting room. The radio was on low: barely audible voices, an interview with a farmer whose chickens had laid so many eggs that he had been declared a Soviet hero. Mama had cleaned the apartment. The red-and-white-checked cloth was smoothed over the table, dust had been lifted off the sideboard and the mismatched armchairs, the cushions on the sofa had been plumped and arranged so that the embroidered kittens and swans were facing out, and the curtains had been pinned open as far as possible. Sofi loved the few hours after the apartment was cleaned. There was a sense of expectation in the air, as gentle yet as unmistakable as the scent of furniture polish.

Sofi went to the window. It looked directly across at the next apartment block, but in the space between the two buildings she could see down to the street. Summer rain, rainbow pools of leaked car oil on the uneven pavement, umbrellas moving like cumbersome beetles. A car pulled up, a dinted beige monster that miraculously fitted in the gap between a garbage truck and a belching bus that waited for damp passengers to climb aboard. The doors opened and her uncle and cousins climbed out.

'They're here!' she said to Mama.

Mama joined her at the window, her mouth set in a firm line. 'Ah, so they are.' She turned Sofi's face to hers gently. 'You take the little girls into your room, show them where they will sleep, keep them occupied with a game. Papa and I need to speak about important things with Uncle Viktor. Understand?'

Sofi nodded. 'Does the building superintendent know they're coming? Will he let them in?'

'Yes, and we have permission for them to stay.' She moved to the bathroom door and knocked quietly. 'Ivan, it's time.'

They were wet when they came in the apartment's front door. Lena, long hair dripping, wore a mournful expression. Natalya, whose chestnut curls still gleamed despite the damp, was impatient with her sister, calling her horse-face and skidding her suitcase along the floor with her foot. Behind them loomed Uncle Viktor, handsome but dark and sallow, and reeking of tobacco and vodka. Sofi did as she was told and took her cousins with her into her bedroom.

It had been a squeeze to get in the two thin mattresses, one parallel to Sofi's bed and the other arranged so that its corner had to be lifted for the door to open fully. Mama had left space for Sofi's art tray, her paints and her boxes of beads. She looked forward to sharing the space. All of her friends at school had siblings, and were crowded on top of each other. It sounded like fun. Though she did wonder how she was going to pull up a chair next to her art tray with the mattresses in the way.

'This is your bed, Lena,' Sofi said, leading the little girl to the mattress next to her own bed.

'I don't like it,' Lena said, shaking her head.

Natalya pushed Lena onto the other mattress. 'She can see under your bed from there,' she explained. 'Monsters. She'd never sleep and we'd never hear the end of it. Go, Lena, have that bed instead. I'm not afraid of monsters.'

As if to prove it, Natalya stored her suitcase under Sofi's bed and crashed onto the mattress with a sigh and a toss of her pretty hair. Lena propped her suitcase up against the art tray, and sat down on her mattress to pull off her muddy boots gingerly. Outside the bedroom door, Sofi could hear adult voices, urgent, rapid. But not a word was clear to her.

Lena had already found Trushka, Sofi's raggedy-cat doll, and was making her drink imaginary milk from a tea-set dish. Soon, all adult seriousness was forgotten as they drew the blind and Trushka was forced to confront the monsters under Sofi's bed – this made Lena laugh and cry in equal measure – until they were squealing and giggling, damp-cheeked.

Then a sharp, rasping voice cut through their merriment. It was Uncle Viktor. 'Don't tell me how to raise my girls!'

Placating tones, and the conversation continued, dull now. Sofi glanced from Lena's face to Natalya's. Both were frozen, uncertain.

Then the door cracked open and Mama stood there, a forced smile on her lips. 'Lena, Natalya. Come out and say goodbye to your father.'

Lena's mouth turned upside down and she began to sob. 'But Papa said he'd stay a week with us.'

The tight expression returned to Mama's face. 'He's decided it would be best if he got away earlier. He has a long trip ahead of him.'

'Where is he going?' Sofi asked.

'Vladivostok, for a job,' Natalya said with a sniff.

'A very important one,' Lena added.

Uncle Viktor joined Mama at the bedroom door. 'Well, now, you girls. Behave yourselves. None of your nonsense. Lena, wipe your nose. A man has to work; your tears make me feel guilty.'

Lena scrambled to her feet and clung to his waist. Viktor glanced away, patting her shoulder lightly. 'There, there. Aunt Stasya will look after you. Nothing to cry about. I'll be home in time for your birthday.'

Natalya hung back, trying hard to look brave, defiant. Sofi knew it was a performance. She felt so glad to be in her own home, with her own mother and father, and decided that beauty was not a charm for good fortune after all.

Before Natalya and Lena's arrival, Sofi's childhood had been quiet. Almost sedate. But now the tiny apartment was filled with noise and long hair and elbows. Sofi's feelings about the new situation changed from hour to hour. Sometimes she loved it: there were games and laughter. Sometimes she just wanted to sit down, shut them out and draw. Her cousins did their best to fit in to the new family routine, though Natalya's approach to chores was slapdash to say the least.

Every Saturday night was games night. Usually Mama, Papa and Sofi played their favourite card game – The Fool – on a folding table set up near the bathroom door with a blanket on the top so the cards couldn't slip away. This Saturday, the first since the cousins' arrival, Papa invited Natalya and Lena to sit up with them and play.

'I'm sure your father has taught you this one,' Papa said, carefully removing the low cards from the deck.

Lena, at mention of her father, went mirror-eyed with sadness.

Natalya shrugged. 'He didn't teach us anything, Uncle Ivan.'

Papa frowned and dealt the cards. 'Is that so? We always played it as children. I'm surprised he didn't pass it on.'

He began to explain the rules. Lena looked blank and Natalya's brow furrowed with concentration. Sofi picked up her cards and looked at them: a mediocre hand; she began to strategise.

'So, Lena,' Papa said, 'you go first.'

Lena stared at her hand, then ventured to put out an ace in the trump suit.

'Not that one, silly,' Sofi said.

Lena's hand collapsed, her lip began to quiver. Papa pulled her into his lap and kissed the top of her head. 'I think this one is too little to play,' he said. 'Here, Lena, you can share my hand.'

Natalya went next, with a six of diamonds. Sofi defended with an eight of diamonds. Natalya played a seven of hearts. Sofi defended with a six of spades.

'That's lower,' Natalya protested.

'It's a trump,' Sofi explained.

'What does that mean?'

A brief argument ensued. Natalya was concerned that everyone had seen her cards now and the game was no longer fair. Papa shuffled and dealt again. This game proceeded more smoothly. Sofi was the first one to hand in all her cards. Natalya looked as though she would be the last, the Fool, but then Mama played the wrong card.

'Oh, is that the trump suit? How silly! I really do deserve to be the Fool,' she said, as Natalya played a ten of hearts and Mama had nothing left to defend with.

Sofi knew Mama had lost the game on purpose so that Natalya wouldn't. The irritation itched in her stomach. Her parents had never, *not once*, played badly to let her win. Papa always insisted she had to think things through, pay attention; he had even encouraged her to count the cards in her head to deduce what might be left. If she lost, she lost. She was the Fool. And here was Mama making a mistake as silly as the one Lena had made.

On the next hand, Papa leaned over Natalya and showed her which cards to play. Natalya struggled and struggled with the rules, remembering sometimes and forgetting others. After four hands, Papa suggested it was time to pack up.

'But we usually play until eight o'clock!' Sofi protested.

Natalya had already shot away from the table, and Lena was gratefully climbing down from Papa's lap.

'Hush, my child,' Mama said softly, stroking her hair. 'Things are a little different at the moment, that's all. You must understand.'

An urge to cry overwhelmed her. Her cousins had only been here a week and everything was different. She had to share her room, her toys and her parents. And now games night was ruined. 'I don't want to understand,' Sofi said. 'I just want to play cards.'

Mama glanced at Natalya and Lena on the sofa, heads bent together, giggling, then back at Sofi. She crooked a finger and beckoned Sofi to come with her to the bathroom, where they would be out of earshot. She sat on the edge of the bath and held Sofi between her knees.

Her voice echoed softly. 'Lena and Natalya have no mother. Their father is far away. They have lived in a dozen different homes. We must be kind to them.'

'But what about me? What about games night?'

'Perhaps we'll do it again sometime. Or you and I can play quietly together. But it's not right to make your cousins feel lost and foolish. Their lives are already so uncertain.' Mama grasped Sofi's wrists softly, pulled her hands to her lips and kissed her knuckles. 'I still love you as much as I always have.'

Sofi felt a tear pop out and roll down her cheek.

'Papa does too,' Mama said.

Sofi nodded.

Mama stood, pulling her close. Sofi buried her face in the hollow between her mother's breasts, breathed the warm scent of her. She tried to understand, and promised to be kinder in her thoughts towards her cousins.

That summer was particularly humid. Lena found the nights unbearable. With the window to the bedroom closed, she would perspire until her sheets were wringing wet. But to open the window was to let in the mosquitoes and midges that bred in the swamps around the city. She knew she shouldn't scratch the bites, but she couldn't help herself, knocking the tops off them until they bled. Then Aunt Stasya would order the window be closed and the sweat would sting the wounds, and Natalya would roll her eyes and call her a baby for scratching.

Apart from that, she liked staying in Leningrad. Aunt Stasya was kind, and Uncle Ivan – who looked a lot like Papa – was a reassuring presence. Sofi made up the best games, and Natalya didn't pick on her so much when there were three of them. Every Thursday afternoon, Aunt Stasya worked late at her job in the bakery. Uncle Ivan took the three girls walking and she came to know the wide avenues of Leningrad, its overgrown gardens, its vast grey public squares decorated with bright red splashes of Soviet banners and posters, and its sour-smelling canals. She admired with awe the gleaming cupola of St Isaac's Cathedral and the many statues of Soviet heroes, especially one of Lenin with his resolute face and swirling coat. Uncle Ivan bought them ice-creams in square cones to eat outside on the street while he went into a bar and had a drink or two with friends. Then they would make their way back in the endless afternoon, to eat huge bowls of fresh *pelmeni* that their elderly neighbour, Irina Petrovna, had cooked in the communal kitchen while they were away.

But Lena did not forget that Papa would be back soon, and secretly counted down every day on the calendar hung on the back of the bathroom door. Papa had said he would be home in time for her birthday, August the nineteenth, and she marked off the days with her eyes, anticipation tight in her chest.

When Aunt Stasya tucked her in the night before her birthday, Lena was almost too excited to sleep.

'Your birthday tomorrow, little one,' Aunt Stasya said, smoothing her hair away from her forehead. 'Six years old. Such a big girl.'

Lena loved Aunt Stasya's hair, which was fair and thick and always bundled up in a knot at the back of her neck. She reached for it impulsively, loosening a strand to twine between her fingers.

'I'm looking forward to Papa coming home,' she said.

Aunt Stasya smiled, but it wasn't her usual easy smile. The first tingle of alarm touched Lena's heart. 'I'm sure it will be a lovely day,' her aunt said, climbing to her feet.

Lena watched her go to Natalya's mattress, then to Sofi's bed; she always lingered the longest there, stopping to sing a lullaby with a haunting tune: '*Bayushki bayu*'. The dim room, the faraway sounds of cars beyond the windows, Aunt Stasya's melancholy voice – all of it impressed itself deeply upon her, and she *longed* for Papa's warm arms and gruff voice. She felt dislocated, a long way from home, and, remembering Aunt Stasya's strained smile, began to worry that Papa wouldn't come for her.

She tried to reassure herself. He had made a promise, he wouldn't let her down. But then she remembered all the times he *had* let her down. She had never noticed before: she was small, he was Papa. Perhaps she was old enough now to see him as fallible; all of the little disappointments he had wrought returned to mind. Selling her bicycle to pay a debt, the countless times he had been late to pick her up from the babysitter, the hurried goodbyes at another relative's house for another long separation.

Since they had been staying with Aunt Stasya and Uncle Ivan, Papa had not been in contact. It was true that she could barely read a letter, and that there was no telephone. But usually he sent a cheerful card with a few words on the back, renewing promises to arrive on a certain date and to bring presents (which were always lost in transit).

As Aunt Stasya left the room and shut the door, pulling all the light out with her, Lena wondered for the first time, with a desolate hollowness, whether Papa would be back at all.

The sun was weak outside the curtains, but it was definitely morning. Lena stretched her mind back as far as she could, but she couldn't remember turning five. Today, she was six, a terribly big number that made her feel tall, and a little frightened. She tried to guess what time Papa would arrive, and if she would seem noticeably bigger to him. Over breakfast, she imagined what he might say. 'Lena, you're as long as I can remember,' was always one of his favourite complaints if she had her legs stretched out across the sofa or under the table. Perhaps he would say that. Imagining it made her feel safe: if she could hear it in her mind so clearly, then it would probably happen. He would come, he would say it, all would be well. In no time they would be packing their suitcases and heading home – wherever that would be – with Papa.

Uncle Ivan and Aunt Stasya went to work, but the girls were home for the school holidays. Irina Petrovna from next door came over to watch them. She brought Lena a gift, a packet of coloured pens and a little notebook with stiff white pages. Lena thanked her, kissed her cheek (avoiding the stubbly mole near her ear), and returned to the window. She had pulled up a seat and now knelt on it, watching for Papa.

After lunch, Sofi tried to encourage her to come down and play.

'No, thank you,' Lena said, eyes not leaving the road. If she kept watching, he would come. If she looked away, even for a moment, her lack of faith might somehow make him dissolve, disappear.

By four o'clock, Natalya had grown impatient with her. 'Will you get down from there?' she said, pulling Lena's hair hard.

'No. Then I won't see Papa.'

Natalya stormed off, and Lena knew it was because Natalya was frightened Papa wouldn't come.

Aunt Stasya came home with a pie from the bakery with Lena's name and age carved into the crust. Uncle Ivan brought with him a present, a tambourine wrapped in lilac paper as pale as the summer evening outside. Reluctantly, she was coaxed away from the window to eat under the dusty hanging light in the communal kitchen. But after dinner, she returned to her position. By now, the twitch under her skin had become acute.

He *would* come. Wouldn't he?

She knew that Aunt Stasya and Uncle Ivan were murmuring about her behind her back. She knew that Natalya was hiding in the bedroom, that Sofi was making a show of reading a book while she secretly stole pitying glances at Lena. But Lena kept believing. If she couldn't believe in Papa, then what could she believe in?

The evening light went on forever. Finally, Aunt Stasya approached her. 'Lena,' she said.

Lena turned, had trouble keeping her mouth right side up.

'It's time for bed.'

'I would like to wait up, just a little longer, and see Papa when he comes.'

Aunt Stasya looked at Uncle Ivan, who stood and moved towards Lena, an expression of sadness on his brow. Then he stopped in the space between them and squared off his shoulders. 'Lena,' he said in a very stern voice, 'your aunt has given you instruction. Do as you're told and go to bed at once.'

All the sadness in the world welled up inside her. Shuddering sobs in her chest. Tears spilling over and running down her cheeks. She cried like a baby. Aunt Stasya put warm arms around her, tried to shush her. Uncle Ivan grabbed his key from the hook by the door and left the apartment. She couldn't imagine how she had made him so angry. Lena pressed her hot face into her aunt's soft cotton shirt and called her papa silently, over and over. Knowing he would never hear her.

CHAPTER TWO

Seven weeks after Papa had gone missing – Natalya liked to think of him as being missing rather than having simply run away – the first of the cold winds of autumn began the business of stripping bare the lime trees along their street. The small round leaves gathered in the courtyard of the apartment building, rotting in the moulded corners. The girls were playing outside, having been thrown out of the apartment for being rowdy.

Lena heard a car engine and climbed on top of the courtyard's brick wall to see who it was. Natalya knew that Lena thought it was Papa; that every car, every footstep, every letter collected in the mailbox raised her hopes anew. Natalya could not bear her sister's hope and disappointment. Unlike Lena, she knew that Papa was not a good man, or an important one. He had gone to Vladivostock to work the fisheries; he had probably liked being shed of his paternal responsibility, and now he wasn't coming back. Papa was gone, it was easier to accept that. Natalya didn't like to feel unhappy, so she didn't think about it, and grew increasingly irritated with Lena for wanting to talk about it constantly.

Sofi sat on the bench – carefully avoiding the loose bolt that poked up through the wood – creating a necklace fit for a princess. Because that was what Natalya was in this game: an American princess, who lived in a palace and starred in movies about her life. Natalya put the finishing touches to her castle, which consisted of old sheets tied to the back of the gate and secured on the legs of the bench. Sofi held up her creation and Natalya gasped with pleasure.

'It's beautiful!' she said, eager fingers reaching for it. It was made of wool and plastic beads, but it was deliciously perfect for a princess: an intricate interweaving of strands, knotted and beaded in gradated colours.

'Let me put it on you,' Sofi said, standing up to fasten it around Natalya's neck. Natalya held her long hair out of the way while Sofi's clever fingers did their work.

'Look, Lena,' Natalya called.

Lena climbed down from the wall and joined them. 'It's pretty, Sofi. Can I have one too?'

'I only have odd-coloured beads left,' Sofi replied. 'Maybe Natalya will let you wear it later.'

'Only if we play American princesses all afternoon, and I get to be the princess and you are the servants.'

Lena bristled. 'I don't want to be a servant.'

'It's only a game,' Sofi said, giving Lena a good-natured shove. 'Come on.'

They fell into play, inside and outside the castle. The afternoon shadows grew long too quickly now, and the pressure of time's passing made their game frantic, stupid, giggly. Natalya could hear her own voice grow raucous as she shouted imperious commands at her two servants. Eventually, a window opened in the building above them and a red-faced man called out for them to be quiet.

After he'd shut his window, Sofi turned to Natalya soberly. 'Let's not annoy him. He's an official with the district Party committee.'

But it was almost impossible for Natalya to be quiet when she was a princess. Ten minutes later the red-faced man appeared at the gate to the courtyard. As he pushed it open, the castle collapsed and Natalya suddenly found her own sobriety. Her face was hot.

The red-faced man stood in front of them, his hairy forearms folded across his belly. Natalya smiled at him brilliantly; her secret weapon. Most people softened towards her as soon as she smiled, but not this man.

'I have been listening to you girls,' he said, scowling, 'and I am ashamed of what I have heard. America? Princesses? Do you not know that princesses grow fat on the blood of workers? You are not princesses, and girls who are not princesses do not survive long in the capitalist paradise they dream of. They are bought and sold by wicked men. Shame on you, all of you. I will let the building superintendent know that you've violated house rules by disturbing your neighbours. Pack up this silly game and go home.'

Lena burst into tears, and Sofi quickly untied the sheets and folded them. But Natalya was frozen with anger. How dare he ruin their game?

'Come on, Natalya,' Sofi said.

Lena pulled her hand. 'Natalya? Can I wear the necklace now?'

The red-faced man was still watching them. 'Not now, Lena,' Natalya muttered, taking the sheets from Sofi and bundling them under her arm. 'Aunt Stasya needs help with dinner. We should go.'

As she entered the dim staircase, though, her imagination returned to the fantasy of never having to help with dinner or set a table, of necklaces made of gems rather than beads, and palaces that Party officials could never tear down.

That night, while she was supposed to be drying the dishes, Natalya faked a tummy-ache and went to the bedroom alone. Under her mattress, pressed flat and cool, was her special scrapbook. She turned the stiff, crackling pages lovingly. One of Papa's friends had once given her a stack of foreign magazines and she had cut the pictures out of them – models and movie stars – glued them neatly in the book and decorated them with coloured borders or carefully drawn ribbons. As she couldn't read English letters, she had no idea who the people were. But she was in love with them all, the women as much as the men: their glossiness, their addictive beauty. Lena was always trying to get the book off her, but to Natalya it was sacred.

She went through it now with an ache of longing in her chest. What the red-faced man had told them wasn't news to her. They learned at school all about princesses and palaces and the evils of the decadent west. Two weeks ago, Uncle Ivan had taken them to an art gallery that had once been a palace; now it had been restored into the hands of the people. But she had been awestruck by its size and its opulence and, even though she was fearful that somebody could read her thoughts, had imagined herself living there. Why couldn't she be a princess, or at least a very rich and beautiful and famous lady? She had seen the old, bent woman with the birch broom who swept the gutters on their street and knew that she definitely didn't want that for her future. Was it so wrong to want pretty things, a nice life?

Sighing, Natalya closed her book and slid it back under her mattress. She felt guilty about not drying the dishes and about Aunt Stasya's concerned face. She supposed she should go back and help, but for now she just wanted to lie here and imagine the biggest, brightest life she could for herself. Surely that was more important than housework.

After seven months at Sofi's school, Natalya was dropped back a grade. One December afternoon, as early dusk crowded the windows, Sofi looked up to see her cousin standing uncertainly in the door to the classroom. Natalya was seized by the teacher and plonked next to Sofi, who was then charged with the responsibility of 'helping your cousin to learn'. Sofi was partly pitying of her cousin and partly irritated. Natalya never spent a second on homework, excusing herself by saying she wouldn't need to know maths when she was a movie star. Sofi did not like to feel as though she had to work hard enough for both of them. But on the other hand, she had heard Mama tell Papa that Natalya was simply unable to concentrate, that a skittish mind had been given to her at birth along with her pretty face, and that she was vain because she was insecure.

Still, Sofi was annoyed, and on the walk home that afternoon everything Natalya did or said bothered her. Her voice was like a prickle stuck in her sock. She was ungrateful, stubborn, selfish. Sofi walked a few paces ahead, and then, when Lena and Natalya lingered over a stray dog on the soft edge of the canal, she walked even further ahead until she lost sight of them. *Ha, serve them right.* She had the key and they didn't, so they would have to plead with the superintendent to get in, and he had been cranky with them all since the red-faced man had complained.

She let herself into the dark foyer of the building, checked for mail – none – and climbed up the narrow staircase. The smells of the building were trapped in the staircase: an unpleasant blend of cooking odours and cat urine. The light was out in the hallway again, and only the grey light from the window at the end of the corridor lit her way. She approached the door to the apartment and saw that it was already slightly ajar. Curious, she pushed it all the way open.

A large man, with hands like blocks, rose from the sofa on her arrival. She stopped, wondering for a moment if she was in the wrong apartment. But she wasn't. There was the lamp her grandmother had given them, the painting of the sea hanging over the sofa, the black armchair with the rip in the vinyl. And now, as she turned her head to make sure she *was* in the right place, she saw that her mother's bedroom door was half-open, and that Mama lay on her side on the bed, very still. Why was she home from work? Sofi's heart jumped. Was she dead?

'Mama?' she called.

The man took her elbow gently and met her eyes with a softness at odds with his stern voice. 'Leave your mama be. She is having a rest. She has just come home from the hospital.'

'Hospital?'

'I am Vasily Ilyich Gergiev, the site superintendent at your father's workplace.'

Sofi had lost the ability to speak. Something terrible was happening; bad luck had gathered around her the way that ants gathered around a scrap of food. She knew she was about to be carried away by it and so she clutched the back of the sofa to try to pin herself down.

In the background, the radio burbled softly. A terribly cold winter 'for the record books' was predicted.

'Your father fell at the construction site today,' Vasily Ilyich said. 'He fell a long way.'

Her blood was hot, deafening in her ears. 'Is he dead?'

He glanced away. 'No. But he is not expected to live.'

Sofi turned her gaze once again to Mama, and could see now that her back heaved softly with stifled sobs. She had turned onto her front, face buried in her hands. Her usually tidy hair spilled out over the pillow. Sofi wanted her mama, her warm embrace and cool reassurances. But she was terrified of walking through that door, of joining Mama in that position of grief and suffering on the bed. If she just stood here, hanging on to the sofa, and closed her eyes . . . There, now perhaps none of it was true. Perhaps it was just a bad dream that would clear away when she woke.

Voices in the hallway. Natalya and Lena.

'Why didn't you wait for us, you –' Natalya's words cut off abruptly.

Somebody nudged Sofi and she opened her eyes. It was Vasily Ilyich. 'Your mother needs you,' he said. 'Go to her.'

And so it was real, and her cousins were gazing at her in wide-eyed confusion and fear, and her heavy, heavy feet were dragging towards Mama's bedroom, and Mama was turning to her, arms outstretched, and crying and crying – *oh, my Sofi, my child, my child* – and Sofi curled up next to her on the bed. Although Mama's body was close, she was lost in her own grief, leaving Sofi miles and miles from comfort.

Sofi watched as the sky came all the way down and settled on the street. Soupy grey clouds, laden with snow. Behind her, Irina Petrovna knitted, the needles click-clicking against each other rhythmically. Papa had been in hospital for two weeks, and Sofi had barely seen her mother. Mama stayed as long as she could by Papa's side, catching the last tram home in the freezing dark. Irina Petrovna watched the girls, cooked dinner with them and ate with them, but it was up to

Sofi to get herself and her cousins bathed and into bed. Sofi couldn't sleep without Mama in the house. She always forced herself to keep her eyes open until the moment she heard the keys in the lock. Only then could she release her muscles and drift off to sleep.

Sofi visited her father too, of course, and it was clear to her that he wasn't coming back to them. Papa had never been an energetic man, but his stillness now was odd, unnatural. He didn't speak; his face was hidden by bandages and tubes. But she wasn't able to tell Mama that she knew Papa would die. Mama still held out hope, rubbed his hands vigorously, spoke to him in a quick, breathless voice. She feared Mama's grief almost more than she feared the loss of Papa.

'Looks like snow,' Irina Petrovna said.

Sofi turned. 'It does.'

'You go down and bring Lena and Natalya back up with you. They'll freeze their blood solid out there in the courtyard.'

Sofi hopped down from the chair by the window and moved to the door.

Irina Petrovna stopped her. 'Sofi, why didn't you go and play this afternoon?'

'I don't feel much like playing,' she said simply.

'Life will go on,' the old woman replied.

Sofi hesitated. She had heard that Irina Petrovna believed in God, observed all the Orthodox traditions. Secretly, of course. 'Do you think Papa will go to heaven?'

Irina Petrovna's cheeks flushed. 'Heaven? Who believes in heaven?'

'You do.'

She shrugged. 'As to whether I believe in it, well, that's not important. But if there is heaven, then I can't see why your papa wouldn't go there.'

A gust of wind rattled the windows.

'Go, get your cousins. The weather will be very bad by nightfall.'

Sofi ran down the stairs, heart thudding. She liked the idea that Papa might go to heaven and, from there, watch over them. Always be present, somehow. But she had been raised an atheist. Religious people were ridiculed, harassed. It was hard to start believing now. So what would happen if he died? Nothing. He would just be gone. The emptiness of life, the futility of it, sideswiped her. Happiness seemed just a dream, something she had felt once that might never return.

As she crossed the courtyard, calling her cousins' names, the first flake of snow fell. Light, bright, crystalline, landing on her shoe. She looked to the sky, the swirling grey. Wind gusted in the bare branches. A great cold was coming.

Forty days after Uncle Ivan's accident, he finally died. Natalya guiltily admitted a sense of relief. She had endured countless trips to the freezing hospital to sit beside her uncle's frightening, silent body. She had watched flurries of snow intensify into blizzards that kept them inside, away from the hospital and the rest of the outside world for six days, while Aunt Stasya paced and gnawed the skin on her fingers. She had felt all the colour drain from her life as her two best friends – Lena and Sofi – became consumed by the awful gravity of the waiting.

The forty days had been brutal for Aunt Stasya, who barely slept, and whose tense body throbbed like an inflamed nerve in the apartment. Now that death had come, she had adopted a manner of extreme calmness, organising with officials to have Uncle Ivan's body taken to the crematorium, filling out what seemed like hundreds of forms, and greeting with a hard face each well-meaning visitor who came with straggling posies, forbidden blessings or cruel curiosity.

In the afternoon after the cremation, Natalya sat at the sitting-room window watching the snow fall and fall onto the grey street below. She touched the window pane. It was icy. Lena appeared, tear-stained, at her elbow and Natalya pulled her close.

'Papa is gone, Uncle Ivan is gone,' Lena said. 'Aunt Stasya is so sad it frightens me. Who will look after us now?'

'We have each other, sister,' Natalya said against Lena's hair. Then the thought popped whole into her head: who would look after Sofi?

Her poor cousin; her pale, freckled face permanently frozen in an expression of disbelief and misery. 'Come, let's find Sofi,' she said.

She was in bed, the blankets pulled up so only the top of her fair head was visible. Natalya and Lena lay down on either side of her. Lena peeled back the covers, but Sofi wouldn't open her eyes. Lena kissed her face.

'Sofi?' Natalya said.

Sofi shook her head. 'Don't ask me to speak,' she whispered. 'I'll start crying and never stop.'

Lena began to whimper and cough, and this set Sofi off, and Natalya couldn't hold her own tears in any longer. They sobbed until their faces were hot. Finally, afternoon eased into night and Natalya's fingers searched out one of her cousin's hands and one of her sister's.

'We will take care of each other,' she said hoarsely. 'Nothing will ever come between us. Swear it.'

'I swear it,' Lena said promptly, shaking her head for emphasis.

'I swear it too,' Sofi managed.

So they clung to each other in the icy dark, with the idealistic certainty of children that such a promise could be kept forever.

CHAPTER THREE
1987

Lena hung back in the doorway, watching across the corridor as the American visitors managed their suitcases out the door. *Americans*. It was only her third week on the job at the Hotel Moskva. She had seen plenty of Swedes, Finns, Germans and the occasional Middle Eastern businessman, but these were her first Americans. She checked the hallway: nobody around. Opportunities like this would be rare. Her heart thudded softly. She had to speak to them, but it was important not to be seen by anyone else.

In her arms was a bundle of dirty sheets for the laundry. She stuffed them into her trolley, knocking over a tray of shampoo bottles. She wiped nervous hands on her apron, checked the long corridor left and right. Doors stretching off for miles. In her first week working here, the corridors had grown nightmarish. Room after room to be cleaned, until her shoulders ached from making beds and her hands turned red and began to peel from using cleaning products. She had regretted her decision not to sit a university entrance exam, as Sofi had done. But Natalya, who worked in a second-hand shop, talked about getting an apartment of her own. Lena had loved the idea, and decided to get a job too. Her good English had made her suitable for work with foreign visitors, but she had been strictly warned about what was appropriate and inappropriate to discuss with them.

'Excuse me,' she said, advancing into the corridor as the visitors closed their door behind them. A thin, beautifully dressed woman in her forties and an elderly man who could have been either husband or father.

'Yes?' the woman said, curious. Until now, she had probably only been approached by her official Intourist guide, or by furtive young men trying to convince her to sell them her shoes or her T-shirts. The Party was happy to let tourists into the country as long as they never really interacted with the locals.

'I am looking for a man, Viktor Chernov. I think he may be in United States.'

The couple exchanged glances, then the woman said gently, 'There are a lot of people in the States.'

'But you have ways to find him. Phone book. Or perhaps he was in newspapers. I think he defected USSR in 1976.' She heard the lift bell ring softly in the distance and knew she didn't have much more time alone with the Americans. 'He is my father. Please, you help me find him?'

The woman recoiled at the direct request, eyes darting left and right as though wondering if this were a KGB sting.

The man, however, gave her a sympathetic smile. 'Viktor Chernov. That's his name?'

'Yes, tell him to write to his daughters. He knows where we are.'

'It's a long shot,' he said. 'But if I ever come across his name, I'll pass that message on.'

'Long shot?' The phrase meant nothing to her.

'It's very unlikely,' the woman explained. 'You'll have to excuse us. I don't think we're supposed to be talking to you.'

Footsteps in the corridor, and Lena stepped back into the doorway of the room she was cleaning. The floor supervisor rounded the long curve, passing the Americans on her way. Lena backed into the room and made herself busy dusting the bedside tables. When the footsteps had receded, she put down her cloth and went to the window. Traffic fought for space on the street below. Beyond, the Neva River shone like a pale length of satin, early morning mist rising softly from it.

She leaned her head against the glass, closing her eyes and feeling a little foolish. *There are a lot of people in the States.* Of course. But wouldn't a Russian name stand out?

Lena sighed, realising she didn't even know for certain that was where Papa was. In the eleven years since he had left, she had spent a lot of energy wondering about him, asking about him, doing her best to find him. Aunt Stasya had little information to give her. He was headed for Vladivostok to work at the fisheries there. He had promised to write the moment he arrived. But then nobody had heard of him again. When she had turned fifteen, she began to write letters to the fisheries, the officials in charge of movements in and out of Vladivostok. She was mostly answered with silence. One letter, asking for further details, had been discovered by Aunt Stasya. She had been horrified and begged Lena not to write any more. 'We don't want to stand out,' she said. 'People go missing and it's best not to ask questions. We don't want the Party to notice us. Please, Lena, accept that your father is gone and he's never coming back.'

Lena had come up with many theories about Papa's whereabouts, skirting the unpleasant ones and building up the appealing ones in her imagination. Vladivostok was close to the west, just across the way from Alaska. What if he had taken a fishing boat and simply sailed off towards freedom? Perhaps he intended to send for his daughters one day, but communication between the Soviet Union and the west was still fraught. This idea, formed in her childhood, had acquired all the durability of truth. For his sake, she had learned English. Partly from a cassette that Sofi had, but mostly, in the last year, from the English romance novels that Natalya had brought home. The people Natalya worked with dealt in goods that were impossible to get anywhere else, and which were certainly not for sale to the public. Lena started off slowly, but soon began devouring the novels quicker and quicker.

'I thought I might find you here.'

Lena's head snapped up and she whirled around. Then she smiled in relief. It was only Konstantin, one of the other cleaners and, owing to a secret kiss in the broom cupboard a week ago, her new boyfriend.

She moved away from the window and grabbed stiff, fresh sheets off her trolley. 'You frightened me,' she said.

'What time is your break?' he asked, his clear blue eyes fixed on hers.

'Eleven.'

'Ah. I'm at eleven thirty. We'll miss each other. And I'm off the next two days.'

She shook out the sheet, spreading it over the mattress. Her arms were getting used to this movement now, and she had noticed hard little muscles forming on her shoulders. 'I'll see you on Saturday evening, though. You're still coming for dinner, aren't you?'

'Of course.' He closed the door behind him and playfully tackled her, pinning her to the bed.

'Konstant*in*,' she complained, without any real anger.

He kissed her. A little too wetly. But he was her first boyfriend, so she had nothing to compare his kisses to. He was nineteen and gorgeous, that was enough.

'You are very beautiful, Lena,' he murmured against her ear.

She smiled up at the ceiling. She loved to hear it. Growing up, she had developed crushes on a lot of boys, but they were usually only interested in Natalya. It was nice to have her independence in this job, to be free of comparisons with her sister. She was looking forward to him turning up for dinner at her place. Tall, gorgeous, more a man than a boy. Natalya would finally see that she wasn't the only one who could attract male attention.

His hand wandered to her breast. She let him touch her for a moment, but when he tried to move inside her blouse she pushed his hand away. 'No, Konstantin. Let me get back to work. The floor supervisor is around this morning.'

He jumped off the bed and held out a hand to help her up. His lips brushed her cheek. 'See you Saturday,' he said with a smile.

She watched him leave, admiring his square shoulders and narrow hips. It took her a few minutes to collect herself, to shake off the love-struck feeling and get on with finishing the beds and cleaning the bathroom. When the room was restored to neat blandness, she backed out into the hallway with her trolley, colliding with her supervisor.

'Lena,' the woman said with a downturn of her thin lips. 'Did I hear you speaking with the American visitors this morning?'

'No. I mean, yes. They asked me which floor the breakfast room was on. I told them, that's all.'

'Very well,' she said, distracted, checking her clipboard. Then she was on her way.

Lena relaxed. Not so dangerous after all. She would keep her eyes and ears open for other American visitors. She would never accept, as Aunt Stasya suggested, that Papa was not coming back. She knew he was out there somewhere and, one day, she would find him.

Sofi didn't remember them making a conscious decision to reprise their Thursday afternoon ritual of buying ice-creams on Nevsky Prospekt. Once their teenage years had brought them a little more independence, it had just seemed natural. Mama still worked the late shift that afternoon, and at any time of year there was something magical about being on the busy street, lights glittering against dusk skies, birds flying home above the crisscross network of tramlines.

It was early spring, the snow had nearly melted and the days were growing mercifully longer. Sofi and Lena met outside Moscow Station, then headed across to the markets where Natalya worked in a second-hand shop. They entered the cavernous shop with its scarred wooden floors and its rickety trestle tables covered with Party literature, old books, musty mismatched clothes, plastic toys that smelled of sanitising chemicals. Natalya was ignoring the queues forming, and smoked a cigarette while chatting to a tall man whose eyes never left her face. Sofi felt the familiar disbelieving admiration as she regarded her cousin. Natalya was tall and lean, with skin that glowed as if it were polished, and thick chestnut hair scooped lazily into a ponytail. Her eyes were clear and blue, her nose fine and straight, and her mouth a perfect bow. No wonder her companion was mesmerised. Sofi stole a glance at Lena. She, too, had a slender body, shining hair, unblemished skin. But she was slightly shorter than her sister, her hazel eyes less exotic, her smile more toothy. It was unfair, and Sofi acknowledged that. Under ordinary circumstances, Lena would be thought a great beauty. But it was her misfortune to be a shining star positioned next to a supernova.

Sofi had long since learned not to think about her own looks, and to fulfil the role as the clever girl instead. She was in her second year of study at Leningrad State University. Geology. She didn't want to be a geologist, she wanted to make jewellery, but there was no pathway into that career for her. The state had decided she would make a good geologist, and so she did as she was expected to do. Sometimes, in geochemistry class, she would get sidelined into researching the mystical properties of stones and thinking about ways they would work themselves into jewellery designs. But then it was back to soil composition, or learning lists of isotopes.

Natalya saw them and unfolded her lean body, butting out her cigarette beneath her toe. 'I've got a surprise!' she called.

Her companion, a bear-eyed man named Tolya who Sofi suspected was an inveterate racketeer, smiled and held a finger theatrically to his lips, a shushing gesture. Natalya said something to him quickly, gathered up her bag and hurried over, grabbing Lena and Sofi by the wrists. '*General Hospital*,' she whispered. 'Twenty episodes!'

Lena gasped, eyes rounded in delight. Natalya was friends with people who could get anything *na levo*, whether through exploiting contacts, bribery or the black market. And what Natalya and Lena wanted more than anything else was American soap operas. One of Natalya's ex-boyfriends had set up a video player in their apartment and they had both become addicted to *General Hospital*. Sofi had to admit that, despite the awkward Russian dubbing by a single male voice, she found it quite compelling too.

'Can we go straight home and watch them?' Lena asked. 'Aunt Stasya hates it.'

'It's the first warm afternoon of spring,' Sofi said. 'Let's have ice-creams, in memory of Papa.'

Lena conceded quickly, and the three of them made their way out to Nevsky Prospekt, where they bought ice-creams from a vendor and then wandered down across Fontanka Canal towards the Summer Gardens. The snow melt had left a stinking wake of rotting vegetation, but the first tight green shoots on the maples and elms cheered her. Long shadows pulled out of the trees as they found a bench in front of a dirty statue. Two soldiers walked past, tidy in their red-trimmed khaki uniforms and black caps. Sofi remembered, as a child, always thinking the soldiers seemed frighteningly male and aggressive. Now she could see they were often young pale-faced men, with no more of an idea about how the world should work than she had.

When they had gone, Natalya opened her bag to release the loot.

'Here, Lena, more books for you.'

She handed Lena four yellowing paperbacks with lurid covers and English writing on them. Sofi was taking electives in English, but her language skills were nowhere approaching Lena's abilities.

'And here,' Natalya said, pulling out two video tapes in worn cardboard sleeves, 'is Dr Noah Drake.'

Lena put her hand on her heart and faked a swoon. 'My future husband.'

'What about this Konstantin fellow?' Natalya shot back, leaping to her feet and holding the video tapes just out of Lena's grasp.

Lena giggled. 'He's almost as good-looking.'

'I'll be the judge of that Saturday night,' Natalya said, handing the tapes to Lena and sitting down.

'I have something for you too, Sofi,' Natalya said, rummaging again. 'Tolya had them, he was going to sell them but I said I'd take them.' She smiled, a cat who had eaten the cream. 'And Tolya *always* does what I say.' She pulled out a small cloth bag and dropped it in Sofi's palm. 'Go on, look.'

Sofi opened the bag and shook it out. Three polished pieces of quartz crystal dropped into her lap.

'Lucky crystals,' Natalya continued. 'I thought you might need them. You know, for your exams.'

Sofi fingered the edges thoughtfully. Did she need luck? That would depend on how she viewed her life. Losing her father young; having to share a mother who struggled to feed them and keep them on the right path; burying her dreams of a life of art to focus on geology. From that perspective, she was unlucky. Sometimes she felt as though she had been forcibly placed on the wrong train, and it was speeding towards a destination a long way from where she wanted to be. Sofi Chernova, geologist. It was going to happen whether she liked it or not. But then, Mama always warned her against negativity.

She didn't need luck with her exams, she was already topping her class. Instead, she could make something with these crystals.

'Sofi doesn't need luck any more than the rest of us,' Lena sniffed.

'I love them, Natalya,' Sofi said. 'I'll make you a necklace each.'

'Like you used to when we were little. Remember? American princesses.' Natalya twisted her pretty mouth into a bitter smile. 'Maybe I need the lucky crystals, if I ever want to be a movie star.'

'Imagine being on *General Hospital* and getting to kiss Noah Drake,' Lena said, tapping the videos with her knuckles. 'Better than making beds for tourists.'

'Better than selling second-hand clothes to old men,' Natalya agreed.

They sat in silence for a few minutes, brought low by the reality of adulthood, the forced extraction of childish fantasies.

'Hey, cheer up,' Sofi said. 'Everything's changing. We might get to Hollywood yet.' She couldn't make her voice sound confident.

Natalya forced a smile. 'Let's not think about it. Let's go home and watch *General Hospital* instead.'

Sofi jumped when the door to the apartment opened. She had imagined she would have the place to herself for the whole day. The table was strewn with beads, polished stones, spools of shiny wire, tools, and hundreds of tiny handmade loops. Usually the materials were all packed up in a battered sewing basket and stored under Sofi's bed. But once a week – when everyone else was at work and she had no classes – it all came out.

Mama frowned at her. 'I hope you'll clean that mess up.'

'Of course. Why aren't you at work?'

Mama's fingers fluttered over her temple. 'I'm ill.' She pulled out a chair and sat down next to Sofi. 'My head is pounding.' She picked up the necklace Sofi was working on. 'This is beautiful.'

Sofi smiled, pleased to be able to show somebody her work in progress. She leaned over, hooking her arm around Mama's shoulders. 'I'm making three: one for me, one for Natalya, and one for Lena. You see, I've set these polished crystals in a netted bezel I wove myself, and then chosen a bead design for each of us. Blue for Natalya, green for Lena, and purple for me.' She pulled up short of explaining how much work had gone into making the headpins, wrapped loops and eyes, or how the work consumed her: beyond the point where her hands ached from bending and cutting; beyond the point where she closed her eyes at night and all she could see were strands of silver-coloured wire, variegated patterns of glass and opaque beads. 'It's a surprise, so don't tell them,' she finished.

Mama was still studying the necklace: Natalya's, blue to match her eyes. Sofi leaned her head onto Mama's shoulder.

'It's very fine work, Sofi,' Mama said. 'You must have spent a lot of time learning these skills.'

'I do spend a lot of time on it. It's my passion.'

Mama pulled away and handed her the necklace, eyebrows raised. 'I hope you aren't neglecting your studies.' She slipped into a gentle, yet familiar lecture about the importance of securing a good job, about the future of the Soviet Union being uncertain now that the ways were changing, about how pleased she was to have had a secure job for the last twenty-six years and how it had allowed her to provide for the girls even in the most desolate of times.

Sofi nodded through it, fingers itching to get back to her work.

'But Mama,' she ventured, 'don't you get bored at the bakery? You've never done anything different, or had a promotion, or changed location.'

'I'm needed there,' Mama replied firmly. 'I think there are few things as important in life as being needed. People come to me every day to buy their bread. If the bakery was closed because I didn't feel like going to work, what would they do? Today, it took me three hours to convince the baker to let me go home sick. I'm that important.' She shook her head. 'I'm sorry, my dear. I'm sick and cranky. Perhaps I should leave you be and go lie down.'

'Can I get you anything?'

'No, no. I will be fine.' Mama moved off towards her bedroom.

Sofi picked up a set of pliers in each hand and began the task of closing loops inside one another. Mama's ideas about being needed in the community were powerful ones, ideas taught since the first day of school. Sofi had grown up knowing about equality, justice, the supremacy of the collective. But at eighteen years of age, her own individual journey seemed acutely significant.

The necklaces on the table were charms, set with the lucky crystals Natalya had given her. But now Sofi mulled over the notion of luck. It seemed a primitive idea, like the silly superstitions that Mama couldn't shake off: don't loan sharp objects, don't shake hands through a doorway, don't cut your fingernails on exam days. What she needed was not luck. If she wanted to make jewellery, she needed to be somewhere there was a market for it; she needed money and materials. Without those things, she was stuck with soil sampling. She wanted to escape to the west as much as her cousins, though she wasn't caught up in fantasies about movie stars. Everything was changing in the Soviet Union. Perhaps there was something she could do to lift herself out of her circumstances.

The sudden thought of the three of them going, and Mama being left behind alone, gave her pause. But she pushed those feelings aside; she would cross that bridge later. For now, she had to apply her clever mind to the problem, look for an opportunity, and make her own dreams fly.

Natalya first saw the beautiful man at the Gostiny Dvor metro station. She was hurrying home, reluctantly. She'd been having a wonderful time with Tolya and his friends, swigging vodka from a passed-around bottle, smoking rolled cigarettes in the park. She had almost changed her mind, not gone home. But Lena's dinner party was tonight, and her sister was so keen for her to meet this new boyfriend. She couldn't let Lena down.

Then she spied the beautiful man in the concourse, under the wide arched roof, as he was checking in his pockets for change. He had the kind of looks she always appreciated in men: powerfully built, with intense eyes. She may have forgotten him, had she not happened to sit opposite him on the train. It was Saturday afternoon, the carriage was half-empty, so there was nowhere to look but into his eyes. As the train stopped and started, as the carriage emptied the further they went up the line, their gazes became hotter. A woman with a pink-faced baby was sitting next to her. The baby babbled and whined, but Natalya didn't notice. She glanced away and back at the man, and always his eyes were waiting for hers to return. Finally, the woman alighted with her baby. He smiled. She smiled. And he slid over to sit next to her. His thigh pressed against hers, seemed to burn through her skirt.

The last passenger left on the train, halfway up the carriage, was an elderly woman in a blue headscarf. She dozed into her chest. An inspector in a long grey coat, with a round fur *ushanka* on his head, paced down the aisle before letting himself into the next carriage. Natalya felt a tickling sensation at her hip. She looked down; the man – who she guessed was about the same age as her – was stroking her with the back of his hand. She smiled, delighted and scared by the naughty game. She dropped her hand by her side, he caught her fingers in his. Her heart thudded as he casually placed her hand in his lap, edging his folded coat over the top of it so they wouldn't be seen. She could feel a hard lump under the fabric of his pants. Thrilling. She was not inexperienced with men: she'd had dozens of boyfriends. But this man's boldness was intoxicating. So far, she'd had sex twice, once each with two different men, and both times it was an incredible disappointment. Right now, though, she felt she understood what all the fuss was about. She leaned into him and his arm slid around her back, his hand creeping up to cup her breast.

The door between the carriages opened with a clatter and a blast of stale air. The inspector returned and she and the man slid apart quickly. Her pulse was thundering at her throat. She was only one stop from home and she had to – *had to* – find a place to go with the man, to press her body against his and enjoy him properly.

'I have to get out at the next stop,' she said.

'Me too. I'm supposed to be meeting somebody, but . . .'

'We should find somewhere. We can't go to my place.'

'Is there a park? Somewhere secluded?'

She laughed, feeling wild, young. 'You've made me forget all my manners. I don't even know your name.'

He smiled. 'It's Konstantin.'

Aunt Stasya gently shook Lena's shoulder. She turned from the window. Six o'clock had passed an hour ago. It was dark outside. Konstantin hadn't arrived.

'Shall we eat?' Stasya said.

'Can we wait another ten minutes?'

'I'm starving,' Sofi said.

Natalya was silent, sitting on the sofa looking at Lena sadly.

'I don't think your Konstantin is coming,' Stasya said.

She was right, of course. Lena wished she could call him, but he was living in an apartment without a phone. She didn't know what she feared most: that he had been killed in an accident on the way to her place, or that he had simply stood her up. She took one last look down to the street. Headlights moved past, nobody stopped. She dragged herself to their new dining table, crammed into the corner of the sitting room, where Natalya and Sofi already sat. Aunt Stasya went out to the kitchen and returned with a plate heaped with *blini*. Lena didn't have an appetite. She pushed her food around on her plate as the conversation at the table moved on without her.

Eventually, Stasya tapped Lena's hand with the back of her fork. 'You see, this is why I don't think it's a good idea to have a boyfriend at your age,' she said.

'Aunt Stasya, you don't think it's a good idea at any age,' Natalya said.

'That's not true,' she replied. 'But you have to be careful with boys. They all want . . . you know . . .'

Natalya rolled her eyes. 'What? "Intimate relations"?'

This was the term Stasya used to talk about sex. Not that she talked about sex very often; just enough to remind them that marriage should come first.

Lena wasn't a prude, but she did like the idea of being in love before sharing her body with somebody. Lately, she'd imagined that somebody might be Konstantin. And she *knew* he felt the same. Why else would he find her whenever he could at the hotel, cover her in hot, secret kisses? Dread washed over her. If he felt the same, then something bad must have happened to stop him coming. She rose. 'I have to go and look for him,' she said. 'He might be sick, or dead, or . . .'

'Just sit down,' Natalya said gently. 'He's probably fine.'

'Well, if he's fine, why isn't he here?' Lena heard her voice shake, and swallowed back tears.

There was a short silence, then Stasya said, 'Perhaps he's not as interested as you thought.'

A crushing sense of vulnerability overwhelmed her. The three of them looking at her with pitying eyes – especially Natalya, who boys were always interested in – thinking that she had been a fool, that she had imagined Konstantin's interest.

'I'm not hungry,' she muttered. 'Can I go to my room?'

Stasya nodded and waved her away, not meeting her eye. Lena couldn't tell if her aunt was angry with her or ashamed of her. She slipped away towards the bedroom, taking one last glance down at the street. Searching for somebody who wouldn't arrive.

Natalya rested her shoulder on a cold stone wall, smoking, tapping her foot, waiting for Lena to emerge from the front doors of the hotel. Drunks gathered in pairs or groups of three outside the entrance to Aleksandra-Nevskogo station. Periodically, she could feel the metro rumbling below her feet. It was Monday, Lena's first shift since she had been stood up at dinner. Today, she would have asked Konstantin why he didn't come. Natalya didn't know what Konstantin would tell her; she had urged him (under threat) to be discreet. But no matter what he said, Lena would be upset. So Natalya had charmed Tolya into letting her off work early so she could be here for her sister. Tolya was usually pliable.

She leaned her head back, blowing a stream of smoke into the air. A thickset man in overalls stared at her as he walked past. She closed her eyes, ignoring him, feeling oddly guilty that she should attract such attention simply by standing there. The disaster with Konstantin weighed heavily on her. As soon as she'd realised who he was, she had gone cold, jumped away from him, berated him for being so faithless to her sister. She had warned him to stay away from both of them forever, had mentioned her friends at the second-hand shop who would certainly enjoy enforcing her instructions, and told him to let Lena down gently and never to mention meeting Natalya. She had done everything she could to make things right; but they could never be made right. It wasn't her fault, she hadn't meant to, but she had stolen her sister's boyfriend.

Natalya opened her eyes just in time to see Lena, a zip-up cardigan over her uniform, moving away from the huge entrance doors to the hotel. Natalya called out to her, waving. Lena approached, looking wary.

'What are you doing here?'

'I got off early, thought I'd come and meet you.' She touched her sister's shoulder. 'How did it go with Konstantin?'

'He's alive and well, of course,' Lena said with a resigned shrug.

'Anything else?'

Lena's bottom lip trembled, signalling that she was about to cry, just as it had since she was a little girl. Natalya gathered her up and held her close, stroking her hair.

'Sh, sh, little sister,' she said. 'It's all right.'

'It's not all right. He says he changed his mind, he doesn't want to be with me any more.'

'Then he's a pig and you're better off without him.'

'I know that. It's just . . . I feel like such a fool.'

Lena's hot tears spilled onto Natalya's neck, and all Natalya could do was hold her, fighting the guilt swirling in her stomach and vowing that she would be careful in future.

This could never, *never* happen again.

CHAPTER FOUR
1992

Sofi had seen the white-painted windows of the marriage agency a hundred times before. It was on the second floor, and her office was on the third. As she walked up the dim stairwell, she often glanced at the frost-haired woman with the long red fingernails and the hard smile who smoked a cigarette in front of the agency. Sofi had never given much thought to what the American Bride agency did. After all, she was in a secure job with a mining company – and not many had secure jobs any more – and had little need for a husband just yet.

But today was different, and she glanced around quickly to make sure that none of her work colleagues could see her before she pushed the door open and went in.

The idea had come to her two nights ago. An old friend from her first year of university, Anya Bletsky, had phoned to invite her out for a drink. She hadn't heard from her in years; Anya hadn't finished her degree and they had drifted apart.

Sofi arrived at the pizza restaurant, downstairs off Mytninskaya, a little too early. She was studying the menu when perfumed arms enveloped her, and she looked up to see her friend.

Anya was dressed beautifully, adorned with glittering jewellery and her hair was streaked almost white-blonde. She had lost the roundness of her teenage years, and with it had gone the dimple in her cheek, the soft curve of her shoulder. She had with her a man. Sofi's first thought was, how strange to bring her father with her. But no, he was introduced as Barry, her husband, who spoke no Russian. They arranged themselves around the booth, agreed to speak English, and ordered two pizzas to share.

It took a while for their story to emerge. He was American, they lived now in Seattle, they were here to visit Anya's mother. The whole time, Sofi watched Barry with a mixture of fascination and distaste. His lips were plump and moist, and he reminded her of a fish. His gaze did not fix in one place, but rather moved around the room avariciously, lighting on young women. Anya did not seem to notice. As she raised her cigarette to her lips, the gold chains around her wrist clanked against each other. She smoked, the lights catching the facets of the diamond on her engagement finger. At last, Barry went off to the cigarette machine and Sofi asked what she had been dying to ask all night.

'Where did you meet him?' she said in Russian.

'A marriage broker. We corresponded for a while, then he sent me money to come see him. Gave me this . . .' She flashed the ring. 'I said yes and two months later we were married.'

'Do you love him?'

She snorted, and Sofi felt, unaccountably, like a fool. 'I like him well enough. I don't see him that often. He works very hard.'

'And you? Are you working?'

'I don't need to. Oh, we'll probably have a baby in a year or so, but for now I'm just enjoying my time. Reading, going to movies, shopping. A far cry from life here, Sofi.'

Barry was approaching the table. Sofi thought about her friend – young, pretty – having to make love to him. She dropped her voice and said quickly, 'If you'll forgive me for saying, it sounds like prostitution.'

'There's not a prostitute in the world who gets paid as much as me,' Anya said with a smile.

'No Russian,' Barry said, more angrily than he had reason to be.

Anya turned her face to him for a kiss and Sofi looked away. The seed of an idea had been sown.

Sofi had thought the American Bride office would be beautifully fitted out, but it wasn't. There was something almost grubby about it, with its two round tables heaped with photographs of women, its drooping posters of weddings, its dusty framed photographs of smiling young Russian women in bridal attire next to an assortment of much older men. But she pushed aside her misgivings and waited for the woman with the hard smile to get off the phone. She greeted Sofi with barely a flicker of friendliness in her eyes and introduced herself as Regina.

'Now, how can I help?' she said, indicating Sofi should sit with her. She swept a pile of photographs aside with her forearm and one or two fell on the floor. She didn't pick them up.

'I want to know about . . . the process.'

'Thinking about marrying an American man?'

Sofi shrugged, made uncomfortable by the question.

'Well,' Regina continued, 'who could blame you? We have many wealthy, kind men who are looking for Russian wives. American women are hard, greedy, too independent.' She moved to a bookcase and brought back a stack of magazines with English writing on the front. 'We advertise only in quality American magazines.'

Sofi's mouth turned down in doubt. The magazine Regina held out for inspection was called *Hot Cars* and its cover featured a picture of a half-clad woman leaning provocatively over the bonnet of a car. She took it gingerly.

'Page eighty-two,' Regina said.

The phone rang and she was off again, giving Sofi the chance to look carefully at the advertisement. Four photographs of Russian women. Very beautiful girls, not like the hundred nondescript ones whose photographs were falling off the table. Underneath, the caption read: *We are looking for American husbands.* Then there was a paragraph about each girl, her first name, her age, her interests. It finished with *Hundreds more girls to choose from* and the address of the agency.

Regina was off the phone again. 'There are many benefits to you. Life is a much better standard in America. Many of our girls live in mansions. It's not unusual for their fiancés to buy them expensive gifts: watches, perfume, even cars. We offer a life that you couldn't dream about here.'

Watches, perfume and cars were not the stuff of Sofi's dreams. But Regina had hit on a vein of truth. The Soviet Union had fallen. Once, everyone had been poor, but at least the condition was general. Now, a gap had opened up between the haves and have-nots. Businessmen drove up the cost of rents. International companies – like the mining giant Sofi worked for – paid Russian workers a pittance because they knew they could get away with it. She had grown up thinking that hard work would bring her freedom. But it hadn't. Under the old regime it had brought only more hard work. Under the new regime it brought even greater disappointments: freedom had been glimpsed and then denied. She had to get out of Russia, or else she would be poking around in the dirt for the rest of her days.

'How much does it cost?' she asked.

'You pay only for the photography session,' Regina replied, sliding an unevenly cut information slip over to Sofi. The figure for the photography session was equal to two weeks' rent. 'Our American clients bear the costs of introduction. You correspond with your prospective husband until you're sure he's right for you. Then he'll either come here to meet you, or bring you over to him. We assist with all the difficult business: visas, travel arrangements and so on.'

Sofi was lost in thought a few moments.

'Can I book you for photographs?' Regina said.

'I might sleep on it,' Sofi replied. She indicated the magazine. 'Can I take this?'

'No,' the other woman said. 'They cost a lot of money.'

'Oh. Sorry.' She tucked the information slip in her handbag. 'Thank you for your time.'

Regina raised a hand; it could have been a farewell wave or a gesture of dismissal. Sofi headed upstairs to her office, but couldn't concentrate on the file in front of her.

Visas, travel arrangements: she could manage those herself. Photographs: there were plenty of those around. She would have to find an international bookshop to see if they stocked *Hot Cars* magazine or something similar, so she could look up the address to place an advertisement. Sofi Chernova didn't need a marriage broker service, especially if she didn't intend to marry.

'Sofi?' It was her supervisor, a timid woman in her forties. 'Are you nearly finished with the file?'

'Sorry,' Sofi muttered, making a show of moving papers about. 'I'll have it to you by lunchtime.' She pretended to read the documents, waiting to be alone again before placing her head on the desk and making up her mind.

Life wasn't fair. To anyone. She thought about the ad in *Hot Cars* magazine. *We are looking for American husbands.*

If there were rich men in America foolish enough to respond to such advertisements, then she was a poor girl in Russia smart enough to take advantage of them. And she had the perfect bait. Now all she had to do was convince Natalya.

Natalya hurried along the slick footpath, a magazine held over her head to protect her from the rain. A bus lurched past, belching exhaust fumes and splashing muddy water on her ankles. She slipped down the narrow side street that she and Lena now called home. Yellow light glowed in the apartment window. Warm and dry. The apartment was very comfortable at this time of year, though it was an icebox in winter and a stinking humidity trap in summer.

She let herself into the building and made her way up the stairs. With a bit of luck, Lena would have cooked dinner already. Natalya's days were very full at the moment. She worked in a shoe shop during the day: her eighth job in five years. Then she hurried straight from work to the Shining Smile Modelling and Acting Academy, where she was doing a three-month course. It was costing her every rouble she had, and quite a few roubles from her boss and current boyfriend, Valery. He thought if he helped pay her fees, she might sleep with him. He was wrong. She had already tired of him, but couldn't split up with him until she'd found a new job to go to.

The apartment smelled delicious and Sofi was there, making soup while Lena toasted bread. It wasn't unusual for Sofi to drop by; they were all still very close. The space was tiny: a combined kitchen and living space, one bedroom for the two of them, and a poky bathroom with no bath. The walls were decorated with Lena's pin-ups of Charlie Sheen and Natalya's pin-ups of former Soviet models who had made it big in America. Natalya went to the bedroom to dry herself off and change into her pyjamas, and joined them at the table. The girls gossiped while they ate, and Natalya relaxed, putting her worries about Valery out of her mind.

After dinner, when they had squeezed onto the sofa and Sofi produced a block of Belgian chocolate as a treat, Natalya grew suspicious. Sofi didn't like to spend her money on anything but silver wire and coloured glass beads.

'All right, Sofi,' Natalya said. 'Cooking us dinner? Belgian chocolate? What's wrong?'

Lena paused with a piece of chocolate halfway to her mouth. Sofi smiled, indicated she should keep eating. 'I have an idea,' she said. 'I need your help with it.'

Natalya laughed. 'Why do I feel worried?'

Sofi moved from the sofa to the floor so she could see them both while she spoke. She wrapped her arms around her knees and paused for effect, making sure they were listening closely before proceeding. 'Natalya,' she said, 'you want to be an actress, you want to live in glamorous places, be famous.'

'I want that too,' Lena squeaked, and Natalya fought her usual impatience with her younger sister. Why couldn't she find her own dream to aspire to?

'Yes,' Natalya said slowly.

'But you work in a . . . where do you work this week?'

'Shoe shop,' Natalya grudgingly admitted. 'Though I'm looking for something else.'

'And Lena, you've been working at the hotel for five years. I've been working for the mining company for three years. Not one of us is doing what we want.'

Her hand had unconsciously gone to the bracelet around her wrist: a three-strand design of gradated pink and purple beads, with a silver flower hanging next to the clasp. How Natalya had coveted that bracelet, one of the first Sofi had made with real silver instead of wire.

'I'm saving,' Lena protested. 'For a ticket to America.'

'It will be years before you can afford to go,' Sofi responded. 'Especially now you're paying rent on this place. Admit it, we're all stuck. We need to get out of Russia, but we can't. And the longer we stay, the harder it will get. Responsibilities mount up. In five years, any one of us could be married, have children. Then how do we get away? What happens to our dreams?'

Natalya felt as though her throat was closing up. 'I'm doing an acting course,' she said weakly, already knowing that it meant nothing. Each of the other twenty-four girls in her class imagined that they would be 'discovered' while working in their demeaning jobs and magically transported to Hollywood for a life of fame and wealth. She sighed. 'What do you have in mind?' she asked Sofi.

'What are you prepared to do?' Sofi shot back, her serious mouth set in a firm line.

'Almost anything,' Lena said.

'Anything,' Natalya said. 'Absolutely anything.'

By the end of the following month, they had already made twelve hundred American dollars. Using one of Natalya's glamorous photographs taken during her acting course, and the address of a burnt-out apartment in the adjacent block, they advertised for prospective American husbands in an American magazine. Then they charged the twenty men who responded a sixty-dollar 'introduction fee' in cash. So far, not one of them had written back to complain that there had been no introductions; in fact, no further correspondence had eventuated. Perhaps sixty dollars wasn't much to an American man: it was a quarter what a large agency would charge them. But Sofi suspected, too, that these men were too embarrassed to complain. She tried to place another ad, increasing the introduction fee. The magazine refused to take her booking; they'd had complaints. Undeterred, she found another magazine, tripled the introduction fee and did it again.

They were doing well, the money was coming in; surely it wouldn't be long before they started the process of applying for visas, booking plane tickets ... The thoughts filled Sofi with thrilling feelings. But as their success grew, she realised she had to confront her feelings about leaving Mama behind. Her mother had no idea that she would soon be losing the only family she had left in Russia.

And yet, how could she stay? It was natural for children to fly the nest. She and Mama were close, but wore on each other's nerves. Sofi wasn't a little girl any more, she had her own ideas and opinions; and they often clashed with Mama's, who still held by the entrenched beliefs of her Soviet youth. It was well past time for Sofi to move on. If Papa had still been alive, she wouldn't have the slightest qualm about going.

But Papa wasn't alive, and their little family had been crippled by that awful event; and she and Mama had clung together all the harder for it.

At the start of summer, the stash of money under Natalya's bed was growing nicely. But it still wasn't enough. They had very clearly decided what they wanted: enough money for three airfares and six months' living costs in New York or Los Angeles. Sofi didn't intend for their trip overseas to be a holiday; she wanted to stay long enough to start a business. She was in the process of finding another magazine to advertise in when the letter arrived.

Lena brought it over to Sofi's place one afternoon, her face pale as a sheet. 'It's a bad one,' she said.

Sofi quickly scanned it. It seemed they had upset a lawyer, who was now making vague threats about bringing them to justice. Most importantly, he said he had advised the advertising sales departments at forty-four magazine publishing companies. There would be no more ads. The party was over.

'What's wrong?' Mama asked, noticing their ashen faces, the disappointed slump of their shoulders.

'Nothing, Mama,' Sofi said brightly. Then, under her voice, she said to Lena, 'Meeting at your place. One hour.'

The apartment was in semi-darkness when Sofi arrived. Natalya and Lena were trying to save money on their power bill so they only ran one light bulb at night. They sat around the kitchen table with the shoebox full of letters in front of them, while the clock on the stove ticked softly and the muffled sound of traffic moved past outside.

'I have a plan,' Sofi said, realising she was nervous and rolling her shoulders. 'But it's not for the faint-hearted.'

'I'm not faint-hearted,' Natalya laughed, and they both looked at Lena.

'Let's hear it,' she said.

Sofi tapped the shoebox. 'My friend Anya said her fiancé bought her expensive gifts, sent money for airfares, even before he met her. I wonder if there are a few men in here who might be so generous.'

Lena's brow furrowed. 'So you want to take this a step further? Trick them out of more money?'

'I'll do it,' Natalya said, raising her chin almost imperceptibly. She looked noble, queenly. 'We're poor, they're rich.'

'We'll find five or six of them,' Sofi said. 'Lena will write them letters; she has the best English. We'll send more photos, promises. We'll see if we can convince one to send money. Then . . . same as last time. We stop writing.'

Yes, her heart was definitely thudding. Before, it had almost been like a game, where the stakes were low and the rewards matched. Now it was high risk. Not just legally, but morally. Secretly, she hoped that Lena would disagree, shut the idea down.

'Lena?' she said.

Lena glanced from one to the other. 'Can we just choose one man? For a start? I read all their letters. Some of them are unpleasant, but some of them, they're nice. They don't deserve to be treated so badly.'

Natalya rolled her eyes, but Sofi patted Lena's hand.

'Bless you, cousin. You have a big heart.' Sofi flipped the top off the shoebox. 'All right, then. We read every letter, and we find the richest unpleasant man in there. Then we get to work on him.' She had a deep sense of something shifting inside her. Was it her youthful innocence slipping away? The thought terrified her. And yet inside the shoebox was her way out of Russia and into a new life.

His name was Roy Creedy from DeKalb, Illinois, and they found him because Lena remembered him. A racist who had complimented Natalya on not looking 'like a chink like a lot of Russian ladies'; a braggart who had posed like a slug on a silver spoon in his red sports car for the photo he sent; and an undeniably rich man who was very comfortable to talk about the shopping mall that he owned and the over-inflated rents he was screwing his lessees with. He was perfect.

Lena still had misgivings as she wrote the first letter. Some of them were moral. Taking a little money from a lot of men was very different from targeting one. But other misgivings were born of silly old jealousies. She was nominated as letter-writer because of her excellent English and also because her years of reading romance novels gave her a fine vocabulary for love letters. But it was Natalya's photographs they enclosed. Lena knew she was easily attractive enough to entice any man – and certainly a man like Roy Creedy – but it was never suggested. Natalya was the most beautiful; everyone accepted it without hesitation. And, stupidly, she felt overlooked.

As they packaged up the letter and sent it, she found herself hoping that perhaps Roy Creedy wouldn't respond, that they wouldn't have to go through with the scam. Then she found herself equally hoping that he *would* answer, that they would get their money and be on their way to Hollywood.

Lena wasn't sure precisely what she'd do once she got to Hollywood. Natalya was very clear on her desire to be a movie star, and had taken acting lessons. Lena had always dreamed about it too, but in the way a younger sister accepts unquestioningly her older sister's wisdom. She had to admit that, more than dreams of stardom (which would be nice if they came true), she hoped that in America she might finally find her father.

Within two weeks, Roy Creedy had written back.

The three girls sat down in the kitchen with his letter and read it carefully. He confessed to wariness, and suggested they corresponded for a little while before rushing into meeting.

'Let's find somebody else,' Natalya said. 'This could take ages.'

'No,' Sofi responded, twirling a strand of her fair hair thoughtfully. 'He's serious. We want somebody who's serious. The rewards would be greater.' She laughed self-consciously.

Natalya turned her gaze to Lena. 'You have to woo him,' she said. 'Your letters have to make him fall for you really hard.'

Lena took a deep breath. 'It seems wrong somehow.'

'Of course it's wrong,' Sofi said gently. 'But you have a lifetime to make up for this sin. A lifetime in a land of boundless opportunities.'

Natalya was more practical. 'He has a lot of money. He won't miss it.'

'But if he falls in love . . .'

'He won't fall in love. You can't fall in love with someone you've never met. He'll think it's love, but he'll get over it.'

And so the dance began.

He was forty-eight, had suffered through a messy divorce – 'I gave the bitch half a million to shut up' – and was looking for somebody 'more old-fashioned, who wants a man to be a man'. They wrote once a fortnight and, beneath his brittle exterior, Lena thought she began to see his heart. He was hurt, and afraid. That was for certain. She grew to pity him for his unpleasantness, which was obviously a social handicap. She was forgiving of him in her letters and he warmed to her forgiveness. He said that he was in love. Though who he was in love with, Lena couldn't guess. It was

Natalya's photo pinned to his wall. But it was with Lena that he had forged a connection. Every time one of his letters arrived and Natalya or Sofi opened it, she felt that something sacred had been violated.

In the meantime, Natalya posed for more photographs and tried to improve her English. She approached this task through watching *Santa Barbara* and occasionally picking up an English study guide listlessly, before putting it aside and declaring that it would be easy enough to learn once they actually got to America. Sofi, for her part, began gathering forms for visas, started the process of getting passports for all of them, researched work regulations in other countries, set up an international bank account, and went through the shoebox to identify more suitable marks for their next venture.

They were a magnificent team, but Lena wondered how many times they could do this before they all started to get hard and cold.

And as much as she dreamed of a bright future out of Russia, she wondered if the cost might be too high.

Roy Creedy had promised a Christmas present and Natalya became obsessed with speculating what it might be.

'A diamond necklace,' she suggested.

Sofi laughed. 'Nobody sends diamonds through the mail.'

But Natalya could tell Sofi hoped for a diamond necklace too.

Every afternoon after work Natalya checked the mailbox they were using. Every afternoon she was disappointed.

One Wednesday, in the second week of December, when a light snow had frosted the dirty street and made it look almost pretty, she came home to find Lena and Sofi waiting for her. Both jumped off the sofa as the door opened, and Natalya paused, wary.

'What's happened?'

'The present has come,' Lena said. 'I called Sofi right away.'

'It's not what we thought,' Sofi explained. 'And we can't sell it.'

Natalya dropped her bag, wondering why Lena was chewing her lip nervously. 'Why not? What is it?'

Sofi brandished a slip of papers. 'It's a plane ticket. Your name. He's given you a couple of months to get organised with a passport and so on. February fourteenth. In America, this is Valentine's Day.'

Natalya snatched the ticket from Sofi's hand. There was her name, printed on a plane ticket to Chicago. A return flight with no return date yet set. The thrill started in her toes and surged up through her.

'We'll understand if you don't want to go,' Sofi was saying. 'We don't really know him, you'd be by yourself and your English isn't great. If only he'd sent money instead, we could have –'

'Of course I'll go,' Natalya said brusquely.

There was a moment of shocked silence, then Lena said, 'Really? Without us?'

'I'll be fine.' She waved the ticket. 'I'm going to America.'

CHAPTER FIVE

Lena was sorting reservation cards during a quiet moment on the front desk when the shadow of her supervisor fell over her.

'Lena,' he said, his stern features set in hard lines, 'I need to speak with you.'

Alexei Andreev was a presence to be feared. So far Lena had only met him twice. Once when she'd had her interview for the front-desk position, and the second time when she'd arrived late and he'd had to fill in for her by checking in a busload of Japanese tourists. He had roared at her, oblivious to the shocked expressions on the tourists' faces. With his immaculate suit, his imposing height and his rumoured underground crime connection, he had become like a bogeyman in her imagination.

She followed him meekly to his office, where he indicated she should sit down. He sat opposite, turning a white card over in his fingers. She saw what it was immediately and squirmed.

'I can explain,' she started, but he shook his head and made a gesture that suggested she should keep her lips closed.

He held the card in front of him, slipped on his reading glasses and, with a theatrical tone, read from the side printed in Russian: 'Viktor Ivanovich Chernov, born 1943. Dark hair, brown eyes, medium build. Please contact Lena Viktorovna Chernova, Oleg-Vladimirsky pl. apartment 11B, Leningrad.' He took his glasses off slowly and fixed her in his icy gaze. 'Do you want to know how I got this?'

She remained silent.

'An American guest complained to me. She said you had given it to her, forced it on her. I think you've forgotten that the Americans are still wary of Russians; they think the KGB still watch everything we do. She thought you might be some kind of spy.' He laughed, flicking the card towards her. 'I told her you hadn't the intellect for espionage. You haven't even corrected your address. Leningrad has been St Petersburg for years.'

Lena picked up the card. She didn't explain that it had cost her a lot of money to have the cards printed so changing the city name was not an option. Nor did she tell him that she had given one of the cards to every American tourist and most English-speaking Japanese tourists (Vladivostock was, after all, very close to Japan and perhaps Papa had taken his chances there) since she had had them printed two years ago. Instead she said, 'I'm sorry. I know I shouldn't have done it. I won't do it again.'

'I assume this man is your father?'

'He is.'

'If he disappeared in 1976, the likelihood is that he upset somebody in the Party. Many people "disappeared". But you think he's still alive?'

'Yes. I do.' Even as she said it, she knew that she could not hold on to that hope much longer.

His pity took the edge off his anger. 'Lena Viktorovna, I would be pleased if you would leave the guests to enjoy their holidays without harassment. If I discover you continuing with this nonsense, I will dismiss you from employment.'

She hung her head. 'Yes, Alexei Andreev.' She cared little about the job, but knew she should hang on to it just in case. Until the day they bought their plane tickets. Then she would tell Alexei Andreev exactly what she thought of him.

'I want you to bring to me all of the cards you have. I will destroy them so you won't be tempted.'

She returned to her locker and reluctantly handed over the cards. A busload of Swedish tourists kept her busy afterwards, and it wasn't until she was making her way home that she thought about Papa again. It had been many years since he had disappeared. She barely remembered him any more. She had one bent photograph that she kept in the drawer with her underwear; Natalya had refused to let her have it in a frame in the apartment. In the same drawer, she had more cards, over a hundred. She doubted she would be able to resist slipping some into her handbag tomorrow; nor resist offering one occasionally to a friendly-looking American. A lifetime's quest was not so easily abandoned.

Viktor Chernov prised his boots off at the front door to his Moscow apartment, dislodging caked mud that shattered as it hit the cracked tiles. Within, he could hear Ulyana moving around in the kitchen and smell onions cooking. He sighed, pulled the little white card out of the pocket of his overalls and read it again.

The American tourist had been almost apologetic. He explained in broken Russian that the woman had been insistent. When he saw the name on Viktor's badge, he felt compelled to give him the card. Viktor had glanced down at his badge, part of the uniform that the large international company he now worked for had insisted upon. He was only a gardener. He travelled an hour every day from his home on the clattering, dingy outskirts of Moscow to keep the flowerbeds at the Moscow Travel-Inn tidy. The woman who had given the tourist the card – no, it wouldn't do to think of her as 'the woman'; she was still his daughter – also worked at a hotel. He stopped himself from reflecting on the coincidence. He stopped himself, too, from feeling any pity for her. All these years later and she was still looking for him. He'd assumed his children would have forgotten him long ago.

'Get me a drink, Ulyana,' he said as he fell into the torn vinyl sofa.

'Get it yourself,' she replied, draining the remains of her own glass. He eyed her from his vantage point as she bustled in the kitchen. Her wide thighs straining at the material of her pants, her brassy blonde hair growing grey at the roots. Had she ever once been the temptress? The woman who had convinced him to shed his family commitments and disappear?

She poured him a large splash of vodka anyway, and set it at his elbow. 'Tough day? You look tired.'

He always looked tired. He *was* tired. Tired of life, worn down by it. Sometimes, when he thought that he might have another thirty years left to live, he went cold in the stomach. He held up the card to show to Ulyana. She read it quickly.

'Where did you get this?'

'A tourist at work. It's from my daughter, the younger one.'

She recoiled, her mouth turning down in distaste. 'The children?'

'They're not children any more. They'd both be in their twenties.'

'Really? Has it been that long?'

He knew, from the way she dressed, that she still thought of herself as twenty-five. Their years together had been a bright, brief haze to her, trapped in a bubble of alcohol.

'What are you going to do?' she asked.

'Nothing.'

'You don't want to see them?'

He shook his head. 'Oh, no. That's all over.'

'Good.'

He smiled at her. 'Maybe if one of them became a millionaire I'd get in touch.'

She laughed, and for a moment he caught a glimpse of the woman she used to be, before stained teeth and drooping eyelids. Ah, who was he to complain? A balding gardener who reeked of tobacco and trembled if he went eight hours without a drink.

'Make sure you do,' she said. 'Get us out of this place. Because we certainly can't do it ourselves.'

Natalya knew how to look noble. It was one of her best faces. A lift of the chin, slowed blinking, perhaps even a patient downturn of the gaze at the two little boys crawling noisily around the floor of Chicago's O'Hare international airport, shouting at each other in English. She had already collected her bag and cleared customs, and still Roy Creedy wasn't here. Had she misunderstood the instructions in the last letter? Or had there been a subsequent letter, a changed mind, new plans? But she wouldn't let anyone see how concerned and confused she felt, so she retained her noble aspect, knowing that Roy Creedy's first glimpse of her was the most important.

People jostled past, dragging suitcases and reluctant children alike. The two little boys were called sharply by their mother; a blind man walked past with a guide dog. The whole place seemed to be moving, making noise. She tried not to glance around nervously, instead focusing on snatches of conversation that swirled around her, testing her English comprehension. She wasn't clever; she knew that. But she had worked so hard on her English the last few months. So it disappointed her that most people spoke too quickly or too imprecisely for her to understand.

'Natalya?'

She turned, keeping her eyes calm, and saw him. He approached fast, his eagerness hastily concealed. He was taller than she'd imagined, a meaty man dressed in jeans and a checked button-up shirt, his belly puffing over a large, gleaming belt buckle. A gold ring was trapped behind his knuckle and a chunky gold bracelet rattled against his watch. Long strands of hair had been combed artfully over a shiny pate, and he had spectacularly white teeth which made his smile very engaging. He was neither attractive nor unattractive; and when he took her hand in his bear-like grasp and shook it firmly, she found herself predisposed to like him.

'I'm sorry I was late. The I-94 was ice, and it was bumper to bumper as soon as I left the tollway.'

She smiled, hiding confusion and panic. 'Ah, more slow, please. I have trouble to understand.'

His smile fell slowly. 'Trouble to . . . ? But your letters. Your English is perfect.'

This line she had rehearsed many times. 'I have help with writing letters. I dictate them to my sister. She has very good English.'

She watched his face as he reassessed their correspondence. It was important to smile now, to charm him back to her. 'You be so very patient with me, Mister Creedy? I am just silly girl.'

'No, no, not at all,' he said, taking her suitcase and motioning her towards the doors. 'You're not silly. You're . . . beautiful. We'll get along just fine. And call me Roy.'

'Thank you, Roy,' she said, smiling shyly. 'You are kind man.'

He led her into the parking area, to a hulking station wagon. The sports car in the photographs was nowhere in sight.

'Where is red car, Roy?' she asked, as she settled into the passenger seat and buckled her seatbelt.

'My pride and joy? I don't take her out much, and I definitely don't let women ride in her. She's a Corvette ZR1 hardtop, special edition. Too special. I save her for times when I need to blast up the highway, solo only.' He smiled. 'Don't worry, this is a good car too. Can you drive?'

Natalya had understood less than half of what he'd said. But the last question was clear enough. 'I can drive. I have no paper.'

'No licence?'

'That's it. No licence.'

She started to get the hang of the language as they conversed in the car. He told her about the ranch-style house he'd built south-east of DeKalb: the town, he told her proudly, where barbed wire had been invented. They drove through wide fields ploughed to black, snow melting from them in uneven shapes. The sun had started to set and the sky was pale above the stretching horizon, birds travelling in flocks to get home before dark. Occasionally, she would see an endless train making its way across the flat landscape. She was tired. Her brain couldn't keep up with Roy's small talk. It had been a very long day, and she had crossed enough time zones to make her feel popped out of her natural rhythm. She was simply waiting to come to rest. Unknowingly, she started to doze.

Some time later, she didn't know how long, he was shaking her awake. She started, confused. His large male presence gave her a sudden primal surge of adrenaline. She gasped before she could stop herself.

'Hey, hey, it's okay, we're home,' he said in a soothing voice. The sky was dark now and the car had stopped. 'I won't hurt you, Natalya. You can trust me.'

She watched in the rearview mirror as he went around and opened the back to get her suitcase out. *Yes*, she thought, *but you can't trust me.*

The next morning, she woke to sun streaming through a crack between the curtains in the sumptuously appointed guest bedroom. It took her a few moments to get her bearings, check the clock and realise that she had slept very late. The previous night had been confusing. Her brain had been too tired to keep up with English, the meal he had served her too salty to eat. The house was gigantic. She felt trapped in a fairy tale. He had shown her through with pride, muttering all the time. She had caught only a few phrases. Something about his cleaner, and not needing her any more soon. She nodded through it all, longing for bed, then collapsed onto her pillow and fell into dreamless slumber.

Now she pulled the curtain open and found herself looking through french doors onto a balcony and beyond to an uninterrupted view of green garden and black fields. A leafless maple tree stood in the centre of the wide, flat lawn, flowerbeds crowded at its feet. The sky was pale blue and cloudless. She thought about home: the tiny apartment crushed on all sides by other dingy buildings, the long days when she didn't even see the sky, the endless sticky humidity of summer, the dirty rain and snow of winter. And the idea glimmered into her mind: maybe it wouldn't be the worst thing in the world actually to marry Roy Creedy and live in this paradise forever. It was what she wanted after all: to be rich, live in a big house in America.

She knew that fame was a long shot, really, and here, right in front of her and available right now, was the kind of life she had long dreamed of.

A gentle knock at the door.

'Yes,' she called in English.

Roy Creedy opened it, his eyes slipping to the front of her nightgown. She gently grasped the collar, drawing her arms over her chest.

'Ah, hi,' he said. 'It's getting late. I thought you might want some breakfast.'

'Yes, this is good,' she replied. 'I will make my clothes and come now.'

'Great,' he said. 'I have a surprise for you.' He withdrew, taking his greedy gaze with him.

She quickly dressed and brushed her hair, stopping to put on some mascara for good measure. In the dining room, a plate of bacon and eggs awaited her. Beside the plate was a small velvet box. Her heart picked up its rhythm.

'I've already eaten,' he said, gesturing to her to sit down and taking the seat next to her. 'I'm up very early most days. Successful businessmen don't wait for office hours.' He grinned proudly. He was wearing precisely the same outfit as the day before, except the shirt was a different colour.

'You look nice in blue, Roy,' she said as she picked up her fork, pretending to ignore the box.

'And you . . . you'd look good in anything.' His voice dropped to a whisper. 'Or nothing.' He pushed the box towards her. 'Open it.'

Her fingers trembled as she slowly lifted the lid. Inside, a huge sparkling-cut diamond on a gold ring. She drew in her breath.

'You like it?' he said, plucking the ring out of the box and offering it to her left hand.

'Is real?'

'Oh, yes. Of course.'

She thrust her hand forward, but then he snatched the ring back and his smile was gone.

'A few things I need to make perfectly clear first.'

She nodded, her ears ringing slightly as she tried very hard to concentrate on what he would say next.

'I don't like independent wives. I already had one of those and she screwed me for a lot of money. If you marry me, you agree that I'm the boss.'

'Of course,' she said, quickly abandoning any idea that she could actually marry him. She would stick to Sofi's plan. The diamond looked to be worth a lot of money, and once it was on her finger it was hers and she could do what she liked with it.

'And you do the things a wife's supposed to do. The cooking and cleaning, keeping my house nice. I'll allow one baby, but I don't like babies and I don't have the energy for them, so I'm not looking after it. That's a woman's work, and I don't want to be bothered.'

'I have no idea for babies,' she said. 'No babies is okay.'

'You say that now, but you'll change your mind. Just so we're clear. Only one.' He held up his finger and wagged it, a gesture more suited to a small child.

She nodded.

'And last: there are certain duties a wife performs that . . .' He blushed and she almost laughed. 'In the bedroom, I'm the boss. What I say goes.' Now the bluster returned to his voice. 'I get what I want, when I want it.'

'Yes, Roy,' she purred. 'But not until after we have marry.'

'Old-fashioned girl, eh? I like that.'

She offered him her hand again, smiling prettily.

'Sweet Jesus, you are beautiful,' he sighed, then slid the ring onto her finger. 'I'll do the paperwork. No big wedding, okay?'

She pouted. 'But pretty dress? And I only bring some of my thing. I need to go back to Russia to –'

'No. No "go back to Russia", you stay with me. I'll buy you new clothes. If there's anything you really want or need, you can send money to your sister to package it up and post it.'

'My sister? She can come to wedding?'

He frowned, then shrugged in concession. 'I suppose. We can buy her an airfare.'

Natalya thought about other things to ask for, other costs that could mount up and force him to give her a lump sum of money. But she didn't want to push her luck and knew she needed to keep his trust. She leaned her head on his shoulder and sank into him. 'You are kind man, Roy. I am very happy.'

He turned her face to him and kissed her; too wet, lots of tongue. Ah, well, it wasn't the first time she had been kissed badly.

'We'll be happy together,' he said, 'as long as you mind what I say.'

He pressed her against him and she gazed over his shoulder and through the kitchen window to that magnificent view. She could go now. She had the ring. But if she just stayed another week . . . there might be another opportunity to get more out of him, enough so that they wouldn't have to repeat this process too many times. She admired the diamond, shining brilliantly on her finger, and was very pleased with herself.

CHAPTER SIX

It took five days for him to leave her alone.

Natalya knew he was wary; that was why he had forbidden a trip home to Russia, after all. But she had charmed her way under his defences, playing up her inadequate English to make herself seem almost naive, a quality he seemed to admire above all others. Or *almost* all others. He was spellbound by her looks, that much was clear. She quite enjoyed the attention, and did her best to dress demurely yet be provocative all at once. A forgotten button on her blouse, a casual hitch of her skirt when sitting next to him in the car, a smile imbued with meaning over breakfast.

He had been busy entertaining her and needed to get on with his work. He owned a shopping mall in a neighbouring town, and a problem with the heating system required him to be out of the house for the day.

'I will be fine by myself,' she assured him. 'I will cook traditional Russian dinner for you.'

He shook his head. 'None of that foreign crapola for me. There's steak in the freezer.'

She smiled brilliantly, although she was amused. All he ate was steak, usually with potatoes, sometimes with bread and bacon and fried onions. Natalya had a stomach-ache from the fare she'd been eating so far.

'Yes. I will make you steak,' she said, all the while knowing she wasn't going to make him anything, that she would be gone before he returned.

He added a baseball cap to his usual ensemble and let himself out of the house.

An hour after he'd left, when she was very sure she was alone, she packed her suitcase and looked up the phone number for a taxi. She intended to get to the nearest town, then find a bus to the airport. She had a small amount of American dollars for the fare, but she hesitated before she picked up the phone. The diamond ring would be worth a good amount, but it seemed a long way to come, a lot of work to do, to be leaving with so little. She left her suitcase in the kitchen and walked down the long, quiet hallway to his bedroom. The door was shut. She tried it. Locked.

Bastard.

Urgency gripped her. If it was locked, then there was something in there she wanted, she knew it. She crouched down, jiggling the handle, trying to peer through the crack between the door and the jamb. She sighed, almost defeated. Then remembered the balcony that led off her own bedroom. She hurried through, and found herself standing outside the french doors to his bedroom. Of course they were locked too, but there was nobody in miles to see her pick up a rock from a pot plant or to hear the glass shatter. She carefully slid her hand through the broken pane – caught the skin of her wrist on a jagged edge – and opened the door. Her heart thudded. She felt like a thief. She *was* a thief. The blood began to drip off the cut on her arm and she grabbed a handful of tissues off Roy's dresser to press against the wound. She waited a moment for her heart to still, then put the tissues in her pocket and started the search.

The room smelled musty and male. It seemed he didn't let the cleaner in here: clothes were strewn about and a layer of dust covered everything. He had a television on top of the dresser, and an en suite bathroom where his towel lay untidily in a puddle. She opened his wardrobe, not sure what she was looking for. She found only clothes and shoes, baseball caps lined up. She went to his dresser. More clothes, belts, half-empty bottles of aftershave, a whole drawer of socks: not matched, just thrown in together. Nothing of value.

She crouched down and looked under his bed. A large box. She pulled it out and flipped open the lid. It was full of pornographic videos and books. Nasty ones. A quick glance at a few of the covers indicated that anyone who promised Roy Creedy that they would follow his instructions in the bedroom would come to regret it very much. Two handguns were tucked into the box. Her heart skipped a beat. Stuck in the corner with a sticky blob was a key. She pulled it out and looked around her again. A key to what? She had checked everywhere.

Perhaps not thoroughly enough. She ploughed through the sock drawer, the underwear drawer. Clothes flew everywhere, but she found nothing to unlock. In the distance, she could hear the phone had started to ring. She ignored it at first, then realised it might be Roy checking up on her. If she didn't answer he may come home – to broken glass and rummaged drawers. Would he then find good use for those two handguns? She ran around back through her own bedroom and picked up the phone in the hallway.

'Hello?' she said, trying not to sound breathless.

'That's not how you answer my phone,' he said, and there was nothing good-natured about his voice. 'You say "Creedy residence, Natalya speaking". What took you so long?'

'I did not know if I am allowed to pick up phone,' she said. 'But then I think, what if that is my darling Roy? And it is you, so I am glad I pick up.'

He chuckled softly. 'Are you being a good girl?'

'Yes, of course,' she answered.

'Well, let's go out for dinner tonight. Some of my business associates are meeting in town around seven. I'm gonna show you off.'

'Oh, that's nice. I like to go to dinner.'

'I'll be home by four so we can go shopping, buy you something pretty.'

She felt a real twinge of sympathy for him then, but realised she had gone too far to back out. 'I see you then.'

Moments later she was back in his bedroom, looking for what the key unlocked. She turned her attention once more to the wardrobe, to the row of caps lined up on the shelf. She reached up, pulled them down one by one. Under the last one she found it: a square iron box with a lock on top. The key fitted. She turned it.

And struck gold, quite literally. Four thick gold chain bracelets, a gold watch studded with diamonds, gold rings that his fingers had outgrown, a gold pen, and a gold-and-diamond keyring attached to a car key.

Natalya held it up in front of her face, watching the key spin left and right.

The red sports car.

She took the box, emptied its contents into her suitcase, then found the internal door to the garage. Of course it was locked too, but it was an old-fashioned keyhole lock and twenty minutes' concentrated fiddling with two metal paperclips popped it. Twenty minutes during which she could have changed her mind – she had enough – but she just kept going, blocking all thoughts of regret, fear, guilt, ignoring all consequences.

The garage door to the outside world was automated. She hit the button, letting the light stream onto the car's gleaming red bonnet. *My pride and joy.* Natalya reflected on her early schooling, how they had learnt about American capitalist pigs and their love of consumption. Roy fitted the description perfectly and, deep in her childish communist heart, she decided that this was just redistribution of wealth. She unlocked the car, slid into the white leather driver's seat and started the engine. A tiger. She revved. It felt nothing like the old Ford that she had driven around Vyborg when Tolya was teaching her to drive.

She slipped it into gear and took off. Couldn't quite manage the speed and lurched to a stop. Told herself to be calm and concentrate. Deep breath. The tiger growled into life again and she was away. She flicked on the radio, chased country music across the dial, then flicked it off. She had no idea which way the airport was, simply felt the need to get far away quickly.

An hour later she pulled over at a gas station just off the highway. At first she wondered if they were closed. The cement was rutted and the shop was in a state of disrepair. The rusted steel roller doors on the adjoining workshop were closed. But a bird-eyed man ambled out of the shop and approached her car, rubbing his bristly chin. A name badge woven onto his overalls read *Russell*.

'Can I help you, lady?'

'I need to find car shop.'

'Car shop?'

She cursed her poor English. 'I need to sell car.'

Russell stood back, running his eye over the car's sleek body. 'Hmm, is that right? And this car is yours, is it?'

'Of course,' she said.

'You've got the paperwork and all to go with it?'

'I . . . no.' Her heart sank. Naive little fool. Of course there would be papers involved, registration and so on.

He turned from her and called over his shoulder towards the workshop. 'Jim! Open up!'

Natalya wasn't sure what to do, what they intended. She thought about putting the car back into gear and driving off, but if she did she would knock the man over. From within, somebody was hauling up the chains on one of the roller doors.

Russell turned back to her. 'Drive on in. I think me and Jim might just be able to help you.'

Natalya nodded once, and backed the car into the workshop. Within moments, Jim was at work removing the numberplates.

'Hey!' Natalya protested.

'Hush, now,' Russell said. 'I thought you wanted me to help you?'

She felt keenly her foreignness, her inability to explain or ask for explanations. 'What are you doing?' she said.

'This ain't your car, sweetheart. But me and Jim, we know how to make it ours. All that remains is for you to give us a price.'

Natalya began to understand. She had no idea what to ask for. 'I need money, not cheque.'

'Cash? Got it.'

'I need somebody take me to airport straightaway.'

'Got it.'

She looked at the car, uncertain. 'Ten thousand dollars?'

Russell laughed. 'Do you know how much this car is worth?'

She felt foolish, shook her head.

'Looks like we both got lucky today, lady. I'll give you your ten thousand dollars, cash, and take you to the airport. You've gotta come with me to the bank –'

'Not DeKalb,' she said. 'Big trouble for me there maybe.'

'No problems. Jim, you get on with that. I'm taking the lady to her plane.'

He loaded her into a rattling pick-up truck and they headed out amongst the wintry cornfields. He didn't feel a need to talk to her, so she was left mercifully alone with her thoughts. Ten thousand dollars. Plus the diamond ring, plus whatever the gold jewellery would fetch. She had done it. With one mark, she had set herself, her sister and her cousin on a path towards their dreams. She could barely keep the smile off her face. They rattled into a town and pulled up in a monstrous car park outside a shopping mall.

'Wait here,' he said, taking the keys with a smile. 'Don't steal mine too.'

She did as she was told. The engine of the car ticked quietly. She looked around her, then her heart jumped. Diagonally opposite was Roy's station wagon. She recognised the nodding dog toy on the dash. This must be *his* shopping mall. How could she have been so stupid, insisting Russell not take her to DeKalb? Roy wasn't in DeKalb, he was here.

Her instinct was to get out of the car and run. But what if he spotted her? And what about her ten thousand dollars? She slid down into the footwell, among dirt and empty soda cans, wrapped her arms around her knees and tucked her head down. An eternity passed, and every footstep she heard outside she was sure belonged to Roy.

She tried to think up explanations, but fear had confused her so she just sat, curled in a ball, and hoped the horror would be over soon.

The door opened. Russell laughed.

'Who you hiding from?'

'Please? We go now?'

'You going to get back in your seat?'

She shook her head.

'Have it your way. Here.' He gently threw a fat envelope at her. 'Pay day.'

As they backed out of their spot, she risked a peek at Roy's car. It still sat there, waiting for him. To take him home to his plundered house, to a disappointment he didn't know was coming. Natalya felt tears prick her eyes, and she wasn't sure who they were for. She just wanted to get to the airport quickly and go home.

CHAPTER SEVEN

Sofi passed the Borodinskaya-22 art gallery on her walk home from work every day, and kept an eager eye out for new exhibitions. She loved to amble across the polished floorboards, through the mazelike exhibition rooms, and contemplate beautiful art. On the day that she met Julien, she was so wrapped up in thoughts of Natalya's trip to America – wondering if she'd arrived safely, if Roy Creedy was treating her well, if she'd got any money out of him yet, and if Sofi could ever forgive herself for the scam – that she almost didn't see the poster. But then a fair-haired man in his mid-thirties stepped out in front of her without looking, nearly knocking her over.

'I'm sorry,' he said in heavily accented Russian, before distractedly turning away.

'It's fine.'

She glanced up and noticed that the man had been pinning a poster under the glass display case at the front door of the gallery. A new exhibition, French artist Julien Blanchard. One of his paintings took up half the poster: a sumptuous feast of rich colours, a woman's reclining body. She paused. The man had moved on to the other display case. Sofi went in.

She found Julien Blanchard's paintings in the second exhibition hall, where the international artists displayed. His paintings spoke to her soul. They had the composition, richness and romance of Pre-Raphaelite art, but were rendered in an almost expressionistic style. The woman at the centre of the first canvas, an exhibit nearly as tall as Sofi, had blue-white skin that looked soft as butter; her fingers were feathered into her scarlet hair; and she lay upon a deep green chaise longue whose edges blurred into a collection of pastoral shapes and colours. Sofi stood for an age admiring the way the colours borrowed beauty from one another, the way the movement of the painting made her feel content and almost drowsy, then moved to the next canvas. It was equally spellbinding. His work had the nineteenth-century sensibility that she was always trying to capture in her jewellery: something that looked traditional, antique, richly detailed, and yet made use of modern materials and techniques.

The man who had been pinning up the posters appeared at her elbow, and she sensed that he was looking at her.

She turned, tried a smile. He looked back at her with clear blue eyes, almost icy. He didn't smile. Instead, he said, 'What do you see?'

Taken aback, she didn't know how to answer. 'They are beautiful,' she said simply.

'I painted them.'

Now she became even more flustered, in the presence of the artist himself. 'Really? My goodness, I'm honoured to meet you. You are . . . an inspiration.'

He looked at her blankly. 'I'm sorry, my Russian is not good. Do you speak French?'

She shook her head and they fell to silence, considering each other for a moment. Then he turned and walked away, disappeared into a back room marked for staff. She returned her attention to the paintings, but the spell had been broken. All she could think about was the artist, Julien Blanchard. About life in France, being a painter. About how fortunate he was, and how unaware he seemed to be of this good fortune. She idly played with the cuff of silver wire and glass beads that she wore around her wrist, wondering if one day something she created would mean as much to somebody as Julien Blanchard's paintings meant to her.

Sofi was sitting at the dining table, her beads spread out around her, turning a postcard of one of Julien Blanchard's paintings over in her fingers, when Mama came home.

'Everything all right?' she asked, dropping her bag by the door. She approached Sofi and glanced at the postcard. 'That's pretty.'

'I met the artist,' Sofi said, knowing she sounded starstruck. 'A real, live artist.'

'I suppose he eats, sleeps and breathes just like the rest of us,' Mama said.

The phone rang and Sofi leapt up to get it.

'Natalya's back.' It was Lena's voice.

'What? When? She didn't call us. Did it go all right? Is she well?'

But Lena cut her off. 'No time. We need you to help us pack up. Natalya's got a friend coming later tonight to move our stuff out.'

'Move already? Why?'

'Just come. Quickly.' And the phone cut off.

Mama frowned. 'Who was that?'

Sofi was already at the door, gathering her coat. 'Lena. I have to dash. See you later.'

She hurried down to the metro and made her way to Pushkinskaya, desperate to know what had happened, why they were packing their things in such a hurry, hopeful and terrified all at once. A thick cover of cloud trapped the pale glow of streetlights. People in overcoats and fur hats bustled past her, and the smell of grease frying in restaurants penetrated the damp, cold air. She headed through a tunnel of scaffolding covering an old Italianate stone building – so many scaffoldings through the city now – and down the last uneven lane that led to her cousins' apartment block.

Lena let her in with a breathless hello. Their apartment was in disarray. Clothes and books in piles everywhere, boxes stacked precariously on top of each other.

'What's happening? Where's Natalya?'

'Here,' Natalya answered, emerging from the bathroom with a packing box. 'Make yourself useful. Put those books in those boxes.' She indicated with a shrug of her slender shoulders.

'I'm not doing a thing until you tell me what's going on.'

'I'll tell you everything,' Natalya said. 'But just start packing. Tolya is coming in one hour with a van.'

So Sofi started packing books, while Natalya told her the incredible story of charming and robbing Roy Creedy, before stealing his car and running away. Sofi was horrified and thrilled all at once. Ten thousand dollars and a quantity of gold jewellery! As guilty as she felt, the bubble of hope that the story aroused in her could not be burst.

'We won't need to do it again,' Lena concluded. 'Isn't that great?'

'But we have to get out of here immediately,' Natalya said. 'If he comes to the address over the road, well, that's too close for comfort. He might see me. I've little doubt that he could be dangerous.'

'Where are you going to go?'

'With you. Aunt Stasya's.'

Sofi opened her mouth to say there wasn't room, but of course there was. They had shared a bedroom before; most of the furniture in this apartment wasn't theirs; and, besides, within a very short time they would be off, away, out of Russia, on paths to new destinies. She felt a pang thinking about Mama, so unsuspecting.

The collection of packed boxes grew. Sofi's stomach grumbled, and she wondered if her cousins had eaten. A celebration would be nice; a restaurant and a bottle of smooth *mukuzani*.

'Is it all right if I give Tolya the jewellery too?' Natalya asked. 'He has plenty of contacts to sell things.'

'No, no,' Sofi said. 'I know a vintage jeweller. They'll have a better idea of the value. Tolya will take the first offer that comes along. I'll go tomorrow. The sooner it's sold the better.'

'Yes, then we can all move to Hollywood,' Natalya said, without looking up from the box she was packing.

Sofi considered her a moment, and Lena also stopped to watch them both. Natalya looked up, a crease of puzzlement between her eyebrows. 'What's wrong?'

'Shall you tell her or shall I?' Lena said.

Sofi took a deep breath. Natalya hadn't realised the obvious and was going to be very disappointed. 'We can't go to America, Natalya,' she said.

'What? Why? I thought this was all about . . .' She trailed off, realisation dawning. 'Oh. *He*'s in America.'

'And you stole his car, among other things,' Lena finished for her.

'But it's a big country,' Natalya wailed.

'If he's alerted the police, they'd know when you came back into the country. Even if they didn't, do you want to be feeling all the time that your past is going to catch up with you?'

Natalya shook her head, pouting prettily. 'But I want to be a movie star.'

'Then pick another country that makes movies,' Sofi said. 'France?'

'None of us speak French,' Lena said.

'Then it has to be England.'

'London,' Natalya said, as though trying it on her tongue to see if it tasted as good as 'Hollywood'.

'London,' Sofi echoed. They had enough for travel, for rent of a little flat, a few necessities to get them started. Her imagination crowded with images of promise and it felt as though she was expanding, out and out of herself, into a new world where anything was possible.

But first she had to tell her mother.

Mama didn't talk to Sofi for two weeks. Not a word. The presence of her cousins only served to make the situation more awkward. Sofi had explained, as quickly as she could while Lena and Natalya had brought their things into the little apartment, that they had been saving their money and now it was time for them to go, to leave St Petersburg and Russia. Mama said nothing, and added nothing to it over the coming days.

After the initial two weeks, the ice thawed a little. But still Mama only communicated with her when absolutely necessary. Despite all her efforts, as the months went by and the tortuous business of organising the visas consumed her spare time, Sofi could not shake her mother out of this mood. She felt cut adrift. Her heart wanted to share all the excitement and frustration of this process with the person dearest to her. She needed Mama's calm practicality; but Mama kept her at arm's length.

Finally, finally, the visas were approved. Sofi's English had improved vastly from going through the process, but Natalya's still languished. They set a date, they bought their tickets. A one-way fare was not allowed, so they set the furthest return date they could and vowed to have some reason to apply to stay beyond that first twelve months. They packed, each trying to fill only one suitcase but her cousins finally stretching to two. As the day drew closer, the feeling of melancholy grew and grew until it enveloped Sofi. Leaving this city – the place of her birth, the only home she had ever known – would be easier if she could at least hold her mother and cry on her shoulder.

Two nights before they were due to leave, Lena and Natalya went out to give Sofi and Mama some time alone. Sofi stayed in her room a little while, cleaning out the box that contained all of her old university papers. Mama was sitting on the sofa watching television when Sofi returned from the rubbish bin. She approached, stood hesitantly behind the sofa.

'Mama?'

'Hm?' She didn't look up.

Sofi strode to the television and turned it off. 'Mama, we have to talk.'

'Hey! I was watching that.'

'Don't you think this is more important?'

Mama sniffed, averting her eyes. 'You and I do not agree, obviously, on what's important.'

Sofi sat next to her, reached for her hands and leaned forward. 'Mama, please. Please don't be so cold with me.'

Mama fell silent.

'Can you at least tell me why you are so angry with me?'

Another silence. This was as far as she ever got with Mama. She certainly wasn't expecting an answer this time.

But, in a small voice, Mama said, 'I don't know.'

Sofi's pulse quickened. At last, she was going to talk.

'Can we talk about it?'

Mama sighed. 'Really, Sofi. I don't want to.'

'You must. I don't want things to be so strained between us when I'm going to be so far away.'

Mama shifted on the sofa, leaning away from her. In the soft lamplight, Sofi could see the lines deepening around her mother's mouth.

'I'll miss you, Mama. Will you miss me?'

'Of course,' she said gruffly.

'Do you feel left behind? Is that it?'

'I do feel left behind, Sofi,' Mama sighed. 'But not by you particularly. I feel left behind by the world.'

'What do you mean?'

'I used to know where I fitted. Under the old system. But now it seems to me that nobody *needs* anybody any more.'

'I still need you.' Sofi didn't remind her that daughters grew up and left home all over the world every single day.

'I knew where I stood,' Mama continued, her voice growing impassioned. 'But that certainty has been taken away from me. I work longer hours for less pay and I don't know who to complain to. My rent keeps going up and up. I phone the letting agent to tell them about the broken tile in the bathroom and nothing gets done. I'm the only person who still uses the communal kitchen; everyone else has stoves in their apartments. I don't know who my neighbours are any more except for old Irina. And now . . . I lose my daughter.'

'You aren't losing me. We'll write. We'll see each other again. You can come to visit.'

'How? How would I afford to come to London? With you gone, my rent will double. I'll have to take in a boarder. Today, Sofi, I feel like a fool. I have spent my life sacrificing myself . . . for the collective, for my child, and for my brother-in-law's children. This sacrifice has rewarded me with nothing. I am forty-eight years old, I am used up. This is it.' She gestured around her hopelessly. 'This is my life.'

Sofi's throat constricted with holding back tears. 'I'll send you money, Mama. When I'm a big success. You can come and live with me.'

'I don't want money, and I won't accept money,' Mama said. 'Besides, it's all written with a pitchfork in the river. Big success? Who says you will be?' She shrugged. 'And I'll be here waiting when you get back.'

I'm not coming back. Sofi stilled her tongue. She fell into Mama's arms and held her tight a long time. Mama cried and stroked her hair, and Sofi felt the full weight of the goodbye. She even thought about staying, but then decided that a better thing to do was to leave and to make something wonderful of her life, to show her mother that it was possible.

CHAPTER EIGHT

Natalya tried not to be home too much in the evenings now. Aunt Stasya was fractious about them moving back in without asking, so Natalya stayed behind at the shoe shop, then walked along the canals until late, smoking and trying to keep every inch of St Petersburg in her memory. Sometimes she didn't get home until Stasya had gone to bed.

It was unlike her to be melancholy, and she knew it. Some days she grew hugely impatient with Sofi, who seemed to be taking forever to organise their visas. She just wanted to be away, gone. But other days she wondered how she would fit in in a new city. Here, she knew everything, she was somebody. There . . . who knew? And on other days, she had to repeat her adventures in America over and over in her head, almost as though trying to convince herself that they'd really happened. It was a blur now, and she could hardly believe that she'd robbed a man and sold his car, which she'd since discovered was worth at least five times what she'd taken for it. Perhaps, then, she was also walking out her guilt. She knew Sofi and Lena had struggled with it too.

Natalya finished a cigarette by the plinth of Peter the Great's statue on Senatskaya Square. She wouldn't miss the metallic sourness of the canals and exhaust fumes, but she might miss the decaying grandeur of St Petersburg, its golden lights. She looked about for Tolya, who was supposed to meet her here. Another uncomfortable swirl of guilt, this time for her sister and cousin. She had kept the engagement ring. Not because she wanted a diamond, but because she felt she was owed something special, something particular to her, given that she had taken the biggest risks. She had asked Tolya to sell it for her. There would be auditions to go to; she needed great clothes and shoes. Sofi had taken charge of the money as though it were her own, determined to make it last the whole year without them having to take jobs that would distract them from their goals. All Natalya wanted was a little something for herself.

She was about to light another cigarette when she saw Tolya's familiar hulking shape approaching. She waved, and he hurried over.

'Natalya,' he said, smiling, his breath steaming from his lips. A streetlight caught his unshaven cheek. He chuckled. 'I'm sorry, but it's funny.'

'What's funny?' she asked warily.

He pulled from his pocket a familiar box: the one she'd given to him with the engagement ring in it.

'Couldn't you sell it?'

'No,' he said. 'Nobody wanted it.'

She was annoyed. Tolya usually did everything she asked. 'Well, I'll take it somewhere else then. I'll –'

'Natalya, it's not real.'

'What?'

'You heard. Open the box, have a look what happened when the jeweller inspected it.'

Natalya flipped open the lid. The 'diamond' hung half out of its setting.

'The ring's not even real gold. The best offer I got for it was one hundred roubles. I thought you might prefer it as a keepsake.'

She felt a short, sharp burst of anger and betrayal. But then she was laughing like Tolya. Laughing and laughing until her eyes were wet and her stomach ached. Roy Creedy had given her a fake diamond engagement ring. It was beautiful, hilarious; and any guilt or shame or pity she'd felt evaporated at once into the chilly sky.

Lena woke early. Too early. But the excitement – the fear – of the coming day would not let her sleep. At two o'clock that afternoon, she would be climbing on a plane with her sister and cousin, heading to London. It seemed like a dream, and as Lena lay in bed, trying to get back to sleep, she felt disconnected from reality. Finally, she admitted she wasn't going to sleep another moment, and she rose quietly and dressed.

Natalya woke, sat up and said softly, 'What are you doing?'
'Can't sleep.'
'Keep trying. It's three in the morning. It will be a long day.'
'I'll be fine.'

She slipped out of the bedroom, found her shoes and handbag at the door and, as quietly as she could, left the apartment, hit the street and began to walk.

It was July, and the sun was not far below the horizon. The sky was pale pink, gradating to soft blue above her, and the city's monuments were black shapes against it. The streets were quiet, but not empty. Insomniacs, tourists and teenagers were out, experiencing the white night. It was a curious feeling – dreamlike, almost – walking through a city where night had never arrived. She wandered for a while, then realised that she was heading towards the apartment she had shared with Natalya. The address she had listed on the cards, the address that she hoped would one day fall into her father's hands. It was a route she had taken a number of times since they had moved out. She couldn't bear the thought that he would contact her and she wouldn't know. So she went back every week or so, to lift the mail slot and check for communication from him.

A mosquito settled on her cheek and she swatted it away. The streets were blessedly light on traffic, so the air was fresh and cool. She waited for a sense of melancholy, for the foretaste of homesickness, but found none inside her. Curious. She knew Sofi felt it, and even Natalya had become fond of talking about things they might never see or do again. Certainly, Lena felt the itching nervousness of taking on a big change; but for her, losing her father had been the event that had unseated her. Leaving St Petersburg could never be as hard as that.

Eventually, she arrived at her old apartment block. She still had the key to the security door and let herself into the foyer. A white envelope poked out of the mail slot and her heart leapt. But it was only a letter for Natalya, the logo of a clothing company printed on the corner. Advertising, perhaps. She slid it into her handbag, despondent. She glanced up the stairwell. Maybe somebody new had moved in and they had collected a letter from him? But she dismissed the thought as soon as she had it. Natalya's letter was here; nobody had cleared the mail. The apartment was still unoccupied and she had to admit that none of her little cards had ever found her father.

Lena sat on the bottom step and leaned her head against the iron balustrade. So, was it time to give up? Was it time to be an adult and admit the truth? That her father was either dead or, more likely, had abandoned her and Natalya? She sighed. Going to America wouldn't have helped, and perhaps she always knew that. A new life waited, and a new life required new thinking. Perhaps she would be a movie star after all, or a model, or something. Someone important, who would meet a wonderful important man and forget about her father, her first love, altogether. She closed her eyes and tried to visualise Papa the last time she'd seen him. The features of his face wouldn't resolve; she realised she barely remembered him.

'Goodbye, Papa,' she said, opening her eyes. She rose. Who knew what the future held? Anything was possible. Anything except her father coming back.

As she let herself out to the street, she glanced across at the other apartment block, the one with the burnt-out flat whose mailbox they had used for their Russian bride scam. Guiltily, she glanced around her. Poor Roy. They had used him terribly, and Lena knew from the correspondence they had shared that he wasn't a bad man, despite Natalya's protestations that he was dangerous. He had the same flaws and vulnerabilities as anyone. On impulse, she crossed the road and checked that mailbox too, wondering if he had tried to contact them.

This time, she was rewarded. A cream envelope with Roy Creedy's familiar handwriting on the front. She picked it open and read.

Natalya, you bitch, I'm glad you're gone. I trusted you. I LOVED you. But now I see what you really are, a lying whore. Burn in hell, whore. You've broken my heart. Burn in hell. Roy.

The handwriting was driven into the page with great passion. His sense of anger and betrayal was palpable. Lena read it over and over. *You've broken my heart.* Beneath the rage, there it was, that vulnerable spirit that Lena had always discovered in his letters. Even though it was Natalya who had stolen his things, Lena felt that she had betrayed him the most. They had connected in their letters; she felt she knew him. Now this.

She began to walk again, turning the thoughts over and over in her tired mind. *Go home. Go back to bed. Sleep on it.* But if she slept on it, when would she have the opportunity to be away from Sofi and Natalya today? And they would never let her do what she was thinking of doing.

Her mind made up, she sat on the brick windowsill of a hairdressing shop and rummaged through her bag. Here was a pen. She knew she had stamps in her purse. But paper to write a letter on? She ripped open the envelope addressed to Natalya that she had found earlier. As she suspected, it was a sheet of advertising. The reverse side was blank. Lena began to write in English.

Dear Roy. I owe you an explanation at the very least . . .

She paused. How much to tell?

Natalya isn't entirely to blame. I am her sister, Lena, and I wrote the letters. Our cousin, Sofi, organised everything. We are desperate and poor and I know that doesn't excuse our actions, but perhaps it will help you to understand them. I enjoyed writing letters with you. I think you are a nice person. I hope you find true love with somebody else. I am very, very sorry. Lena.

She read it and re-read it. Convinced herself that it was the right thing to do, that he deserved some communication that acknowledged his anger, apologised for the trouble they had caused him. Nothing bad could come of it – they would have left St Petersburg long before he got the letter, and he was unlikely ever to find them – and perhaps even a little good could come of it. He would be careful in the future. He would know that they regretted their actions.

She slid the sheet into the envelope his letter had come in, peeled off the address label and wrote his in its place. She put all the stamps she had on it; she wouldn't need Russian stamps any more. She posted it on the way home, feeling positive.

Ready for a new start, a new life. Somewhere else.

II

CHAPTER NINE

Natalya was tired of budgets. Or rather, she was tired of Sofi's budgets.

Here she stood, in the office of Hanson & McCall's modelling and extras agency on Tottenham Court Road, with Veronica Hanson herself saying she thought Natalya had a bright future, and yet Natalya couldn't commit to paying the folio fee.

'I have to ask my cousin,' she admitted. 'She is very careful with our money.'

Veronica, an ageing beauty in her early fifties, smiled benevolently. 'Tell her you'll make the money back in a month. I have a few castings right now that you'd be perfect for.'

'Modelling or acting?'

Natalya had been hugely disappointed to find that most modelling agencies imposed a five-foot-nine minimum before taking on new girls. She was half an inch too short. Nobody at the Shining Smile Academy had ever pointed out this deficiency to her.

'Both.'

Again, Natalya was pleasantly surprised. Other agencies had said her Russian accent was far too thick for acting jobs.

'Don't delay,' Veronica said, handing her a business card. 'Call me tonight.'

Natalya headed up to the Goodge Street underground, and made her way back to Fulham where they had rented a tiny flat. She still wasn't used to the English letters on every sign. It felt as though she were wandering in a textbook, all the concepts far too difficult for her to understand. They had been here two weeks, and every day she had dragged herself to agency after agency without success. Usually, Lena came with her. It irked Natalya that her sister insisted on pursuing the same goal as her. A remnant from their childish past. 'Me too!' So many things Natalya had been obliged to share. So this morning she had left the flat quietly, alone.

She bought a packet of chewing gum at the greengrocer on the corner of their street. She had thrown away her cigarettes – again at Sofi's insistence – and was finding it very tough. She knew she'd be able to concentrate better if she could smoke; her English would be better, everything would go smoother. But Sofi had added up a year's worth of cigarettes and discovered it was equivalent to three weeks' rent.

'Do you want to have to get a job, or go home early, just because of cigarettes?' she had asked.

Natalya hadn't answered. She wasn't getting a real job or going back to St Petersburg ever, so the question was pointless. But she gave up smoking anyway, telling herself that when she was rich she could take it up again.

Sofi was sitting on the sagging sofa looking at a glossy catalogue. Lena was nowhere in sight.

'Where's Lena?' Natalya asked, as she hung her handbag behind the door.

'She went for a walk. A secretive one. Like you this morning.' Sofi put the catalogue down, and now Natalya could see it was full of pictures of beads and clasps and jewellery wire.

Good, Lena was out. 'I need to talk to you,' Natalya said, sitting on the coffee table in front of her cousin. She brandished Veronica Hanson's card. 'I've found an agency willing to take me on.'

'You went without Lena?'

Natalya waved the question away. 'Lena doesn't have to tag along with me everywhere. This has always been my dream. She has to find her own.'

Sofi had turned the card over, saw the figure written on the back. 'Oh, my. This is the fee to join?'

'Yes. But she says I'll make it back very quickly.' She dropped her voice low. 'You understand, though, that Veronica Hanson wants me, not Lena.'

'What do we know about this agent? Is she reputable?'

'She seems to be.'

Sofi sighed. 'I suppose there's no point coming all this way and not taking the chance.'

'So I can have the money?'

'Yes, on one condition. We all need to start speaking English, even here at home. We won't survive long without it.'

Natalya winced, but agreed.

'I need a little money too,' Sofi admitted, handing Natalya the catalogue. 'Real silver wire, some glass beads. Not as much as you, but... I've found out about an open market. I think my things will sell.'

'No point coming all this way and not taking the chance,' Natalya echoed. 'But Lena will want her share too.'

'Of course she will.'

'I know it's fair,' Natalya said, 'but Lena has never really been sure about what she wants to do.'

'She wants to be an actress.'

'Does she? Have you ever seen any evidence of that, except for her just going along with me?'

Sofi smiled patiently. 'In any case, once you and I have made this money back, it will have to be her turn next.'

The front door opened, making Natalya and Sofi guiltily cut off their conversation. Lena let herself in and kicked off her shoes. Her straight, dark hair was tied back in a ponytail, making her look like a teenager. Natalya felt a surge of protective instinct for her. Then she noticed that Lena had a lightness about her step, a smile lingering in her cheeks.

Natalya knew her sister: she had met a man.

'Hello,' Lena said. 'You two look very serious.' She headed into the kitchen and opened the refrigerator. 'Is there any milk?'

Sofi rose. 'At the back. Make coffee for all of us.' She paused, dropping her voice to a serious tone. 'We need to talk to you about the money.'

As they drank coffee, Sofi explained. Natalya perched on the edge of the armchair – as hard as the sofa was saggy – and watched Lena's face for signs of that familiar expression of her childhood. The left-out look. Any moment now, she would say, 'Me too.'

But Lena surprised her. 'I suppose that makes sense,' she said with a shrug.

'If Natalya manages to pay back the fee as quickly as she expects, then you can be next,' Sofi said.

'Fine, then. I trust you.'

'You're in a very good mood,' Natalya said.

Lena raised her coffee cup to hide her smile. 'I've just been offered a job three afternoons a week at the newsagent on the other side of the square.'

'A job? I didn't know you wanted a job,' Sofi said.

'I didn't think I did. But I'm bored, and I'll get a chance to practise my English.'

Lena was notoriously reluctant to talk about her love-life, but Natalya could fill in the blanks: the man who had put the smile on her face must work at the newsagent.

In a roundabout way, it seemed they had all got what they wanted today.

Lena stood in a cavernous, smoky pub at St Albans, shifting from foot to foot because her legs were growing tired. She was surrounded on all sides by people dressed in op-shop clothes, batik prints, flannel shirts and Doc Martens boots, and she felt embarrassingly overdressed in a floral print dress and high-heeled shoes. She had wanted to look nice for Sam, but he had brought her to a place where looking nice was not appropriate.

Sam's band, Velvet Ponies – Sam on guitar and vocal, Chris on drums, and James on bass – had secured a spot in the St Albans Battle of the Bands competition. Lena had driven up with the band that afternoon in a van loaned to them by the drummer's father. It was exciting: sitting in the back seat with Sam in a cigarette haze, music blasting on the radio, listening to Sam and his two bandmates plan their set list and fantasise about what they'd record if they won the main prize. Lena and Sam had been on only one date before this, had exchanged a kiss outside the front entrance to her apartment block at midnight. But already it felt as though they were meant to be together. Sam had slid out of his seatbelt to crush up next to her, kissing her ear and stroking her arm.

They had met at the newsagent. He was out front, changing the magazine posters in their perspex displays. She had been walking past and her first glimpse of him . . . well, it had been enough. She faked a need for pens, went inside and lingered a while. While she was at the counter he'd brushed past, smiled at her. That smile – all boyish and languid – had been like a first taste of a wonderful drug. She'd asked the manager if there was any work going; he'd offered her a few hours a week. And she had successfully thrown herself into Sam's world.

Lena shifted her weight again. They'd arrived at the pub at five o'clock. Apart from half an hour sitting down to eat indigestible pork sausages for dinner, she had been on her feet – in her high-heeled shoes – for nearly six hours.

The band on stage clattered to the end of a song. Cheers and whoops filled the vacuum. Warm arms slid around her from behind. Sam.

'Hello, beautiful,' he said in his lilting northern accent.

'When are you on?' she said, turning to him.

'After these lads. They have two more songs.'

The music burst from the PA system again and Lena had to shout. 'Good luck.'

He leaned in to kiss her, the world stopped, then started again as he moved away.

At last, just when she thought she couldn't stand for a moment longer, Sam's band took to the stage.

'How are you doing tonight?' Sam said into the microphone. Drunken shouts responded. Lena realised her hands were balled into tense fists. She knew how much this competition meant to him. She took a deep breath, tried to relax. The band started playing.

Sam had come from a little town on the northern coast to London to be a pop star. He slept on the sofa in his bass player's flat. They were going to be big, he knew it in his marrow. Lena believed him utterly; his passionate conviction seemed to her so noble. But as she listened now, she couldn't hear the spark of genius that she'd expected. They sounded like every other band that had played that night. She chided herself. Clearly she knew nothing about this kind of music. Being hidden away behind the Iron Curtain during her teenage years had left her at a disadvantage.

She watched Sam, his long curls catching the coloured lights, his face studious as he backed away from the microphone to play a guitar riff. Gorgeous, utterly gorgeous. A fantasy formed in her imagination: she was the girlfriend of the English pop star. Living in a mansion in the country, travelling the world first-class, dressing in designer fashions. Now she imagined Natalya with her, a film star; two glamorous sisters with expensive shopping bags hanging from their arms. Then her old insecurities gripped her. Natalya had made it clear that she thought she was the one with the looks and the ability to succeed in that world. With a guilty twinge in her stomach, she wondered what would happen if Natalya's dreams foundered while her own came true. But then she quickly screwed her eyes tight and banished the thought, fighting the superstition that her childish nastiness had the power to affect the world.

The song ended. The crowd cheered. Lena clapped as hard as she could, as if the force of her applause could banish her guilty thoughts and her uncertainty over whether Sam's band were actually any good.

Of the six bands that performed that night, three were chosen to go through to the next round and Velvet Ponies wasn't one of them. Lena sat in the van waiting while Sam and his bandmates morosely loaded their gear into the back. It was after midnight, and the last stragglers of the audience were making their way home drunkenly. Sam slid into the seat next to her, still smiling.

'I'm sorry you didn't win,' she said as he snuggled up against her.

'Ah, they'll regret it when we've sold a million albums,' he said dismissively.

The front doors opened and Chris and James got in. The van started and they were backing out onto the quiet street, and speeding back towards London.

Nobody felt much like talking so Sam and Lena kissed – the way teenagers kiss – all the way home. The journey was a blur of sensations. The strobing effect of streetlights speeding past; the thumping music from the radio; the smoke from Chris's cigarettes and the cold fresh air that gusted in the window that he had left cracked open; but most of all Sam: his soapy smell, his hot lips and tongue, his long tickling hair, his warm hands over her breasts, but only on the outside of her dress. It was like a dream, a warm sweet dream from which she never wanted to wake.

At length, he sat back. She caught her breath, watching the empty streets.

'So,' he said quietly, 'did you like the music?'

'Oh, yes,' she enthused. 'It was marvellous.'

'You're a doll,' he said, kissing her forehead. 'We've got a long way to go.'

'But we'll get there,' James said from the front. 'Never give up.'

'What do those judges know?' Sam said, leaning forward onto the front seat.

'They don't know shit,' Chris said.

'Yes, they do,' James said. 'They gave it first prize.'

The three of them burst into uproarious laughter, and Lena was reminded of her relationship with Sofi and Natalya and the silly private things that could make them all laugh until tears ran down their cheeks.

Ten minutes later, they were pulling up outside Lena's apartment building. She opened the door and Sam moved to follow her out.

'What are you doing?' she asked.

'I'll see you to your door. I don't like leaving you out on the street.'

'No, it's fine.'

What was she afraid of? Sofi might still be up, but Natalya wouldn't be. Would she? Lena imagined her, looking sleepy but still beautiful, maybe in those soft cotton pyjamas that showed her nipples as obvious shadows under the fabric. She couldn't let Sam anywhere near her.

'Sofi and Natalya will be asleep. I don't want to wake them.'

'I'll be quiet.'

'No . . . I'd rather not.'

His smile faded. 'Lena? You're not . . . ashamed of me, are you?'

'No! Of course not.'

She suddenly saw herself through his eyes: overdressed, primly insisting he didn't touch her below the waist, not wanting him to meet her family. She seized him around the neck and yanked him forward, gave him a slow, passionate kiss. When she released him, his smile was back in place.

'I'll explain everything another time,' she said.

He slapped his chest over his heart and pretended to swoon back into the van. Lena waved and hurried up the stairs. The van was speeding away as she let herself into the dark hallway, heart thumping, Sam's contagious smile still lingering on her lips.

Sofi wondered if she would ever stop feeling guilty about not working. Or at least not earning any money. In the three weeks they had been in London, her English had improved dramatically. With her qualifications, she would have no trouble getting a job; in fact, she had seen one advertised just this morning in the newspaper. But she hadn't come here to be a geologist and so she resisted the urge.

Her time was for designing, for threading beads, winding silver wire, finishings. That was why they had taken so many risks; not so she could sit in the office of a waste disposal company and write reports about ground contamination. They had a year, and to honour the promise to herself she had to stay with her art.

In that frame of mind, wandering through the National Gallery at Trafalgar Square could almost be counted as hard labour. Sofi checked in her backpack and began her journey through the centuries.

She had been through almost all of the major galleries in London, but she kept coming back to this one, with its endless rooms of masters. Some paintings – Delaroche's *Execution of Lady Jane Grey*, or Turner's *Hero and Leander* – could hold her transfixed for long, silent stretches of time. The colours and textures would seep into her mind, and later at home an idea would come to her in a flash: gold chains and white ribbons; or silver, mother-of-pearl and midnight colours. She would sketch furiously, hours slipping by, while Natalya and Lena banged in and out of the flat, occasionally arguing with each other.

If she wasn't in a gallery, she was in a jewellery shop, memorising designs with her eyes, judging every other designer in the world cruelly but at the same time certain that they must be better than her. Their jewellery was selling in shops, hers wasn't.

But there was time for all that. She just needed to build up some stock, get enough pieces to take to the markets. See if anyone besides herself was interested in them.

Sofi wandered through the gallery. It was a Thursday morning, early and quiet. A group of Australian tourists was just ahead of her, so she took a different route, found herself in a room of seventeenth-century paintings. She stopped in front of them one by one, soaking them in.

One, by Nicolaes Maes, held her for longer than the others. A woman peeling a parsnip into a wooden bowl on her lap, while her small daughter looked on. This time it wasn't the colour or the composition that arrested her, it was the fact that the woman reminded her of Mama. With her hair scraped back, eyes down and concentrating, working by the dim light of the outside world in their flat in St Petersburg.

Things hadn't ended comfortably. Mama had been distressed on the morning they'd left, but trying to hide it. Sofi, excited and dying to get away, had pretended not to notice. And so, many things had gone unsaid. Since then, Sofi had written a cheerful but superficial letter every week, but hadn't heard Mama's voice. It was strange, after twenty-four years, for Mama not to be around.

Sofi felt in the pocket of her pants. Change for the train home. Or she could walk and call Mama. She shook her head; it was five miles, a warm day. And yet to hear Mama's voice suddenly seemed more important than sore feet.

She hurried towards the entrance and found a public phone. Fed some coins into the slot and picked out the familiar number.

Mama answered. Lovely, comfortable Russian.

'Mama, it's me.'

'Sofi.' She sounded surprised, pleased, but guarded. All that in one little word.

'Did you get my letters?'

'No. I haven't had any.'

The Russian postal system. Sofi felt the sting of guilt. She should have realised, should have phoned to say they'd arrived safely.

'I've sent three,' she said sheepishly. 'You'll get them in time.'

'You're well? Natalya and Lena?'

'Fine. We're all fine.' She realised she was on the verge of tears. 'I miss you.'

'And I miss you, child. But you are having your adventure. Despite me, despite the old sourpuss.'

'You're not a sourpuss.'

Mama made a dismissive noise. 'Enough of that, tell me about London.'

So Sofi did, and Mama told her the news from home: how Irina Petrovna was keeping her company, how her job at the bakery kept her busy; and Sofi was so glad she had called to put things right. She fed her money through coin by coin. First the train money, then the money for milk and eggs, then finally she realised she would have to hang up or they would have no money for coffee. Lena and Natalya would never forgive her for that.

'I'll write every week, Mama,' she said. 'As long as you do too.'

'I have nothing to write about,' Mama replied. 'Life here is very dull to you, I suppose.'

'No, not at all. I love hearing about home, about you. Promise me you'll write?'

'Of course I will,' she said. 'I love you, Sofi.'

'I love you too, Mama,' Sofi said, just as the final coin dropped through the slot.

CHAPTER TEN

The rain was hammering against the narrow windows of their flat as Sofi unpacked her first shipment of stock. Thousands of glass beads, spools of silver wire and rattling boxes of clasps; she would no longer have to make her own. The phone rang and she thought about ignoring it, wrapped up as she was in the moment of promise. But Natalya's new modelling agency had sent her on a lot of jobs in the past four weeks, and she didn't want to miss a call that resulted in work. She scooped up the phone. It was Natalya herself.

'You have to come down here straightaway,' she said breathlessly in Russian.

Sofi was so used to speaking English that it took her a moment to adjust. 'Down where?' Natalya had left early that morning for a shoot.

'I'm at Clapham. It's not far. Catch a taxi. It's urgent.'
'What's wrong?'
'I don't understand what they're saying to me.'
'Natalya, your English has to –'
'They're so angry at me. You have to come. I'm afraid.'
Sofi glanced at the downpour, sighing inwardly. 'All right, what's the address?'

Of course there were no taxis in sight, so Sofi jumped on a bus at Fulham Broadway and found a seat. Damp raincoats on either side of her. She flipped open her London A–Z and traced the streets with her finger. The bus rattled along and she tapped her feet anxiously. Why would Natalya be afraid? Wasn't this a professional engagement? Though, Sofi had to admit, most of the work Natalya had done so far was modelling underwear and swimsuits for direct mail catalogues. She was making good money, but it seemed a little demeaning.

Within two minutes of walking, Sofi's umbrella had blown inside out. She was soaked when she arrived at the address Natalya had given her, but still she paused on the street, uncertain. It was an ordinary block of residential apartments. Not a studio, or even an office. She checked the address she had written down again, then went in.

Up on the fourth floor, she found the right apartment and knocked. Natalya opened the door a half second later. Her face was thick with make-up, her hair teased out. She wore a dressing gown, tied tightly around her narrow waist.

'Thank you, thank you!' she whispered, dragging Sofi inside.

The main living area of the apartment had been cleared. A sofa pushed against the wall supported a coffee table, a television unit and dozens of books. Other furniture was stacked next to it. Lights on poles were arranged around a single wing-backed chair in the centre of the room draped with a large square of fake tiger fur. In the kitchen, four men mumbled between themselves.

'My cousin is here now,' Natalya announced in thickly accented English, and Sofi despaired of her ever being able to master the language sufficiently to be an actress.

One of them, a lanky bearded man wearing a black T-shirt and jeans that sat low beneath an overhanging belly, approached, brandishing a piece of paper. Sofi deduced this must be the photographer.

'She signed it! Time is money! I have to pay my assistants!'

Sofi took the piece of paper and said in quiet Russian to Natalya, who stood behind her shoulder, 'What's going on?'

'They want me to take my clothes off.'

Sofi's head snapped around. 'What?'

'They have nothing for me to model. No swimsuits or underwear. They just want to take photos of me naked.'

Sofi returned her attention to the work contract that Natalya had signed. A clause had been ticked: *I understand nudity may be required for this engagement.*

'Did Veronica tell you about this?'

'She didn't say anything.'

'Natalya can't read English,' Sofi explained to the photographer. 'She didn't know what she was signing.'

'I have a legally binding contract here,' he roared, his face suffusing a purply shade. 'I have already outlaid a lot of money in setting up the shoot. She agreed to it. She can't go now.'

Sofi turned to Natalya. 'Go and get dressed.'

'Don't you dare,' the photographer said.

Natalya stood uncertainly, a deer in headlights.

'Go and get dressed,' Sofi repeated in Russian, forcing steel into her voice. Natalya scurried off to the bedroom. Sofi handed the contract back. 'She was unaware of what she was signing; she isn't taking her clothes off.'

'It's not my problem if she can't read English!'

'And nor is it hers. Your complaint is with her agency, not with Natalya herself.' What was Veronica Hanson thinking? But then, if Natalya had been willing so far to strip to her underwear... Sofi began to realise that the modelling her cousin had done may have purposes other than to sell clothes. 'We're going home.'

The photographer shouted at her, spittle flying from his lips. 'She's not going anywhere!'

The other men from the kitchen began to gather and Sofi was put in mind of a pack of snarling dogs. Natalya emerged from the bedroom, dressed in her own clothes.

'Call Veronica Hanson and take it up with her,' Sofi said, clutching Natalya's hand and trying to still her pounding heart.

'Sofi?' Natalya said.

'We're going.' Sofi strode to the door, Natalya trailing behind her.

The bearded man seized Natalya's hair and yanked it violently. She stumbled, yelping. Sofi helped her up, sliding an arm around her waist.

'Get away from her,' she shouted. 'Get away from her or I'll call the police.'

The man stepped back, swearing, but didn't follow them. They made it down to the street before Sofi's knees buckled underneath her and she had to support herself against the outside wall of the apartment block. The rain poured off the eaves. The damp air made Natalya's hairstyle sag.

'I thought he was going to kill me,' Natalya gasped in Russian, rubbing her head with a wince.

'English, *please*, Natalya. This is how you get yourself into these problems.'

'Veronica will be angry. She won't send me on any more jobs.'

'That's a good thing, don't you see? She let you go to that job without telling you what was involved. She knows you can't read English well. She was betting on you doing as you were told.'

Natalya mused on this a few moments. A pair of young men in black raincoats walked past, their necks nearly bending backwards to stare at Natalya.

'If you ever want to work seriously as a model or an actress, you must preserve your reputation. No more modelling in next to nothing.'

'But Veronica –'

'Forget Veronica. You're sacking her. Find a new agent.'

Tears squeezed out of Natalya's eyes. 'I can't. I am so bad at English. Especially the writing. I look at the scribbles, and I try to say the letters out, but all the words are spelt so strangely.' Two tracks of black mascara made their way down her cheeks. 'It hurts my head. This is too hard. What if I end up in the same situation again?'

'You won't,' Sofi replied. She remembered Mama's words from all those years ago. *You are not beautiful like your cousins, but you have a good brain. When they get themselves into trouble, they will need you to help them out.* 'You won't, because I'm going to manage you.'

Sam, Sam, Sam. There wasn't room for other thoughts in Lena's head. Just Sam. Just his smiling eyes, his long curls, his warm, warm hands. Days blurred by in a love-struck haze. She had forgotten about wanting to be a movie star; she had forgotten about Russia and her father; she had forgotten the urgency about establishing herself in some way in her new city. Everything that used to be important was caught up in the all-consuming present.

Every Wednesday evening, she and Sam finished work at the same time and made their way to the rehearsal room. Situated above an empty shop that had once been an Indian takeaway, the room and its unfinished floorboards were still imbued with the scent of cardamon and chili. The drummer's unpredictable uncle owned the building, and the band was constantly under threat of being thrown out. For the time being, though, their gear was safely locked up there between rehearsals; along with a few other creature comforts like an old sofa, a cheap coffee table and a heavy ceramic ashtray that was always overflowing with butts.

The long summer days were now behind them and a new chill in the air marked the arrival of autumn. They arrived at rehearsal late – the last customer at the newsagent had taken forever to pick lottery numbers – and discovered the room in darkness. Sam switched on one of the lamps – it was artfully draped with a paisley scarf – and Lena found the note pinned to his amplifier.

Chris can't make it. I'm shagged. Rehearsal's off, okay? See you back at home. James.

'Oh, bugger,' Sam said, picking up his guitar anyway.

Lena sat on the sofa. 'Isn't this the third or fourth time that Chris has cancelled?'

'Fourth.' He sat next to her. 'I don't know how serious he is. But he's a good drummer.' He began to pick at the strings, which sounded tinny and quiet without amplification.

Lena watched his fingers move, hypnotised.

'You like it?' he said, noticing her watching. He meant the music, which she could barely hear.

'Um . . . yes.'

He reached over to switch his amp on and played it again. This time he sang. It was quiet, pretty. A love song of sorts, though not a big aching ballad. Lena grinned stupidly when he got to the chorus. *My Russian girl*, he sang. The song was about her. She immediately lost all objectivity: it was the best song she had heard in her life. When he finished she threw her arms around his neck and kissed him.

'Thank you, it's so beautiful.'

'So are you.' He disentangled himself to prop his guitar against the amp, then returned to her embrace. His chin was warm, stubbly, and he spoke very close to her ear. 'You're the best thing that's ever happened to me.'

She allowed him to kiss her gently on the earlobe, on her cheek and chin.

'Lena? We're alone here tonight. Do you think . . . ?'

She had so far declined to sleep with him and, as two months had passed since they'd met, he was growing impatient. Not that he showed his impatience to her. He was gentlemanly in all things, told her he could wait as long as she needed. But how long did she need? She was not a virgin. On her twentieth birthday she had taken care of that, determined to have it over with. But since then she had been very cautious about sharing her body. Usually with good reason. Two other boyfriends had been driven away by her refusal to sleep with them; and she knew this meant they weren't good men in the first place. Was she worried that Sam would leave her too? Was it a test of his honour?

Now, with his lips at her throat, she trusted him completely. And desire was swirling up through her, bending her will.

'Come on, Lena,' he said, his grey eyes fixing on hers. 'When do we ever get time alone?'

She pushed her hair back off her face. 'All right, yes.'

He smiled and her heart flipped over. 'Really?' he said.

'Yes, really.'

He reached out to touch her face, running his fingers in a soft caress around the line of her jaw. 'I'll be so good to you,' he said.

Then he was kissing her and she was melting into him, and time slowed as he undressed her by the lamplight, his lips following his gaze all over her soft flesh. His skin was hot and smooth, pressed against hers, and she closed her eyes and gave herself up to the sensation he was creating with his fingers. An aching tide of pleasure swept through her, like nothing she had ever felt before. Then the tide released, rocking her body so that she shouted out. A moment later, she was embarrassed that she had been so vocal.

'Sorry,' she said, catching her breath.

'Don't be sorry,' he replied, covering her body with his. 'Is this your first time?'

She shook her head. 'No. But I've never felt like *that* before.'

He chuckled, then positioned himself and slowly slid inside her, collapsing across her so his curls trailed over her face. She clung to him, wanting to hold on to this moment forever. The old sofa, the scarf over the lamp, the smell of stale cigarette ash and Indian spices – all of it seemed impossibly romantic. When she remembered with alarm that they hadn't protected themselves, she pushed aside the thought. Tonight was their first time, a moment to warm their memories when they were old. She didn't want practicalities to intrude.

Afterwards, as they lay entwined on the sofa, an old blanket pulled out of the kick drum keeping them warm, Lena was starting to doze when Sam said, 'Lena. I think I love you.'

She sat up, looked down at him. 'I *know* I love you.'

He smiled and pulled her down to kiss him. She felt as though she was in a huge sunny bubble of happiness. He loved her. Love, which she had read about in books and watched in movies a thousand times. Love, which had always seemed to elude her. But here it was, here in Sam's arms.

'When am I going to meet your sister and your cousin?' he asked.

She hesitated. He loved her; Natalya couldn't charm him away. But that wasn't what she was afraid of. Here, now, she was beautiful. The most beautiful girl in the world. But once he saw Natalya, he'd know that she wasn't.

'Lena? You've gone quiet.'

But still, she couldn't keep him a secret forever.

'Lena, you're going to have to explain this reluctance to me. I'm starting to think that you don't want your family to know about me.'

'No, no,' she said quickly. 'It's not that at all.'

'Then what?'

She sat up again, pulling the blanket around her breasts. Took a deep breath. No point in being in love and not telling the absolute truth. 'My sister, Natalya, is really, really beautiful.'

'But so are you.'

'More beautiful than me. I have known it all my life.'

Then he was laughing, shaking his head, pulling her close. 'Beauty doesn't work like that, Lena. We have an expression in English: beauty is in the eye of the beholder. You ever heard that?'

She nodded. 'Yes, I have.'

'Well, it's true. Old men still think their wives are the most beautiful things they've ever seen, even when they're all wrinkly.' He squeezed her. 'If I'm lucky enough to still be around when you're old, I'll prove it to you.'

Tears pricked her eyes, but she wasn't sure why. Relief? Or was it the way her heart was made weak by the idea that they might grow old together?

'All right,' she said. 'You will come and meet Natalya and Sofi. I'll arrange it with them.'

'Good girl,' he said, kissing her bare shoulder. His body began to tense. 'Lena? Are you up for it again?'

'Of course,' she said. 'I'm all yours.'

The nights belonged to Sofi.

After the chatter and chores of dinner, after her cousins had gone out or had watched their television shows and finally gone to bed, she brought out her crate of beads and wire and spread out on the dining table and, by the light of a lamp bent over her, worked until her hands ached.

She had asked at a few of the market stalls on Camden High Street if they would take half a dozen pieces of her jewellery. All of them said the same thing: 'Rent your own stall.' She felt a fool for not understanding the system, and was anxious at the amount of work it would take to make enough jewellery to warrant her own stall. But she had to admit there were enough designs in her head; and Natalya and Lena were happy for her to buy supplies. So all she needed was the time.

Her days were consumed with organising Natalya. First it was finding a new agent, which had taken more than a week. There were plenty who would take her on to do the same kind of work Veronica Hanson had sent her for, and plenty more who would charge her a lot of money and not guarantee any work. Finally, she had found an agency at Regent's Park who were casting for a chewing gum television commercial and thought Natalya might have the perfect face for it. No speaking, so her thick accent wasn't a problem. All she had to do was shake two pieces of gum into her hand and pop them in her mouth with a smile. They signed her up, she got the part, and Sofi had thought she was on her way.

Four weeks later, there had been no more work.

The agency sent Natalya on dozens of casting calls, and her beauty would see her survive the first cull. But then the time would come to read her lines – carefully rehearsed over and over with Sofi – and they would stop her as soon as she opened her mouth.

'It's not fair,' Natalya would wail. 'Other girls get discovered just walking along the street!'

Sofi did her best to help Natalya with her English but her progress was slow, and Sofi realised that learning English in the company of her Russian relatives was not ideal. So she had convinced Natalya that she had to get a regular job, like Lena, just for a short while. Immersing herself in a constant stream of English was the only way she would pick it up properly.

Natalya was hugely reluctant about the idea, right up until Sofi found the ad for the tearoom job at STC, one of the television stations. The interview was on Monday.

Sofi yawned and sat back. She had finally finished the delicate work of encasing a series of coloured shells in net bezels. Tomorrow night she'd begin joining them together into a bracelet. She pushed them around on the table: pink, cream, peach . . . no, peach, pink, cream . . . She couldn't decide, but getting the colours in the right order was always difficult. She wondered how much she should sell the bracelet for. She had little idea of the value of her work, but she knew that shells and glass beads were cheap. One day, she hoped to work with gems: rose quartz, pink topaz, kunzite and tourmaline would give this bracelet a pleasing weight, a presence in the world.

She kept sliding the shells around, her eyes growing heavy. It wasn't just the late nights, it was her own constant efforts to grapple with the new language. Lena was fluent already, was having no trouble at all adapting to their no-Russian rule at home. But Sofi still translated everything in her head, which meant she was thinking twice as much as she ordinarily needed to. She also had to struggle with all the paperwork. Leases and bills, contracts and pay forms.

Finally defeated by tiredness, she packed her things away. The door opened quietly and Lena appeared. Her face was flushed from the cool air outside. She met Sofi's gaze and smiled.

'Still awake.'

'I'm just going to bed now,' Sofi replied.

'Can I talk to you?'

Sofi nodded, and Lena pulled out the chair opposite her.

'Sofi, I'm in love.'

Natalya had already told Sofi she suspected Lena was seeing someone.

'We know.'

Lena's brows shot up. 'You do?'

'Natalya guessed. Someone at work.'

'Yes. Sam. He's . . .' She trailed off, lost for words.

'When will we meet him?'

'Soon, soon. It's difficult. Natalya . . . she's so beautiful.' Lena laughed self-consciously. 'I worry, you know?'

Sofi was glad, then, that she was no beauty herself. It seemed it entered one into a competition that brought nothing but anxiety.

'You shouldn't worry,' she said, patting her cousin's hand. 'Not if Sam loves you too.'

'He does. He says he does.' The flush in her cheeks deepened and Sofi knew it wasn't from the autumn chill. 'He makes me forget myself, Sofi. He makes the world stop.'

'Bring him for dinner. We'll cook Russian food. He'll be yours forever once he's tried your *cheboureki*.' Sofi stood and stretched. 'Coming to bed?'

'In a few minutes.'

Sofi left her cousin sitting pensively in the dark. As she made herself comfortable on the inflatable mattress on the floor, she thought about Lena's insecurities. She could safely say that no man who would be interested in her could ever be interested in Natalya. No lover of beauty was going to choose Sofi, and for that she was grateful.

CHAPTER ELEVEN

The tearoom at the STC building, which sprawled over half a block at Acton, was in dire need of redecoration. Or so Natalya thought as she went on her rounds, clearing away clattering teacups and wiping tables with a foamy solution that made the skin on her fingertips peel. If they would just paint the dim scuffed walls and replace the blue-and-white swirling linoleum and the dusty baroque hanging lamps, it could look as sleek and modern as the rest of the building. Then, perhaps, she wouldn't be so depressed about working here.

It was her fourth week on the job and her English had improved rapidly. Sofi had been right. Surrounded by it every day, without her sister and cousin to bail her out if she found herself stuck, she had acquired new words, sentence structures, even the ability to read, very quickly. But despite this benefit, she could find nothing to like about her job. Certainly not the hideous striped apron she was forced to wear, nor the way she had to pull her hair back severely in a ponytail. Not clearing away the lunch scraps of the television news presenters with their imperious expressions and heavy make-up. Not even spotting the celebrities that came through – and there were many, on their way to film the comedies they starred in or to be interviewed on variety shows – because she wanted to *be* a celebrity, not just to see one and feel so acutely the gulf between her life and theirs. She noted with displeasure how few of the female television stars were as attractive as she was. And yet they were famous and she wasn't. They all treated her as though she were mud on their shoes. She had to endure it all – which she did sullenly – and keep longing for something to change.

She had been on several more casting calls, but the agency had started to realise that she was being rejected repeatedly for the same reasons. While the camera loved her exotic looks, the advertisers didn't love her exotic accent. She had done one more job for them: a photo shoot advertising toilet paper where she'd had to pose as a long-suffering but glamorous mother whose child had unwound a whole roll. A mother! With her flat stomach and dewy complexion! Worse, she still hadn't been paid for it. Sofi was negotiating with the agency every day about the missing money. In the meantime, Natalya was stuck in the dingy tearoom with cracked fingers and a perpetually damp apron, worse off than she ever had been in St Petersburg.

Lena wouldn't listen to her complaints. 'I have to work too,' she would say; but Lena was working with the gorgeous and charming Sam, who had been over for dinner every Saturday for the last six weeks. Their situations could hardly be compared.

'Natalya?'

She looked up. It was her boss, Carmen, a waif-like redhead with a burst of dark freckles across her face.

'I'm off for a smoke. Would you watch the counter for me?'

It was three o'clock, there would be hardly any customers. Natalya nodded and, balancing a tray of dirty cups and plates on her hip, returned to the counter. She knew Carmen would be gone for at least twenty minutes, so she ground some coffee beans and made herself an espresso. She was sitting on a stool behind the drinks fridge, trying to look inconspicuous, when a beautifully dressed man with thick platinum hair appeared at the counter.

Natalya put down her cup and approached, unsmiling. 'Can I help you?'

He looked at her, almost as though he were stunned. She realised that his hair wasn't white with age. Rather, it had been dyed that colour. He was probably in his late forties, with narrow dark eyes and a thin, pointed nose. He wore a dark grey suit over a black poloneck, and his face and beautifully manicured hands were deeply tanned.

'Is Carmen on today?' he said at last. 'I always stop by for one of her coffees when I'm in.'

Natalya shook her head. 'She's having cigarette. I make you coffee.'

'Carmen makes very good coffee.'

'So do I.'

'Ah. Well, I shall trust you then,' he said. 'Double shot macchiato. To take with me.'

As she made the coffee, she could feel his eyes on her. She was used to being stared at, but this was different. It was as though he were assessing her, not falling in love with her. It made her feel uncomfortable given the grubby state of her apron and her unforgiving hairstyle.

She handed him the coffee cup but he didn't offer her any money. Instead, he said, 'I'm Rupert Palmer.'

'Natalya Chernova,' she replied warily.

'Hm. Polish?'

'Russian,' she said, a burst of offended national pride making her pull her shoulders up.

'You don't know who I am, do you?'

She shook her head, curious but keeping her face neutral.

'I'm the creator of *Lonely Shores*.'

Once again she masked her expression. Inside, her heart began to thump wildly. *Lonely Shores* was a popular English soap opera. She and Lena watched it every night. She produced a slow smile for Rupert Palmer. 'I like *Lonely Shores* very much,' she said. 'Is very good show.'

'Thank you. Unfortunately our advertisers aren't feeling quite as positive at the moment.'

She didn't understand, so said nothing.

'Never mind,' he said with a relaxed smile. 'Natalya Chernova, we are casting this afternoon for a new part. Bridget Connell's niece is arriving on the street, and we need somebody with a fresh face. A beautiful face. Will you come down with me for a screen test?'

This time, no amount of trying could hide her feelings. She knew she was standing there completely exposed, a little 'O' of surprise fixed to her lips.

'Natalya?'

She was pulling off her apron and shoving it under the counter. 'I come.'

'Do you need to tell your boss?'

Natalya waved the comment away. 'Is not as important.'

Rupert laughed, in a very appealing full-throated way, and grasped her hand. 'Come on then.'

He took her down a winding, carpeted hallway, through the glass-ceilinged atrium that sat at the heart of the building, and to the other side where the studios were. They approached a queue of pretty girls lined against a wall, studying sheets of script.

'Here we are,' said Rupert.

Natalya thought he was going to put her at the end of the queue, but he didn't. Still clutching her hand, he pulled her past all the girls – whose eyes followed her with unsheathed resentment – and through a crash door into a huge room under miles-away roof beams. A big roll of paper hanging from a metal frame unfurled onto the floor in front of two very bright lights. A camera was set up in front of it.

'Ginny? Dan? Quickly.' Rupert gestured to a man and a woman who were laughing with each other by a trestle table set with pastries and teapots. 'I've pulled this poor lass away from her post back at the tearoom. Can we give her a quick test?'

The woman, Ginny, hurried back with a brisk step, while Dan stacked a couple of pastries in his hand before taking his place at the table in front of the lit area. Natalya could see they had a television monitor set up in front of them. She stilled the butterflies in her stomach and smiled at them. 'I'm sorry, I have no lines to say.'

Ginny's face immediately became stern. 'Rupe? The accent.'

'Just let her have a chance,' Rupert replied. 'Look at her face!'

The familiar sinking feeling. Her accent. She would have to try hard, so hard, to sound English.

'On the red mark over there,' Rupert said to her. 'I'll tell you what to say.'

Natalya was glad for the bright lights because it meant she couldn't see Ginny's disapproving expression. She freed her hair from the ponytail and smoothed it over her shoulders. Rupert explained that she was meant to be a young woman who knew a secret that Bridget Connell, a very popular regular on the show, was desperate to keep. Ginny said Bridget's lines, and Rupert prompted Natalya with what she was to say in response. She concentrated harder than she'd ever concentrated in her life. He had a very distinctive accent and she tried to copy it. Two lines in, she heard a titter from the table. She hesitated.

'I'm sorry, Rupert,' Dan said, bursting into loud laughter. 'But listen to her!'

'Natalya, darling,' Rupert said soothingly, 'ignore my very rude colleague. Say the lines again in your own voice. Don't try to sound English, you're not.'

Puzzled, Natalya did as he said. How could she possibly get a part as an English girl if she sounded so Russian? A few minutes later, the screen test was over and Rupert was leading her back to the door.

'I'm sorry,' he said. 'But you aren't right for this part.'

Natalya swallowed hard on her disappointment.

'You do make very good coffee though,' he said brightly as he opened the door for her to leave.

She scowled at him and stormed off, keeping her head high past the long queue of pretty *English* girls who had the advantage simply through the luck of their birth. Well, she couldn't spot a single face more beautiful than her own, and they all knew it.

Back at the tearoom, Carmen pounced on her. 'What the hell do you think you're doing?'

'Rupert Palmer came by, he took me for screen test.'

'Rubbish!' Carmen answered. 'You never, *never* leave the counter unattended. People will come and steal things. I'm going to dock you an hour's pay for that.'

Natalya fixed Carmen in her gaze. The quick elevation of her hopes and the equally quick letdown, the certainty that she could never be an actress because of her cursed accent, the demeaning position of being told off by Carmen in the depressing tearoom... A wave of nihilism rolled over her.

'Fuck you,' she said, very pleased with the way the English swearwords sounded in her mouth. 'Fuck your tearoom. I go now. I not come back.'

'You can't go, you have to give me at least two hours' notice. I'll dock your pay. You'd better not try to change your mind...' Her voice faded into the distance as Natalya, keeping her back very erect, walked away.

Lena couldn't drink her champagne. She berated herself for being so petty, for being a slave to the acute jealousy that had created the seasick feeling in her stomach. It was a Thursday afternoon, and Natalya's chewing gum commercial was scheduled to air for the first time at four thirteen. Sofi had bought champagne, invited Sam over – he was becoming a fixture at their flat – and instructed Lena to take the afternoon off work for the big event.

Of course Lena was happy for Natalya. She was her sister; Lena loved her. But old childish feelings haunted her. Natalya was going to be on the television; strangers all over England would admire her beauty. *Sam* would admire her beauty. How could he not when he saw her all made-up, packaged, glamorous? Up until now, Sam had been friendly but studiously unnoticing of Natalya. Probably to make Lena feel better. But today, Natalya was necessarily the centre of attention. Her stomach surged again. There, she had gone and made herself sick with jealousy. What a baby.

Sofi checked her watch. They were deep in the middle of a cooking show. 'It must be the next commercial break,' she said.

Natalya's eyes were glued to the screen. She didn't seem to be taking much pleasure in the event, but then she had been a misery for the last week. Ever since she'd quit her job at the television station. Typical Natalya. Couldn't stick to anything for long.

'Ah!' Natalya squealed, as the cooking show cut to a break and her own face appeared on the screen.

Sam started laughing and Lena had to admit it felt surreal. Her sister. Hair pulled back to reveal exotic cheekbones, eyes painted with smoky colours, shaking two pieces of gum onto her palm and popping them in her mouth. She chewed, and the voiceover explained the benefits of sugar-free gum. Then she smiled brilliantly.

'Did they paint your teeth?' Sofi asked. 'They look very white.'

'I think they did,' Natalya said, leaning close to the screen. The commercial ended abruptly. It was all over.

Sofi clapped, and Sam joined in. Lena lifted her hands, then a huge wave of nausea hit her. Instead, she put her hands to her mouth and ran for the bathroom to throw up.

'Lena? Are you all right?' It was Sofi, outside the bathroom door as Lena leaned against the toilet bowl, waiting to see if her stomach would settle.

'I think so,' she replied.

Sofi let herself in, closing the door behind her. 'Can I get you anything?'

Lena shook her head. Sofi flipped the lid down and helped Lena to sit. The swirling in her stomach had settled a little.

Sofi crouched in front of her, brushing Lena's hair behind her ears. 'How long have you been feeling sick?'

'All day, really.' As she thought about it, she realised that the unsettled feeling in her tummy had actually been hanging around longer than that. She shrugged. 'Must be coming down with something.'

Sofi's eyebrows pulled down hard, making her look cross. She wasn't, but it was a familiar expression to Lena. She was thinking, thinking hard.

'What is it?' Lena asked, afraid that she was transparent and that Sofi had seen all the way to the sick envy in her heart.

'Lena, is there a chance you could be pregnant?'

Lena shook her head, the denial emerging before her brain could process the question. 'Of course not.'

'Really?'

This time, Lena considered the question. Realised that she couldn't remember the last time she had had a period. From that one fact, all the other evidence dropped into place. She had been very tired, finding it impossible to get started in the mornings. The nausea had been hanging around for more than a week. Her stomach went cold. 'But we're careful. We use condoms.'

'Every time?'

Lena nodded.

'Every single time?'

'Except the first time.'

'How long ago?'

Lena counted back. 'Eight or nine weeks,' she managed. 'Oh, God, Sofi. What have I done?'

Sam appeared at the door, smiling, unknowing. 'What's wrong with you, sickie?' he said with a laugh in his voice.

Darling, gorgeous Sam. He would smile through this, Lena knew it. He would hold her hand and tell her everything was all right, even though it wasn't. But even knowing this, she couldn't bear to tell him, because his life was about to change forever and she didn't want to be the one who changed it.

Sofi rose. 'I'll give you two some time alone,' she said.

Sam looked confused. 'What is it? Is everything all right?'

Lena smiled weakly and took a deep breath.

CHAPTER TWELVE

Sofi had been blessed with a perfectly clear, cool autumn morning for her first day behind the market stall at Camden Lock. The smell of frying onions drifted in waves, making her stomach growl. She had been too nervous to eat breakfast, but her fears were not warranted. People browsed, chatted to her, admired her work. She had decided to call her jewellery business Anastasia Designs, after her mother, but also to evoke the exoticism and mystery of the last Russian royal family. She had even designed a logo – the Russian letter Ч, which was the first letter in her surname – and marked it on tiny paper tags that she tied to each piece. The jewellery sold quickly, and she realised that she had set the prices far too low. In the end, unsure, she had decided to calculate her costs and set prices that covered them with no mark-up. She had expected to be lucky to sell even one item on her first day at the markets, but so far she had sold eleven. Another jewellery stall that she had passed on the way up here was selling pieces made with fishing line and glue for comparable prices. The work that Sofi had put into her jewellery, with its handcrafted settings and chains, was monstrously undervalued. She wasn't terribly worried by this, though. It was only her first time. She would know better next time.

All around her, chattering voices, music, children calling to each other. The sun sat at an angle to catch the coloured kites for sale at a nearby stall, and the breeze flapped their tails. She had been chatting to the elderly woman at the next stall all morning, a seamstress who made little elf and fairy costumes for children. Sofi had a strong sense, for the first time since she had arrived in London four months ago, that she was in the painting rather than viewing it from the outside.

She looked up from rearranging her jewellery on the black cotton backdrop, and saw a figure in the distance that looked vaguely familiar. She frowned, trying to recall where she had seen him before. Then, just as he slipped from view behind a stall, she remembered. Julien Blanchard, the French artist whose exhibition she had fallen in love with back in St Petersburg. She still had the postcard of his painting taped to the mirror on their dresser. Her blood jumped. He was in London, just as she was. She was gripped by an intense desire to go up to him, say hello, ask what he was doing in England. It seemed too rare an opportunity to miss, and yet she didn't know him. More importantly, she needed to sit right here, behind this stall, selling jewellery. While he wandered away, maybe forever . . .

She straightened her back, craned her neck to see if he was still in view. Perhaps she should just let him go.

But she couldn't. The thought made her feel sad, though she didn't know why.

'Monica,' she said to the woman at the fairy stall, 'I've just seen . . . someone I know. Could you . . . ?'

'Keep an eye on the stall for you? Certainly.'

Sofi nodded a thank you, then slid out from behind her stall and hesitated over which way to go. Finally, she turned left with determination, and ran directly into him.

'Oh,' she said, looking up and seeing him almost on top of her.

'I beg your pardon,' he said, not meeting her eye.

'Monsieur Blanchard?' she said, then had no idea what to say next.

Now he stopped, stood back, considered her. Her hand went self-consciously to her hair.

'We have met?' he asked.

'Yes. In a way. Some time ago in St Petersburg. I was at your exhibition. Your paintings. Your beautiful paintings.'

He smiled and his blue eyes crinkled at the corners. 'I am sorry to say I have no recollection.'

'Well, I couldn't speak French and you couldn't speak Russian.'

'But we both speak English, so now we can communicate.' He laughed softly, and glanced over her shoulder. 'This is your jewellery?'

'I . . . yes. Yes.'

He bent to inspect a necklace of black glass beads, each set in a hand-wrought clasp and joined to the next with eyes and headpins, finished with a silver flower she had woven around a larger chunk of glass. 'This is very nice,' he said. 'Glass?'

'I would love to do it in onyx. Or amethyst.'

'You admire the nineteenth-century jeweller, I see. The grand jeweller, with his eye for mourning wear.'

She smiled. 'Yes, precisely. This piece is based on a portrait I saw of Queen Victoria.'

Julien straightened, smoothing his fair hair. He stood only an inch taller than her, so their eyes were almost level. The skin on his face looked very soft, as though he might have trouble growing a beard. 'Can you take a break from your stall? Come with me for coffee?'

Sofi hesitated. She very much wanted to go with Julien, but her jewellery would take ages to pack up . . .

Monica had been watching the whole exchange. 'Go on,' she said. 'I'll look after your stall for you.'

'Thank you,' Sofi mouthed, grabbing her handbag.

'I'm sorry,' Julien said as they moved away from the stall, 'I do not know your name.'

'Sofi,' she answered.

'It's my pleasure to meet you, Sofi. Again.'

They found a table at a crowded café overlooking the lock, and Sofi fought the anxious twitch in her veins. She wasn't particularly good at talking to men at the best of times, and Julien Blanchard was a famous artist. She would have to concentrate very hard if she didn't want to get completely tongue-tied.

'I tried to tell you,' she started, 'when we were in St Petersburg. I tried to tell you how much I love your paintings.'

His brow furrowed. 'Yes? That makes me happy. Today, it is not such a good day. Every brush stroke seems amiss somehow.'

Sofi was amazed that he could have any doubts about himself. Perhaps they had something in common.

They fell into conversation, sometimes made amusingly confusing by their newness to English. Julien was in London for six months on an artist's residency, but he wasn't enjoying his stay much. London was too grey and crowded for him, and he told her in rapturous tones about his home in the Loire Valley.

'The town is called Richelieu,' he explained. 'A seventeenth-century town with walls and a moat, though the moat is grass now. My house is a *maison ancienne*, some walls are original stone from the 1600s. I inherited from my mother when she died three years ago.'

As he wove his tale – of warm summers and mild winters, of a village market under original chestnut and oak beams, of a garden terrace where he set up his easel in July and painted while dragonflies buzzed around him – she realised with alarm that she had spent her whole life in cities. She wondered if this meant her soul had never been able to expand, to float over sunlit fields of waving grass. If, instead, it had contracted to a hard, dull object inside her. Surely that wasn't good for an artist?

'I do not live a fancy life,' he said. 'I have only a little money. But I live a beautiful life, and not many can say that.' He sighed, gathering himself. 'Ah. I have been too long away from my work, Sofi.'

'You have to go?' The disappointment was acute.

He drained his coffee. 'I think we both have to, yes? Your jewellery might not sell without your sweet face behind it.' He stood, and nodded. 'Thank you for your company.'

Sofi opened her mouth to say, 'Can I see you again?' but realised she couldn't. Instead, she said, 'I had a lovely time.'

He moved away, then stopped and came back. 'Could I please have your phone number, Sofi?'

'Of course,' she said, smiling. 'As long as you promise to use it.'

'Hold it still.'

'I am.'

'It's no good, Natalya. Give it to Sofi. Her hands are steadier.'

Sofi took the long piece of cotton, upon which Lena had threaded a needle, and held it as steadily as she could above Lena's exposed stomach. Lena lay on the bed with Natalya and Sofi kneeling either side of her.

'Don't bump, Natalya,' Sofi said.

'I'm not bumping,' Natalya replied in Russian, the default language she always fell back to when the three of them were alone together.

Sofi held the thread, Lena and Natalya stilled. Eyes glued to the needle as it started to swing.

'A girl,' Natalya breathed.

'Hmm,' Sofi said, as the arcs of the needle grew rounder and rounder. 'I think it's going in circles.'

'A boy?' Lena said.

'Well, you sleep with your pillow to the north, so that's a boy,' Natalya said.

Sofi sighed, winding the thread around her fingers. It felt as though they were all still teenagers, playing one of their silly games.

Natalya flopped on the bed next to Lena and gave voice to Sofi's thoughts. 'It doesn't feel real, does it?' she said. 'That there's a baby in there.'

Lena smoothed her blouse over her still-flat stomach. 'Maybe it will feel more real to you when I start to show,' she said. 'But I assure you, throwing up constantly makes it very real to me.'

Natalya smiled weakly. 'Well, life here in London hasn't gone precisely to plan, has it?'

Sofi didn't point out that as far as her plan went, she was right on track. Her early success at the markets had buoyed her. She was building up her stock, and hoped to start taking it around to shops in the New Year. Already, she had two boutiques and a small accessory chain in mind. The special bonus to all this was her date with Julien coming up in one week. An acquaintance of his was exhibiting at a small gallery near Greenwich and he had asked her to accompany him to the opening.

Sofi frowned now as she remembered the phone conversation. He hadn't really said it was a *date*, had he? Perhaps he was only interested in friendship. Sofi was hopeless at reading such signals, and found the whole business of dating and romance terribly confusing and stressful. She'd had one boyfriend so far in her life: a classmate at university. It had lasted nearly two years, but she had known from the first week that he wasn't really right for her. But she had persisted because she hadn't known what else to do. Finally, he had finished his degree and been sent for his mandatory two years of service a long way from the city. Sofi, the top graduate in her class, had been able to choose a local job. Distance had forced her hand; she'd let him go. With relief.

Lena bristled at Natalya's comment. 'I'm not unhappy about this pregnancy,' she said. 'I love Sam, and we would have got married and had children one day anyway.'

'But you're not going to be a movie star now, are you?'

'Are you?' Lena shot back. 'Or is one chewing gum commercial your limit?'

Sofi watched them, fascinated as always by how they could be so sharp with each other. It was their proximity: as sisters they trusted each other enough to argue. They were always softer and kinder with Sofi; warier of her perhaps. In every trio, Sofi imagined, there was always a duo who were stuck like glue, leaving someone slightly – almost imperceptibly – on the outer.

Natalya sat forward to retaliate, then burst into laughter. So did Lena. Finally, Sofi joined them.

'You're not to worry about me,' Lena said, sitting up and stroking her stomach. 'In a way, I've got what I wanted. I've found the love of my life. Imagine if we'd gone to Hollywood. I never would have met Sam.'

'And I'd be doing time in a women's prison,' Natalya joked. 'I wonder if Roy Creedy bought himself a new car.'

Sofi resisted the urge to check that nobody was behind her, listening in. They never spoke about Creedy, about the scam. It was as though they had dropped the memories into the Baltic Sea on their way over, so that they would never surface again. Hearing his name spoken aloud felt dangerous.

Natalya laughed. 'Sofi, you don't need to look so worried.'

'You shouldn't laugh at him,' Lena said. 'You stole his car.'

'*We* stole it,' Sofi said. 'We were all in it together, so don't blame Natalya. But yes, I don't think we should laugh at him. I'm not even comfortable talking about him.'

'Yet he made it all possible,' Lena said.

'He made it possible for you to get pregnant accidentally and for me to make a fool of myself when given the opportunity of a lifetime,' Natalya said, rolling her eyes. 'Excuse me for not thanking him.'

'Come on, let's cheer up,' Sofi said. 'Imagine a couple of years from now. Natalya, you're a movie star, and Lena, you're a pop star's wife. You're both on the red carpet, wearing my jewellery, of course.'

'I like that story,' Natalya said, settling back on the bed. 'Tell it to me one more time.'

CHAPTER THIRTEEN

Natalya was doing sit-ups in front of the television when the knock at the door came. Every morning now she did at least an hour of exercise – stretching, toning, star jumps – in the hope that she could lose a little weight. She was convinced that if she were thinner, she'd look taller; then she might get more modelling work. It was a desperate wish, really. She was certain that her career was over before it had begun. Begging Sofi for money for acting classes hadn't helped. Sofi had suggested another job, another month or so improving her English, before committing to spending that much money. Natalya understood that Sofi's plan was probably the most reasonable, but the thought of taking another demeaning job filled her with rage and panic all at once. How long could an actress spend being a waitress before she had to accept that she wasn't an actress at all? She had already seen Lena's dreams of being something special crushed under the weight of a job, a boyfriend – though, admittedly, he was a profoundly attractive one – and now an unplanned pregnancy. Lena had never considered ending the pregnancy. Her head was full of romance. Didn't she know that her youth would flee all too soon? Her beauty would be past its best by the time she was free of the child. Didn't she know that dreams were fine as gossamer; it wasn't wise to put anything heavy on top of them.

Natalya didn't answer the door. She was only up to three hundred and twenty sit-ups, which meant she had one hundred and eighty to go; and it was probably just the nosy woman across the hallway wanting to borrow sugar. The knock came again, more insistent.

Natalya sighed, flopping back on the floor. 'I come,' she called. 'Please wait.'

She stood. The heat was on too high. Sweat patches stained her T-shirt. She opened the door and was momentarily stunned. Rupert Palmer stood there. She quickly assessed the situation and found the right face for it. Charming, even a little aloof. After all, he had rejected her.

'Good morning, Rupert,' she said, flapping the bottom of her T-shirt in the hope it wouldn't cling to her quite so damply. 'I have not expect to see you again.'

'You have proven very difficult to find,' he said, removing his black sunglasses and perching them on top of his platinum hair. 'May I come in?'

'Of course,' she said, standing aside.

He assessed the tiny space, the mismatched furniture. Natalya closed the door and leaned on the back of a chair, waiting for his eyes to return to her.

'Well . . . shall we have a coffee?' he said.

'No,' she replied.

'Ah. No?'

'I am actress, not coffee maker. You understand? Last time I make you coffee, things not so well for me.'

He smiled, and she smiled in return. But she didn't sit, and she didn't offer him a seat. She suspected he had developed a crush on her: so many men had in the past. If all he had to offer her was his desire, then she didn't want it.

'So, you have found me. What now?'

'You quit your job. The day I auditioned you. You didn't have to quit. I would have explained to Carmen why you weren't there.'

'I didn't like job anyway.'

'I had to track you down through employee records. I suppose I could have phoned you, but I did so want to see you again.' He smiled, shook his head. 'I don't blame you for quitting. You were better than that job. It was demeaning.'

He was saying exactly what she wanted to hear, and Natalya could see right through him. Coming over in person immaculately dressed in an Italian suit, assessing how poor she was, telling her she was too good for a job in a tearoom. He was trying to manipulate her, which amused her. She was used to being the one in that position.

'You come all this way to tell me only this?' she said, keeping her voice deliberately cool.

'No. I came all this way to tell you something else. I watched your screen test, over and over again.'

'Did you laugh? Everybody enjoy big laugh on the day.'

'I did not laugh. Not once.'

She waited.

'Natalya, I am the creator of *Lonely Shores*. I can do what I like. And I would like to offer you a part.'

A dull pulse of electricity jolted her heart.

'You'd be terrible for the part of a local, but perfect for what I have in mind. It's for a short contract – twelve weeks, I'm thinking – but it's an important part. You will play Tatiana, a Russian girl who comes to work as Mrs Bradley's cleaner, and winds up seducing her husband into an affair.' He frowned here, pulled back the cuff of his crisp suit and checked his watch. 'I do hope you'll say yes.'

'I will be paid properly. My cousin, Sofi, you will tell her the pay.'

'If that is what you want, yes. I'll phone her this evening. You won't be taping until the New Year. Now I also think we should anglicise your name. Natalya Chernova's a bit of a mouthful, and your surname sounds too much like Chernobyl, which is a name nobody likes. How about Natalie Chernoff?'

At that point, Natalya would have agreed to just about anything, but she feigned thoughtfulness before saying, 'If you think it will make things easier.'

'Good. I'll have my assistant producer drop around some scripts in the next few weeks.' He hesitated a moment. 'You can read English, can't you?'

'Of course,' she said, puffing up her chest. 'No trouble.' She would have to rely heavily on Sofi with learning lines.

'Good. We're agreed then. I'll talk to Sofi about your contract.' He tapped his watch. 'I must go. I have a script to write. With you in it.'

She beamed brilliantly, grasping his hand firmly to shake it. 'Thank you, Rupert,' she said. 'Thank you for a million times.'

Sofi fell into the habit of picking Lena up from work and walking home with her. Lena was terribly tired, sick all the time, and Sofi was still under the influence of the protective urge that had characterised her childhood. Lena always seemed a little lost somehow, or in danger of becoming lost at any rate.

Sofi had spent the afternoon combing through op shops, buying old cheap jewellery that she could pull apart and re-use. Her prize find was a tarnished bracelet bristling with silver charms that had only cost her four pounds. She planned to recycle it into a dozen different pieces, and could hardly wait to get home and start prising the links apart.

Lena was grateful to see her as always, complaining about having to vomit in the kitchenette sink that morning and saying once again that she really had to think about leaving work soon. They were still discussing the pros and cons of that decision when they opened the front door of the flat and found Natalya dancing around the living room with a duster, singing an old Abba song at the top of her lungs.

'Come in, come in!' she shrieked in Russian.

'You're cleaning?' Lena asked, astonished.

'I couldn't sit still. The most exciting thing has happened.'

Sofi's heart began to flutter. 'What is it?'

Natalya tripped over her words; her face was flushed with excitement. 'Rupert Palmer came by. He's offered me a role on *Lonely Shores*. Three months, playing a sexy siren. I'm going to be a television star!'

'Oh!' Sofi said, because that was all she could say. It had happened; it had really happened. One of their dreams had come true.

Lena's smile was stiff. 'I'm so happy for you, Natalya.'

Natalya threw her arms around her sister and hugged her wildly, while Sofi stood and let the news sink in. Natalya's dream had come true, and now she believed – *truly believed* – that hers could too. She allowed herself a fantasy: her jewellery in magazines, in stores, on the glossy skin of famous people . . .

Then Natalya was rambling about going out to celebrate, about champagne and dinner – even though Sofi hadn't seen her eat at night-time for weeks. Without waiting for agreement from Sofi and Lena, Natalya disappeared into the bedroom to get changed.

Sofi turned to Lena. Her cousin smiled, but she looked like a little girl who had missed out on a piece of cake at a birthday party. Quickly, Sofi took her hand and rubbed it. 'Don't worry, your turn will come.'

'Will it?' She pressed her hand into her tummy. 'Are you sure?'

Sofi opened her mouth to say something reassuring, but Natalya was calling to them to come and get changed; and, besides, she wasn't all that sure.

Sofi hadn't told her cousins about Julien. Not because she was trying to keep it secret; simply because she grew more unsure by the day about the date. She had managed to convince herself that he probably only wanted to see her as a friend – how could an internationally renowned artist be interested in her beyond that? – and because she couldn't say with certainty precisely *why* she was going out with him, she said nothing.

So when the doorbell rang and Natalya leapt up to buzz him through, no doubt thinking it was her long-awaited scripts about to arrive, Sofi realised her cousins would be puzzled, possibly angry, and almost certainly would tease her mercilessly later.

She went to her room to check her appearance. She was hopeless at putting on make-up, so had settled for brushing out her silky fair hair and pulling on a dress instead of jeans. When she emerged,

Natalya was opening the door to Julien, who was at least two inches shorter than her.

'Hello,' Natalya said. 'You are Rupert's assistant?'

'No, I'm . . . ah, Sofi. There you are.' He smiled at her brilliantly, and Sofi hurried over to invite him in.

'My cousins, Natalya and Lena,' she said, presenting them. 'This is Julien Blanchard. He's an artist. We're going to an exhibition opening this evening.'

Natalya and Lena exchanged glances and knowing smiles.

'Have a lovely time,' Natalya said.

'We won't wait up for you,' Lena added.

Sofi felt her face flush and hurried Julien out. Down on the street, a cab was waiting.

'A cab?' she said. 'I thought we were going to catch the train.'

'The fellowship includes a travel allowance,' he replied, opening the door for her. 'This is a good way to spend some of it.'

For the entire cab ride, Sofi tried to discern whether Julien's interest was platonic or otherwise. But he offered her no hints. The seatbelts kept them a polite distance apart; her own hesitation kept the conversation superficial. They compared winter rain patterns: France, England, Russia. It was like a school assignment. By the time they arrived at the gallery, they had spoken of nothing but the weather and she had the sinking feeling that she was so boring that Julien, if he had ever had any interest in her, would certainly have changed his mind by now.

The gallery was on a narrow lane one block back from the river. A crowd spilled out onto the footpath – smoking, talking, laughing – huddled in their winter coats against the late autumn chill. As Julien and Sofi got out of the cab, a dozen sets of eyes were trained on them, assessing them: were they worth knowing? Julien seemed beautifully oblivious to all this, taking her under the elbow to propel her gently towards the front doors. Sofi caught a whiff of cigar smoke, of the metallic smell of the Thames, then they were inside, in an overheated space with bare floorboards and white walls. A bespectacled youth crossed their names off a list and indicated they should go through.

'And may I just say, Monsieur Blanchard,' the young man said, 'that I am a fan, a very big fan, of your work.'

Julien smiled and nodded, but didn't respond. Sofi was painfully aware that so far he had not taken her hand. That was a clear sign, wasn't it? Her hands felt suddenly warm and heavy, hanging there, unused . . .

'Ah, there is Simon. Excuse me.'

And with that, he was off through the crowd, finding his old friend and shaking his hand warmly. Sofi stood a moment, then decided that such uncertainty was embarrassing and moved with purpose to the refreshments table. Champagne in one hand and ribbon sandwich in the other, she began a slow circle of the room, stopping to assess each painting.

She had heard of Simon Phillips-Pritchard, but never seen his work. It was impossible not to compare it to Julien's. They shared an expressionistic influence, but where Julien had used it to find beauty, Simon seemed to have used it only to represent discord. Dark geometric skies over cowering cities, narrow alleys with sinister shadows waiting in them, industrial wastelands. She gave each painting her full attention, aware that it may be a long evening if she simply sat on the sidelines and waited for Julien to return. The cumulative effect of looking at the works was a vague feeling of hopelessness.

She was standing in front of one particularly disturbing painting when a red-haired woman in a red dress spoke to her. 'What do you think?'

Sofi turned to the woman. She had a thick row of pearls around her neck. Plain pearls always seemed to Sofi such a waste. Their smooth sheen was made for contrast, in her opinion. She stopped redesigning the woman's necklace in her mind and answered the question truthfully. 'They're ugly.'

The woman leaned closer. 'Go on.'

'I mean, he has a talent, but why not turn it to beauty? These paintings are just depressing.'

'In your opinion.' Her voice was sharp now.

'Well, of course it is only an opinion,' Sofi said, already regretting having spoken.

The woman glanced at the painting, then back to Sofi. 'My husband painted them,' she said. 'You'll forgive me, I don't agree with you.'

Sofi watched her leave. She felt as though she could cry. It would get back to Julien now, of course. *That blonde woman over there – the one who hasn't bothered dressing for the event – she said your paintings are ugly and depressing.* She would have to leave. That was all there was to it. It was stupid of her to think for a moment that she belonged in this world. She took her half-empty glass back to the table and headed towards the door.

'Sofi?' Julien's hand was on her wrist, firmly but gently. She hadn't realised, but she'd walked right past him on her way to the table. 'Come with me, I want you to meet Simon and his wife.'

Sofi turned, opened her mouth to speak. No words came out. Instead, she managed a sad gasp.

Julien tilted his head, puzzled. 'Is everything all right?'

'I . . . no, it's not.' She quickly explained what had happened.

To her surprise, Julien burst into loud laughter. He clapped his hand over his mouth to stop, then said, 'This is true? You really said that?'

Sofi nodded, sick with embarrassment.

'Well,' Julien said after a theatrical check over his shoulder, 'it's about time somebody said it.'

Sofi hid a smile.

'I have seen enough. You and I, we will go to have dinner. Somewhere nice. And you can tell me freely what is ugly and depressing about Simon's work, so that I never accidentally repeat the offence in my own.'

They escaped. Through the busy night-time dark and finally into the refuge of a Chinese restaurant above a midnight pharmacy. Julien shrugged out of his coat and hung it behind him, and Sofi took a moment to admire his profile. Then he caught her looking and she looked away, willing herself not to flush.

'So, here we are,' he said. 'A Russian woman and a French man in a Chinese restaurant in England.'

She smiled. 'Funny, isn't it.'

'Not as funny as you telling Jacinta Phillips-Pritchard that her husband is a morbid madman.'

'I didn't say that!'

'But it's true, Sofi. You have such an ability to read a painting. Tell me, what was it you saw?'

Sofi realised that Julien needed to be reassured that his own work was better than his friend's. She was happy to oblige because at last they were talking. Talking about art, about beauty, about ways of looking at the world and re-interpreting it. Wine arrived, meals came and were eaten and cleared away, and still they were talking. His passion and energy for their conversation was a stark contrast to his restrained body language towards her. He sat very erect in his chair. When his hand bumped hers while pouring wine, he pulled back as though stung. Sofi even imagined he was avoiding meeting her eyes directly, though she did catch him staring at her – with intense blue focus – while they were splitting the bill at the front counter of the restaurant. By the end of the evening, she still had no idea how he felt about her.

The cab pulled into the kerb outside her apartment building, and she turned to him and smiled.

'Thank you for a lovely evening,' she said, and realised she was still hopeful that he might show his hand one way or the other.

He seemed about to say something to her, then turned to the driver. 'Please wait,' he said. 'I will see the lady to her door.'

The driver nodded his assent, and Julien climbed out after her. An icy wind had whipped up, carrying with it the smell of rain. They hurried to the front door. Sofi turned to him, tucked her hair behind her ears. He touched her shoulder. She stood very still.

'Sofi, I will have to ask you because I cannot tell. Do you want me to kiss you?'

For a confused moment, she wondered if she'd heard him right. 'That depends. Do you want to kiss me?'

'I do. But I am troubled in trying to guess your feelings.'

Sofi nodded emphatically. 'Yes. I want you to kiss me.'

He leaned in. Their noses bumped. He pulled back, realigned himself, and kissed her. Warm lips. His hand went to her hair. He made a noise in his throat; a relieved sound. Rain began to fall. He pulled back, reluctantly.

'I will call you again,' he said.

'I'd like that.'

Then he was hurrying to the cab and speeding off into the night. Sofi put her hand over her heart, realised she was smiling too broadly. Natalya and Lena were going to see that smile and make fun of her until bedtime.

But she didn't mind at all.

CHAPTER FOURTEEN

'You will get married, though, won't you?'

It was the third time that day that Sam's mother had asked the question. This time, they were in the hospital cafeteria, waiting for two o'clock and Lena's first appointment with a midwife. She would have much preferred to be alone with Sam. She was nervous, she felt vulnerable. But Wendy had only arrived the day before, along with Sam's sister, Becky, and, as Lena was learning, Sam found it impossible to say no to his mother.

'We'll come,' she had squealed with delight. 'I want to be very involved in the life of my first grandchild.'

Wendy was an attractive woman in her early forties; she had been only eighteen when she had Sam, twenty at Becky's birth and had raised them alone. Her hair was a rich red-brown and her make-up was applied with a tidy hand. Her fingernails were long and painted with elaborate decals. A leopard-print blouse strained over her impressive bosom, and she wore tight denim jeans and high-heeled boots. Becky, by contrast, was scrubbed free of make-up and wore her mousy hair very short. She was impatient with everything her mother said or did. On this occasion, it was Becky who answered Wendy's question.

'For God's sake, Mum, will you stop banging on about a wedding.'

'Well, you're not likely to give me one, are you?' Wendy snapped. She turned her eyes to Lena. 'Our Becky here has decided she prefers girls to boys.'

'Oh,' Lena said, struggling to find an appropriate answer in any language.

'Mum, we haven't talked about getting married yet,' Sam said, impossibly patient with her. 'We're just doing one thing at a time.'

Lena slid her hand under the table and squeezed Sam's. The cafeteria was a noisy, miserable place, full of people waiting to see doctors or sick friends. Dusty tinsel and sagging foil Christmas trees were strung from the ceiling. The smell of roasted potatoes and brewed coffee mingled with the smell of damp coats. Rain came down heavily outside. The vinyl tablecloth was clammy under her forearm.

'You should come and live with us,' Wendy said. 'I can look after the wee one while Lena goes to work.'

'We're going to stay in London,' Sam answered firmly. 'Lena's going to look after the baby herself.'

'You'll never manage on one income. And what's she going to do? Sleep on James's sofa with you?'

'I'm looking for a place. We'll be fine.'

Lena glanced at the clock on the wall above the counter. Five minutes. Her stomach hollowed out. 'We should go,' she said to Sam.

'We'll walk you up there,' Wendy said, draining her cup of tea and pushing back her chair.

Lena just wanted to be alone with Sam for a few minutes before the appointment, but it wasn't to be. The midwife was running half an hour late, and for the entire time in the waiting room Wendy offered her endless advice about babies. Sam and Becky, obviously used to her, tuned out by reading magazines. No such escape for Lena, who was forced to nod and smile and say 'thank you' again and again. The room was crowded with women with bellies of various sizes. Lena pressed her hand over her stomach, unable to believe it would stretch that much.

Finally, her name was called. As she and Sam stood, so did Wendy. Lena looked at Sam in alarm.

'No, Mum,' he said. 'Wait here.'

'But what if they have one of those ultrasound machines? You'll see the baby for the first time. Doesn't a new granny deserve to see the baby too?' Her voice had become plaintive, and Lena wasn't sure if it was put on for effect or genuine.

The midwife gestured to Lena. 'Please, come in. We're running very behind today.'

'Can relatives come in too?' Wendy asked.

'If you like.'

'No,' Lena said, finally finding her voice. 'It's very private for me.'

Wendy stopped in her tracks, mouth turned down. 'Oh. I see. Well. We'll wait here then.'

'Mum,' Becky said in an exasperated tone, 'just leave them be, will you?'

Sam's hand in hers, Lena followed the midwife to a wood-panelled consulting room. A pinboard over the desk was covered in photographs of newborn babies: red, screaming, grasping. Lena felt a swirl of fear. Once, when she was five, she and Natalya had taken big pieces of cardboard to the grassy slope near their grandmother's house. Natalya had gone down first, sitting on the cardboard. Lena had followed, but hadn't realised how steep the decline was. That feeling, of the world falling out from under her, returned to her now. She wondered why she hadn't terminated the pregnancy. Sam had made it clear that he would have been comfortable with that too . . . but Lena couldn't. She intended to be with Sam forever, to have children with him one day. How could she make the choice to end the life of *this* child just because the timing was inconvenient? She would always wonder which genetic material the child would have borrowed from each of them. Sam's curly hair or her straight hair? Sam's olive skin or her white skin? Sam's grey eyes or her hazel eyes? Besides, she had always felt a little like terminations were murder. Though she'd never confess it to Natalya, who had strong opinions otherwise.

The midwife asked dozens of questions, some of them Lena felt almost too personal to answer in front of Sam. But, of course, now they were going to be parents. There would be very little mystery between them any more. Finally, she led Lena and Sam to an adjoining room and put Lena up on a narrow bed.

'It's a bit early to hear a heartbeat,' the midwife explained, preparing the ultrasound machine. 'So if you wait here, the obstetrician will be in to have a quick look and confirm that baby is there and he or she is okay.'

Time stood still as Lena lay on the narrow bed, waiting. Finally, a beautifully groomed doctor walked in and, with only a few words of greeting, was probing her private parts. Lena tensed every muscle in her body as she waited for the image to appear on the screen. When it did, it was a grey blur that she couldn't make sense of. The doctor leaned close to the screen and said, 'Hm.'

'Is everything all right?' Sam asked.

'Oh yes. See this?' She pointed to a white blob. 'That's the head. And this?' She pointed to a similar shape. 'That's the other head.'

Lena didn't understand at first. She assumed she must have missed some English idiom. But Sam got it. His face went pale, and Lena caught a glimpse of how he might have looked at eight years old. He was a boy for that second, so very young. Then he found his voice and said, 'You're joking? Twins?'

'Oh yes. Two babies.' The doctor winked. 'Congratulations.'

She left them alone for a few minutes while Lena straightened her clothes. The anxiety peaked and she began to cry. Sam put his arms around her.

'Hey, it's all right. We'll be all right.'

'Two babies. How will we manage?'

'We'll get a little place. I'll take more hours at the shop.'

'What about the band?'

'I'll keep doing the band. There'll be evenings, weekends. And when we get signed we'll be able to move to a bigger house. We'll hire a nanny. It might be tough at first, but things will work out for us.'

Lena allowed herself to be cheered. Sam was probably right. If Natalya could get a job on a television soap, then Sam's band could get a recording contract. Thoughts of Natalya made her anxious again: what had happened to her own dreams? She had been so quickly and easily distracted from them. Now, she knew, the tide had carried her too far away to get back to them. She would have to make sure Sam didn't abandon his ambitions so easily. Her fantasy of being a pop star's wife would have to change a little, that was all. Perhaps she would be shopping at Harrods for baby clothes instead of designer clothes.

She managed to smile. 'You're right. We'll be fine.'

The midwife returned with a photo of the babies. Lena still couldn't make out the various body parts, and wondered if this meant she was a bad mother.

'To show your mum,' the midwife said, handing it to Sam.

'She's going to fall over backwards,' Sam said.

'She's going to say we have to come and live with her,' Lena warned.

'Don't worry,' Sam said. 'Won't happen. I promise.'

The weather was chilly but clear as Sofi and Julien sat in a park across the road from the girls' apartment. Winter had lately arrived. The trees were bare and the nights had grown longer. Sofi watched as mothers ambled by with babies in pushchairs, as joggers sped past, as dogs straining at their leads pulled their owners along. She dared not disturb Julien, who sat on the bench with his sketchbook in his lap, dispiritedly sketching lines that were mysteriously inadequate to him. The sky was pale blue and the sun shone weakly. Julien had complained repeatedly about the cold all morning, but Sofi had laughed at him. If there wasn't snow up to her ankles, then it wasn't really winter.

They had come out seeking fresh air and privacy. His own bedsit, paid for by the artists' council who had granted him his residency, was thick with the smell of oil paints, which gave her a cloying headache. Her apartment was full of people. Lena, the first swell of her stomach becoming visible, sat on the sofa looking through catalogues of baby equipment with Sam. Natalya carried around her script, marked up heavily in Russian, pausing every thirty seconds to clarify something with Sofi. Sofi was wearied by Natalya's demands, and Julien couldn't work with her cousins around. On days when Natalya and Lena were both out, it was wonderful. He and Sofi would sit at the table together, both engaged in their art, for uninterrupted silent hours. But more and more her cousins were home: Natalya obsessively memorising lines, Lena too sick or tired to go to work.

Sofi felt mean casting her problems with Natalya in financial terms, but the truth was that Natalya was going to be paid a lot of money for her twelve-week stint on *Lonely Shores*; and that for every hour spent helping her translate lines or fill out forms, Sofi was not working on her own project. She was making jewellery painfully slowly, then selling it pleasingly quickly. Because she didn't have enough stock to warrant a weekly stall at the markets, she had convinced Monica at the fairy stall to share a little space with her occasionally, for a fee. But her business could be going so much better were she not continually on call to help Natalya.

Julien sighed in exasperation, flipped the page over. 'The lines will not behave themselves!'

'I'm sorry to hear that,' she said, smiling.

'You have such a quality in your work, Sofi, you are decisive. I never see you dither as I do.'

A warm glow of pride in her heart. Even though they had been seeing each other for weeks, she couldn't shake the feeling that he was the famous artist and her opinions and abilities should be secondary to his. For his part, he never implied such secondariness. He was genuinely interested in her and what she did. Natalya called him, in a derogatory tone, Napoleon. But there was nothing of the tyrant in Julien; only compassion and gentle acceptance.

Only three months remained on his residency, and then he would be returning to France. An uncomfortable length of time: not long enough to fall in love and decide to stay together forever, but too long for a brief passionate affair. Sofi almost laughed out loud at this thought. Julien's passion was saved for art. She didn't mind. She had heard Natalya talk about boyfriends showering her in rose petals or taking her for moonlit walks, but none of those men had been trustworthy or kind.

Julien's gaze went across to the apartment block. He frowned, a common expression of his. He had a permanent downward line between his eyebrows. 'Is that your cousin?' he asked.

Sofi followed his gaze. Sighed. 'Yes.' Natalya. Again. She was waving now, the ubiquitous script in her hand.

Julien picked up his sketchbook and stood. 'I'm sorry, I cannot be disturbed.'

'It's all right.'

He moved off to the next bench. Natalya glanced at him and hesitated. Then kept walking, and slumped down next to Sofi.

'What is it this time?' Sofi asked.

'You don't need to be angry with me,' Natalya said, handing her an envelope. 'I bring you letter. This came in post. From Aunt Stasya.'

Sofi picked the letter open, wondering what she would find inside. Two weeks ago, she had nominated one piece of jewellery to be Mama's, intending to put a very high price on it. If it sold, she would forward the money on. Luckily, a tanned young woman with a Spanish boyfriend had fallen in love with it and convinced him to buy it on the spot. Even small amounts could make such a big difference to Stasya, who struggled along with extra hours at the bakery and a boarder that she didn't like.

Sofi laughed as the pieces of the torn-up cheque fell out of the envelope. She didn't need to read the accompanying letter; she would save it for later, when she was alone. Next time, she would just send roubles. Even Mama wouldn't tear those up.

Natalya was already flipping to a page of her script and jabbing at lines. 'I don't understand this, Sofi,' she said. 'It must be wrong. Tatiana says to Mr Bradley that she is admiring him all the time above other men. But Mr Bradley is old man, nearly sixty. Tatiana is young. Is she saying this only to have his money?'

Sofi, who had read the whole script repeatedly, shook her head. 'This isn't real life, Natalya.' Here she felt a twinge, Roy Creedy's earnest handwritten letters coming to mind. 'Besides, age is unimportant if you find somebody attractive.'

'How old is Julien?'

'Thirty-five,' Sofi responded, wondering why she felt defensive.

'So he is older. Not sixty, though.'

Sofi laughed. 'His age doesn't matter to me.'

'So I should act here I am really in love? Not pretending in love?'

'I'd say so, yes.'

Natalya frowned.

Sofi switched to Russian to chide her. 'Natalya, you really must improve your reading. If you read the whole thing a few times, you'd understand your character better. Just memorising snatches of it here and there is not working.'

'I'm trying,' Natalya said. 'I'm trying so hard, but it makes my brain hurt. Look, I made a list of words, all spelled the same, all said differently.' She flipped the script over and showed Sofi the list: *Cough, enough, though, through*. 'In Russia, a word is almost always spelled as it is said!'

'The more you read, the better you'll get at it.' Then Sofi took a deep breath and said what was on her mind. 'I'm spending so much time helping you, Natalya, that I'm not doing my own things.'

Natalya's eyes widened as if realising for the first time that Sofi had needs. 'Oh. I'm sorry. Of course.' Then, petulantly, 'But you said you'd manage me.'

'I didn't realise it would be so time-consuming.'

Natalya pressed her lips together a moment, thinking. A breeze rattled overhead, and from the corner of her eye, Sofi saw Julien tighten his scarf around his neck. Finally, her cousin spoke, bravely once again in English. 'Sofi, a manager should be paid. That is problem, yes? You are working all for nothing?'

'I . . . yes, I suppose that is the problem.'

'So it is easy to fix. I pay you half of my money.'

'Half? That's far too much, Natalya.'

'Half of half then. That is fair.'

'A quarter of your earnings?'

'For this role. You agree?'

Sofi considered the offer. It would be a solid amount of money, which she could then invest in her business. Her mind lighted on the possibilities: onyx, amber, amethyst and turquoise; wound in finely wrought silver patterns. But could she take Natalya's money?

'Please, Sofi, I need you very much.'

'All right,' Sofi said. 'Yes.'

'I shake your hand then. This is business contract.' Natalya grasped Sofi's hand in her long pale fingers and shook firmly. Then she stood. 'I go and try to read some myself. Understand Tatiana better.'

'Good idea.'

Natalya moved off, and Sofi joined Julien on the other bench. The page in front of him was filling up now. She sat and waited for him to finish, to notice her.

'Natalya is gone?' he said, looking up at last and blinking as though he had just woken from a dream.

'Yes.'

'She's very thin, you know. Does she ever eat?'

'Breakfast and lunch. Never dinner.'

'It's a pity. If she put some weight on, she'd be almost beautiful.'

Sofi laughed, throwing her arms around his neck and kissing him.

'Careful, careful,' he said softly, putting his sketchbook aside. 'Don't bend the pages.'

Life without him would be too barren. She rested her head on his shoulder and willed time to slow down.

CHAPTER FIFTEEN

Natalya sat with Sofi at the table while a miserable drizzle fell outside their windows. She had her hips swung to the side so that she could press her feet against the radiator. Together, they were reading aloud the entire pile of scripts, start to finish. Rather, Natalya was reading them while Sofi corrected her repeatedly. Natalya hated it. She hated feeling as though she were back in school, not quite keeping up with the class, puzzled and distracted all at once. She wasn't stupid, though she knew people believed this of her sometimes. In fact, in her opinion, she was really very sharp. She had always been able to read a situation quickly, work out from their body language and tone what people expected or desired and adapt herself to suit. She could make anyone like her, and when people liked her they did things for her. Well, almost anyone. She hadn't had much luck with the self-obsessed little Frenchman Sofi was dating. What did her cousin see in him?

'Your mind is wandering again,' Sofi said, much more patient now she was being paid for her time.

'I'm sorry. I need cup of tea. You?'

Sofi stretched her arms above her, yawning. 'Yes, please.'

'Did you stay up too late again last night?'

She nodded. 'I'm trying to finish enough pieces to take to the market this weekend.'

The phone rang and Sofi rose to answer it. Natalya crouched in front of the cupboard, looking for sugar. Then changed her mind. No more sugar in her tea and coffee. She had to think like a television star.

A moment later, Sofi was standing next to her. 'Natalya, it's Rupert.'

Rupert. Natalya didn't know why her heart jumped. Did she expect he had phoned to change his mind? She had a contract, he couldn't fire her now.

Sofi laughed and whispered, 'Don't look so worried. He's called to ask us out for afternoon tea.'

Natalya went to the phone, relieved. 'Hello?'

'Natalya, I've just asked Sofi if she and you would like to come to afternoon tea at the Ritz. She's turned me down, but I do hope you'll say yes.'

'I . . . yes, I would like that very much.'

'Good. I'll pick you up out the front of your building in thirty minutes. Dress code is formal.' The phone clicked off and Natalya hung up the receiver.

'You don't want to go?' she asked Sofi.

'I don't think Rupert was really interested in me going,' Sofi answered. 'I'll stay here and do some work.'

Half an hour later, sheltering her sleekly styled hair under an umbrella, Natalya waited for Rupert to pick her up outside the apartment block. A silver Jaguar rounded the corner and pulled up to a smooth halt in front of her. She settled herself into the soft, cream leather and shrugged out of her coat.

'Good afternoon,' Rupert said as he rejoined the traffic. 'Seatbelt, please, we're not in Russia.'

Natalya smiled, fastening the seatbelt. She felt very pretty in her only good dress, a low-cut black gown with three-quarter-length sleeves she had found at Selfridges.

'I normally put on a Christmas party for the whole cast,' Rupert explained as the windscreen wipers beat a quiet rhythm. 'But you aren't one of them yet, so I thought I'd take you out for some special treatment. Oh, and to ask how things are going with your preparation.'

'I am learning all my scripts,' she said.

He stopped at a red light and turned to her. 'Good, because we . . . Good lord, what are you wearing?'

Natalya looked down, confused. 'This is my best dress.'

'It's hideous. You looked better in your apron, or your workout clothes. The top is cut too low, you look like a tart.'

Natalya's first instinct was anger. How dare he call her a tart? But then she realised the anger was covering up embarrassment. She had thought she looked great, but she obviously had a lot to learn. She didn't like feeling so uncertain. The car moved off again, and Rupert – seemingly unknowing of how much anxiety he'd caused her – kept speaking.

'I was at the Dolce and Gabbana fashion show in New York a few months ago. Lots of nice things for you there. Riding coats over lace skirts and so on. Classy, timeless. That's what you should be wearing.'

'I have no money for Dolce and Gabbana.'

'Never mind. Once the publicity starts, I'd be surprised if designers weren't throwing clothes at you. With your body.'

'I am too short for model.'

'Rubbish. I could get you modelling work like that.' He snapped his fingers. 'But you don't want to model. Models don't get any respect. You're above it, my dear.'

He fiddled with the radio dial and a burst of Andrew Lloyd Webber's music filled the car. They continued along in silence for a while, Natalya feeling lost and out of her depth. Finally, she asked him, 'Rupert, is it all right for me to wear this dress to Ritz? Will they let me in?'

'What? Oh. Yes. Many women wear ugly dresses. You won't stand out.'

By the time they had arrived, the valet had swept off with the Jaguar, and they had been seated in the glittering gold-and-cream Palm Court, Natalya had become so fixated on how inappropriate her dress was that she sat with one hand on her shoulder so her forearm hid her low-cut neckline.

'Relax, Natalya,' Rupert said. 'That's an order.'

She released her arm, but still felt terribly exposed. She glanced around her, trying to reassure herself that others were dressed badly too. But she realised she couldn't really tell. She had the sense of being in water up to her chin, unable to reach the bottom with her toes and desperately paddling to stay afloat.

'Are you admiring the decorations?' Rupert said.

Natalya followed the direction of his gaze. Golden Christmas trees with pink decorations. 'Is my first English Christmas,' she told him. 'We had no Christmas the same in Soviet Union. And Russian Christmas is in January anyway.'

'Ah, we know how to do Christmas here in London,' he said. 'Perhaps later we'll take a walk through the streets. Look at the lights.'

She began to cheer up. A very polite waiter arrived and asked her to choose her tea. She had no idea, so had the same as Rupert. It arrived with a silver three-tiered serving platter of sandwiches, scones and pastries. Rupert helped himself eagerly, but Natalya picked.

'Good girl,' he said to her. 'The camera is very unforgiving of lumps and bumps.'

She felt both pleased and insulted at the same time.

He dusted his hands and leaned forward on his elbows. 'Now, Natalya. I must talk business with you.'

'Yes, Rupert.' She put aside a half-eaten scone.

'Our ratings at *Lonely Shores* have been less than spectacular of late. We've decided that to coincide with your arrival on the show and also another character – the one you originally auditioned for – we're giving the show a bit of a makeover. New opening credits, re-recording the theme song... to give it a slightly younger, sexier feel. We've a national ad campaign planned and we hope to generate some publicity, so you could be expected to do interviews and so on.'

Natalya glowed. *Interviews.*

His voice grew stern. 'But all of this relies on you being up to the task I've given you. If we encourage people to watch, and you are very bad at your part, then we've wasted a lot of money. Do you understand?'

'I will not be bad,' she exclaimed, stricken that he should suspect it.

'I need you to be *brilliant*. I'll be honest with you. You're a risk. Ginny and Dan didn't want me to hire you at all. But I saw something in you . . .' He trailed off, his soft grey eyes locked to hers. She glanced away, embarrassed. 'In any case, you'd better not throw your chance away. Many, many girls would kill for the opportunity you have.'

The feeling of flailing around in water came back to her. It was her dream to be in this world, but she didn't seem to know the rules yet.

'Rupert,' she blurted, before thinking better of it, 'I need your help to be good actress.'

'Of course, Natalya,' he answered smoothly. 'I'm here for you. Is there anything in particular that's bothering you?'

She didn't mention the fact that just reading the scripts was the biggest challenge. 'I don't understand . . . I can't make my character to love an older man.'

'Ah. I see.'

'Mr Bradley is . . . I watch show and cannot see why Tatiana would admire him most.'

Rupert levelled that grey gaze at her again, and she squirmed under it again. 'Natalya,' he said, 'you have the heart of a true actress. So many would just learn the lines and say them, but you need to feel what goes on beneath.'

'Yes,' she said, realising she sounded a little breathless.

'Craig Bradley represents something Tatiana has never experienced. He's wise, he's in control of his life, he's powerful. She suspects he would be a wonderful lover, a man with many talents learned over years of experience.'

Natalya didn't interrupt to say that, actually, the bumbling Craig Bradley didn't come across as wise or powerful or a skilled lover, because she was fairly sure they weren't talking about Craig Bradley any more. Rupert was trying to seduce her – she knew the signs. And she was flattered. Stupidly flattered. She smiled, probably too broadly.

'What do you want, Natalya?' he said, serious.

Confused, she shook her head, her smile fading. Had the rules just changed again? 'What do you mean?'

'What is your dream? What wish have you nursed in your heart since you were a child?'

The words *American princess* came to mind, but she didn't say them. 'To be an actress.'

'An actress? Or a star?'

'A movie star,' she answered solemnly.

He didn't speak for a few moments and she wondered if she'd been foolish to say it out loud. But then he answered. 'You know that I have the power to make it happen. It will all depend on how you go. Don't you let me down. Don't you let yourself down.'

'I won't,' she promised.

He checked his watch and frowned. 'You know, I don't think I'll have time for a walk with you this afternoon. In fact, I've just remembered something important I have to do across the other side of town. You understand, don't you?'

'I . . . of course. You are busy man.'

'*A* busy man, Natalya. You've got to put articles in your sentences.'

'You are *a* busy man,' she replied dutifully.

'I certainly am. Here . . .' He fished in his pocket and pulled out a fifty-pound note, casually dropped it on the table. She wondered if others in the room would think he was paying her off, like a whore. 'Take a cab home, my dear. I'll see you on set in three weeks.'

The chill outside was a distinct contrast to the warm, close air in the cinema. Lena and Sam emerged into Leicester Square, then pulled on gloves and scarves to keep them warm. Noise surrounded them. Dull, thudding bass from nightclubs, merry-go-round music drifting from the far end of the square, voices talking and laughing, a carolling band of teenagers in red and white smocks. Christmas lights competed with lights from shops and bars, a blur of colour. The rich smell of roasting chestnuts awoke Lena's appetite, and she realised it was the first time in months that she *didn't* feel nauseous. She was so relieved that she remarked on it to Sam.

'A Christmas Eve present,' Sam replied with a laugh. 'That's great, let's get pizza.'

So they bought pizza by the slice from a narrow shop and wandered through the square. It had rained earlier, though it was clear now, and golden light was caught in all the puddles. Sam wanted to sit down, but they ambled for ages before they found a seat that was dry enough. By that time, the pizza was sitting awkwardly in Lena's stomach and she wished she'd not eaten so much of it, nor so fast.

'Lena,' Sam said, turning to her with a grave look on his face, 'I need to talk to you about something important.'

Lena braced herself. He was leaving her; that had to be it. All of the excuses about not finding a place for them yet – lack of money for bond, James disputing with him about who owned what furniture, waiting to hear back about a better-paying job with the drummer's father – suddenly revealed themselves starkly as lies, ways of appeasing her while he worked out how he could extricate himself from the relationship. But even as she had these thoughts, Sam was taking her hand, sliding off the bench to bend on one knee in front of her . . .

She caught the collar of her shirt in her right hand. 'Sam?'

'I love you so much, Lena. You are the best thing that's ever happened to me.' He fished in his pocket with his free hand. 'These babies will join us together forever, but I wanted to propose to you, like this. Because you deserve to be asked, and you deserve this.'

He pulled out a small blue box, which she took with shaking fingers and opened. Inside, a single small diamond on a silver band. Thoughts whirled through her head: how could he afford this if he couldn't afford bond for a flat? But also the relief, the *sheer blessed* relief that he wasn't going to leave her; that, in fact, they were to be married, and she would not be sent home by herself to Russia with two babies to care for.

'So,' he said with that smile of his, the smile that warmed the frosty London evening as though the summer sun were shining on her. 'Lena, will you marry me?'

'Oh, yes,' she said, pulling him up into her arms. 'I will.'

She slid off her gloves and he pushed the ring onto her finger. It was slightly loose and the diamond slipped around to nestle against her palm. Sam promised he would get it refitted, and Lena had to ask him how he could afford the ring in the first place.

'I borrowed the money from my grandad,' he said. 'He's loaded.'

Lena knew that Sam's mother and sister lived with his grandad, but the way Wendy had constantly complained about money had led Lena to believe they were struggling. Sam explained that Wendy asked Grandad for nothing now, because the old man was suspicious about people wanting his money and she didn't want to be cut out of his will.

'She's going to inherit the lot one day, so she bides her time. She looks after him, gives him his pills, runs him about to the clinic. He's only seventy but he smoked like a chimney his whole life and he's always sick. I think Mum's waiting for him to die so she can get her money and go shopping with it.' He laughed. 'She'd kill me if she knew I borrowed from him.'

That word again: *borrowed*. Did that mean they would have to pay him back? And if a loan was so easy to get, why did Sam not borrow the money for them to set up house together? She brushed the thoughts aside, angry with herself for being ungrateful on such an evening. She didn't want the coming responsibilities to displace her romantic spirit. She adjusted the diamond on her finger and admired it in the glow of Christmas lights.

'Do you like it, Lena?' he asked, hooking his arm around her middle and pulling her close.

'I love it,' she replied and it was the truth.

CHAPTER SIXTEEN

Lena woke in the early-morning dark. It seemed she couldn't get through an entire night without having to make a trip to the toilet. The worst part was that, once she'd been up, she found it almost impossible to get back to sleep.

On her way back from the bathroom she stopped at the kitchen for a drink of water and to check the clock: 3 a.m. Sighing, she took herself back to bed and began the long wait for sleep.

Natalya and Sofi slept on, their soft breathing mocking her. She was the one who needed the most rest; why was it so impossible for her to get it? If she'd known how tired she would get, she would never have . . . but, of course, she'd not intended to fall pregnant at all, had she? It was a little mistake with enormous consequences. Sometimes, alone like this, when she wasn't trying to convince Sam, or her sister, or Sofi, that she hadn't screwed up spectacularly, she let herself feel the regret fully. She prayed that once the babies came, the feeling would go away. She didn't want either of them to look in her eyes and see even the barest shadow of regret.

Lena flopped over on her front, pushing a pillow underneath her. Her tummy was starting to grow and she wouldn't be able to sleep in this position for much longer. She closed her eyes tightly and tried to clear her mind. But dark thoughts circled. She had been to see the midwife the previous day, and everything was progressing normally, but they had talked about the topic Lena had assiduously avoided thinking about until now: giving birth.

'Of course, there's no way of knowing what kind of labour you'll have really,' the midwife said. 'Though a lot of girls ask their mums. If your mum had good labours, you probably will too.'

Lena had been speechless for a few moments, prompting the midwife to lay a cool hand on her wrist.

'Are you all right?'

'My mother died giving birth to me,' Lena said.

The midwife, nervous eyes scanning the folder in front of her, clucked and huffed her way out of the conversation, reassuring her that medicine was very different in England in the 1990s compared to Soviet Russia. Lena had allowed herself to be reassured. But now, in the dark, her thoughts turned to her mother's death. Why did she die? It frustrated her that she couldn't ask anybody. The knowledge was urgent now. If only she could ask her father. She had an impression – perhaps Papa had said something in her youth – that her mother's death had been violent and bloody. Or perhaps that was merely a memory of a morbid childhood imagining.

There was no chance of her sleeping now. She rose quietly, went to the kitchen and put the kettle on. Sofi had forbidden her from drinking coffee because of the insomnia, so she made a cup of camomile tea and turned the television on. Her eyes ached. She couldn't concentrate on the screen, her mind kept returning to her mother, babies, blood . . .

Aunt Stasya might know. She finished her tasteless tea and moved to the telephone. Sofi left a little address book by the phone; next to Stasya's number were instructions on how to convert the time. Stasya would be up now, having breakfast, getting ready for work. She hesitated. Had Sofi told Stasya yet that Lena was pregnant? Even now, as an adult, she feared her aunt's bad opinion.

Lena steeled herself and picked up the phone. Generally, they didn't make long-distance calls. Sofi wrote to Stasya once a week, saving phone calls for special occasions. Well, this was a special occasion. If she didn't speak to Stasya, she mused, she might never sleep again.

'Good morning, it's Stasya Mikhailovna Chernova.'

Stasya always used her most polite voice to answer the phone, and it made Lena feel vulnerable for her. She was so old-fashioned, cared so much about what others thought.

'Aunt Stasya,' Lena said. 'It's Lena.'

A short silence, then, 'Well, Lena, do you want congratulations or commiserations?'

So Sofi had told her. 'Congratulations?' Lena said in a meek voice. 'I'm having twins, and Sam and I are getting married.'

First, of course, they had to find somewhere to live. Sam was dismissive: the right place would turn up. But Lena didn't want still to be living with Sofi and Natalya when she had two babies to care for.

'Hmm, I think that should be the other way around. It was in my day. First marriage, then babies.' Her voice softened. 'But I do wish you all the best, child.'

'I'm sorry to ring you so early,' Lena said, 'but I'm having trouble sleeping and you were the only person I thought of who could help.'

'How so?'

'Do you know anything about Mama's death?'

Stasya sighed sympathetically. 'I'm afraid not. All we knew of it, we heard from your father. Lena, don't concern yourself so. You will be fine.'

Lena thought about all those little cards she had given out with her father's details on them. And not one of them had reached its destination. Had she given up too easily on finding him? Now she was in England, she might have access to other ways of locating him.

'If only I could find him,' she said.

'You don't want to find him,' Stasya said, her voice cooling several degrees. 'Even if he's still alive, he wouldn't be much use to you.'

'But he could tell me how Mama died. Then I'd know if it was something hereditary.'

Stasya made a dismissive noise. 'He wasn't there when you were born, Lena. He was off drinking with friends. That was all he told Ivan about the birth. He came home to find Natalya had been left with the neighbours, and a motherless infant was waiting for him at the hospital. He didn't know a thing.'

Lena digested this piece of information, not sure how she felt.

'She had Natalya without any problems, Lena. Put it out of your mind.'

After the conversation, Lena turned off the television and the lights and crept back to bed. Natalya turned over, cracked open an eye and said huskily, 'Are you all right?'

'Yes,' Lena replied, flopping over on her tummy again. 'Just can't sleep.'

Natalya rolled onto her side and began gently stroking Lena's hair. 'Then don't sleep. Just lie there and relax.'

The soothing gesture, the soft dark, began to erode wakefulness. She was starting to drift . . . when she felt it.

Like a stream of bubbles, bursting against the wall of her tummy.

She took a quick intake of breath.

'What is it?' Natalya whispered.

'The babies. I felt them move!'

'Really?' Natalya's arm snaked around her middle. 'Could I feel it yet?'

'Not yet, I think. It was very soft.' There, again. A series of soft little bumps. Tears pricked her eyes. *Babies. Two dear little babies.* She let out a sob of happiness.

'Are you crying?' Natalya said, pulling Lena over so she could search her face in the dark.

'For happiness,' Lena said.

Natalya grasped her hand and snuggled up next to her. 'I'm glad,' she said.

At last, the day had come, and the butterflies in Natalya's stomach were beating their wings madly. Over and over in her head, she repeated her lines as she waited for the car to pick up her and Sofi, while their breath fogged in the air and the distant sound of traffic rippled over the pre-dawn streets. On the long drive to Haysbridge-on-Sea on the southern coast, where the set for *Lonely Shores* was already abuzz with a bewildering array of people: rough-mouthed men running cables; camera operators; boom operators; a bossy woman with a light meter around her neck; and others without evident purpose, hurrying around, shouting to each other, making jokes, eating currant buns. In the make-up chair, while the strong smell of coffee and cigarette smoke from the catering room next door mingled with the faint odour of paint and oil from the sets. In wardrobe, as a very young, very pretty woman dragged clothes on and off Natalya's body until settling for a plain blue button-up dress not unlike the one she had worn to her original audition.

Sofi was annoyingly solicitous. 'How are you feeling? You remember your lines? Do you need any help with anything?'

But Natalya just wanted to be inside herself, silent and still, to combat the whirr of sound and movement. Her gaze moved continually around her, searching for Rupert. He was nowhere to be seen.

Lonely Shores had been running on STC for four years. Rupert Palmer was the mastermind behind it, having graduated from producing two well-received game shows on the same channel. He had gambled the last of his company's profits on buying five neighbouring houses in the reluctant village of Haysbridge-on-Sea and converting them into sets. This meant no expensive location shoots: two units could be inside filming while the third was outside. The soap had been a big success, generating miles of newspaper and magazine coverage, increasing tourism to the area, making stars out of its cast, especially the much-loved Bradley family. Natalya's role was to embroil them in a compelling affair-separation-reconciliation subplot.

'Tatiana, can we have you on set with unit one at number twenty-five, please?'

Natalya looked up from where she sat as the wardrobe assistant tried shoes on her feet. 'Now?'

'Yes, now.'

With Sofi at her elbow, Natalya made her way out onto the street and into number twenty-five. The set was so brightly lit that it made her tired eyes ache. She had thought she would be shooting her first scene first, but apparently that wasn't the case. They wouldn't be shooting her arrival at the front door until midday, when the sun was at its highest in the sky. It threw her: she had learned her lines in order. But Sofi rubbed her arm and told her she'd be fine.

One of the people who had been at her original audition – he introduced himself as Dan Ellison, unit one's director – came to get her, and positioned her on the set: a kitchen, authentic down to the last detail, with magnets holding school notices on the fridge. And yet, it was only half a kitchen. Walls had been removed to make space for camera runs, electrical cords hung from the ceiling, the sink was dusty because water had never been run in it, and the floor was streaked with scuff marks. Just off set, stacks of equipment and props were stored. A tall man repositioned her, checked the light. Another of the actors arrived, a soft-skinned woman in her forties. Natalya recognised her from the show as Meg Bradley. She smiled and said hello, but the actor merely gave her a nod and kept drinking her coffee. Now, Natalya had a surge of confidence. She had played out this scene with Sofi dozens of times. In fact, she thought she was capable of some of her best acting. Once again, she wished Rupert was here to see it. She was going to be brilliant, just as he had told her to be.

It took a long time for everyone to be ready. People came in, went away again. Somebody fetched her an apron. She tied it on only to be told to take it off again. Disagreement followed.

'She should only wear an apron if she's cooking. She's not cooking, she's cleaning.' This was a disembodied voice from beyond the bright lights.

'Cleaners wear aprons.'

'Since when?'

'My cleaner wears an apron,' the actor playing Meg Bradley said helpfully.

'Viewers associate aprons with cooking, not cleaning.'

'Does she cook?'

'Not in this scene.'

'But will she cook? Later?'

Scripts were thumbed. Natalya was frozen, too afraid to answer. Finally, she piped up. 'There is scene much later, where Tatiana cooks for Mr Bradley some Russian food.' *Borshch*. That's what they had written. If she were trying to seduce a man, she would cook him lamb *shashlyk*, or a sticky *sharlotka* layered with custard. But not beetroot soup. 'Not in this episode,' she continued.

'Apron off.'

'Give her a scarf.'

Another delay as the hairdresser was called and spent ten minutes arranging the scarf on Natalya's head so that it looked authentic and yet beautiful at the same time. Then, finally, they were ready to shoot. Somebody called action, the clapperboard was slapped together, and Meg Bradley said her first line.

But it wasn't a line that Natalya recognised. Bewildered, she looked towards the cameras. 'I'm sorry. Dan?'

An impatient 'Cut' somewhere from the dark. 'What is it, Tatiana?'

Natalya wasn't sure if they didn't know her real name, or if it was customary to call an actor by their character name. 'This line is not in my script.'

Dan hurried on to the set with a script, showing it to her. English letters and words swam in front of her. She concentrated very hard. The lines were definitely different.

'You mustn't have been sent the script updates. Here.' He handed her his script. 'Everybody, take a twenty-minute break while Tatiana learns this scene.'

A rush of heat burned Natalya's heart. Learn a scene in twenty minutes? But it wasn't fair! She had practised and practised.

Dan gave her an apologetic smile. 'Sorry, happens sometimes, especially with new cast. You probably weren't on our drop-off list. I'll make sure you're on it, and I'll get you a copy of the latest scripts to take home.'

'But I learn all the other ones already.'

'You'll get used to it,' he said over his shoulder as he left the set.

Natalya realised she was starting to perspire. 'Is Rupert here today?' she asked desperately.

'Usually gets in around midday,' somebody said from the dark space beyond the lights.

Sofi joined her on the set. Her freckles stood out starkly under the bright light. 'Come, Natalya, we'll sit down together and learn those lines.'

'I can't,' Natalya hissed. 'Is not enough time. I have still other lines in my head.'

'You have to. Don't worry, I'm here to help.'

Natalya was frozen to the spot.

'Come,' Sofi said again, leading her off. They found the sitting-room set, dim and empty, and sat on the Bradley family's sofa.

'This isn't fair,' Natalya said.

'You can complain about it, or you can learn your lines,' Sofi replied sternly, tapping the page in front of her.

So they started reading. Natalya tried to put her sense of injustice aside, but it affected her concentration. The lines weren't markedly different; just different enough to be confusing. Two pieces of conversation had been transposed and new material had been added. Most annoyingly, the part Natalya had loved, where she spoke about the town she had grown up in, was gone. She crammed the changes into her mind, trying not to be overwhelmed at the prospect of re-learning the rest of the week's lines.

From the other room, Dan started calling, 'Tatiana? Where are you?'

She took a deep breath. Sofi squeezed her hand.

It was disastrous. Because she had learnt the other script so well, it kept popping into her mind. She stumbled over words; English felt as foreign now as when she had first arrived here. She had no opportunity to be brilliant: all her effort was concentrated just on saying the right lines in the right place. Impatience surrounded her. Dan's voice became sharper. The boom operator who had been holding a microphone above them for ages began to complain about his shoulder. Meg Bradley was flapping her shirt to dry out the sweat. The bright lights and blooming adrenaline were like a bad dream to Natalya. When Dan called, 'Cut, *still* not right!' for the eleventh time, she burst into tears.

Sofi was with her a moment later. 'It's all right, it's all right,' she said soothingly.

'Who is that?' Dan called. 'Get her off the set.'

Sofi took her hand, led her off again.

'Where are you taking my Tatiana?' Dan said, approaching them.

'She's having trouble learning the lines so quickly,' Sofi explained. Natalya marvelled at how she could be so cool. 'We'll need more time.'

'There isn't more time. Is she an actress or not? Because she won't last long in the business with this attitude.' He rounded on Natalya. 'I knew it was a bad idea to hire you.'

Sofi stepped in again. 'Natalya was not given the script changes. You noted that yourself. She is at a disadvantage, and you should make allowances for it.'

'Every other actor I know can learn a few lines – especially when they're not that different from the old ones – in short order. Is she stupid?'

'Not at all. But Natalya still has difficulty reading English.'

Natalya kicked Sofi's ankle, but it was too late.

'Are you serious? We've hired an actor, for a soap, who has difficulty reading English? Does Rupert know?'

'What's going on here?'

Natalya looked around to see Rupert striding towards them up the hallway. She held back a sob: now it was all going to fall apart. She would be going home, never to return. And all because of her defective brain and its inability to master those English letters and words. Maybe Dan was right. Maybe she was stupid.

Sofi, doing an admirable job of protecting Natalya's interests, was on to Rupert in a second. Complaining about late script changes, about bullying, about insults. Rupert listened with a stony expression, then turned his gaze on Natalya. A moment from her childhood flashed into her mind: her father, angry with her for breaking a glass, glaring at her. But Rupert didn't fly into a rage as her father had. Instead, he said quietly, 'Natalya, I'd like to speak with you. Alone.'

'Natalya won't speak to you without me,' Sofi said.

Rupert frowned his disapproval, and Natalya brushed her off. 'No, no, Sofi. It's all right. I will go.'

She wasn't sure why. Perhaps she was tired of being spoken about as though she wasn't there. Or perhaps she was embarrassed at the thought that Sofi would see her being fired. But she suspected that she agreed to go with Rupert simply because he had asked her to.

Sofi shook her head, but Natalya held up her hand. 'I know what I do. I am not stupid.' She cast an accusing glance at Dan. 'Despite what everyone think.'

'Good girl,' Rupert said in a soft voice as he led her away, and the compliment soothed her. He took her to a locked room near the front of the house. Inside, the floorboards were bare and every corner was crammed with cardboard boxes overflowing with props, neatly coiled electrical cables, stacks of aluminium cases full of gear. Bay windows looked out onto the street, where another unit was setting up.

'All right now, Natalya,' Rupert said, closing the door behind him and pressing his back against it. 'What's the story?'

'I learn all my scripts,' she said. 'I worked so hard, and now director tells me . . . now *the* director tells me that there are new scripts, new lines to learn.'

'And is it true? What I heard Dan say when I arrived? That you can't read English?'

'I can read English. But I am slow.'

He ran a hand through his thick white hair, fixing his eyes on the ceiling. 'You have let me down, Natalya,' he said with a sigh.

Her heart felt cold.

'I distinctly remember you telling me, when I offered you this part, that you would have "no trouble" reading the scripts.'

'I need little help, that is all. *A* little help.'

Now his gaze moved to her face. She noted, with some amazement, that she was less concerned about being fired than she was about arousing his disapproval. His expression softened.

'Do you know what I'm thinking, Natalya?'

She shook her head.

'I'm thinking, is she worth the trouble?'

Natalya remained silent.

'And then I look at you . . . you're so . . . beautiful.' Here he looked away, almost bashful. For some reason, the gesture aroused a flutter of excitement in her.

Now he was straightening his cuffs over his tanned wrists, his businesslike manner restored. 'I'll have a word with Dan. It wasn't your fault that you didn't get the new scripts in time. He'll have to make allowances.'

'Thank you, Rupert,' she gasped. 'I will try so hard.'

'Ensure that you do.'

'Sofi will help me, she –'

'Ah, Sofi. Is she going to be here every day?'

Natalya nodded. 'Well, yes.'

'Not a good idea, Natalya. You don't want to be so indebted to her. Besides, English isn't her native language either. I'll bring in a coach. A coach can help with your accent too. I'll have that organised by the end of the week, so tell Sofi she needn't accompany you.'

'You are too generous.'

'It's a business decision,' he said dismissively. 'Back to work now.'

Natalya followed him back to the set. She realised she was a little disappointed that he hadn't offered to coach her himself. But then, he was a very busy and important man. Far too old for her. If only he were twenty years younger. Or even ten. She just might find herself falling for him.

Sofi tried to still her heart. She knew she should be excited, not fearful. But she wasn't experienced at these things. Nakedness was reserved for baths.

'I'm ready,' she said, in a voice she knew was too small, too unsure, in the candlelit room.

Julien, who had been sitting on the other side of the bed covering his eyes, removed his hands and smiled at her. She crossed her arms over her stomach while he regarded her. She wore no clothes, but had covered herself in jewellery, her *own* jewellery. Beaded armbands, a silver and glass choker, a long chain with a single turquoise caught in a woven silver net the shape of a star.

'Ah, you come to me covered in jewels,' he said, pulling her down next to him and starting to unbutton his shirt. 'I will remember this forever.'

'Will you?' she breathed, closing her eyes and raising her arms above her head, forcing herself to let go of her awkwardness. His hands closed over her breasts and his lips found her navel. The mineral smell of paint was strong in the room, and dust from the bedspread made her nose itch slightly.

At length, he spoke. 'I am not much of a lover, Sofi. I have known only two women like this before you. I promise, I will remember.'

She opened her eyes. He was still dressed from the waist down. His skin was very pale and his body lean. A few dark hairs sprouted on his chest.

'But now,' he said, 'everything must come off.'

He reached for her arms and slowly slid off the first armband, then the second. He unclasped the choker, trailing the silver chain over her breasts as he removed it. She shivered, goose bumps rising all over her body. His hot lips warmed her skin again, and she sighed, letting her eyelids flutter closed.

'I was trying to be more beautiful,' she said. 'For you.'

'Under the skin, we are all human, and that is beautiful,' he said. 'So varied, so alive, so hopelessly flawed and endlessly well-meaning. I see a spark in you, Sofi. It glows, fierce as diamonds.'

She felt him lift off the necklace, and knew that she was now truly naked before him. The thought filled her with delicious tremors. She opened her eyes to find him gazing at her face, a dreamy expression in his eyes.

'Come to me only as you are,' he said. 'Not as you think I want you to be.'

She smiled; he kissed her.

'I will,' she said.

CHAPTER SEVENTEEN

Late-afternoon sun clung to the curtains in Julien's bedsit. The space was now tidy and blank. All the canvases had been freighted back to France, the bed had been stripped, his belongings had been packed and now sat in two battered suitcases at his feet as he re-examined his plane ticket. Sofi watched him, fighting down the desperate surge of longing, the ache that had characterised her days in the last few weeks. He was going; she had to accept it.

He tucked the plane ticket away in the pocket of his jacket, and looked up to smile at her. 'Well, Sofi. I go now to the train.'

'You won't let me pay for a taxi to the airport?'

He shook his head. 'I like trains. I find inspiration on them, in the movement. You keep your money, spend it on your jewellery.' He stood, bent to pick up his cases. Then hesitated, sat down again. 'Sofi?'

Her heart thudded dully. 'Yes.'

He interlaced his pale fingers, tilting his head. 'I did not paint you. I did not want to paint you. Perhaps a more romantic man would have.'

She laughed. 'I expected nothing like that.'

'I want to explain why. In case you or your cousins ever stop to ask why there was no token of our parting. Why the artist did not lay you on a chaise longue of blues and purples, and pattern sunlight in your hair.' He reached out and touched her hair. 'It is because you are real, Sofi, and that is good for me. I live so much of my life in my imagination. I do not want to take you in there with me. Do you understand?'

'I think so,' she said.

'Through you, I have connected with the world. It is a good feeling. I will miss it.'

Tears – traitorous, unhelpful tears – pricked at her eyes. The ache was back and, with a bolt of clarity, she realised that she loved him.

His voice became quiet. 'I do not speak easily of my feelings,' he said.

'It's all right.'

'You could come with me.'

The statement hung in the air. She had wondered if he would ask, and she had already thought it through and rejected it. Natalya required a great deal of attention at the moment. Sofi had still been accompanying her to the set two or three times a week; she didn't trust Rupert and wanted to make sure she kept up a strong presence. Then there was organising her for interviews and photo shoots. Some days Sofi spent hours on the sidelines of a photographer's studio, dreaming of being with Julien while insincere people fawned around Natalya. She had also taken over managing Natalya's money because her cousin was hopeless and didn't understand it. Natalya would spend it all in a week if Sofi let her, so Sofi had set up bank accounts and investments in the hope that Natalya would still have some money to tide her over when her contract ran out. Her big television debut was the following night, and *BritSoap* magazine had featured her on their March cover. Now her contract with *Lonely Shores* was over, there would be new offers to field, new film sets to get her to, new lines to help her with. And then there was Lena, six months pregnant now and still Sam hadn't found them a suitable place to live together. One excuse after another, and Sofi wondered if Lena had yet figured out that Sam was going to make an unreliable husband.

Perhaps it wouldn't matter: two babies were coming, she hadn't much choice. In any case, Sofi couldn't abandon her now either.

'I can't. Not now. But I would like to.' She smiled at him and he smiled in return.

'Listen now,' he said, 'for I will say it only once. I love you, Sofi Chernova. There. I have said it. You will not hear it from me again.'

'Will you tell me if you stop loving me?' she teased.

'No,' he answered, with no humour. 'For it won't happen.'

She fell into his arms and he pressed her close. 'The time, the time,' he muttered against her hair. Then he was pulling back, picking up his cases again. 'I will write to you often, and try to make you change your mind about coming to me.'

He handed her the key to the bedsit. She had offered to return it to the letting agent for him, so he didn't have to go across town and back with heavy suitcases. 'Goodbye, Sofi.'

'Goodbye.'

He leaned in and kissed her. Time stopped. Sunlight and the warm beat of his heart.

'Goodbye,' he said again, turning and heading for the door.

She lay on the stripped bed, clutching the keys in her right hand. The window was open, the promise of spring breezed in, making the curtains flutter. She hurried to her feet, looked down to the street. There he was, a suitcase in each hand.

'Julien!' she called.

He looked up.

'I love you too.'

'I thought so,' he called in return, and continued on his way.

She watched him down the long grey street until he moved from sight.

Natalya peered close to the mirror in the little bathroom of their apartment, double-checking that her make-up was blended properly around her jaw. Linda, in make-up at *Lonely Shores*, had taught her a lot. She now looked back on her old technique with embarrassment. Had she ever really put blush in the hollows of her cheeks? She stepped back, cursing that she didn't have a better light to get ready by. Still in this apartment, still sharing a bed with her rapidly expanding sister. And yet she was a soap star. Or at least, she would be after this evening.

She'd thought that when Lena moved out with Sam, they could all leave the apartment and find somewhere better. But Sam was still sleeping on his bass player's sofa, and Lena was still mooching around the apartment. Now, with Natalya's contract having run out just four days ago, there was no guarantee of more money coming in. She breathed deeply, trying not to let it bother her. There would be something. She hoped.

Her dress for the party was laid out in the bedroom. Chanel. It had arrived on set for her on Friday. Wardrobe had handed it to her, telling her that Rupert had sent it. Ankle-length, white, diaphanous, with bell sleeves and embroidery across the skirt. Feminine and sexy. She had already bought a dress for the occasion – a black velvet evening gown – but if Rupert wanted to see her in Chanel, then she would wear Chanel. She slid into the dress, longing for a full-length mirror.

Above her bed was pinned the advertisement that had run in *BritSoap* last week. On one side of the page, a photograph of Craig and Meg Bradley, beloved regulars on *Lonely Shores*. On the other, Natalya herself: in a French maid costume, with her hair cascading over one shoulder, her lips painted dark red. In between her and the Bradleys, bold against the white background, was the word *Re-Vamp*. And underneath, a shoutline for 'the new look *Lonely Shores*' commencing March fourteenth. Tonight. The party was being held at Rupert's London office, and she knew that it might be the last time she saw him. The thought generated powerful feelings. Rupert had been her champion, her saviour in many ways. Although they hadn't spent a moment alone since her first day on the set, she always felt that she might be special to him. He would often come to watch her filming, and she would try her hardest to do well to impress him. Then he might wink at her, or offer her a special smile before checking his watch – always checking his watch – and ducking off. She had found herself asking around. Was he married? No. Was he gay? Definitely not: he'd dated a string of attractive women, but wasn't seeing anyone presently. How old was he? Estimates placed him somewhere between forty-nine and fifty-four. *Fifty-four*. She had just turned twenty-six: less than half his age. But whatever strange feelings were stirring in her, he didn't encourage them and she didn't express them.

Natalya slid open the wardrobe door and crouched down to go through her shoeboxes. A lot of her money had been spent on shoes. Rupert had given no indication what kind of shoes would go with this dress and she was terrified she would get it wrong. Gold stilettos? Or flat brown sandals? She considered both in the dim light of the bedroom. Then put on the stilettos. It was a party. They were party shoes.

A light knock at the door. Sofi entered, her face lighting up when she saw Natalya.

'Wow. You look like a princess.'

Natalya twirled for her. 'Are you sure you don't want to come to the party?'

Sofi shook her head. 'I'd be out of place. Besides, I want to stay here with Lena and watch it on the television. Like we do every night.'

Natalya shook her head. 'I can't believe it's real sometimes.'

'I have something for you,' Sofi said, going to her side of the chest of drawers.

'What is it?'

When Sofi turned around, she had a necklace in her hands. Natalya's heart sank.

'You made it?' Natalya asked.

'Yes. Look, I've wrapped the amethyst in a silver flower. Took me ages.'

She offered it to Natalya, but Natalya didn't reach for it.

'It would have gone nicely with my other dress. But . . . Sofi, this is Chanel.'

Sofi blinked, then dropped her hand, swinging the necklace slightly. 'Oh, of course.'

'It's by a famous designer. I can't really wear homemade jewellery with it.' What would Rupert think?

'I'm sorry,' Sofi said, putting the necklace back in the drawer. Did Natalya imagine that she slammed it shut? It wasn't like Sofi to get angry; or at least, it wasn't like her to show her anger.

Natalya, discomfort making her mute, left the room and gave Lena a kiss goodbye before heading down to the street to catch a cab.

Rupert's Soho office was small but beautifully decorated, with rich red paint, framed black-and-white photographs and gleaming track lighting. The desks had been cleared of papers to make way for platters of gourmet food. She noticed there was even a platter of *pirozhki*, to honour her Russian character. Her stomach rumbled but she didn't dare pick up anything to eat. No food after five o'clock. The room was crammed with people, most of them gathering around a large television in the corner. Natalya greeted her fellow cast members, noticing with satisfaction that she was wearing the most beautiful dress. Air kisses were exchanged, but she had never really warmed to her castmates and they had never warmed to her. She lifted a glass of champagne from a waiter's silver tray and her eyes searched the room for Rupert. He was nowhere in sight. She asked one of the cameramen, who said Rupert hadn't arrived yet. She mingled, drank more champagne. Her resolve weakened by alcohol, she surrendered to a tiny canapé topped with caviar. A ripple went around the room. It was nearly time for the show to air. Where was Rupert? Was he going to miss her debut?

Then she saw him, by the door. He had just arrived and was swamped by people. Of course. Everyone loved Rupert, everyone wanted to impress him. Her heart jumped: he was with someone. A woman. She edged closer to have a better look. A young woman hung on his arm. She was beautiful, with fair hair cropped close to her head and a generous smile painted vibrant pink. Natalya had a glimmer of recognition and thought she might be a pop star. Rupert saw Natalya and strode over.

'Natalya, the dress suits you well,' he said. 'This is Zoe.'

'Pleased to meet you,' Natalya said, not meaning it at all.

Rupert leaned close. 'Your shoes are a disaster,' he said, before moving on.

Natalya stood, half a glass of champagne in her hand, feeling her heart sink all the way to the floor. Now his hand was on the small of Zoe's back. What made her so special? What made her so deserving of Rupert's total approval, his firm touch?

'Tatiana? It's about to start.' This was Dan, who had still not used her real name once.

She drained her champagne, picked up another, and found herself a viewing position near the television. A hush fell over the room. Someone flicked off the overhead lights. A commercial finished, then the music burst into life: the familiar *Lonely Shores* theme remixed with a rock beat and new vocals. The opening sequence was different too, with footage of each family on the street as though they were posing for a photographer: squabbling, or cuddling, or ignoring each other, and then stopping to pose and smile. Natalya wasn't in the opening credits as she wasn't a permanent character. Her eyes flicked to Rupert and Zoe, then back to the screen.

She was on a few moments later, arriving at the Bradleys' front door in a plain blue dress and with her hair scraped back. She looked thin and regal, even in her ordinary clothes. The gathered crowd cheered. Natalya smiled. Someone patted her shoulder.

'I come about the cleaning job,' the Natalya on the television said. Craig Bradley's eyes nearly fell out of his head, and then they were inside, and the scene cut to another part of the action.

Natalya watched the show with mingled pride and anxiety. She looked good and she sounded good, but she had already filmed Tatiana's last lines. Meg Bradley, having discovered the affair, had thrown her out. She had already filmed Tatiana's last shot: taking her suitcase and walking away from the street. Everyone else in the room still had a job tomorrow. She didn't.

Sofi had told her not to worry, that there would be different offers now. But in Natalya's imagination she would be back to auditioning for non-speaking commercials, stuck in that apartment with her pregnant sister and her pious cousin . . . She pinched herself. *Don't be nasty.* She realised she must be drunk. She always got morose and angry when drunk. Just like her father. She upended her glass of champagne in a nearby pot plant.

Finally, the closing credits ran while the gathered crowd applauded and catcalled. She forgot to look for her name and felt a pang of disappointment; then remembered that it wouldn't be her real name listed in any case. It would be Natalie Chernoff, which luckily rhymed with a brand of vodka that just happened to be sponsoring advertising on the show. Then the crowd was dispersing and she found herself standing uncertainly by the television, which still flickered but was now muted, as the lights came back on and the party kept pulsing.

'Well done.'

She looked up. It was Rupert. She smiled, but knew it hadn't been convincing. 'Thank you. Where's Zoe?'

'She had to go home. Has an early start in the morning. She works in television.'

'Ah. I thought I'd seen her before. The morning news.'

'That's right.' He touched her shoulder, fingering the sleeve of her dress. 'I knew this would look good on you.'

'Sorry about the shoes.'

'You have a lot to learn. You probably need a stylist for parties and public events. I'll give you a few phone numbers.' He dropped his hand and, for an uncomfortably long time, just stared at her as though he were thinking.

She gathered herself, tilted her head and produced a more confident smile this time. 'What is it, Rupert?'

'I think we need you back on *Lonely Shores*.'

Her heart leapt. 'Really?'

'Let's find somewhere quiet to discuss it.' He took her hand and looked around. 'Come on, there's a room down this way.'

He led her down the corridor and dropped her hand to pull out a set of keys. He took her into a storeroom, empty except for one metal shelf holding two boxes of photocopy paper. He switched on the overhead light, which was far too bright for comfort, and leaned against the shelf. Natalya stood in front of him, arms folded self-consciously. Her heart thudded, hopeful.

'Imagine this,' he said with a spread of his hands. 'Meg Bradley thinks Tatiana has gone back to Russia. But Meg's son, Trevor, who has been away at university in London, returns to the street with a girlfriend: one he wants to marry. And it's Tatiana.'

'Does Meg have a son named Trevor?'

'Oh, yes. We give every character lots of relatives in other cities, in case we want to introduce them at some point. We'll have to cast for him. But the break between Tatiana's departure and her return is perfect: you'll be off the screen for a few months, but that will add a touch of realism. She goes away, she finds Trevor, they fall in love. Can you imagine the chaos that would cause?' He began to pace the small room. 'I have a feeling about Tatiana. We know we're going to see improved ratings with the Bradley family embroiled in an affair. This is a fabulous way to carry it on for months. How about another contract? Another six months at least, same arrangement as before?'

Natalya opened her mouth to say yes, then remembered Sofi. She would be angry if Natalya agreed to anything without speaking to her first. Sofi might be able to get more money, or other advantages. 'You'll have to phone Sofi,' she said.

Rupert's brows drew together. 'No, I'm not going to phone Sofi. I'm making you an offer now. Do you want to take it or not?'

'Of course, I –'

'Then leave your cousin out of this. It's very unprofessional to have a member of your family represent you, Natalya. Especially someone who is foreign, and who knows nothing about the entertainment industry.' He placed his hand over his heart. 'I give you my word, I am offering you a brilliant deal, one that any aspiring actress would walk through fire to be offered. You don't want to seem ungrateful, do you?'

She had a sense that he was working her over, but her mind was fogged by alcohol and ambition. Being a working actress was one thing, but it was the benefits that she was addicted to: photo shoots and interviews, parties, designer clothes, a stylist, being close to Rupert... She lifted her chin. 'I am not ungrateful. I know how far I have come. I will take your offer, with pride and with pleasure.'

He smiled slowly and reached for her cheek, grazing it softly with the back of his fingers. Her heart lurched. 'I'm very pleased,' he said. 'But there's one more thing I want to ask you.'

'Yes?'

'Can I turn out the light in here?' He didn't wait for an answer. He switched off the light and took her hands in his. It was so unexpected that she tensed. 'What's wrong?' he asked in a forceful tone.

'Nothing... I... What about Zoe?'

'Zoe who?' He laughed. 'Do you want to do this or not, Natalya?' His thumbs were making circles on the soft flesh of her wrists. 'I think you do.'

He gathered her towards him and kissed her hard. Her resistance melted away in an instant. All she felt were his strong arms, his passionate lips, the commanding confidence of his caresses. She sighed against him, allowing him to have his way. Her dress was removed, deliciously slowly. He laid his jacket on the carpet for them and took his time in pleasuring her. She had never known so experienced a lover, and all of the things that had been blocks to her finding him attractive ceased to matter.

After, in the minutes before they had to re-dress and return to the party, she stroked his shoulder and stared up into the dark space above them.

'Do you know what this means?' he said gruffly.

'What does it mean?' she asked, turning her face to kiss his cheek.

'It means you're mine.'

She couldn't see him, so didn't know if it was a joke. 'I am?'

'Oh yes,' he said, gripping her hand firmly and bringing it to his mouth to kiss. 'You belong to me now.'

She laughed lightly in the dark, but he didn't laugh in return. 'If you say so,' she replied. 'I don't mind belonging to you.'

'Good,' he said. 'We have an agreement.'

CHAPTER EIGHTEEN

Lena was doing her best to avoid Sam's family. It was Easter Monday, and they were visiting Wendy's rented house in Briggsby, an unremarkable town on the north Yorkshire coast. Lena had been seized by her usual bout of afternoon tiredness and had retired to the mattress on the floor of the dingy front room to rest; while Sam had gone out to visit an old school friend. She lay on the mattress, her gaze tracing the damp pattern in the corner of the ceiling. The window was closed and the curtain was drawn, but she could still hear the rattle of a lorry going past, just a few feet beyond the narrow pebbled courtyard. Weariness seeped through her. Not the kind of tiredness that could be solved by a few early nights, but a bone-deep exhaustion that – as far as she could predict – would end only after she had managed to get these wriggling babies out of her. Until then, she just wanted to lie in one place and stare into middle distance.

Privacy was nonexistent here. The room they were sleeping in was actually the dining room. The table and chairs had been crammed into the sitting room for the duration of their visit, but the sideboard, china cabinet, linen cupboard and Wendy's sewing box were all in here. There was no door to separate the room from the rest of the house, and Wendy was in the habit of shouting 'knock, knock' before barging in at any time to get tea towels or buttons or some other unnecessary thing. The bathroom was a thousand miles away, and to get there Lena had to sneak past Grandad's door – which was always open – lest he call her in and keep her standing there on her tired, swollen feet for ages as he recounted pointless meandering tales of the town's history, all the while slowly gasping on the air through his oxygen mask.

Lena let her eyes close and listened to the rhythm of her heart. She was starting to drift off when the familiar, overly bright voice said, 'Knock, knock.'

Lena jolted.

'Oh, sorry, love. Didn't realise you were sleeping.' Wendy walked briskly to the linen cupboard with an armful of folded towels.

Lena sat up. 'I'm just so tired all the time.'

Wendy laughed. 'Get used to it. How are you going to be when you've got two of them demanding to be fed all night?' She came to stand by the side of the mattress. 'Come on, hop up. We never get time alone. Let's go for a walk down to the cliffs.'

'I really don't think –'

Wendy had grasped her upper arm and was pulling her gently. 'Here, let me help you. The sea air will do you good.'

Lena climbed to her feet, not wanting to be rude to Wendy who had been very kind since their arrival. She had made all their meals, done all their laundry, and returned almost daily from the second-hand shop in town with tiny little clothes for them to take home for the babies. Lena pulled on her shoes and followed her out the front door, and they walked side by side down the narrow footpath that led to the cliffs.

Briggsby had no beach, and so was a common omission in guidebooks to the area. Instead, there were plunging cliffs and miles of tide pools. When the tide was high, like today, the waves crashed and roiled almost deafeningly on the rocks at the bottom of the cliffs. The long yellow grass alongside the footpath bent in the sea wind, and snowy gulls circled. The sky was grey and spring still seemed a long time away. Lena wished she'd brought her hat to keep her ears warm.

'So,' Wendy said as they walked along the cliff path. She grasped Lena's hand, a girlfriend's gesture that seemed forced. 'Nice to talk to you alone.'

'Yes,' Lena managed.

'Have you and Sam thought of names for those babies yet?'

'Ah, it's hard, you know. We have to come up with two girl names and two boy names, and then only use half of them.'

'I like Anna. That was my mother's name. Sam was very close to his grandma.'

Lena didn't mention that Sam hadn't suggested this name at all. 'My father's name was Viktor, and I would like that for a boy, or Viktoria for a girl.'

Wendy pulled down her lips in an expression of distaste. 'Erk. I don't know about that. And a girl would get called Vicky. Do you like Vicky?'

'I don't mind it.'

'Any other names? Ones that aren't foreign?'

'Well, I am Russian, so most of the names I like are from Russia. Anatoly, Ivan, Anya, Katria.'

'No, I don't like any of those. You can't send a boy out into the world named Anatoly. What about Sarah? Simon? Matthew? Jessica?'

'Matthew is nice. Sam likes that. But we'd like at least one name that's Russian.'

Wendy clicked her tongue: tsk-tsk. 'Then you'll have one who thinks he's yours and one who thinks he's Sam's. Here, do you want to sit down?'

She indicated ahead, where the path led into a park and a picnic bench stood under cover. It didn't look particularly comfortable, but it was better than walking.

Once they were settled, Wendy fixed Lena in her gaze and said, 'I need to talk to you about something quite serious.'

A tendril of apprehension touched Lena's heart. 'Yes?'

Wendy laughed loudly, revealing all her fillings. 'Lord, you needn't look so worried. Nobody's going to die . . .' She shrugged. 'Becky is moving out next month. She and a friend,' she emphasised the word with exaggerated quotation marks in the air, 'are getting a flat in Leeds. I'll have a spare room.'

Lena guessed the rest of the request and was already shaking her head. 'No, we're staying in London.'

'Has Sam found you a place yet?'

'He's looking.'

'Slowly?'

Lena couldn't help but smile. 'A little slowly, yes.'

'I think he's spooked, Lena. If you said you wanted to come and stay here, he'd say yes. I know it. He's a big boy now, but he still needs his mum around.'

She rummaged in her handbag for a cigarette and carefully cupped the end to light it. She flicked the match away, and three seagulls rattled down to peck at it, before deciding it wasn't edible and flying away. Wendy blew a stream of smoke into the air and the sea wind whipped it away.

'I don't think that's right,' Lena ventured. 'His band is in London. He can't leave them now.'

'His band, pah! They're never going to get anywhere. Tell me the truth, are you sick of living with your sister and your cousin?'

'I love them. Dearly. We get along great.'

'But you'd rather be living with Sam. Maybe even seeing if he's going to make good on that promise to marry you.' Wendy tapped the diamond ring. There had been a terrible row over it; as Sam predicted, Wendy had lost her temper at the idea of Grandad being asked for money. 'I'm telling you, if you move up here it will all work out. I'll help with the babies, you can go back to work a bit sooner, Sam won't feel so much pressure.'

Of course Lena wanted to be with Sam. And of course she had wondered over the past few months if he really did intend to marry her. But Sam moved at a different pace from everyone else. The pregnancy was flying by for her, but for him it was still early days. There would be time. A friend of his was vacating a flat in Greenwich soon and had offered to sublet to them. But he wasn't sure about when, or how much, and so the weeks dragged out with nothing happening.

It was true, too, that Lena wasn't happy living with Natalya and Sofi, despite her love for them. Actually, it was only Natalya that was the problem. Natalya with her shining, slender beauty. Lena had watched her own body stretch and stretch, until angry red streaks had clawed across her belly and her once-firm breasts had become soft and overly full. Seeing Natalya every day, unchanged, only added to her misery. The fact that she was on the television every night, in magazines at the newsagent, that she had started wearing an endless array of designer dresses to endless late-night parties, was almost too much to bear. Lena needed to get away from her, just so she wasn't standing in quite so long a shadow.

'I don't think you two know how much hard work babies are,' Wendy continued. 'You'll need my help. I have the room.'

Lena thought it best to put an end to the conversation. She rose, hand in the small of her back. 'Your generosity is appreciated so much, Wendy. You have been nothing but kind. But our lives are in London.'

Wendy muttered something; perhaps it was, 'You'll change your tune.' Her tone was not generous or kind.

'I'm sorry?' Lena asked.

'Never mind,' Wendy said, forcing a smile and taking a drag on her cigarette. 'Let's stop on the High Street for afternoon tea.'

They walked away, linked uncomfortably arm in arm, as the grey sea swirled on the dark rocks behind them.

Rupert Palmer's flat was in an Edwardian mansion block at Mayfair. Sofi buzzed the bell and waited. She suspected Natalya was in there, and she needed to speak to her urgently. She leaned her back on the doorframe and surveyed the neat hedgerows, the cobbled path, the shiny new cars parked along the street. It was May, and the warm weather turned her thoughts to getting out of London, going somewhere with long waving grass and quiet village lanes. It was

Julien's fault. While his frequent letters had not directly repeated his offer for her to come to Richelieu, they were full of the implication. Long passionate descriptions of laneways lined with tall elms, sundrenched stone bridges over still lakes, vast fields of yellow wildflowers. Sometimes he would unwittingly slip into French – a language Sofi was doing her best to learn – as though his love for the region overrode his ability to translate it.

Sofi rang the doorbell again. Natalya was avoiding her. She had tried to phone first, but it had gone to Rupert's answering machine. She hadn't left a message; that would only have warned Natalya that she was coming.

This time, Natalya's voice emerged from the intercom. 'Yes?'

'It's Sofi.'

A short pause. Then, brightly, 'Come on up.'

The door clicked and Sofi pushed in, and took the lift to the fourth floor.

Natalya, dressed in a T-shirt and designer jeans, her feet bare, led her through the entrance hall to the enormous sitting room. A line of double-glazed windows allowed a view out over Oxford Street and the rooftops beyond. Natalya sat in a leather armchair and invited Sofi to do the same.

'Where's Rupert?' Sofi asked.

'He's out at a meeting.'

Sofi was relieved; she found him unpleasant, with cold eyes and an insincere smile. Natalya obviously felt differently about him. Sofi knew that Natalya was sleeping with Rupert, even though Natalya, coyly, kept trying to hide it. She crept in early in the mornings with a variety of improbable excuses – late-night shoots, falling asleep on sofas at parties – before taking fresh clothes and disappearing again. Sofi wasn't sure why Natalya wasn't open about the relationship. Was it Rupert's age? Or was it that Natalya knew deep down that it was unwise to sleep with a business associate, especially one with so much power over her? Sofi hoped it was the latter; but Natalya's decisions lately had been unwise in the extreme. Hence the visit. In today's post, along with letters from Julien and Mama, was a contract that Sofi hadn't seen before.

'I wasn't expecting to see you,' Natalya said, pulling her feet up under her. She was wearing a gold anklet, and Sofi felt a small pang. Natalya had continued to refuse to wear Sofi's jewellery, not realising that a few photos of a rising star wearing her work could make a vast difference to the trajectory of her business. But then, what business? She had let it all languish, wrapped up in working for Natalya and helping out with Lena.

Sofi pulled the contract out of her handbag and laid it on the coffee table. 'It's about this.'

'Did you open my mail again?'

'You've always encouraged me to open your mail because, until very recently, you couldn't read it. Also, as I understand it, you employ me to manage this kind of document.'

Natalya shook her head, forcing a laugh. 'Don't look so cross, Sofi. You go quite red and flushed.'

Sofi fought the uncomfortable feeling that she was starting to dislike Natalya. 'It was one thing to accept an offer of work from Rupert without consulting me.' That had really stung. Sofi would have asked him for more money, better conditions. But Natalya had verbally agreed to whatever Rupert wanted and now it was too late. 'But I'm over that, because that's what you wanted to do and I understand that. But this . . . Natalya, we talked about it; we decided it was a bad idea.'

Natalya had been asked to pose for *Shutter*, a high-class magazine that purported to be for photography enthusiasts, but which featured a lot of naked women.

'You haven't come all this way to take your clothes off in front of everybody.'

'I changed my mind. Their photos are always very tasteful, artistic.'

'It's not even about the nudity; it's the lying. We discussed the offer, we rejected it, and then you signed a contract with them without telling me.'

Sofi leaned back, watched Natalya. Her cousin never stopped being an actress. In most situations she put on a front of some sort, but Sofi had become adept over the years at reading her real feelings underneath. Natalya's face was blankly reasonable, but Sofi knew she was angry.

'What is it, Natalya? Spit it out.'

Natalya switched to Russian, as she always did when she needed to express herself. 'You're too controlling.'

'You asked me to do this.'

'Rupert says –'

'Rupert? Your employer? Or Rupert your lover?'

Natalya drew her full lips into an angry line.

'Tell me something,' Sofi continued, 'did Rupert think taking your clothes off for *Shutter* was a good idea?'

'Yes,' Natalya conceded, 'and I trust his judgement because he's very particular about me posing tastefully and having the right clothes –'

'Even if you're not wearing any?'

'You make it sound cheap. They are art photographs. The female form is beautiful. Your little Frenchman is always painting it.'

Sofi took a deep breath, changed back to English. 'We must sort this out, Natalya. We are at each other's throats and I don't like it. You employ me to help you make good decisions, but I can't do my job properly if you aren't honest with me.'

Natalya was silent.

'Please, Natalya, speak to me. What's on your mind?'

Natalya leaned forward, her long hair falling over her shoulder. 'I think it might be unprofessional to have a family member represent me. Especially as you are foreign and you don't really know anything about the entertainment industry.'

'I see,' Sofi said.

'I need to take advice from somebody who knows the industry really well.'

'Someone like Rupert?'

'Well, yes.'

'But you understand, don't you, that Rupert has his own motives?'
'He wants to look after me.'
'He employs you. His feelings for his business might very well come first.'

Natalya shook her head defiantly. 'No, Rupert cares for me.' She dropped her eyes coquettishly, an expression that Sofi recognised from her television show. 'He says he loves me.'

Sofi fought with conflicting feelings. On the one hand, a choking sense of anger gripped her: how did Rupert dare to manipulate Natalya this way? Her cousin was being a fool. But on the other hand, it looked like she would finally be free from Natalya's demands. Time, again, to focus her energy on her own work. Her own heart.

'I'm sure he doesn't love you, Natalya,' Sofi said gravely. 'But if you would like him to take over managing you, then just say so.'

Natalya pushed her hair behind her ears. 'But the money, Sofi. How will you manage without it? I can keep paying you, if you like. I don't mind. I just –'

'Hush,' Sofi said, holding up her hand in a stop gesture. 'I don't mind about the money. I've saved a lot. I even invested some.' She frowned. 'Which reminds me, I'll have to explain all the accounts I've put your money in.'

'Just send the paperwork to Rupert,' Natalya said dismissively.

'Don't be so foolish. Mind your own money.'

'He's not Koschei the Deathless,' Natalya said with a laugh, referring to an evil Russian folktale character who preyed upon young women. 'He's a good man.'

Sofi regarded her. There she sat, surrounded by wealth and luxury, a television star on the rise. But Sofi could see beneath the poised beauty to the little girl beneath. The little girl who pretended it didn't hurt when her father abandoned her. And she felt such a pang of fear for her that her anger evaporated.

'Please be careful, Natalya,' she said softly.

Natalya softened too. 'I will be. I'm sorry if I've let you down.'

'You haven't,' Sofi answered. 'In a way, you've set me free.'

CHAPTER NINETEEN

'So this is the nesting instinct, is it?'

Lena turned to see Sofi standing at the door to their bedroom, a wry smile on her face.

'I don't think so. It's just that now Natalya is gone, I have more room in the wardrobe. So it's nice to tidy it up.'

Sofi came in and lay down on the bed.

'Besides, I'll need to know where everything is so that I can pack.'

The bedsit in Greenwich was, at last, going to be their new home. Sam's friend who currently rented it would be moving out within a week. Which left only three weeks before the babies came in which to rent bassinets and fold away tiny clothes. Natalya had reminded her of the Russian superstition that it was bad luck to buy baby clothes before the birth. But Lena simply needed *something* to be done, because everything else was up in the air. Despite the tight deadline, the time was dragging. She felt as though she was carrying a boulder between her legs, and could not believe that her belly could continue to grow another four weeks without exploding.

The phone rang and Sofi leapt up to answer it. Lena envied her grace. A moment later, she was back. 'It's Sam.'

Lena dropped the blouse she was folding and waddled out to the phone. The tone of his voice alerted her immediately that something was wrong.

'I'm sorry, Lena. He's pulled out. He's going to stay here, after all.'

The bedsit. It had fallen through. 'But . . . we have nowhere to live.'

'It's all right, I'll find somewhere.'

Anger, long held at bay, bubbled up inside her. 'Sam, I am having two babies in less than a month. You promised me you would find us a place. What's wrong? Were you lying? Do you not want to be with me? With us?'

His voice was instantly placating. 'Of course, of course. I'm just . . . so disorganised. I'm such a dud, Lena. I can't . . . time has flown and I was so sure, so *sure*, that he was going to move and . . . I'm sorry, I'm sorry.'

Hearing the self-recrimination in his voice halted her anger. 'It's all right. It's all right. We're both struggling with new things, Sam. I'm sorry I got so angry.'

'You were right to be angry.'

'We must find somewhere, this weekend.'

'I know, I know. I'm sorry. I'll make my way back to your place now. There's a bus leaving in ten minutes. Might take a while. It's rush hour.'

Lena said goodbye and replaced the receiver. Sofi stood nearby, watching her with concern. Lena shook her head, pressing her lips together so she wouldn't cry.

'I've had an idea,' Sofi said. 'I'll leave and Sam can move in here with you.'

'Where would you go?'

Sofi shrugged. 'Maybe to France.'

Lena was filled with sudden sadness. 'We're splitting up, aren't we? The three of us, we've been so close. We've been through . . .'

The words got stuck in her throat. Their history flashed across her memory: Sofi's games to distract her from the loss of her father; the night that Uncle Ivan died; helping each other with homework around a table in the communal kitchen; sharing dreams about movie stars; cooking together in Natalya's apartment; and then the thrill and guilt of the business with Roy Creedy, their escape from Russia.

Sofi rubbed her forearm. 'Look at you. All emotional. You forget that we came here so that we could have our adventures. They were always going to lead us in different directions. When Sam gets here, I'll ask him if he wants to take over this lease.'

'He can't afford it, Sofi. Not without taking more hours at the newsagent. And then what would happen to his band? We have to get a bedsit, and it has to be further out. I just hope we can find something soon.'

'I could help you out with money.'

Lena was about to refuse when she was suddenly hit by a sharp pain in her side. Almost immediately, a huge gush of water splattered on the kitchen floor between her feet. Her first thought was, *I've finally popped.*

Sofi looked at the puddle on the floor, then back up to Lena's face. 'Is that . . . ?'

'I don't know,' she managed.

'Are the babies coming?'

'It's not time.'

Sofi dashed off to get towels. Lena was frozen to the spot, unable to think clearly. They weren't due yet. She didn't want to have the babies tonight; she had too much to do.

'Should we go up to the hospital?' Sofi asked, dropping a towel on the puddle and handing Lena a second one.

Lena shook her head. 'I'll wait for Sam.'

'He could be hours.'

'The average first labour is twelve hours. Longer for twins, probably. I . . . just because my waters broke doesn't mean –' Her sentence was cut short by a deep shaft of pain. She gasped.

Sofi led her to the sofa. 'You should sit down.'

Lena rested on her side until the pain went away, then said, 'If I have to put up with twelve hours of that . . .'

'It's all right. I'm with you.' Sofi brushed her hair off her face, sitting silently next to her as the clock over the stove ticked loudly. 'I think you should go up to the hospital,' she said finally.

'Not without Sam. I don't want to do this without him.'

'But the babies are early . . .'

'It will be ages, Sofi. I'm waiting for Sam.'

Pressure began to gather around her tailbone again, spreading up between her legs. She grunted and, unable to bear sitting still, scrambled up to lean over the back of the sofa. She tried to relax her body as the pain arced through her. Sofi rubbed her back and made soothing noises.

When the contraction stopped, she collapsed forward, breathing deeply a little while.

Sofi said, 'There were only three minutes between them.'

'No, it was longer than that.'

'I timed it.'

'You must have timed it wrong.'

'Lena, you are *not* waiting for Sam.'

Lena had never felt so helpless. She shivered with fear, completely unable to make a decision, while sickening pressure gathered again low in her body.

Sofi, sensing a crack in her resolve, said, 'Come on, put your shoes on. We're going to the hospital.'

'Call an ambulance,' Lena managed, just as the next wave hit her. 'I can't go on the bus like this.'

Sofi scurried off, and Lena became lost once again in the whirlpool of pain and pressure. Deep, guttural sounds emerged from her throat, and she had a primitive, animalistic urge to bear down. Sofi was there again, rubbing her back, speaking to her reassuringly. Time fogged as she was possessed again and again by the cruel rhythm: crashing waves of pain, then blessed stillness. Sofi spoke of the ambulance, how it was on the way, but Lena barely heard her. She battled the pain, which grew and grew, until one of the waves went on and on and Lena was sure she would die. She screamed, but then it faded off and there were a few calm minutes of respite. She climbed down onto the floor and lay on her side again, catching her breath. Time ticked on.

'Has it stopped?' Sofi asked.

As if in response, it hit her once more, even stronger. A steam train was passing through her, terrifyingly fast.

'Sofi,' she gasped, 'they're coming.'

'No, no. It's been only half an hour since it all started.'

With the next wave, she got to her knees and began to push. There was no resisting it. Sofi helped her out of her jeans, the calmness in her voice now completely evaporated. Somebody was shouting. Probably her. Far, far away, the sound of a siren. Was it for her? Not only was Sam going to miss the birth, so was the ambulance. She pushed, running on instinct, desperate to get this large, hard object out of her.

White-hot pain.

'I can see its head,' Sofi cried. Her voice seemed to be coming from a long way away, through water.

Then the baby slithered out, and Lena collapsed to the floor, crying.

'It's a girl, it's a girl!' Sofi shouted, picking up the slick, bloody infant and plopping it on Lena's chest.

The baby opened her mouth and began to bleat. Lena was amazed and horrified all at once. She'd imagined newborns would be quiet little dolls, not this wriggling noisy creature. She touched the baby tentatively. It didn't seem real. Then the thought came: *I made it, I didn't die.*

'What do I do?' Sofi was asking. 'Do I cut the cord?'

'I don't know. Where is the ambulance. Is it –'

The urge to bear down returned. And in a moment, things took a turn for the very worst. The second bag of waters broke and, along with the fluid, bright blood gushed out of her. Stars of alarm crowded into her mind. She thought she heard a voice whispering, 'It was the second one that killed her.'

'Sofi!' she screamed.

Sofi took the little girl and wrapped her in a towel, the long purply cord still attached. Lena didn't think she had ever seen Sofi look panicked, and it frightened her.

'I need to push,' she said, struggling to her knees, the primitive instinct taking over again.

'There's a lot of blood, Lena.'

But there was no stopping it. She bore down with all her might. Liquid gushed out of her. Her vision spangled. Sofi told her to hang on. The doorbell rang. Ambulance.

'Stop pushing!' Sofi shouted over the noise of the first baby crying. 'I can see a foot, the rest of the baby isn't coming.'

Lena opened her eyes to look down, and saw such a pool of blood that it iced her heart. She lost her balance, fell on her side, and reality blurred as she passed out.

There were moments, made lucid by extreme pain, that flashed brightly out of the darkness. Sofi's pale face, an ambulance officer speaking to her as though she were a child, not being able to make her tongue move to speak, speeding through the darkness, a mask being brought down over her face. Then, a gap. Not like sleep, like death. Finally, sound faded back into her consciousness. Footsteps, clattering trays in the distance. She opened her eyes and found herself hooked up to an IV drip, in a crisp hospital bed, in a clean nightgown. The light was dazzling. She turned away from the window, to see Sam sitting there. Next to him, in a plastic bassinet, one tiny baby.

He leapt to his feet. 'You're awake!'

Sudden awareness was upon her. 'Where's the other one?' she cried.

'He's fine.' Sam's eyes filled with tears. 'They're both fine. The little boy came through like a champ. He's in special care, but they say he'll be out in a day or two.'

'A boy?'

'And a girl. You did it, Lena. You nearly died, but you did it.'

'I nearly . . . ?'

'You've had a blood transfusion, an emergency caesarean under a general anaesthetic.' The scientific words sounded awkward coming from his mouth. 'But we have the two most beautiful babies in the world.'

Lena glanced around. Other beds were curtained off. She could see a nurse's sensibly shod feet under one of the curtains. The light seemed brighter than ever; she felt dizzy and weak.

'Can I hold her?' she asked.

'I'll get a nurse,' he said.

A moment later, a prim-faced nurse bustled up to the bed. Lena moved to sit, but pain forced her to be still.

'Don't try to move,' the nurse said in a practical voice. 'I need to check you over, but I'll give you five minutes alone with the wee one.' She dislodged the pink-wrapped bundle from the bassinet and nestled it against Lena's right side. 'I'll be right back,' she said, and left.

Sam sat on the bed, and Lena gazed with wonder at her little girl. She was sleeping, one tiny hand curled up near her face.

'She's six pound two, he's five pound fourteen,' Sam said.

'She is so perfect,' Lena breathed, almost afraid to touch her.

'Sofi's gone to get Natalya,' he said. 'They'll be here any minute. But there's something I have to say.'

She could barely tear her eyes off the baby. The little girl was rousing, her mouth opening and closing as her head turned this way and that. 'What is it?'

'You're going to need looking after. It was a major operation. And we're going to need help with the babies. And we have nowhere to live . . . We're being idiots. Let's just go to Mum's.'

Lena looked from Sam to her beautiful daughter. *Her daughter.* She almost laughed. Sun streamed in the window and she could see the tops of the elm trees that surrounded the hospital rippling and bending in the spring breeze. A soft feeling of contentment seized her, and she decided nothing could possibly be wrong if they were all together.

'Are you sure that's what you want?' she said. 'What about the band?'

'It's not going anywhere at the moment. The drummer never shows for rehearsals. James is getting tired of it. Mum's dying for us to go to her, to look after us. Let's just let her.'

'All right,' she said. 'As long as we're together.'

CHAPTER TWENTY

Sofi's mattress had been moved into the centre of the sitting room to make way in the bedroom for two hired bassinets. Natalya had immediately moved into Rupert's apartment to escape the endless nights of crying and pacing, but she was back this evening. She and Sofi sat on the mattress in front of the television watching *Lonely Shores*. Lena fought her own battle with two sleepless babies behind the bedroom door. Anna and Matthew, Natalya's niece and nephew. Natalya would have felt sorry for Lena if she wasn't so sick of listening to that sound: like petulant cats. She had seen enough of babies in this last week to know that she never, *ever* wanted any.

'Lena's missing the show,' she said.

'She has other things on her mind,' Sofi replied smoothly, reminding Natalya – because she needed reminding quite often, she knew – that she wasn't the centre of the universe.

The episode finished and the credits rolled and still the crying went on. This time, only one little voice. Finally, the bedroom door opened and Lena emerged with a noisy blue bundle in her arms.

'He won't sleep,' she said. She was a picture of tired harassment: in her pyjamas – already, or still, Natalya didn't know – with her dark hair in disarray, shadows under her eyes and shoulders stooped with misery. 'I think he's still hungry.'

'It's all right, Lena,' Sofi said over the crying. 'Bring him out. He can join the party.'

She indicated with a sweep of her hand the bottle of Bollinger champagne – Natalya had bought it on Rupert's recommendation – and three empty glasses that sat on the coffee table next to a plate of Russian *zakuski*: pickled mushrooms and cucumbers, sliced apple, rye bread, and fatty pork *kolbasa* that Natalya would never dream of eating.

Lena shuffled to the sofa, sat down and yanked up her top. Two seconds later, the baby was suckling quietly.

'I'm so tired,' Lena moaned.

'It will get better,' Sofi reassured her. 'Once you're with Sam's mother. She'll be a lot more help than we are.'

'Look, he's asleep already. It took ten seconds. He just needed to suck.'

'Get him a dummy,' Natalya said.

'Wendy says dummies are bad for their teeth.'

Natalya had met Sam's mother at the hospital: an overbearing bully who loved the sound of her own voice. How she'd ever had a son as sweet as Sam was a mystery. 'He doesn't have any teeth.'

'Bad for their mouths then.' Lena ran a hand through her hair, then gently eased the baby off her breast and let him sleep, arms flopped above his head, on her lap. 'There, sleep, little one. We have a big trip ahead of us tomorrow.'

'The other passengers on the train are going to love it,' Natalya said, reaching for the champagne.

Although she'd intended her remark to be ironic, Lena smiled and nodded. 'Who wouldn't love them? They're so perfect.'

Sofi grinned at Natalya and raised her eyebrows.

Natalya reached out to touch Lena's wrist. 'You dear thing,' she said. 'Now. Champagne.'

'Wait, Natalya, the cork will –'

Pop. Little Matthew's eyes flew open and he immediately began to scream. Lena bundled him up and began to walk him and rock him. Natalya poured the champagne. She needed some bubbles in her blood. The crying was jangling her nerves.

'Here,' she said, offering Sofi a glass. 'We need to toast our last day in the apartment together.'

Lena returned to the sofa, applied her baby to her breast again, and brought sweet quiet. 'You see,' she said, taking a glass from Natalya, 'all is quiet as long as my breast is in his mouth.'

'Typical man,' Natalya laughed, raising her glass. 'To us.'

'To us,' Sofi said.

'To us.' Lena took a chaste sip, then put the glass aside.

'You aren't going to drink it?'

'Wendy says I shouldn't drink alcohol, it will go into the breastmilk.'

'Yes, and that will make the babies sleep. A good thing.'

'Perhaps I'll have one more sip,' she said, picking the glass up again. 'It's very nice.'

Sofi and Lena began to dig into the food. Natalya longed for one of the pickled cucumbers wrapped up with cheese in bread. But she dared not eat, especially not cheese. In three weeks, she had to take her clothes off in front of cameras and bright lights for the *Shutter* photo shoot, and there could not be the faintest curve of fat across her belly or hips. She knew that Sofi and Lena would complain, however, if she ate nothing, so she put a few items on her plate and picked them apart, to look as though she had eaten. It was much easier at Rupert's: he was on her side. He understood how important it was to stay thin in this business. In many ways, moving away from her cousins would be good for her. She would not feel like the poor Russian girl who dabbled in television; rather, she would be right at the centre of the industry, surrounded by the people and the parties. They would all understand each other; she could stop feeling guilty and faintly embarrassed.

'I think he's finally settled,' Lena said, loosening Matthew from his hold on her breast and rising carefully. 'I'm going to put him down. No more champagne corks, Natalya.'

Natalya watched her go, trying not to stare at her figure. She had seen pictures of celebrities a week after birth who looked elegant and thin, but Lena still looked six months pregnant. Natalya knew she shared Lena's genes; another good reason not to have babies. That would probably suit Rupert. He was in his fifties: too old for children. She gulped champagne, pushing the thought aside. His age was just a number. There were many other things about Rupert to admire.

'What time is your flight to Paris tomorrow?' she asked Sofi.

'Late afternoon. I'll see Lena gets away first. She might need my help getting organised on the train. She's still in pain from the operation.'

'That's what Sam's for.'

'I know. But do *you* trust him to do it right?'

Natalya laughed, glancing over her shoulder to make sure Lena wasn't listening. 'Naughty, Sofi. Sam's adorable.'

'I don't dislike him,' Sofi said. 'But he's a boy, not a man.'

The bedroom door opened, and Lena tiptoed out and closed it slowly and gently behind her. She gave them a thumbs-up gesture and returned to her spot on the sofa. 'At last,' she said. 'With luck they'll sleep three or four hours now.'

'When do they start sleeping through the night?' Natalya asked.

'Mama always told me that I didn't sleep through the night until I was two,' Sofi said.

Lena groaned. 'I will *die* if I have to do this for two years.'

She reached for her glass, but didn't drink. She seemed lost in thought for a few moments, and she looked so tired and defeated that Natalya rose and sat next to her, pulling her close for a hug.

'Is everything all right?' she asked.

Lena forced a smile. 'I've been thinking about us. Being so far apart. I don't want us to drift away from each other. The three of us . . . we've been through so much.'

Sofi leaned forward, sliding her empty glass onto the coffee table and bringing her knees up to her chest. 'I've been thinking exactly the same thing,' she said.

'Letters and phone calls aren't enough. Why don't we arrange to get together, every single year, without fail?' Lena said. 'No matter what. We'll meet here in London with Natalya, or up at Briggsby, or in France with Sofi. Just for a week. Just so we can be with each other, so we don't lose each other.'

'We'd have to make it the week between Christmas and New Year,' Natalya said. 'It's about the only time of year I can guarantee I won't be working.'

Lena sat forward eagerly. 'Yes, every winter. Like that first winter... do you remember? When Uncle Ivan died.'

'I'll never forget it,' Sofi said.

'We swore to take care of each other,' Natalya said, and the years seemed to collapse down to nothing. She was a little girl, sitting on Sofi's bed, who had already seen enough misery to last a lifetime. 'We swore that nothing would ever come between us.'

'Not families, or careers, nothing,' Lena said forcefully. 'A *zeemoy sobraniye*. Our yearly Winter Gathering. It's decided. Where shall we meet this year?'

'We'll come to you,' Sofi said. 'The babies will still be too little to be apart from you.'

'We will do it every year,' Lena said. 'And nothing will stand in our way.'

Sofi did a last check of the wardrobe, the chest of drawers and under the bed. Nothing. They had lived in the apartment for nearly a year and now no trace of them was left behind. She smiled, remembering the day they had arrived: the excitement overwhelming the still-fresh guilt. So much had happened since then. Well, it had happened for her cousins. One of them had two children and was living by the seaside; the other had become a television star and moved into a luxury apartment in the centre of London. As for Sofi...

She glanced over her shoulder at her two suitcases. One of them, the one she had brought with her from Russia, contained her clothes. The other, newly bought for the purpose, was filled with her bead stock, her growing collection of semi-precious stones, her spools of silver wire and her crafting tools. Where she was going, there were no cousins to need her, no distractions to distance her from her ideas. Her fingers itched. It was her time, at last.

She would miss her cousins, of that there could be no doubt. But Julien waited for her. Her future waited for her.

Now, as Sofi locked the door to the apartment for the last time, she tried to imagine that future. The years, marked by the meetings with her cousins – what would they bring? She picked up a suitcase in each hand and headed down the hallway to the stairs. She couldn't wait to find out.

III

CHAPTER TWENTY-ONE
1996

Natalya pretended to be asleep. It never worked, but there was no harm in trying. Rupert's caresses grew firmer. He didn't care if she was asleep or not. He was used to getting anything he wanted. Daily sex was one of those things.

At first it had been romantic. Exciting. Sometimes it was twice a day, and Natalya had enjoyed playing the part of the gorgeous, willing girlfriend who would try anything adventurous, respond to any request. She had assumed he would tire of it – she had thought that men as old as Rupert had low sex drives – but he hadn't. Her enjoyment, something he had prioritised at the start of their relationship, had slipped into second position. In response to his growing impatience, she had found herself feigning pleasure. Now, two years into their relationship, her only real pleasure was in seeing him satisfied and happy.

If he wasn't satisfied and happy, she became anxious.

She applied a smile and rolled over towards him. At least if she submitted to his desires now, it would be over for the day.

Afterwards, she showered and dressed in her underwear, returning to the bedroom to find clothes. Rupert was hosting a movie producer friend for brunch. Liam Franks. He had been nominated for a Golden Globe award the previous year, and was making a movie about

Mata Hari. Natalya wanted the part very, very badly. Of course, she wouldn't have entered his mind even dimly as a possible leading actress: she was a television star and she had played one part in her entire career. Not to mention that award she had received from one of the tabloids the previous year: *Tastiest Crumpet Who Can't Act.* But Natalya *could* act. The material she was given to work with was poor, that was all. In two years on *Lonely Shores*, Tatiana had seduced nearly everyone on the street, some of them twice. Her lines read as though they were dashed off in a very great hurry, and she never had time to learn them properly. Her character's motivations were inconsistent and rapidly changing, so there was little chance of getting beneath her skin. But with the right material, she knew she could shine. She had read about Mata Hari and felt an affinity with her; she ached at the thought of anyone else playing her and took this visceral response as proof that she was meant to have the part. She had convinced Rupert to organise a low-key social event, just so Liam Franks could meet her and hopefully glimpse her potential as a big star. It was important to look good: something stylish, but casual. She didn't want to seem to be trying too hard to impress.

Rupert had opened the curtains, allowing soft morning light into the room. He lay in bed, the covers pulled up to his waist and his arms folded behind his head, smiling at her.

'You're beautiful,' he said.

She needed to hear it. She would soon turn twenty-eight. *Twenty-eight!* Not young any more. 'Thank you, Rupert,' she said, reaching for a pair of Diesel jeans.

'Jeans again?' he said disapprovingly.

'They're Italian,' she protested.

'I think you're taking the casual chic thing too far. Why not pop on a pretty dress?'

She slid the jeans back onto the shelf and opened the next door of the wardrobe. She could feel his eyes on her, almost as though he were challenging her to choose the right thing. A baby-blue dress with three-quarter sleeves. She had bought it at a boutique in Paris.

He smiled approvingly. 'That's more like it.'

She slipped the dress on and buttoned it, then perched on the end of the bed. The sunlight highlighted the handful of grey hairs among the black ones on his chest. She pretended not to notice. 'Can I make you breakfast?' she said. 'Or shall we wait for brunch?'

'Let's just have coffee.' He moved to get up, but she stopped him.

'No, no. Let me get it for you.' She leaned across, kissed his shoulder. 'If you can convince Liam Franks to let me test for the part, I will be your willing slave forever.'

'You're already my willing slave, Natalya,' he said without the hint of a smile. 'I'm not doing it for favours, I'm doing it because I love you.' He threw back the covers and rose to go to the shower.

It always surprised Natalya how comfortable he was with his nakedness. She left him whistling in the bathroom and went to the kitchen to switch on the espresso machine. While it heated up, she idled over to the front door to pick up the mail and the newspapers. At the long granite kitchen bench, she flicked through tabloid pages, leaving *The Times* for Rupert. On page eight, she was pleased to see a photo of herself. One of her early publicity shots, her head tilted to the side so that her hair tumbled over her shoulder, eyes turned to the camera seductively. She leaned closer to read the article.

And her heart went cold.

Soapie Vamp Natalie Chernoff Fools About With Male Model.

Below her own image was a small headshot of an attractive man with a strong jaw. She had never seen him before in her life. His name was listed as Stefano Raffadali. She quickly scanned the article. A 'source' said they had been seen together at Ministry of Sound, kissing in a corner, then had disappeared together very early in the evening. It went on to point out that Natalya was in a relationship with 'ageing millionaire' Rupert Palmer.

This was bad. Very bad. Natalya did not enjoy clubbing; Rupert frowned upon it. And yet on the night named in this article, she *had* been at Ministry of Sound. Rupert had grudgingly let her go with two of her castmates for a birthday celebration. There was just enough truth in this story for Rupert to doubt her. She hurriedly closed the paper and moved to the bin to dispose of it. Rupert emerged at precisely that moment, dressed in a silk housecoat, and marched to the coffee machine.

'Don't let it heat up too much,' he complained.

'I'm sorry,' she said, feeling the paper burning her fingers. She inched towards the bin, about to drop it on top . . .

'Anything interesting in the news?' he said, indicating the paper.

'I . . . ah. *The Times* is over on the bench.'

Rupert moved towards her and snatched the newspaper. 'Really, Natalya, you're an actress. You can do better than that. What have you seen that you're trying to hide?'

Natalya's stomach hollowed out with fear. Now she had made it much, much worse. *Idiot!* If she had just been up-front, showed him, laughed about it . . . sure, he would still be in one of his moods after, but it might have defused the situation. With a dry throat she managed to say, 'Page eight. It's not true.'

Rupert held her gaze with his own. She had heard the expression 'a cold stare', but realised now that she had never actually seen one before this. He was a million light-years away from her. She reached for his hand, but he brushed her away, settling at the kitchen table with the paper.

'Coffee,' she muttered to herself. 'I'll make coffee.'

He liked her coffee, he always said so. After complaining (every morning) that she let the machine overheat, after warning her (every morning) not to put too much milk in, he would finally drink his coffee and pat her bottom and tell her that, should she ever fail as an actress, she would still be welcome in his house as a coffee maker. And every morning she smiled through it, and somewhere around the first year it had stopped being an annoying, vaguely insulting joke and had become, instead, evidence of his love for her.

She stilled her mind, focusing on the task at hand. He was reading the whole article; she had only skimmed it. Perhaps it wasn't that bad. Perhaps he would turn around now, smile with a shake of his head and tell her, as he always did, that the tabloids were full of rubbish.

She approached with his coffee in her hand. 'Rupert?' she said.

He turned, made a noise. A snarl. 'Why did you try to hide this from me?'

'Because I knew it would upset you. I –'

'Because it's true?'

'No! I've never seen him before in my life. It's fiction.'

'You were there, weren't you? That night?'

'Somebody must have seen me there. But not with a man. Never with a man. I'm yours, Rupert, I love you.'

'Love!' He knocked the coffee cup out of her hand.

Searing liquid splashed up her forearm, drops of it stained her blue dress. She didn't feel it. The cup shattered on the slate floor.

'How dare you talk about love?' he said, leaping to his feet and towering over her, his face flushing deep red with rage.

'It's not true,' she pleaded, her hands, palms up, in front of her chest. 'Please, calm down.'

'If you have nothing to hide, why were you hiding it?'

What to say? *Because I am terrified of your temper*? That would make him even angrier. 'I didn't think,' she said. 'It means nothing. The story isn't true. You know they make up these things. You have to believe me, Rupert, I can't bear you to be angry with me.' A sudden bolt of clarity. 'Phone Kelly. And Ann-Marie. They were with me all night. They know it's not true.'

He quieted. Took a deep breath. 'All right. I will. Though I don't trust either of those ninnies particularly, I know for a fact that Kelly despises you so she'll tell me the truth.'

'Thank you, thank you,' Natalya said.

He stormed off to his office and shut the door behind him. She fetched a tea towel to clean up the coffee on the floor, noticing for the first time three blotches of red against the perfect white skin of her left arm. Burns. She went to the pantry for a potato, sliced it open and pressed the moist starch onto the largest burn, just as Aunt Stasya had treated burns in her childhood. Her dress was splattered too, so she went to the bedroom to change. Only this time, Rupert wasn't there to tell her what to wear and it seemed an impossible choice. What was precisely the right thing? To keep him happy? To please the director coming for brunch? She remembered, vaguely, that she had once known very clearly what she wanted, in nearly all situations. But now the indecision overwhelmed her so she flopped on the bed in her underwear, still rubbing potato on the burns, waiting for Rupert to come back and tell her she was forgiven.

A half-hour passed.

She finally got up. Pulled on her dressing gown and went in search of Rupert.

The flat was completely silent. In the kitchen, the light still flashed on the coffee machine. She switched it off. Eyed Rupert's office door. Wished she could run away.

She approached. Knocked softly.

'Come in.'

She cracked the door open, peered in. 'Rupert? Did you . . . ?'

He didn't turn to face her. 'Kelly and Ann-Marie both insist you were with them all night. You left the club around one. I know that you came home before two, so it seems this is simply a matter of a tabloid newspaper having some nasty fun with you.'

'I'm so glad, I –'

He turned, and she saw his gaze was still cold. 'I don't appreciate having to phone members of my staff and reveal to them my insecurities. How dare you bring this nonsense into my home? Into our relationship? You've made a fool of me.'

'But I didn't do anything.'

'You insisted on going to that ridiculous nightclub. You're nearly thirty, Natalya. You're not a young woman any more. It's embarrassing for you to be tarting yourself up to hang around with people ten years younger than you. Grow up.' He noticed she was in her dressing gown. 'Where are your clothes?'

'I got coffee on them,' she said. 'I don't know what to wear for our meeting today.'

'Meeting?'

'Brunch.'

'Oh, that. I cancelled it. I don't feel much like being social today. Not after being publicly humiliated.'

Natalya felt the floor fall away from her feet.

'I don't care what you wear, Natalya. Really. You must be able to make your own decisions about these things. I'm far too busy to be bothered with every little detail of your life.' He turned back to his desk. 'Go on. Go and find something to do.'

She hesitated on the threshold. He was calm; that was good. Perhaps it would be best to get out now, let him spend the rest of the day finding his usual benevolent and appreciative self. But Mata Hari . . .

'Rupert, I know you're feeling upset, but I really, *really* need to meet Liam Franks. I was born to play Mata Hari, and if I could meet him I could convince him.'

'Don't be an idiot, Natalya. Liam isn't going to cast you as a lead in his film.'

'But you said –'

'I said I could convince him to test you. But he'd never hire you. Not in a million years. A soapie actress? It would destroy the film's credibility.' He made a shooing gesture. 'Go on. Go shopping or something. My Optima card is in my wallet by the bed.'

Natalya felt tears pricking her eyes.

'What *is it?*' he said impatiently.

She lifted her chin, the wounded heroine who would prevail. Hoped he'd notice and leap to his feet, fold her in his arms. He didn't. He did not behave at all like the characters in his television show. She turned and slammed the door behind her, knew he would be laughing at her ineffectual temper. Well, damn him. She was going to go and spend a truckload of his money.

As Lena turned into the street and headed up the hill towards Wendy's house, she calculated that the walk home represented the only child-free twenty-five minutes of her day. Matthew had had her up at four with a screaming fit; by seven she was at work at the Little Darlings Day Nursery where she wiped the bottoms and noses of toddlers all day; and now, at four, she was returning home for the frantic shift: dinner, bath, bed. She wished she could be more pleased about seeing Matthew and Anna. They really were the most beautiful little children, twenty months old now and full of life and laughter. But she had been worn down by other people's children all day, by their irrationality and dependence. She just hoped Sam had managed to get them to sleep in the middle of the day. Matthew, particularly, became whiny and clumsy if he hadn't slept.

She found them both sitting on the sofa, drinking juice out of bottles and watching cartoons. No adults in sight. She hung up her coat and bag. Matthew looked up, saw her and immediately burst into tears.

'Mummeeeeeee,' he wailed, chubby little arms in the air and hands clutching at nothing.

'Oh, dear,' she said, scooping him up. 'Daddy didn't get you to have a rest today, did he?'

Wendy bustled in. 'Sorry, I was just on the phone. Sam's not here, I've been watching them.'

Lena forced a smile. That would explain the juice. And the television. 'Did Anna sleep?' she asked, stroking pale silky hair out of Anna's eyes.

'Neither slept. They didn't seem tired. I put the telly on about two. They've just been having a rest there on the sofa.'

Two hours of television. While Lena was fingerpainting and reading stories with other children, her own had been babysat by Thomas the Tank Engine. She ached. Matthew had flopped his head on her shoulder and was breathing heavily through his mouth. His warmth, his trusting littleness, made her catch her breath, as they always did. She sat next to Anna and gave her a kiss on her smooth forehead. The little girl kept her thumb in her mouth, her gaze never breaking from the television screen.

'Where's Sam?' Lena asked.

'He said he had a band meeting. That fellow phoned him . . . what's his name?'

'David? Or Tony?'

'Tony. That's him. The dodgy one.'

Lena knew what Wendy meant. Sam had hooked up with a new band here in Briggsby. The bass player, Tony, had very little musical talent but was always promising that he knew people, that he could make deals, find gigs. So far, little of it had come true. Sam, for his part, seemed quite taken with Tony. He spoke of him with a tone of awe. She had learnt, in the brief space of their marriage so far, that Sam was not always the best judge of character.

'Mummy?' Matthew sniffed. 'Dinner?'

'I'll make you something,' she said, reaching for the television remote and switching it off. It was like a spell had been broken on Anna and she started asking for food too. Lena found them a box of Duplo to play with and went to the kitchen. The crate in the pantry reserved for her and Sam's food was looking frighteningly empty. He had forgotten to go shopping today. She found some pasta and put it on the stove, intending to make macaroni cheese.

'Wendy, would you mind watching them for just another ten minutes while I have a quick shower?' Lena said. 'One of the kids at work squashed a banana in my hair this morning.'

'Good for split ends,' Wendy joked, sitting at the round kitchen table and lighting a cigarette. 'Here, your sister's in the paper today. Want to see?'

Not really. But she couldn't say that, because it could only be taken the wrong way. She loved her sister, she was proud of her, she wanted the very best for her. But the miles of distance between their fortunes terrified her. If Natalya were right here, in the room, she would be delighted to see her. But to see the public Natalya – that almost-stranger Natalie Chernoff – reminded her too acutely of everything that hadn't gone to plan.

It was too late in any case. Wendy had opened the paper and thrust it across the plastic tablecloth. Some tabloid rubbish about Natalya having an affair with an Italian model. Lena glanced at the glamorous photograph of Natalya and tried not to think about the banana in her hair, the paint under her fingernails, the sensible shoes on her feet.

'What a life she's got, your sister,' Wendy said. 'Fancy clubs and Italian boyfriends.'

'I guarantee you this isn't her boyfriend,' Lena said, handing the paper back. 'She's with Rupert. And my sister isn't a cheater.'

'I didn't say she was.'

'You said she had an Italian boyfriend. You believe the article, that she's fooling around behind Rupert's back.'

Wendy rolled her eyes. 'Don't go all serious on me. It's just a bit of fun.'

Lena sighed. 'Sorry, it's been a long day. I'm going to the shower.'

She headed down the narrow corridor towards the bathroom. Grandad's door was ajar and she took a quick peek in. He sat in his chair by the window, one of the twins' old baby blankets across his knees. The droop of his shoulders made her sad. He was waiting to die; she could see that. Wendy was waiting for him to die too, and he probably knew it.

'Hello, Grandad,' she said softly, from the threshold.

He glanced up. His mouth was permanently turned down and a jowl of displeasure hung on either side. 'Those children of yours have been noisy all day,' he said.

'I'm sorry. Sam was supposed to be watching them.'

He faced the window again. Lena came in and straightened the blanket on his lap. 'It's cold out,' she said.

'It's always bloody cold,' he wheezed.

'Do you need your oxygen?'

He waved her away, and she let him be. She knew, though, that he must appreciate her time and care, even if he couldn't show it. She had once thought him a crotchety old bore, but now she had glimpsed the soul under that crusty shell and she couldn't let him rot in this back room without company.

By the time she was out of the shower, Sam was home, finishing off the macaroni cheese. Both children were in their highchairs. Matthew was screaming at the top of his voice while Anna banged a spoon on her tray. From now until bedtime would be a blur of activity and noise, finally dying off with Matthew's last mournful cries as he went to sleep behind the curtain that divided Lena and

Sam's bedroom in half. Only then did Lena and Sam have time for each other.

Lena could never have guessed how much work two babies would be. If somebody had tried to warn her, she would have dismissed them as liars or fools. But in the black first three months, deep in the night when she was all alone with her regrets and her desolation, she came to learn the truth: her life would never be her own again; she was now a servant to those two squirming bundles. Her own desires to sleep, eat and shower were insignificant, let alone any dream she'd once had to act. That childish fantasy seemed ludicrous now. When one of the little tyrants whimpered, she had to respond. It was that simple.

Anna had discovered her thumb around three months old and started to sleep through until dawn. But Matthew held on to his night-time feeds with a deathlike grasp, until Lena finally admitted defeat and gave up breastfeeding just so that the midnight feed could be shared with whomever could mix and hold a bottle. He still routinely awoke before dawn most days, and could only be soothed by being deposited in the bed between Sam and Lena, where he would sprawl his chubby limbs so that his parents were forced to hug the edges of the mattress. Lena felt her brain had been permanently altered, stewed by endless nights of interrupted sleep. Physically, she was once again slim, but her stomach was traced with silvery-purple lines and her skin would not sit tight over her muscles. A visual reminder that things would never be the same again.

'We're going to the pub, Mum,' Sam called as he handed Lena her coat. Every second Thursday, Sam got paid – he worked part-time in a greengrocer shop – and they went out for fish and chips and a couple of drinks at the Briggsby Arms. Lena had often suggested they save their money for other things: their car insurance bill, or to reduce the interest on that credit card they'd put their wedding expenses on. But Sam pointed out that their time together was just as important as bills. Lena, although she knew he was probably right, still found she was tense until the first swirl of red wine softened the edges of her thoughts.

The Briggsby Arms was a cosy, family-run pub with a tiny firelit lounge where a jukebox was permanently stuck on seventies' ballads. Lena shared her day with Sam and he made her laugh about it, as he always did. The firelight made his warm skin glow, and he caught her looking at him, slid across to sit next to her and slung his arm around her shoulders.

'You happy?' he said, kissing her cheek.

'Yes.' Right at that moment, it was the truth. Sam's physical presence always soothed her.

'Tony and Dave and I had a good talk today. About the future.'

'Oh, yes?'

'We think we should record an album.'

'Shouldn't you try to get some gigs first?'

'Well, we are trying, but nobody's booking us. But if we had an album, then they could hear us first. And we could send it to record labels. Independent ones. It could be the start of something big for us.'

Lena sat back, rolling her shoulders to release the tension. 'It sounds expensive.'

'Not really. Not when it's cut three ways. Tony has a friend with a studio in his house, just up in Whitby. He says he could do it for us for six thousand quid.'

Lena was stunned into silence. Did he really think that they could gather together two thousand pounds? They were nearly that much in debt. Sam picked up his pint and finished it. Rod Stewart was still 'Sailing' in the background.

'You think it's a bad idea, don't you?' Sam said with a grin.

'I don't think it's a bad idea. I just don't see how we could afford it.'

'Ah, that's where you come in.'

She bristled. 'I'm already working full-time. I –'

Sam punched her arm lightly, chuckling. 'No. I don't mean you have to go out and get a second job. As if! You think I'm that irresponsible?'

'Then what?'

'Grandad. He loves you. If you ask him for the money, he'll give it to you.'

Lena drained her wine. 'I'm going to need another one of these,' she said.

'I'll go up and order us some food,' Sam said, checking his wallet. Lena saw a single twenty-pound note in there. She was going to have to make a choice between food and alcohol.

'Just a plate of chips for me,' she said.

While he was away, she leaned back in her chair and considered his request. She had many reservations. The first was that she simply thought it was wrong to ask Grandad. Certainly, everyone pitched in with helping him, but that didn't mean he owed them anything, and she would hate for him to think she was only nice to him in the hope he'd give her money. The second was that she feared Wendy's opinion. Wendy was fierce in her protection of Grandad's money. She had taken care of Grandad for eight years now, and she believed she had earned the inheritance when it came. Any little bits and pieces that trickled away were, in her opinion, being stolen from her directly. Most of all, she felt the sting of injustice that Sam's first solution hadn't been taking more hours at the shop, saving the money himself. But then, that wasn't fair either. How would he be able to write songs and rehearse with the band if he was working all the time? And who would look after Anna and Matthew? Wendy was always willing, but Lena didn't like to feel she owed her mother-in-law anything.

Sam came back with another glass of wine and a table number. She took a sip. They talked about other things for a while. Food came. More wine. The pit of her stomach was lined with warmth and goodwill.

'I'll ask him,' she said at last, as he probably knew she would. 'It's important to you, isn't it?'

Sam leaned forward. 'It's so important, Lena. I turn on the radio and I hear other bands and I think, why aren't we on the radio? Why are Oasis millionaires while I'm selling lettuces? We're good, Britpop is big, the time is right.' He leaned back again, smiling sheepishly. 'Sorry if I sound like a nutter.'

'No. You sound passionate, I've always loved that about you.' She reached out to ruffle his long hair. Her gorgeous pop star husband. 'I want you to be a big success.'

'It's all for you, Lena,' he said, grabbing her hand and kissing it fervently. 'I want you to have beautiful things, a big house, a flash car.'

Lena opened her mouth to say that she didn't want those things, that all she wanted was for them to be together with the kids and grow old happily. But it would have been a lie.

CHAPTER TWENTY-TWO

Sofi wandered the market in a daze of happiness. She stopped at a flower stall and picked up a sweet-smelling bunch of lilies. She smiled too broadly as she paid; the French words spoken to her washed over her. Her mind was too full of other things for translations. She filled her cane basket with pumpkin, asparagus, courgette, corn, anything that looked fresh and ripe and tasty. The basil smelled sweet; she threw a bunch in too. She still hadn't decided what to do with it all. A special dinner. The details were for later. She bought bread, wrapped in paper, from the baker. Hesitated over a bottle of Chinon wine, then put it in her basket. Julien could drink it, even if she couldn't.

This morning had given no hint of the starry joy the day would bring. She'd had a long drive to make, and driving made her nervous. A boutique in Tours had sold out of her jewellery and asked if she could bring more. The boutique sold exclusive handmade clothes and was favoured by rich wives and the occasional French movie star. It had been one of her best outlets, so she had gathered together whatever she could to comply. Not for the first time, Sofi had started to think about hiring somebody to help her one day a week. With paperwork at first, but with a view to training them how to do simple tasks to help speed up the process.

After visiting the boutique, she had stopped at a café nearby, intending to buy a coffee. But, somehow, the thought of coffee didn't appeal; her stomach swirled slightly at the thought. Two seconds later, the moment of realisation. She and Julien had been trying to conceive for only a month. What was the date? She rushed to the nearest pharmacy, bought a pregnancy test, and begged for the key to the staff rest room. Two minutes of waiting, sitting on the closed lid of the toilet. And then, two lines. One was bold, one was faint, but there were definitely two lines. Her first instinct was to run to the nearest public phone, to call Mama and Natalya and Lena and sob joyfully, 'I'm pregnant!' But there was a right order for these things, and Julien had to be told first. Over a special dinner.

She walked home as the shadows stretched out along the cobbled Rue des Gaulthiers, past potted plants that stood sentinel outside shops, and under the overhanging lanterns and signs that lined the street. The sky was streaked with clouds and she thought she detected the faint scent of rain on its way. Her cat, Masha, miaowed loudly at the front door.

'What's that, Masha?' she said, shrugging out of her light coat and hanging it behind the door. 'Did Julien forget to feed you again?'

The cosy sitting room was tidy and empty. She turned on a lamp, illuminating the clean lime-washed walls and the spotted brass fittings. The kitchen was empty too. Not a single used coffee cup or plate on the bench, nor a single crumb on the white tiles or chequered rug. Everything was just as it had been when she'd left in the morning. Julien must have been working all day. He often had times like this, when inspiration seemed to pour into him faster than he had the skill to keep up. She had learnt to leave him alone at such times. But today was different, and he'd have to stop to eat at some stage.

She unpacked her shopping, put the lilies in water, and started cooking. After fifteen minutes, music burst into life behind her. Julien had put the stereo on: American jazz, his favourite. He slid his arms around her and kissed her neck.

'What are you cooking?' he asked in English. They had stuck with it out of habit. Sofi found French hard going, as though her brain were already too occupied with two other languages.

'Quiche. I bought wine if that's what you're looking for.'

He went to the cupboard for glasses, and began to pour.

'Not for me,' she said, trying to keep a blank face. She wanted to surprise him at dinner, accompanied by candlelight. But it was no use.

'No wine for Sofi? While she's cooking?' He considered her. 'That's unusual.'

'Yes,' she said, unable to keep from smiling.

'Ah,' he said. 'So, our endeavours have been successful?'

She laughed. 'You could put it that way.'

He gathered her into his arms and hugged her tightly. 'My dear, you are twice as precious today.'

They held each other for a few moments, then she felt his body become restless. 'Do I have time to paint some more before dinner?' he said. 'The good news has made me feel inspired.'

'Go on,' she said. 'I'll call you when it's ready.'

Julien painted in the downstairs spare bedroom, with the folding glass doors open onto the terrace. She heard him whistling along with the music as he worked.

Life in France agreed with Sofi for the most part. Richelieu was a pretty walled and moated village, a humble semi-precious stone in amongst the fairy-tale châteaux and vast flowering fields of the Loire Valley. She loved their house, its bright green garden and its cosy warmth. She certainly loved the weather, and her business was growing steadily. But Julien was not everything she had hoped for, although she loved him dearly. She thought about what he had just said: 'twice as precious'. The thing was that she rarely felt precious to him. He said it, but she didn't *feel* it. She could see that his art was precious to him, and she knew she very much played second fiddle.

She set the table and called out to Julien. Five minutes later she called again. He mumbled, 'Just a moment.' She served up, garnished the plates, poured him another glass of wine. He still didn't come.

Sighing, she covered his food and put it back in the oven to stay warm. He wasn't coming; he was too wrapped up in what he was painting. She knew better than to insist he interrupt his flow. The early evening was just warm enough to eat outside, so she took her meal onto the terrace. The wild wisteria vine that had tangled itself around the wooden railings was starting to sprout leaves; the earth-scented red geraniums had flowered. She ate as the night deepened and the moon glowed behind the thin cloud cover, and fantasised about the arrival of somebody new for her to love; somebody who might love her passionately in return.

Lena waited until Tuesday night, when Wendy went out for her regular ladies poker night. The children were settled and sleeping, and Sam took off for band practice. In her heart, she hoped that Grandad might have gone to sleep early, as he sometimes did, with the oxygen mask over his face. But as she passed his room, the light was still on. He sat in the armchair by the window in his tartan dressing gown, a pen clutched in his stained fingers as he did the crossword puzzle in the local newspaper. She hesitated near the door, then knocked lightly.

'What is it?' he said gruffly, not looking up.

'Can I come in, please?'

He put the paper aside and beckoned her. 'All right then, if you must.'

She sat on the edge of the bed. The musty smell of his dressing gown mingled unpleasantly with the oily smell of newspaper. 'How are you feeling?'

'What do you want?'

She could have laughed. Instead, she spread her hands and sighed. 'Sam needs money.'

He snorted. Lena thought it might have been a laugh. Then he started coughing, and took nearly a full minute to regain his composure. Lena offered to open his window, get him water, fit his oxygen mask, but he waved her away and kept coughing. When he stopped, he said, 'How much and what for?'

'Two thousand pounds. He needs it for his band.'

'He didn't come himself?'

She decided that being honest would be best. 'He thinks you like me.'

Grandad frowned. 'I do. I *did*.'

A barb of guilt.

He continued. 'And you'd come and ask me for that much money? Not for you or your children, but for his band?'

She shrugged. 'It's what he wants. He's very committed and –'

'Tell me something,' he said, shifting in his chair. 'When you stop by every afternoon to ask how I am, when you straighten my rug or bring me the paper, are you doing that to keep me onside? Because you want my money?'

'No!' she said, bristling. 'Of course not.'

'You needn't sound angry with me. It's a fair conclusion to draw when you're standing here asking me for two thousand quid.' He coughed again, but only briefly.

'I am genuinely concerned about you, Grandad,' she said. 'I promise.'

He pressed his lips together, considering her under the harsh yellow light with his faded blue eyes. 'Everyone is after my money,' he said. 'Admit it. You are too.'

'No.'

'Admit it and I'll give you the two thousand.'

At first she thought she hadn't heard right. 'I'm sorry?'

'Admit the truth: you've been softening me up the last few months. Go on, just say it. I'll write you a cheque straightaway if you do.'

Lena opened her mouth, not at all sure what she would say. Nothing came out. Something stirred inside her and she couldn't, she simply *couldn't*, admit to such a thing. It wasn't true, and she wanted him to know that. But the money . . . Sam . . .

'Well?' he said.

'Will you tell Sam?' she asked.

'Not a word of it.' He smiled, already sensing he had won.

'I will go without the money then,' she said, feeling relieved and guilty all at once.

He rubbed his papery hands together and laughed. 'Good girl.'

She stood, leaned over and kissed his forehead. He seemed genuinely taken aback by the gesture.

'Goodnight, Grandad,' she said.

'Goodnight, girl,' he muttered into his chest.

She went to the sitting room to turn the television on. A talk show. The chatter and laughter washed over her. She had done the right thing, she knew it in her bones. So why did she feel that she had let down Sam, ruined his dream? If she'd taken the money, it wouldn't have been the first time she had done something terribly wrong: the Roy Creedy affair still recurred to her deep in the night sometimes, making her toss and turn with guilty anxiety. But becoming a mother had weakened what little armour she'd had, made her almost unbearably vulnerable. Grandad knew he was a burden to his family; she couldn't have him think that her kindness was just an act. Her kindness was all she had to give.

Rosemary Simons was a small woman with a large voice. Sofi, who was nervously hovering in the sitting room, heard her approach from a distance. Masha got under her feet as she went to the door and opened it to peer out onto the cobbled street. Rosemary was on a mobile telephone, talking very loudly in a crisp English accent as she walked, dressed immaculately in a pale pink suit. Her long blonde hair dipped over one eyebrow, like a forties movie star. She looked up and saw Sofi, smiled and waved, still talking.

'I can't . . . you're breaking up . . . the service out here is shocking, can you repeat . . . oh, bother.' She switched the phone off and dropped it inside an oversized leather handbag. 'Sofi, is it?'

'This way,' Sofi said, pushing the door wide open and showing her through into the dim entryway with its scuffed parquetry floor.

'Thanks for seeing me on such short notice,' Rosemary said, then took an alarmed step back from Masha. 'Oh, I'm allergic.'

Sofi picked up the cat and gently put her outside before closing the door. 'It's my pleasure. Would you like coffee?'

'Tea?'

'Of course. Sit down.'

Sofi went to the kitchen. Julien peeked out of his studio with a questioning look. Sofi nodded, and he disappeared again to leave her to do her business. Rosemary Simons was the jewellery buyer for the big European chain store Chantilly, which specialised in fashion jewellery and top-end accessories. She had called Sofi that morning from Tours, where she was sourcing stock for the following year's spring collection.

'I've seen your work and I just *loooove* it,' she had enthused. 'Can I meet you? Today?'

Sofi, who was used to working at her own pace and certainly not used to buyers contacting her, had been taken aback but had agreed. Of course. A big buyer like Chantilly could mean a turning point in her business.

'Come out onto the terrace,' she said, as she emerged from the kitchen with a tea tray.

'That cat?' Rosemary said, with a pretty wrinkle of her nose.

'If she comes around, I'll lock her in the bathroom.'

Rosemary sprang to her feet. 'Lovely then.'

They settled at the table on the terrace. Sofi had always loved the battered hominess of their house and furniture, but she couldn't help noticing that Rosemary was eyeing it all very closely. Sofi and Julien were not wealthy, but they were not poor either. For Sofi, a lifetime of making do had resulted in her being extremely frugal. Julien was too busy painting to spend money. And so their house was not the redecorated dream of track lighting, leather and chrome that it could be, but fell short too of offering much rustic charm. Apart from the paintings that hung on every wall, it was ordinary, and Sofi had always liked that. Now, she wondered if Rosemary thought she wasn't arty or sophisticated enough to be a jewellery designer for Chantilly.

The summer sun was hot, and the garden smelled of lemons and gardenias. The grass was overgrown again, and bugs skimmed about over it, the sun catching silver on their wings. Beyond the garden wall, the huge chestnut trees were in flower.

'This is lovely,' Rosemary said, but Sofi didn't know if she meant the garden, the tea or the company.

'Thank you,' she said anyway. In the bright outdoor light, she could see that Rosemary wasn't in her twenties, as she'd first thought, but a very well-preserved forty-something.

'When are you due?' Rosemary asked.

Sofi's hands went, as they always did, to her ripening belly. 'September.'

'Lord, not long now.' Rosemary took a sip of tea then put her cup down. 'So, that accent. You're not French.'

'Russian,' Sofi said. 'My husband is French.'

'Those are his paintings inside?'

'Yes. Julien Blanchard. You may have heard of him.'

'The manager of the boutique in Tours told me about him. He's quite famous, I take it.' She picked up her cup again. 'All of this would look great in our catalogue. Gorgeous little French village, overgrown garden, married to a painter, Russian heritage. We can send a photographer to get the best aspects of your house. Anything else marketable about you I should know?'

Sofi took a breath to tell her about Natalya, then remembered that her cousin had been wary about being associated with Sofi's jewellery. 'No, not really.'

'I love your work. *Looove* it,' Rosemary continued. 'It's precisely what I'm looking for. Handmade, beautiful materials, unusual but classy. I can sell loads of it, I know. Would you like to talk about filling an order for me?'

'Of course.' Sofi realised her heart had picked up its rhythm. It was really happening. Anastasia Designs was about to break through to the next level. 'I have about thirty pieces currently in stock. We can look shortly, when we've finished our tea.'

'Thirty? I'm going to need about three hundred.'

Three hundred. The number reverberated in her head and she felt such an awful, sodden sensation of disappointment that it almost made her cry. If Rosemary wanted three hundred pieces for the spring catalogue, that gave her seven months at the most. And she had a baby due in two. She averaged three pieces a week. It was a mathematical impossibility.

Rosemary was still talking, oblivious. 'We're just about to open our twenty-third store, in Vienna. The business is growing so fast we almost can't keep up. It's really difficult to find good-quality, high-end accessories, especially fashion jewellery. We don't do diamonds. We need great designers like you who –'

'I'm sorry, Rosemary. But I'm one person. Well . . .' She patted her belly. 'I'm nearly two. There's no way in heaven that I can make three hundred pieces in time for your spring collection.'

'Oh? You don't have an assistant? A workshop?'

Sofi indicated behind her with a wave of her hand. 'A spare bedroom upstairs.' Now she felt like a fool. No wonder Rosemary had been looking around curiously. She had expected a business, a shopfront, a team of jewellery makers all working off Sofi's designs. 'I'm sorry, I hope I haven't misled you.'

'Oh, no, not at all,' Rosemary said. 'I came down here knowing nothing about you, and now I do. Only, you see, thirty pieces . . . even sixty. One or two per store? It wouldn't work.'

Sofi nodded. The baby squirmed suddenly inside her. Reality reasserted itself. There wasn't time to hire assistants and train them before the baby came. And, besides, she could hardly leave her business in the care of strangers with such an important order to fill. There was no way around it; she would have to turn Rosemary Simons down.

'It was a wonderful opportunity and under other circumstances I would have loved to say yes. Maybe in the future . . . ?'

'I understand. I really do. As for the future, I can't offer any guarantees.' Rosemary placed her teacup, still half-full, in the saucer. 'Here's my card. It was a pleasure to meet you. I wish you luck with the little one.'

After she was gone, Sofi slouched upstairs to her work space and sat heavily at the scarred table where she made her pieces. A half-finished necklace was laid out. Shades of amber and smoke: tourmaline, agate, whisky quartz, some round, some cylindrical, and interspersed with silver flowers that she had woven painstakingly herself. It was beautiful, just the kind of thing that would look good in Chantilly's spring catalogue. She allowed herself to imagine it: photographs of Richelieu, of Julien's paintings, crisp black pages, her jewellery photographed under perfect lighting . . . But there was only one of these necklaces, and Chantilly needed twenty-three.

Julien came in. 'She's gone already?'

'She wanted three hundred pieces by spring.'

He laughed and crouched next to her. 'Doesn't she know you cannot rush an artist?'

She leaned her head on his shoulder. 'I could have done it. If I wasn't pregnant. I could have hired somebody, worked longer hours, met the order. It would have been the making of my business.'

He stroked her back. 'Never mind. You're making plenty of money with the small orders you have at the moment.'

She grew irritated, pulled out of his embrace. 'It's not about the money. It's about making a mark in the world. About being more than a person who makes necklaces in a bedroom.'

He smiled at her, bemused. 'Temper.'

She wouldn't be cheered up. Julien loved that she was artistic, was always interested in her jewellery-making, but somehow in his opinion it had become something she did for spare cash. Of course he'd think that: he was an internationally acclaimed artist. He won prizes and grants, reviewers struggled with superlatives in trying to describe his work.

Julien reached out to touch her hair. 'It will be all right, Sofi. Soon, you will have a little baby to fawn over, and this will fade into the background. Perhaps the opportunity will come again. You must relax.'

Sofi picked up the necklace and fingered one of the smooth stones. She tried to be comforted by Julien's words, but couldn't help feeling that she had just been forced to make a choice that Julien, nor any other man, had ever been forced to make.

CHAPTER TWENTY-THREE

Natalya knew she wasn't the most important person in the room, and it bothered her.

It was London fashion week. She knew that if she went to a Donna Karan or Tommy Hilfiger show, she would be competing for attention with pop stars and film stars. She had a very new and very big engagement ring on her left hand, and she was desperate for somebody to notice it and leak the story to the press. So she had insisted that she and Rupert attend this off-schedule show at a converted warehouse gallery on Clink Street at Southwark, in the hope that she would be seated in the row beside the catwalk. No such luck. A buzz had been building about the young designer, who was straight out of Central Saint Martins, and it had attracted a swarm of A-listers. Natalya was a big star; one of the biggest stars on television. She was a regular in the TV guides and soap magazines; a staple in the celebrity events spreads in the papers; had posed on the cover of *Loaded* dressed only in a fur bikini and a *ushanka* with a red star on it; just the week before had been the subject of a six-page 'at home' photo shoot in *OK!* magazine, barefoot and in skin-tight Guess jeans; had been stopped on the street countless times to sign autographs; been followed by photographers when she walked out to get her morning coffee or go to the gym. She was famous, damn it. But she was television. Not serious television either; she was soap crumpet. And so, when she and Rupert were shown to their seats, she found herself once more in the second row.

The lights dimmed, the music pumped. She could see that she was almost directly in front of a photographer, so she shifted in her seat so her face would be visible in the gap between the two heads in front of her – a football player and his over-bleached wife – and adopted the appropriate facial expression: a slight smile indicating enjoyment, a focused gaze indicating intensity, and a noble lift of the chin to indicate that she was independent, exotic and in no way concerned with the camera trained on her. And all the while, she curled her left hand under her chin so the ring was visible. She held this expression for a while, then the photographer moved on and she relaxed. The seat was uncomfortable, a furniture buyer's cruel joke to play on famous women with no fat on their backsides. She didn't much like the fashion on display either: swathes of printed cloth hung haphazardly on bony models. But she smiled and clapped. Rupert squeezed her hand and leaned over to kiss her cheek, and she snuggled up against him as the music thumped on. Second row was not too bad; there were some people sitting in the last row. Nobodies and has-beens. At least she wasn't one of them.

The lights changed to blue, a smoke machine kicked into action and the men's fashion took to the catwalk. Natalya had to try very hard to look interested. Rupert had flexed forward. Today he was wearing Armani, his favourite. A charcoal suit. He had so many Armani charcoal suits that it was almost like a uniform. She glanced around surreptitiously, trying to see who was sitting behind her. She caught a glimpse of an actress who had worked on the first two seasons of *Lonely Shores*. Rupert had told Natalya that she had left to pursue a singing career, then was never heard of again. She looked tired and bloated.

Rupert pinched her arm and she faced the front again. A trio of scythe-cheeked men were marching down the catwalk in blue velvet suits, chests bare underneath. At first Natalya didn't notice, but then one of their faces registered its familiarity. It was Stefano Raffadali.

The model that she had been accused of fooling around with. Panicked, she glanced at Rupert. He didn't seem to have noticed. Perhaps he didn't remember Stefano's face. It was months ago, after all.

Rupert turned, smiled at her fondly. She smiled back; the panic melted away.

At the cocktail party afterwards, Natalya was pleased to note that most of the A-listers had drifted away, probably to catch one of the scheduled shows. The centre of gravity in the room seemed to turn towards her. Eyes, smiles, introductions were directed her way. Rupert hung on to her tightly, both possessive and protective. A photographer circled, snapping. Natalya knew just how to pose for such photos. Head back and tilted, tongue held behind her teeth while she smiled to avoid crow's feet, hips square and shoulders provocatively angled. It wasn't comfortable, but experience had taught her that comfort meant nothing in a photograph. The first snaps of her in the society pages had appalled her. She had looked like somebody's pretty but half-witted sister from the country, trapped like a deer in the bright headlights of celebrity. She quickly learned that even when she was being photographed relaxing, she had to work hard for it.

'Is that an engagement ring?' the photographer asked. 'Have you got something to announce?'

Natalya smiled enigmatically, theatrically hiding her hand behind her back. Official announcements of pending marriage were dull and rarely got much mileage in the press. Keep them guessing, that's what Rupert had told her.

The photographer moved on, Rupert disengaged from her to talk to a business associate, and Natalya found herself chatting with one of the models, a Ukrainian girl who said that Natalya was her idol and the reason she had left the Ukraine to come to London. Natalya was caught between the glow of adoration and horror of feeling old enough to inspire somebody, when a soft hand touched her elbow.

She turned. It was Stefano.

'Excuse me,' he said, in an accent that wasn't even approaching Italian. It was closer to East End London. 'You're Natalie, right?'

There was nowhere to hide. He was standing directly in front of her, talking to her, and at any second Rupert would see them and come raging over and . . .

'I'm Stefano.' He extended his hand and all she could do was shake it. Her stomach had gone cold and her vision had tunnelled. She was vaguely aware that it was not a good sign to fear her partner so deeply.

'I'm pleased to meet you,' she managed.

The Ukrainian model slipped away, leaving Natalya to deal with Stefano alone.

'I don't want to be rude or make trouble for you,' he said, smiling. His face was impossibly beautiful: an angel's face. 'But I thought it was a bit of a laugh, don't you? What they said about us?' When she didn't respond he began to stammer with embarrassment. 'Oh, maybe you didn't see . . .'

She took pity and jumped in. 'I saw it. It was months ago. It was nothing and I have forgotten it.'

Rupert was back. A bear in an Armani suit. Next to Stefano, he seemed florid and vain, his Andy Warhol hair ridiculous. He grasped her arm firmly. 'Natalya?'

'Natalya?' Stefano said. 'That's your real name? It's so much prettier than Natalie.'

'I have to go,' she squeaked. 'Goodbye.'

Rupert was leading her away, through the crowd to the front door. 'We're not staying?' she whispered. 'It will look bad if we go.'

In response he tightened his grip and propelled her forward. 'We'll talk about this at home.'

As they made their way home in the Jaguar, neither the luxurious softness of the leather seats, nor the subtle comfort of the heating, nor the soft beat of the music on the expensive sound system could soothe away the pain in her arm where he had grasped her. There would be a bruise tomorrow, she was sure of it. It wasn't just the physical pain that troubled her. She knew that Rupert was dangerous. His power and danger had been part of his attraction at first. But now she had seen the crude underside of it. He was a jealous bull.

She turned to stare out the car window. The leaves on the plane trees in St James's Park were growing tired and dropping. Autumn was well and truly here. For the first time, she allowed herself to think about leaving Rupert. A little voice – a sad, little girl's voice, truth be told – inside her mind said, *But I love him*. Natalya didn't know if that were true any more. She was certainly terrified to be without him: lost; cut adrift.

But marrying him seemed like a very bad idea.

It had been a long time since a man had shown interest in Lena, so at first she didn't pick up the signals.

She was in a smoky nightclub above a pub in Leeds, and Sam's band was on stage. It was crowded, and she found herself avoiding the elbows of a casually dressed and good-looking man in his early thirties, with long brown hair in a ponytail. She noticed he was looking at her, and at first thought she was in his way. But then it occurred to her: he was admiring her.

Conflicted feelings. She was married with two children. But at the same time, she hadn't been looked at in that way for years. Certainly not during her pregnancy. Never while out with Anna and Matthew, or on one of her dates with Sam. Not even by the dads picking up their children from the nursery. But here in a nightclub, dressed in a tight black dress and high heels, somebody had finally noticed that she was still beautiful. So she enjoyed his admiration, but was careful not to encourage it with a glance or a smile.

It was great for the band to play to such a huge crowd, but the huge crowd hadn't come for Sam. They had come for a local band who were on the verge of something big. They'd sold a thousand independently recorded CDs, and somewhere in this seething mass of people were record company executives invited up from London to see them. Tony, finally proving his moving-and-shaking credentials, had managed to secure Sam's band one of the supporting slots. It was an opportunity to die for.

The last song ended and quiet recorded music replaced it. She was about to make her way down to the stage to congratulate Sam, when the good-looking man next to her turned and said, 'Hi, I'm Rob.'

'Oh,' she said, 'Lena.' She crossed her arms and carefully hid her hands. Her fingernails were ringed with orange paint. The kids at the nursery had been doing handprints today, and she'd joined in. Every year, whoever was hosting the Winter Gathering had to make special invitations. Natalya always sent expensive ones and Sofi always sent beautifully designed ones. All Lena had to offer was expertise in nursery art, so orange handprints were making their way through the Royal Mail this evening.

'You from around here?' Rob said.

Lena knew she should just get away, but Sam would be ages packing up yet, and she was enjoying the attention. 'No, I'm from up the coast. Originally, I'm from Russia.'

'Wow, Russia. I wouldn't have picked it; you barely have an accent.'

A tall, thin man with glasses tapped Rob on the shoulder and said something in his ear. Rob shook his head and waved him off. 'Sorry,' he said to Lena. 'What brings you down to Leeds?'

'I'm here to see the band.'

'Ah, The Yellow Dogs? So am I.'

'No, the band that was just on. The Sam Tait Band.'

'Really?' He looked puzzled.

'Yes,' she said.

'What do you like about them?'

This was her opportunity to tell him that she was married, that it was her husband she had come to see. But a seed of interest had been planted. Sam spent a lot of time and effort on the band. She couldn't fault his commitment or his passion. Tony had decided to foot the bill for the recording, so they were up at Whitby two or three nights a week in the studio. Sometimes, though, she wondered if Sam were chasing a dream. She loved his songs, but then she would, wouldn't she? Now was her chance to know what an outsider thought.

'I like their songs,' she said. 'But I'm no expert. What did you think?'

'I don't mean to sound cruel,' he said, 'but there's nothing there of interest.'

'You don't think?'

'Utterly unoriginal. One of their songs has the precise same melody as a Rolling Stones song. The lyrics are awkward, and I don't think the bass player was in tune.'

'Oh. I wouldn't have noticed.'

'Trust me, there's no hope.' He smiled. 'I'm sorry, I don't mean to be rude. Can I buy you a drink?'

'No, no. I have to get going actually. Thanks anyway.'

She moved away before he could try to persuade her otherwise.

The band packed up and they all found a table right up the back of the room behind a pillar. While the next band played, Tony and Dave bitched about them and wondered loudly what all the fuss was about. Sam, who didn't have a bitter bone in his body, didn't join in. She turned Rob's words over in her head. *No hope.* It was just one opinion, of course, but she found part of her hoping that it was true. If Sam put the band aside, he could get an ordinary job and that would ease the financial pressure. Immediately she drove her fingernails into her palm. How could she even think such a thing? This was Sam's dream; she wanted him to keep working at it until it came true.

The night wore on, and she drank a little too much. The room felt claustrophobic; her throat was sore from shouting over the music to talk. It was approaching 1 a.m. – Lena tried not to think about what time Anna and Matthew would wake them up in the morning – when Tony finally got the signal that he could speak with the record company people. Most of the crowd had dispersed by this time, and Lena waited at the table with the guitars while the men went off to do their business. Her heart was beating a little faster, hoping and hoping for some crumb of interest for the band. From where she sat behind the pillar, she couldn't see what was going on, so she stood and peered around. Sam, Tony and Dave stood talking to a tall, thin man with glasses. Recognition glimmered. Then Rob joined them.

At first her concern was only for herself. Would Rob say something about her, about how he had flirted with her? But then full realisation was upon her. Rob and his bespectacled friend were the record company people. Her heart sank all the way to the floor. Was Rob telling Sam, right now, that they were unoriginal, that there was no hope?

She shrank back behind the pillar and waited.

When they came back, they didn't look like men who had had their dreams crushed.

'How did it go?' she asked Sam.

'They said no,' Tony said, jumping in.

'But they were encouraging,' Sam said. 'Told us to keep writing, keep rehearsing.'

'We should keep recording too,' Tony added, squinting as he lit a cigarette.

'Yes!' Sam enthused. 'We can go independent. We don't need the big companies. The Yellow Dogs sold a thousand CDs.'

'You're going to need money to do that,' Dave said, pulling his jacket on.

'Yeah, Sam, you still owe me two thousand quid,' Tony said.

Lena froze. Had she heard right?

Sam was quick to move on. 'Let's not talk business now,' he said.

Tony looked from Sam to Lena and smiled. His piggy eyes crinkled up at the corners. 'Ah, the missus doesn't know, I take it? Well, you'll be wearing your balls for earrings next time we see you. Come on. Let's load out.'

Even through the haze of alcohol, she felt the needling worry. Money. They had no money. They already owed thousands and couldn't keep up. *What was he thinking?*

Sam mouthed to her, 'I'm sorry,' as they picked up their gear and made their way down the stairs and out onto the street. It had rained while they were inside and moonlight shone on the puddles. The fresh, cold air was a welcome change from the smoky interior. Lena held on to her questions, her accusations, her anger, until they got home, not wanting to embarrass him. Besides, she knew what Sam would say: Grandad wouldn't give him the money and Tony would; he would pay it back in time; recording the band was important. She wasn't good at arguing with him – she didn't want him to think she was a nagging wife – so perhaps she would just keep quiet this time.

CHAPTER TWENTY-FOUR

Sofi took a rare moment to sit on the sofa, with her feet up, and open her mail. A long letter from Mama. She put it aside, saving it for later. Cheques from two boutiques. Her business was very slow at present, so it was nice to be reminded that she was still attached to the outside world in that way. And finally, an invitation from Lena. Winter Gathering 1996, on an orange handprint cut out and decorated with glitter glue. She laughed, and rose to pin it on the fridge with a magnet.

From the bedroom, a little hiccoughing cry. Moments later, Julien was behind her, holding the tiny bundle.

'He doesn't want me,' Julien said. 'He wants you.'

Sofi smiled the same misty smile she'd worn since Nikita's birth six weeks ago. She placed her hands around the fragile basket of his ribs, her fingers balancing his head. His little arms flopped by his sides. 'Here, little man,' she said quietly behind his ear as she pressed him to her shoulder. 'Shh, Mama has you.'

The crying stopped. Not that he cried much. Sofi could not help but compare him to Lena's babies, who had wailed from dawn to dusk and back to dawn again. Nikita was almost serious, lost in his thoughts while awake. He slept beautifully, already eight hours at a stretch at night-time. Becoming a mother had not been like being thrown into the deep end, as it had been for Lena. Rather, she had slid into the water willingly and easily. She had asked Mama on the phone if it had been like this for her, and Mama had said, yes, it was beautiful, a hush of awe had settled over their house.

'Then why didn't you have more?' Sofi asked. 'Dozens?' She thought she would like to have more, though Julien quickly skimmed over that question.

But Mama was still old-fashioned, didn't like to talk about reproduction. She simply said, 'We were only blessed once,' and changed the topic.

Nikita was opening and closing his little mouth, searching for food.

'I'll take him to bed for a feed,' she said, stroking his soft head.

'Good, I'm in the middle of an idea . . . you understand.'

'Of course I do.'

Julien disappeared into his studio. He had spent a lot of time in there the past six weeks, with the door closed against interruption. Sofi didn't mind. Julien was right, the baby always wanted her. And she loved to be wanted.

'Is that from your sister?'

Natalya felt guilty, though she didn't know why. She had just pulled the orange handprint out of its envelope and read it. 'Yes,' she said. 'I'm going up to Briggsby for Winter Gathering.'

Rupert took the invitation from her to read. 'Why don't you make them come down here? Why do you have to go so far away? It would be much more convenient for you to have it in London.'

'It's not about my convenience,' Natalya said, pulling her feet up under her on the leather sofa. 'Sofi's coming all the way from France with a little baby. It's already been organised. It's Lena's turn to host us this year, so we will go to her. It's my turn next year.'

'Do you want me to come with you?'

Natalya hoped her face didn't show her alarm. 'It's up to you. But I do like to spend a lot of time with them in that week, as I don't see them for the rest of the year.'

Rupert went to the bar to pour himself a drink. 'I don't like it, Natalya. You staying in some fleapit motel at the end of the earth. You don't belong there. You belong in London, surrounded by lovely things. With me.'

'Well, I'm going,' she said firmly. At least, she hoped it was firm. Her voice had been a little quiet . . .

'I wouldn't stop you, darling,' Rupert said, sipping his drink. 'I'm not a monster. I'll stay here in London and get some writing done, but perhaps I'll drive you up there, to say hello. Drink?'

Natalya thought of the calories and shook her head. 'No, thank you.'

'Good girl. Don't want to bloat.'

He took his drink and headed back to his office. Natalya gazed at the invitation and wondered if she dared confess to Sofi and Lena how unhappy she was becoming. Or would Rupert be able to tell she had spoken ill of him, even at a distance of hundreds of miles?

A sharp rap at the door. Lena jumped off the sofa and ran. Natalya was here.

'Hello, hello!' she shrieked, hooking her arm around her sister's neck and pulling her close.

Natalya, instantly in Russian, said, 'It feels like longer than a year. It feels like a century.'

Lena glanced over Natalya's shoulder into the wintry afternoon. The sky was heavy and grey, the bare trees that dotted the grey street shivered in the gusting sea wind. Rupert, wearing black sunglasses, leaned against the door to his silver Jaguar, a black scarf wound thickly around his neck.

'Is he staying?' she asked Natalya.

'He wants to drive me to the hotel. Coming?'

'Of course.' Lena ducked back inside and found Wendy in the kitchen, smoking and flicking through a magazine. 'I'm just heading to the hotel to help Natalya settle in. Could you give Matthew and Anna something to drink when they wake up?'

Wendy waved her away, smiling broadly. She had been particularly fond of Lena lately, because Lena spent a lot of time helping out with Grandad. She read to him for half an hour every morning before work, and had taken over getting him bathed and ready for bed most evenings. 'Go. Have a nice time,' Wendy said.

Natalya was already waiting in the car; the engine was running. Lena opened the door and slid into the soft leather seat. She couldn't relax, feeling the difference between this car and the old Mazda Sam had bought when they'd first arrived in Briggsby.

'Hello, Rupert,' she said as she buckled the seatbelt.

'Hello, Lena,' he said coolly. 'What nonsense have you got planned for your little party this year?'

Lena wasn't sure what he meant. 'It's not a party,' she said warily. 'And I haven't any nonsense planned.'

'Rupert, you make it sound like a hen night,' Natalya said, laughing self-consciously. 'We just sit around and talk and drink coffee.'

'And Sofi will have a three-month-old baby with her, so we won't have much of a chance to get into trouble,' Lena added. 'If that's what you're asking.' She didn't like Rupert; he was very controlling. But Natalya seemed to love him and it wasn't her place to interfere.

Natalya had booked into the Regency Hotel on the Esplanade, a four-star establishment with wide views out over the grey sea. It was the best hotel in Briggsby, but Rupert turned his nose up at it the moment they pulled up.

'Can't you stay somewhere a little further away that's nicer?' he asked as he helped her get her suitcases out.

Lena stepped in. 'The nearest five-star hotel is at Whitby,' she said. 'An hour's drive away. If you leave the Jaguar here, I'll make sure she gets there and back every morning.'

Rupert's mouth pulled into a thin line, but then he started to laugh. Natalya, Lena noticed, looked very relieved. 'Very funny, Lena,' he said.

A gust of icy wind buffeted them. 'We need to go in,' Natalya said.

'Goodbye, honey-pie,' Rupert said, placing a paternal kiss on Natalya's forehead. 'Make sure you keep your new phone charged up and switched on.'

'I will,' she said, then explained to Lena, 'Rupert bought me a mobile phone for Christmas. Isn't he a darling?'

'Oh, yes,' Lena answered.

Rupert and Natalya embraced and Lena turned away, picked up one of Natalya's bags and started up the path towards the pretty Georgian building. She had the distinct feeling that all of the honey-pies and darlings were strained. She stopped at the front door, turning to gaze out at the restless sea.

'Wait, Lena.'

Lena glanced over her shoulder. The Jaguar was speeding off, and Natalya was hurrying to catch up. She held out the mobile phone. 'What do you think this means?'

Lena peered at the tiny screen. 'No signal. Well, you are at the end of the world up here. Next stop, icy seas. Not like the cosy little town on *Lonely Shores*.'

'Rupert will be so cross,' Natalya murmured, turning around in a slow circle, eyes glued to the screen. 'Oh, there. Look. Now it has a signal.'

'So are you going to stand out here all day and wait for him to call?'

Natalya dropped the phone in her bag. 'You're right. Let's get out of this cold wind.'

They went inside. The foyer was warm, the Christmas decorations still in place. The woman behind the counter saw Natalya and immediately started stammering.

'Oh, my God! It's Tatiana, isn't it?'

Natalya smiled graciously. She clearly loved it. 'Good morning. I have a reservation.'

Was Lena imagining it, or was Natalya playing up her Russian accent?

'What an honour to have a telly star in Briggsby.'

'I've come to stay with my sister. She lives here.'

The woman turned her eyes to Lena. 'How exciting! Your sister is famous!'

Lena smiled at the woman tightly. 'It's booked under Chernova,' she said.

Upstairs, while Natalya unpacked, Lena stood gazing out the window. The panes were laced with salt so the view was slightly obscured. 'Do you mind that it's four-star?' she asked Natalya, turning away from the window. 'Rupert seems to mind.'

'Of course I don't,' Natalya said, as she hung skirts and jackets in the wardrobe. 'But you do get used to having the best and it becomes normal.'

'I'm just thinking about that apartment we used to rent in St Petersburg. With the curtains that were all rotted away at the hem.'

'Did you ever see Tolya's apartment? It was wallpapered with old newspapers.' Natalya shook her head. 'I don't miss those days, Lena.'

Lena wanted to tell Natalya that things weren't so different for her now. She and Sam were thousands of pounds in debt and Wendy's rent had just gone up so they had to somehow find ten pounds a week more in board. Sam's band continued the alarmingly long process of recording up at Whitby, and that meant extra petrol money every week, not to mention the impossible cost of four new tyres on the Mazda which they had been putting off for too long already. Lena had taken to walking the twins everywhere in the pushchair, especially on rainy days, because she was afraid that the car would skid them all into a tree. All week she had been working up the courage to confess the whole sorry mess to Natalya. Her sister had so much, and Lena knew she would offer to help out. But embarrassment held her tongue. Little Lena, always the one who cried and needed rescuing.

'When does Sofi arrive?'

Lena was both relieved and disappointed that the conversation had turned elsewhere. Natalya was now folding clothes into the chest of drawers. She had brought a lot of clothes.

'Early this evening. She'll be tired, travelling all day with the baby.'

Natalya flopped on the bed, suddenly nothing like the poised television star and very much like the little Russian girl Lena had grown up beside. Lena joined her. Natalya was still checking her mobile phone, tilting it this way and that.

'No signal,' she said. 'Rupert's going to be upset. Perhaps I should call on the ordinary phone.'

'He won't even be back in London yet. Call him later, and don't worry. It's not your fault.' She propped herself up on her elbow and gazed at Natalya. 'You're not afraid of him, are you?'

'Of course not,' Natalya said, laughing. 'He's my fiancé, remember?' She waggled her left hand, where a gigantic diamond sparkled.

Lena thought of the tiny diamond on her own left hand, and how they still hadn't paid Grandad back for it, and she made up her mind. She had to tell Natalya, before Sofi got here and made things more complicated.

'Natalya,' she said, feeling embarrassed and desperately uncomfortable. 'I'm so sorry to ask, and you can say no if you want to . . .' She trailed off.

Natalya raised her eyebrows. 'What is it?'

Lena sat up. 'We're in such trouble, Sam and I. We're in debt and the car needs new tyres and . . . You know, I feel like such a fool. I'm sorry . . .'

Natalya sat up too, and squeezed her hand. 'Do you need something? Money?'

Lena couldn't bring herself to speak. Tears of shame squeezed out of her eyes. She nodded.

'Of course! Of course. You only have to ask.' Natalya was already up, bending her thin body over her handbag on the sofa. 'I have a chequebook, I'll give you some right now. Money for tyres? Or more? How much do you owe?'

'Three and a half thousand pounds,' Lena admitted.

'That's nothing,' Natalya said, scribbling in her chequebook. 'Nothing at all.'

Lena bit her tongue, wanted to tell Natalya that it was nothing to *her*. But to Lena it was a mountain. Natalya ripped out the cheque with a flourish, handed it to Lena. *Five thousand pounds*. Lena felt as though the clouds had parted and the sun shone through. Flushed and teary, she wrapped her arms around Natalya.

'Thank you, thank you,' she said, accidentally gathering a mouthful of her sister's glossy hair.

'It's all right,' Natalya said. 'Are things really so bad? Did Sam lose his job?'

'No, no. It's just, we don't earn much, and children are costly and . . . well, it seems to slip through our fingers.' Lena didn't confess that Sam's band was a black hole that a lot of their money went into.

She folded the cheque and tucked it into the pocket of her jeans, trying to fight off the crawling embarrassment that she knew would plague her for Natalya's entire visit.

CHAPTER TWENTY-FIVE

'So, do you like it?' Sam said to Sofi. At least, she thought that was what he said. It was hard to tell over the din in her ears, courtesy of a Walkman's headphones.

Sofi popped off the headphones, restoring the sound of the sea rushing onto the rocks nearby. They were rugged up and walking the cliff path together: Sofi, Natalya, Lena and Sam, whose band Sofi had accidentally shown far too much interest in. They were in the process of recording an album, and Sam had been convinced that Sofi wanted to hear the first song, at volume. Lena was smiling at her knowingly. She would have to learn to be less enthusiastic.

She handed the Walkman back. 'Great,' she said, taking the pushchair from Sam. 'Just like the real thing.'

'You think so?'

Sofi nodded. She had very little idea about pop music; it all sounded terrible to her, so Sam's music didn't stand out.

Sam slid his headphones on and fell into step behind them. Sofi liked Sam. He was like a big friendly dog, with his long limbs and his messy hair. But he didn't act like a man who was married with two children. She glanced over to the wide pushchair that Lena pushed in front of her. Anna and Matthew, now two and a half, were just solemn faces peering out of layers of warm clothes. The cold and the layers seemed to have immobilised them, so that they sat staring straight ahead quietly. Sofi couldn't believe that one day Nikita would be so big, but it seemed Lena's children had grown up in the blink of an eye.

They walked like that a long time, chatting and joking, Sam trailing them, concentrating on his music. Sofi realised there was a special kind of relaxed contentment about their Winter Gatherings: being with people who knew her almost as well as she knew herself. It was a fine day, though the sun still shone from a very long way off and had barely made it above the horizon by lunchtime. Nikita slept in his pushchair, his mittened hands curled either side of his pink face.

Natalya was in the middle of a sentence, reminding them about a crush they'd all had on the same boy back in school, when a strange chirping noise made them all stop in their tracks.

'What's that?' Lena asked, looking around. 'A bird or a bug?'

Natalya frowned, glancing at Sam's Walkman. He kept walking, oblivious.

'It's coming from your handbag, Natalya,' Sofi said.

'Oh!' Natalya exclaimed. 'I think it's my phone.' She rummaged in her bag and pulled out the phone, found the right button and answered it. 'Hello? Oh, hi, darling... what?... I can't... hang on, I'll see if I can get better reception.' She slipped off the path and towards the street. Sam walked ahead.

'Rupert bought it for her for Christmas,' Lena explained. 'A tracking device.'

Sofi laughed. She spotted a bench. 'Shall we sit and wait?'

'Good idea.'

They parked their pushchairs and sat.

'Look at us,' Lena said. 'A pair of mamas.'

'You don't look like a mama,' Sofi said. 'Too glamorous.'

Lena smiled. 'Thank you. I don't feel glamorous.' She indicated Sofi's pushchair. 'He's awake.'

Sofi looked down. Nikita was stretching, his little mouth open in a yawn.

'Does he ever cry?' Lena asked.

'Of course. But he's usually very contented.'

Lena leaned over the pushchair, tickling Nikita's tummy through the layers of blanket. 'I can't remember Anna and Matthew ever being that small.'

'They were smaller,' Sofi said. 'Matthew especially, just a little scrap.'

Lena was still playing with Nikita. 'He's a serious little thing, isn't he?'

'Like his father.'

'I can't get a smile out of him.'

'He doesn't smile yet.'

Lena looked at her sharply. 'Really? Not at all?'

Sofi shook her head, a thread of worry working its way into her heart. 'No. Why?'

'Babies generally start smiling at about five or six weeks. Matthew was a bit late, he was ten weeks. How old is Nikita?'

'Nearly four months.' Her eyes went to her baby; her precious boy. Immediately, the worry evaporated. How could he be anything but perfect? 'But he is very serious, and so is Julien, so I'm sure it's inherited. Every baby is different, after all.'

'Of course,' Lena said, quickly enough that Sofi knew it was a performance of reassurance. 'You know your baby.'

Natalya returned. 'It cut out,' she said, shaking the mobile phone. 'What a piece of rubbish!'

Lena stood. 'Come on, let's catch up with Sam.'

Sofi fell into step behind them. It was cruel of Lena to put worrying ideas into her head. Perhaps she didn't mean to, but perhaps she was a little envious of Nikita. He was a peaceful baby, after all, and Lena's twins had been a terrible handful at this age. It was a shame that such petty jealousies should intrude on their relationship, especially when they saw each other so infrequently. She glanced down at Nikita, who was staring up at her with his dark, liquid eyes. He would smile in his own good time, and when he did, Sofi knew, it would be beautiful.

Natalya was dozing in Rupert's Jaguar. She was so tired, as though her eyelids were lined with lead. She struggled to keep her eyes open. Scenery flashed past outside the car. Wide fields under sunlight. But then it was night already. The moon was a sick shade of yellow. She had forgotten where they were going, and she wanted Rupert to stop, pull over, find her a soft bed to sleep in.

'Stop,' she said, but the word wouldn't come out. She turned to Rupert, but it wasn't Rupert at all, it was Roy Creedy, grinning at her . . .

Natalya gasped as she woke, her heart speeding. She took a moment to reorient herself. It was morning, pale daylight glimmered through the crack between the curtains. She was still in the hotel at Briggsby, and she had overslept. Lena and Sofi were coming for breakfast this morning, before Sofi headed home and Rupert returned to collect Natalya. They would be here any minute.

She leapt up to shower, wishing she could shake the uncanny hangover of the dream. In the bathroom, she whispered the nightmare to the shower head, as she had done since she was a little girl. Her father had told her that was the only way to wash bad dreams away. She felt a little better when she emerged, but still there was a weight on the day. She had time only to brush her hair before the knock at the door came.

'Good morning,' she said brightly, letting them in and closing the door behind them. 'I overslept, sorry. Haven't packed yet.'

'But you ordered breakfast?' Sofi asked. The baby was tied to her chest in a papoose.

'Oh, yes, I did that last night. It should be here at eight. Where are your children, Lena?'

'Sam's got them,' she said, pulling out a chair at the little dining table and sitting down. 'Let's hope he remembers to give them breakfast today. He's a great dad, but very forgetful.'

Lena and Sofi fell into conversation. Natalya wondered that Lena could complain about Sam. Didn't she know how lucky she was to have him? He was so calm and loving, he adored her but not in an overbearing or possessive way, and he supported everything that she wanted to do. The fact that he was gorgeous hadn't escaped her attention either, of course, but as he was her brother-in-law she tried to be blind to his appearance.

Breakfast arrived. Sofi took Nikita out of his papoose and laid him on Natalya's bed to sleep, surrounded on all sides by pillows. His arms were flopped up beside his ears, eyelashes half-moons on his cheeks, as he breathed peacefully. Even Natalya, who was horrified at the idea of having children, had to admit he was beautiful.

They sat down to eat.

'Do you girls ever think about Roy Creedy?' Natalya said, nibbling delicately at a slice of unbuttered toast.

'From time to time,' Lena said. 'Why?'

'Do you ever dream about him? I did this morning. He was driving Rupert's car.' As she said it, she realised that somehow her unconscious mind had associated Rupert with Roy. She felt embarrassed for having admitted it out loud. Rupert was older than her and rich, yes, but he was *nothing* like Roy Creedy.

Sofi saved her further embarrassment. 'We wouldn't dream about him, because we never met him. But I do think about him occasionally. Sometimes, I even think about making enough money to give back to him. But that would involve contacting him and . . . from what you said, it's probably best we never do.'

'I almost can't believe we did it,' Lena said. 'It seems a lifetime ago.'

'We were naive,' Sofi agreed. 'We grew up in the Soviet Union, we knew nothing of the greater world. Now we're older, wiser. I regret it, but I can forgive myself. Look what we've done with his money. We didn't waste it on luxuries, we turned it into something. Three lives: children, careers . . .'

Lena smiled wryly. 'I don't have a career.'

'But you might, one day,' Natalya said quickly, aware of her sister's discomfort. It couldn't have been easy for her to ask for money. 'You're still young and beautiful.'

She stopped short of saying she would ask Rupert to get Lena some television work, because she couldn't guarantee that Rupert would. He had been very keen to separate Natalya's business from

Sofi; she could only imagine he would be equally unwelcoming of her sister.

'Of course,' Lena said. 'Or I might not need one. Once Sam's band makes it big.' She laughed. '*If* Sam's band makes it big.'

'They're great, Lena,' Sofi said. 'I'm sure they'll make it.'

'Really?' Lena asked.

Natalya, seeing her brighten, joined in. 'Definitely,' she said. 'They've just been unlucky so far.'

'Nobody deserves it more than him,' Lena said. 'He works so hard.'

'Would you go on tour with him?' Natalya said. 'Take the children?'

'That would be exciting, wouldn't it?' Lena said, and her face took on the dreamy softness it always had when she was imagining some exciting future. 'What a life that would be.' She shook her head, returned her attention to her breakfast.

Natalya, who was used to the company of actresses and models, was envious of Lena's and Sofi's appetites. They ate and they enjoyed it. Natalya had been on a diet for three years. Rupert had even told her that he found the sight of women eating unattractive. That was the world she was heading back to today.

'So, Natalya, have you and Rupert set a date for your wedding?' Sofi said, almost as if she had been reading Natalya's thoughts.

'No, but it will be late next year, I expect. He'll try to get a deal with one of the magazines to cover it exclusively, so we'll have to fit it in around that.'

'Well, you'll be the first one of us to actually have a big wedding,' Lena said. 'Instead of quietly sneaking off to a registrar the way Sofi and I did it.'

'Winter Gathering's in London next year,' Sofi said. 'Perhaps you could have a winter wedding? Ask Rupert.'

'I will,' Natalya said, knowing she wouldn't. Rupert would decide, and she'd have no say. She checked the clock beside the bed. He would be on his way from London now, coming to pick her up.

And she realised that the weight on the day was not due to her dream of Roy Creedy; it was due to Rupert's imminent return. The realisation only compounded the feeling of suffocation. She could not escape him.

Lena walked up the wintry street, on her way home from seeing Sofi off at the bus station. Rupert had come for Natalya much earlier than expected, and Lena had the distinct impression he was checking up on her. Just before she had climbed into the Jaguar, Natalya had pressed Lena close and said, 'Any time you need money, you just ask.'

Lena had nodded, ashamed, vowing never to ask again.

Sofi had claimed exhaustion anticipating the long trip ahead of her, but Lena withheld her sympathy. Nikita was a dream baby. Until Sofi had experienced two screaming in unison, she wasn't allowed to complain. Lena sometimes wondered if Matthew and Anna could tell – had been able to tell even in the womb – that they were accidentally conceived, and that caused them to be needy. Nikita, carefully planned and deeply longed for, seemed secure in his place in the world.

The house was quiet as she let herself in. Sam sat on the sofa. He climbed to his feet and took her hand. 'Mum's taken them out, Grandad's napping. I have a surprise for you.'

She smiled. 'What is it?'

'You have to close your eyes.' He put his arm around her back. 'I'll lead you.'

Eyes closed, she allowed herself to be guided by Sam's warm hands. 'Am I going to like it?' she asked.

'You're going to love it,' he replied, and she got a warm tingle from the promise in his voice. She heard their bedroom door open, then close again behind them. The soft fragrance of roses.

'All right,' he said, 'open your eyes.'

She opened them. The bedroom curtains were drawn and the lamp next to their bed was switched on. By its soft glow, Lena could see that their entire bedroom was filled with long-stemmed roses. Roses all over the bed, roses all over the scarred dresser and mismatched bedside tables, roses scattered on the floor. She gasped. Her first thought was that his band had been signed, given a huge advance, and this was his way of telling her. But then her rational brain kicked in. Sam wore his heart on his sleeve. He would never be able to keep such news to himself long enough to surprise her. So she knew where the money for the roses had come from. Natalya's cheque must have cleared.

She tried not to let her disappointment sour the mood. 'Sam, it's beautiful,' she said.

He cleared a space for them on the bed. Picked up a rose and plucked off its petals to scatter in her hair, across her collarbone. His lips followed, and he began to unfasten her buttons. She tried to give herself over to the sensations, to enjoy the beautiful gesture and not calculate its cost. As they made love, she allowed herself to imagine, just temporarily, that they had plenty of money, that a roomful of roses was not an indulgence that they couldn't afford. She imagined they weren't in her mother-in-law's dingy house, but in a sumptuous hotel room with a view of the sea. The smell of the roses and the salty taste of Sam's skin mingled addictively, and she forgot the world.

Afterwards, when she opened her eyes, the world came back.

'You shouldn't have, Sam,' she said, tracing a rose over his bare chest. 'We can't afford it.'

'We *can*,' he said. 'Normally we can't. That's why I did it. We never have any money. Today we do.'

'Tomorrow we won't. At this rate.'

'It's going to run out anyway, Lena. At least this way we enjoy it.'

Something was amiss with this logic, but Lena was too tired to fight it. The money was spent, roses couldn't be returned for a refund. She lay quietly with him for a few minutes. The radiator ticked, and a gust of wind buffeted the panes of the window.

'Lena, once we've paid our debts, what are we going to do with the rest of the money?'

'Save it, I suppose. For a rainy day.'

'Tony has this great idea.'

'I'm not going to like this, am I?'

Sam laughed, his beautiful good-natured laugh, and leaned over to kiss her forehead. 'You've underestimated Tony.'

He explained that Tony had grown passionate about releasing their album independently, and he was willing to pay for all of the costs, knowing that they'd make them back quickly when the CD started selling. Sam wanted to take a thousand pounds of Natalya's money to contribute towards professional artwork for the cover.

'People are more likely to buy it if it looks like the real thing,' Sam said. 'And Tony has promised that all of the money we make from the CD will go towards paying you back first. So, if we sell them for five quid each, we only have to sell a hundred and half your money is back. And Tony absolutely guarantees he will wait until you are paid back first. See, he's not a villain after all.'

Lena considered it. Natalya and Sofi seemed to think that Sam's band had promise, even if the record company rep didn't. She had to admit that she'd lost all objectivity. 'And you're sure the money would come back that quickly?'

'We'll put it in a few local record stores, sell it at gigs. Come on, a hundred CDs. That's nothing. It will probably take a week.' He feigned a hangdog expression. 'Or you could get one of your kids at the nursery to draw the cover art for us.'

Lena laughed. 'I suppose it's all right. All we have to lose is a bit of bank interest.'

He grabbed her and squeezed her. 'You are the best wife in the world,' he said.

'Keep your dream alive, Sam,' she said to him softly. *Because mine has fallen by the wayside.*

Sofi liked to unpack as soon as she got home. She laid Nikita on the bed, where he kicked his legs gently and sucked his fists, while she sorted her clean clothes from the ones for the laundry. Julien was cooking dinner for them and the delicious smell of garlic frying in butter filled the house. She loved the peace here at home after the constant round of socialising with her cousins. But she missed Lena and Natalya too. She and Julien had only a few friends and Julien hadn't worked hard over the years to connect with the community. Sofi was trying, but her French wasn't good so she strained to make small talk at the markets or at the park. She got by with extra phone calls to her mother or her cousins, and kept to herself.

That would all change soon. She had advertised for an assistant, somebody to help her with filling orders, which seemed to be growing despite the fact that she had not sought out new business since Nikita was born. But he was becoming more predictable now, and she could imagine working on her pieces while he slept, or while Julien watched him some days. Her fingers itched to work. Everything she saw turned itself into a pattern of stones and silver in her mind.

Sofi slid her suitcase under her bed and lay down next to Nikita. He gazed up at her. She traced a finger over his belly. 'Hello, little darling,' she said.

And he smiled. His lips parted and turned up at the corners, into a perfect gummy smile.

Sofi began to laugh. 'Julien! Come here, quickly!'

Julien hurried in looking wild and panicked. 'What is it? What's wrong?'

'Nothing's wrong. It's Nikita. He's smiling.'

Julien leaned over his son, but couldn't coax another smile out of him. Sofi watched them for a while. Nikita, serious again, and his father, desperately trying to tickle and sing a smile out of him. She was surprised by how relieved she felt, and made a promise to herself not to listen to other people's opinions about her child in future. Nobody knew him as well as she did.

Viktor Chernov got home before his wife, Ulyana, on Wednesday nights, but he never cooked dinner for her. He had tried a few times, but she criticised everything he did: too many cloves, not enough ginger, overcooked and chewy, bland and underdone. So he sat on his sofa and watched the television and waited for her to come home and cook for him. A drink or two made the wait go quicker.

When the door opened, he expected her usual sour demeanour, her defeated shuffle. But today she had a spring in her step.

She had a bundle of magazines with her. She worked in the book section of a big department store in Moscow, and often brought home old magazines that hadn't sold. Most were Russian, but some were German, Swedish or English. They lay around the house for months until Viktor finally got sick of them and put them out in the hallway.

'What are you making for dinner?' he asked her.

'I've got something to show you.' She dumped her handbag on the floor and dropped onto the sofa next to him, the magazines in her lap. She leafed through them, looking for something.

'This had better be interesting, because I am very hungry and you are late.'

'You'll want to see it. Ah . . . here.' She pulled out a magazine from the pile, letting the others fall to the floor in a heap. Viktor knew they would be there for days before anyone bothered picking them up. She found the page she was looking for, bending the magazine backwards to hand to him.

He found himself looking at a picture of a beautiful woman. The writing wasn't Russian so he had no idea who she was.

'You don't recognise her?'

Viktor looked closer. 'Ah,' he said. He often went through Ulyana's magazines for pictures of pretty girls, scantily clad. He had dozens pinned inside the door on his side of their wardrobe. His favourite, a black-and-white photograph of a glossy-skinned temptress wearing nothing but a carefully arranged apron, took pride of place at the centre of this collection. This was the woman he was looking at now, although she was clothed and in full colour. Her eyes were blue. There were many other photos of her, in a gleaming home full of expensive furniture.

'It's your little maid,' Ulyana said, a disdainful frown momentarily pulling deep marionette lines on her face.

'I like her better with less on,' Viktor growled, handing the magazine back.

'You idiot. I didn't show it to you because I want you to add her to your collection. You can't read English, but if you could, you would have seen her name. Natalie Chernoff.'

Vaguely he was aware that something momentous was about to be revealed to him.

'And you would have read her sad story: her mother died when she was two, her father abandoned her in Leningrad when she was seven . . . it goes on. Viktor, it's your daughter.'

Viktor was stunned, cold. 'Is she famous?'

'A television star in England.'

'This is her house?'

'A flat. In London.'

Viktor guzzled the pictures now, calculating his daughter's wealth. 'Oh, my,' he said. 'Oh, my.'

'I'll read it to you later. I'm going to make dinner.'

Viktor couldn't take his eyes off the article. His daughter, a rich television star. She was so beautiful, like her mother . . . Then a sick shame came over him and he dropped the magazine, went to the bedroom and flung open the wardrobe door. Without taking even a moment to consider the photograph one last time, he pulled it down and tore it up, then took it to flush it down the toilet.

Ulyana was standing at the bathroom door when he turned around. 'Are you all right?'

'I will be.' He straightened his shoulders.

Ulyana smiled. Not pleasantly; deviously. 'Do you think she might like to hear from her papa after all these years?'

'I'm sure she wouldn't,' he said. 'But I think her sister might.'

CHAPTER TWENTY-SIX

'Happy birthday to you, happy birthday to you, happy birthday Great-Grandad, happy birthday to you.'

Lena clapped, stupidly proud of Matthew and Anna, who were still a month short of their third birthdays but could sing beautifully in tune. They had it from Sam, of course. Not just from his genes, but from the hours he spent singing and playing musical games with them.

Grandad hid his smile under a demeanour of grumpy patience as he spooned Weetabix into his mouth. He was in his usual spot by the window, which was open a few inches to let in the early spring breeze. He wore over his lap the new rug that Lena had knitted for him and given to him that morning, and the wall above his dresser was decorated with pictures the children had drawn for him. Next to the dresser were three large cartons stacked neatly on top of each other. Sam's CDs. Two hundred and eighty-eight of the three hundred they'd printed were remaining. Put in storage in Grandad's room because there was no space in their own, which was still divided in half by a curtain that the children slept behind.

'All right, you children,' Lena said. 'Off you go and have breakfast.'

Matthew and Anna ran away giggling. Anna's hair had stayed very fair and curly, but Matthew's had grown dark and straight. *A girl for you and a boy for me.* She watched them go, then perched on the painted windowsill.

'How are you feeling?' she asked him.

'I'm seventy-five. I feel old. Don't you have to go to work?'

'I don't have to leave for another twenty minutes.'

'Wendy hasn't been to see me yet.'

'She's busy. She'll come after she's cleaned up the kitchen, I'm sure.'

'She's forgotten it's my birthday.'

Lena suspected that this was the case. And she hadn't reminded her mother-in-law, on purpose. She didn't know why; some inexplicable primitive rivalry.

'Sam has forgotten too,' Grandad added mournfully.

'Sam knows it's your birthday,' Lena answered. 'He's still in bed. I'm sure he'll come to see you when he wakes up.'

'Here you are, not even my flesh and blood, and you care more about me than they do.'

'They love you, Grandad, don't be silly.'

'I'm stuck here in this bedroom, most of the time attached to that machine. Who comes to see me every day? You. Who takes me for a walk by the cliffs? You. Who remembers my birthday? You.'

'And Wendy cooks all your meals –'

'You make my breakfast,' he said, indicating his bowl with his spoon.

'But she does the rest. She looks after you.'

'Only because she wants my money. I'm a burden. You know I am.'

They'd had this conversation a hundred times before. Lena was aware that she shouldn't encourage it, but he was right. She *did* care for him more than his family, and they *were* waiting for him to die.

Two days ago, she had found a brochure for a Volkswagen Golf under a pile of magazines on the coffee table. She had opened it up, only to have it snatched out of her hands by Wendy.

'Are you thinking of buying a new car?' Lena had asked.

'A girl can dream, can't she?' Wendy had said, tucking the brochure under her arm. 'He won't live forever.'

Grandad leaned over to close the window. 'Too cold,' he said.

Lena snapped herself out of her reverie. 'This afternoon, when I come home, I'll take you for a walk. It should be sunny by then.'

She stood and leaned over to kiss his forehead. He surprised her by grasping her wrist with his hand. For an old, weak man, he had a strong grip.

'Lena,' he whispered urgently, 'I have to tell you something.'

Surprised, she crouched in front of him. 'What is it?'

'Swear on your life you won't repeat it.'

Common sense told her not to swear anything, but curiosity had the better of her. Her heart thudded. 'I . . . certainly. I promise.'

He glanced towards the door. Sounds of the radio playing and cutlery being put away in the kitchen. She waited. His eyes returned to hers. 'There is no money,' he said.

A little jolt shook her. 'What do you mean?'

'I have less than a thousand pounds in my cheque account.'

Lena wanted to laugh. But there would be repercussions right through the family – *her* family now – from this. 'Then why does everyone think you do have money?'

'I let Wendy believe it. Because I know her, and she would have put me in state care a long time ago if she didn't think there was something in it for her.'

Lena should have been alarmed by his deviousness, by the cruel glint in his eyes when he said this. But she couldn't feel anything but sorry for him. An unwanted, sick old man who had to lie to get people to look after him. She wanted to gather him in her arms and hold him and tell him how deeply valuable he was as a human being, but at that moment Wendy's cheerful whistling advanced up the hallway. Lena pulled back, Grandad returned his gaze to the window.

'Morning, Dad,' Wendy said, bustling in and going straight to the bed to make it.

Grandad harrumphed. Lena was caught between them; the burden of her new knowledge made itself felt for the first time.

Wendy directed a stern glance at her. 'If you're going to work, you'd better wake Sam up. I don't have time for Anna and Matthew today. I'm having my ladies over for morning tea and I don't want those kids of yours anywhere near the sponge cake I'm baking.'

Lena bristled. 'Sure. I'll do that now.'

She brushed past Wendy, leaning close to whisper, 'It's his birthday' in her ear. Wendy's face froze and Lena moved off, ashamed of the sense of satisfaction that Wendy's distress caused her.

The soundtrack to *The Phantom of the Opera* was on the stereo, pumped through twelve speakers hung in perfect positions all around the sitting room. Scented candles burned in expensive glass holders on bookshelves that held hardly any books. Rupert bought books for their covers, not their contents, and blue tones went with the decor here. The rich aromas of Russian cooking rose from the kitchen. Natalya had insisted. Rupert had wanted to hire a chef; his dislike of the appearance of women eating extended to the appearance of women preparing food. But Natalya was a good cook, and hardly ever got a chance. Tonight was special and she wanted to impress. So she sent Rupert out for the afternoon and indulged herself. The table was already set with plates of fresh apricots, figs, dates and nuts. There was mushroom soup made with rich *zaprashka* gravy for starters, with *pagach* bread stuffed with cheese and potato. Followed by roasted goose, and kidney beans that had been slow cooked since the morning, seasoned with garlic and topped with shredded potatoes, honeyed peas, seasoned cabbage and savoury bread pudding. Natalya knew it would be incredible, and that she would eat hardly any of it.

She splashed a generous serving of red wine into a glass and sipped it, relaxed and happy. Rupert had invited to dinner Glynn Kendrick, a Welsh film director who was building up a solid reputation in Hollywood. He had a number of projects on his slate, and Natalya was convinced that she would have to be right for a part in one of them.

The front door opened and she hurried out of the kitchen to greet Rupert. She pulled up short when she saw his face was a thundercloud. Immediately, she felt guilty. She had done something wrong. Chosen the wrong music – even though it was from his collection; she couldn't stand it – or worn the wrong dress. She glanced down at herself: it was the shoes. What was she thinking? High heels for a relaxed dinner at home!

'I'm sorry,' she blurted, then realised that his face had softened.

He reached for her with one hand. In the other he held a bag with two bottles of wine in it. 'No, *I'm* sorry, Natalya. I'm afraid I have some very bad news.'

Natalya's heart sank. She thought of all her delicious food going to waste. 'He can't come?'

Rupert shook his head. 'Oh, no. Glynn's still coming. It's something else. It's about the wedding.'

She swallowed hard. Mention of the wedding always made her heart fizz with icy bubbles. 'What is it?'

'*Hello!* won't agree to our price. Negotiations have broken down. We'll have to shift the date, look for another magazine to cover it.'

'Shift the date?' Natalya said, performing in a more focused way than she ever did on *Lonely Shores*. 'How far away?'

'I've had preliminary negotiations with *BritSoap*. This time next year. They will pay the price we want for the rights, so I'm afraid there's no choice.' He stroked her hair. 'I'm sorry, darling. Another year.'

Natalya hid her relief.

'But we'll try our best to have it earlier in the year, definitely,' he said, walking to the kitchen to set down the bottles of wine. 'Before you turn thirty. A twenty-something always makes a better bride, don't you think? Women in their thirties getting married always seem a little desperate.'

She didn't answer. A year. Another year to decide what to do. She couldn't imagine not marrying Rupert and yet the permanence of it terrified her. Perhaps that was due to her childhood, being abandoned so young. Perhaps any woman in her situation would feel the same way, and all the problems lay at her feet and Rupert was not to blame. His possessiveness, his overbearing ways.

'Are you all right, darling?' he said. He had returned and was stroking her cheek with the back of his knuckles. 'I've ruined your night, haven't I?'

She smiled. 'Not at all. The important thing is we're still together and we're still happy.'

The doorbell rang. Her heart jumped. 'He's here.'

Glynn Kendrick was young and energetic, with a passion that seeped out of his pores so that every time he spoke he seemed more alive and present than anyone else in the room. His wife was an American ex-model named Roxanne, who ate even less than Natalya. Much of the beautiful food went uneaten, though everyone expressed extreme enthusiasm for it.

As Natalya cleared the plates, Glynn sat back and complimented Rupert. 'That's quite a cook and housekeeper you have there,' he joked.

'And a lovely home,' Roxanne added.

'Even if it was decorated in the eighties,' Glynn said.

Laughter went round the room, but Natalya knew Rupert would take the comment to heart. She sat down again, opened another bottle of wine. Talk turned to work, and Roxanne could not contain herself.

'I am addicted to *Lonely Shores*,' she confessed. 'I've been watching it every night since we got here. Natalya, you have the best character! What's going to happen with the baby?'

Natalya had to think hard. She hardly watched the show any more, and was always filming a few months ahead. She remembered that on screen at the moment she was wearing a ridiculously small prosthetic pregnant belly.

'Oh, I can't tell you,' she said. 'Rupert will kill me.'

'I'll be back in the States by the time the baby's born,' Roxanne said. 'Please.'

Rupert interjected. 'Tatiana wants to give up the baby for adoption, but Mary Peterson –'

'The wife of the man who is the baby's father?' Roxanne asked.

'Precisely. She wants to adopt the child.'

'Even though it's a permanent reminder of her husband's infidelity. Lovely! How do you think of these things, Rupert?'

He surprised Natalya by leaning across and taking her hand. 'I give all the credit to my muse here.'

Natalya blushed and couldn't hide her smile.

'Natalya,' Glynn said, 'that's a very strong accent you have. I must admit that I thought you'd faked it for the show.'

Natalya didn't know how to feel about this comment. To her ears, she was practically a local. 'No, it's an authentic Russian accent,' she said.

'I'm developing a project. It's early days yet . . . but it's set in the fifties in Moscow. A spy thriller. I'd love you to test for the female role. It's fairly standard. A love interest who takes a bullet to the head at the three-quarter point.' He laughed self-consciously. 'But you'd be lovely for it. Natural.'

Every part of her body tingled. 'I'd love that.'

After that, she was on a high. More wine flowed and she drank too much. She even ate dessert, vowing to pay for it the next day with an hour of jogging. Her laughter got raucous, she taught Roxanne how to swear in Russian . . . she suspected she might have even flirted with Glynn. They didn't leave until close to one in the morning. When she had packed the dishwasher and turned out the lights, Rupert was waiting for her in the dark bedroom.

'You had a good time tonight,' he said.

She flopped on the bed, drunk and exhausted. 'I did.'

'My turn to have a good time.' He reached for her, and she felt tired at the thought of having to make love.

'Can it wait until morning, Rupert? I'm so tired.'

'No, it can't,' he said through gritted teeth, and violently pulled her dress off her shoulders. 'I brought him here, you owe me.'

She heard cloth rip and went very still. He was determined, and she hadn't the energy to convince him to let her sleep.

'You were so beautiful tonight,' he muttered in her ear as he pulled himself on top of her roughly, almost as though he wanted to punish her. 'So fucking beautiful.'

She closed her eyes and thought of Hollywood.

CHAPTER TWENTY-SEVEN

Viktor had feared he would end up here.

At first he had gone to the address on the little white card, but the two young men living at the apartment had never heard of Lena. He cursed himself. He had been on a bus since dawn, believing that seeing her in person was the only way to do this right. She could ignore letters, hang up on phone calls, but his physical presence would ensure she didn't reject him. Standing out the front of that apartment building, he had considered what to do, and knew the only option was to go to see Ivan and Stasya, his brother and sister-in-law.

And so here he stood, about to knock on their door. He was sticky with sweat from the walk and had to catch his breath. The long grey hallway was dim under broken lights, the linoleum floor was cracked and scuffed. Ivan would likely refuse to talk to him; the rage in his blood at Viktor's abandoning his children, never contacting his family again, would make all his veins swell. Viktor would stand there and take it. If it meant making contact with his rich daughter, then it was worth it. Viktor's opinion of himself was so low, nobody else's opinion could hurt him.

He rapped. Waited. Footsteps inside. Then the door opened and a familiar, pale face peered out at him. It was Stasya. She had been worn down by the years, but she had never been beautiful in the first place so the change was not startling. In an instant, her mouth had turned down and the door was closing again.

'Wait, Stasya,' he said.

'What do you want?'

'To see my family.' He noticed her knuckles were white where she gripped the edge of the door. 'Please, let me in. I know I've done the wrong thing, but I want to do the right thing now.'

She opened the door and gestured that he come in and sit on the sofa. The apartment appeared little changed from when he'd last seen it, only dingier from years of use. He sat, looking around. 'Is Ivan at work?'

Stasya remained silent, came to stand over him. 'How do you number your regrets, Viktor? Do you have room for more?'

A tickle of unease started in his belly. 'What do you mean?'

Stasya marched to the teetering bookcase, pulled down a clay jar and threw it at him. It landed in his lap. 'There's your brother,' she snarled.

'What?'

'Ivan is dead. He has been dead for twenty years.'

Shock hit him in a wave. His brother had been dead for twenty years? How could he not know somewhere in his gut? He had willingly turned his back on his children, his brother, his mother, for Ulyana, but in some foolish fog he'd imagined they'd all go on living forever, that if he changed his mind he could come back and pick things up where he'd left them. The finality of Ivan's death weighed heavily on him. He gently picked up the urn and offered it to Stasya, feeling genuinely ashamed for the first time in his life.

'So who are you feeling sorry for, Viktor? Yourself or somebody else?' she said as she returned the urn to the bookshelf.

'I . . . I know I've been a fool. I know I've been a bad father. But all that is going to change. News of my brother's death is only part of the punishment I deserve for what I have done. I need to make things right in my life.' He hoped he sounded sanctimonious enough. From what he remembered, Stasya was a sanctimonious woman. 'I want to contact my daughters.'

'Forget it.'

'You should not stand in my way. I am their father.'

'They don't want to see you.'

'That isn't true.'

He pulled out the little white card with Lena's name on it and handed it to Stasya. She peered at it, then went to fetch a set of glasses. Standing by the sofa, she read the card. Considered it a while.

'You see. She wants to find me.'

'She wanted to. I know that. For a long time.'

'I've had this only a few years. She can't have changed her mind that quickly.' He tried a smile on her. 'Please, just give me her address. I'll pop over and see her, and you needn't be involved any more.'

Stasya began to laugh. 'Oh, it isn't walking distance.'

Viktor's heart fell. Had Lena moved to Moscow? Had he come all this way for nothing? 'Where is she?'

'In England,' Stasya said. 'Married, with two children. I'll get you her address.'

England. He couldn't just show up on her doorstep there. He wanted to ask Stasya if Lena was rich too. 'What about Natalya?' he asked cautiously.

Stasya had moved to the kitchen, where she was copying down Lena's address from a small cloth-bound book. 'Natalya never asked about you. I won't give you her address.'

'Is she married?'

'She's engaged. Living in London.' Stasya wasn't letting anything slip about Natalya's fame and wealth.

'And your girl, Sofi? Is she in England too?'

'France. Married with a little boy. Nikita.' For the first time, Stasya smiled as she indicated a chubby baby in a photo stuck to her tiny fridge. 'She's a good daughter, she sends me money. I've bought my own stove now.'

She approached him, offering him the piece of paper with Lena's address on it. 'I'm only giving you this because you showed me that card. I believe in my heart that Lena does not want to see you, so it would be better if you didn't make contact. The girls have their own lives now, they don't need you turning up like a ghost.'

'I'll let Lena decide. I'll write to her.'

'She won't answer.'

That was what he was afraid of. He needed to show up in person, beg forgiveness. But then, how was he to get to England? Ulyana had a little money put aside. She'd never mind if he borrowed it, surely. It was a good investment for their future, because once he got hold of Natalya, he could ask her for money. Her poor old papa. She'd likely give him thousands.

'I can see what you're thinking, Viktor,' Stasya said.

'You have no idea,' he replied. He read the address. Briggsby. Where in hell was that? He'd have to take a few months to organise his trip, learn to read English. 'Don't tell her I've been,' he said.

She smiled as though she knew the answers to everything. He wanted to spit on her.

'Don't worry, I won't. She's been disappointed enough by you in her life,' Stasya said. 'I won't make her any promises.'

He folded the address and slid it into his pocket. 'Well, thanks for your help, Stasya. It's been nice to see you.'

'Rubbish,' Stasya said. 'Go. Pay me back by making sure I never have to see you again.'

Viktor shrugged and rose. That was an easy enough request to comply with.

Nikita loved the park, so Sofi took him every afternoon. Along Grande Rue and past the statue standing at Place du Marché, where Nikita always demanded to stop, his little hands flapping as he bounced in the pushchair. She had to push him around and around its weather-worn stone column while he gazed upwards, transfixed at the way the figure of the little boy on top swirled into the sky. Summer was giving way to autumn, and already the smell of burning leaves hung over the grey stone streets of the village. Out through the towering front gate and into the château parklands, where the leaves were turning and loosening, set free by chilly gusts. Along the dirt paths between rows of tightly packed ash trees, their leaves making a last stand against the sunlight. Finally, she came to a stop at a children's playground, the play equipment standing empty. She released Nikita from his pushchair and took him to the swing.

He had just celebrated his first birthday, and had started to pull himself up to stand. Walking was still a long way off, which disappointed Sofi a little. They were due in London in three months for Winter Gathering, and she hoped to have him toddling around in the photos. But what he lacked in physical ability, he made up for in mental acuity. He could repeat almost any word that Sofi said.

She took him down from the swing and he flapped his hands and made a frustrated noise.

'Roundabout?' she asked.

'Row-d-bow?' he mimicked, copying her exact inflection.

She took him to the roundabout. He didn't like to ride it, but he liked her to spin it for him so he could watch it go around. He sat on the grass, his eyes fixed on it. She gazed off over the park. Another mother arrived with her little boy, who promptly started swinging like a monkey on the bars and jumping about shouting.

'How old is your boy?' Sofi asked her.

'Fifteen months. Yours?'

'Twelve months,' she replied, gazing at her dear baby. He was so peaceful. No screaming and monkeying around. He never gave her any trouble. She grew tired of spinning the roundabout and collected Nikita to bundle him back in the pushchair.

'Mama needs a walk,' she told him. 'She has a big decision to make.'

Off again into the clear, crisp afternoon. It had been a busy year. Orders had started pouring in around March, with boutiques stocking up for summer. Julien had convinced her not to turn work down, but to take on an assistant instead. And so she had hired Francette, a nimble-fingered nineteen year old who lived on the next street. She managed the tedious coiling once the designs were ready; finished the pieces with clasps, hooks, loops and jumprings; strung necklaces to Sofi's specifications; and took care of all the packaging and posting of orders. It freed Sofi's time up to indulge in designing, sourcing stock, making nice with her clients on the telephone. She made sure that she kept a hand in making things, of course. She was a craftsperson who had to use her hands. Julien took care of Nikita in the mornings, usually, while Sofi took him in the afternoons. Except for the last month: Julien had been away in New York, on a residency for a prestigious gallery. He would be away another three weeks yet, and then next year . . .

Well, next year was the problem.

Julien had been invited to Sydney for six months. Sofi didn't want to go, but nor would she stop him. The separation wasn't really a problem for them. They were both able to take the long view: six months was not long when compared with a lifetime, and Nikita was very little and unlikely to remember Julien's absence. They trusted each other, and were well-off enough now to afford daily phone calls. At least that was what she told herself.

But the real problem was that she would have sole care for Nikita, and Rosemary Simons had approached her once again. She wanted five hundred pieces, she wanted to give Anastasia Designs a special corner of each Chantilly store, she wanted to do a feature in the autumn catalogue.

And so Sofi stood on a threshold. She tried not to think of it as a choice between her career and Julien's, because Julien had not asked her to give anything up for him. Though he must have known, surely, that if he didn't go to Sydney then she could say yes to Rosemary readily. Nor did she want to think of it as a choice between work and Nikita, because only Nikita could win. She could hire more staff, but how many more people could be working on her jewellery before it wasn't handmade by Sofi Chernova any more? As well as the order for Rosemary, she had her regular clients to provide for. The quality of the pieces had to remain paramount. So should she hire a nanny? The thought made her want to cry. Somebody else looking after her Nikita? Somebody doing it for payment not love?

She would just have to work harder, that was the answer. Longer hours at night when Nikita was asleep. Get up earlier in the morning.

Bring her notebook to the park to rough out designs while Nikita watched the roundabout. She could do it. It would exhaust her, but Nikita would only be little for a brief time, and opportunities had to be grasped when they appeared.

Sofi stopped and leaned over the pushchair. Nikita gazed up at her with his clear, dark eyes. He was still not a particularly smiley baby, which proved Sofi's point that, all along, he had displayed his serious nature. 'What do you think, little man?'

'Dittle ma?'

She stroked his soft cheek and smiled at him. She would meet with Rosemary in London in December and she would say yes. But both Nikita and her business were too precious to entrust to others. She would have to do it all herself.

Rupert had been rumbling about renovating. Natalya had, of course, noticed that his new interest had started around the same time as Glynn Kendrick's offhand joke about the ageing decor of their apartment. It made Natalya feel sad for Rupert that he could be so easily upset by someone else's opinion. He normally seemed invincible. In any case, interior designers and decorators had been in and out for the last few months, offering opinions and carefully totalled quotations. Finally, he had settled on a project manager and the work was due to start shortly after the New Year.

It was Wednesday, and she wasn't needed on set. Rupert had gone to his office for a day of meetings – *Lonely Shores* was on the verge of selling into Denmark and Sweden – and she had been left with strict instructions to let the cabinet-maker in to measure up the kitchen.

'He's an old friend,' Rupert said. 'I have to have at least one person I know I can trust on the job.'

Natalya spent the morning phoning around nearby apartments to book a place for Sofi and Lena to stay over Winter Gathering. Last time they'd come to London, they had shared the spare bedroom here. But Rupert had been disapproving, and the apartment seemed very small and crowded. It would only be worse with builders coming and going, measuring things. She knew Lena couldn't afford to pay for her own accommodation, so if she just organised it and booked it, then there could be no arguments, no embarrassment.

The doorbell went, and she rose to buzz the cabinet-maker through. She hoped he wouldn't ask her any tricky questions as she hadn't a clue about what Rupert wanted. To her eyes, the kitchen looked wonderful as it was.

She opened the door.

'Hello,' he said. 'I'm Marcus.'

Natalya hadn't expected a young man. She had expected Rupert's 'old friend', a crusty tradesman in his fifties. Marcus was in his twenties, with an easy smile and short dark hair. He was taller than her by a mile, with long, lean limbs.

'Um . . . I'm the cabinet-maker?' he said, a tone of uncertainty in his voice.

She realised she hadn't spoken. 'I'm sorry, of course. You should come in. Rupert told me you were an old friend and I took that . . . literally.'

'Ah,' he said, stepping inside and wiping his work boots on the doormat. 'My father. Rupert went to school with him. He's semi-retired, I do a lot of the hard work these days.' He smiled at her. 'Can you show me to the kitchen?'

'Certainly. This way. But please, don't ask me what Rupert wants. He is in charge.'

'It's fine, he's given very detailed instructions.' He ran a hand along the granite bench. 'This is nice. Why does he want to change it?'

'I'm not sure,' she said, laughing. Then stopped herself. It was a betrayal of Rupert to laugh about him to another man. 'He knows what he likes and he always gets it,' she said.

Marcus turned and raised an eyebrow at her. 'I see. Well, I'd better get to work then.'

She left him to it, glancing back over her shoulder as he pulled out his tape measure. She came into contact with many good-looking men in her line of work, and Marcus was nowhere near as exotic and gorgeous as some of the models she had met. But there was something about him that appealed to her. He seemed real, not constructed. The muscles in his back weren't from hours of soulless repetitions in a heated gym but from real hard work.

He looked up, saw her watching him. Smiled.

Her heart flipped. Immediately, the panic set in. She turned, headed for the door.

'I have to go out,' she called. 'Just pull the door closed behind you. It will lock automatically.'

'No problem,' he said.

She took her handbag and coat off the stand near the door. Fresh, cool air would clear her head, stop her thinking thoughts that would get her into trouble.

CHAPTER TWENTY-EIGHT

It was one week out from Christmas. All day Lena had been singing carols, painting crowns, making costumes for the nursery Christmas concert the following evening. She was exhausted. The long street was cold and grey. It felt as though the sun had not even risen that day. Endless twilight.

Still, soon she would be on holiday. This year for Winter Gathering she was leaving Anna and Matthew at home with Sam. Giddy freedom made her steps light. As much as she loved them, to be in glittering London an unencumbered woman was a dream to be cherished. Natalya, bless her, had already booked them into a holiday flat at Bloomsbury. She couldn't wait to get away.

She noticed the figure on the street when she was still at the bottom of the hill. At first, she'd thought he was standing outside the neighbour's house, but as she drew closer she could see he hovered near her own front door. The lights weren't on in the house and she remembered that Wendy and Sam had taken the children to see Santa Claus at the toy shop on the High Street. Grandad wouldn't answer the door if the house were on fire. So, whoever the man was, he was waiting.

His back was turned to her, he wore a heavy coat and a grey knitted hat. She hurried towards him, the words 'Can I help you?' poised on her lips.

Then he turned.

Years fell away.

'Oh,' she gasped. His face, his bearing, everything about him was familiar. Her heart grew warm and tears burst spontaneously from her eyes. She rushed to him, a little girl again. 'Papa,' she said, embracing him, barely noticing his musty staleness.

'My daughter,' he said in Russian. 'I have found you at last.'

Lena was worried it was a dream. She went about ordinary tasks – turning on the radiators, boiling the kettle, hanging up Papa's coat – all the while battling the surreal conviction that she was somehow hallucinating. *Papa had come back.*

He sat silently on the couch, waiting for her to return with two strong mugs of coffee. Then she sat opposite him and stared at him. He was older than she remembered, of course, but still retained his strong, handsome face. He looked somehow noble, a deposed king. He sipped his tea, then made a grimace.

'Do you have anything stronger?'

She sprang to her feet. 'My mother-in-law has a bottle of whisky. I think she was saving it for a special occasion, but . . .'

'That will do nicely,' he said.

She found the whisky, poured him a glass. It *was* a special occasion, and if Wendy complained, then Lena would simply buy a new bottle to replace it. She wanted to keep Papa happy; she couldn't have him thinking he wasn't welcome.

Papa gulped the whisky and extended a shaking hand with the empty glass. 'Another, please?' he said.

Lena's heart ached for him. He was nervous; he had come all this way and he feared that he would be rejected. That would explain his trembling hands.

'Of course,' she said, filling his glass again, this time leaving the bottle on the coffee table in front of him. 'But you must tell me, Papa, what has happened with you? Where were you? Why didn't you come back?' Her voice cracked, and she took a deep breath to keep it even. She didn't want him to feel guilty.

And so, as dark crowded the windows, he told her the whole story. He had set out for Vladivostok as planned. At the time, the area was heavily controlled. He was never intended to be a fisherman. Rather, he had been recruited to an important position enforcing immigration control all along the coast. He wrote letters to them twice a week, but later discovered that the KGB had not passed them on, worried that the letters would alert their enemies to his whereabouts. Then his senior officer had made a terrible error and a boatful of Russian double agents had escaped through to Japan. He had blamed the error on Papa, who had been secretly tried in a dark room full of KGB officials, then sent to a prison camp in Siberia. There, he served out years and years in hard labour until the collapse of the Soviet Union. All the time, his thoughts had been for his daughters: how could he let them know he was alive, that he still loved them and thought about them constantly? Finally, he was freed. He had telephoned Stasya immediately, but she had refused to give him their address, refused to allow him any contact. She hadn't even told him his brother was dead. She had decided it would be best for the girls never to hear from him again. In the end, he had to pay Stasya money — twenty thousand roubles — before she would give him Lena's address.

Lena experienced a million different emotions during the telling of this story, and her heart was tired after it. Chief among them, though, was anger.

'You mean you would have found us sooner if it weren't for Aunt Stasya?'

'Years ago.'

Years she would never get back. Stasya had always been negative towards her father, and Lena could easily imagine her turning him away under the pretence of protecting her and Natalya. But that wasn't a decision for Stasya to make. Lena was a grown woman, with children of her own. Children who had never met their grandfather.

'Don't be too angry with her,' Papa said. 'She did what she thought was right.'

'She knew how much you meant to me,' Lena said, palming away a tear. 'It's unforgivable.'

He reached for the whisky bottle and, on impulse, she moved onto the sofa next to him and curled up against him. He didn't seem to know where to put his hands, eased his arm awkwardly away so he could refill his glass. Of course, he hadn't been particularly affectionate when she was a child either.

'I love you, Papa,' she said. 'I've always loved you. I waited, and waited, and waited . . .' Again she found herself crying.

'Hush. I'm here now. Don't cry.'

Then the door burst open and Sam and Wendy were herding the kids in. Matthew and Anna were bright-eyed from the evening air and Christmas excitement. Wendy spotted him first and froze.

Lena leapt to her feet. 'It's my father,' she said, English suddenly foreign again on her tongue. 'He's come back.'

Behind her, Papa stood. He nodded and said in pained English, 'I am Viktor Chernov.'

Lena introduced a guarded Wendy, a disbelieving Sam, and finally her two wide-eyed children; all the while, her heart hammered against her ribs. What if they didn't like him? What if he didn't like them? Would he leave again?

'This is your Dedushka Viktor,' she said to her children.

'Come here so I can look at you,' Papa said in Russian, arms outstretched.

Matthew seized Sam's leg and hid behind it. Anna hung back with her finger in the corner of her mouth.

'You haven't taught them Russian?' he asked.

'There's no need for it here in England,' she confessed. Wendy had talked her out of teaching them both languages; now she felt as hot-faced with guilt as a schoolchild confronted with her teacher's displeasure. 'If they want, they can learn it when they're older,' she squeaked.

'Are you staying long?' Wendy asked, ever practical.

'Little while,' he said. 'Maybe.'

'He'll have to come to London with me next week,' Lena said. 'I won't tell Natalya. It can be a surprise.'

'Well, then. If you'll be here for a few days, we'd better find you somewhere to sleep.'

As the days slipped by, Sam and his family were accommodating, if grudgingly so. As well as offering the sofa to sleep on, Wendy set an extra place at the table for Viktor every night, including for Christmas dinner. Sam's sister, Becky – visiting for Christmas – refused to speak to him at all, and complained to Lena that he smelled bad. Sam's opinion had been typically noncommittal.

'It makes you happy that he's here, doesn't it?' he asked in bed one evening, after sitting patiently by while Lena and Papa spoke rapid Russian to each other all night on the sofa.

'It's like a dream,' Lena tried to explain. 'As a child, I imagined the moment of his return over and over, until he became like a fairy-tale prince with magic powers.'

'You can see that he's not?'

'Of course,' Lena admitted. Her father had lost his hair, he drank too much and was bloated around the middle, he was little interested in taking baths and cleaning his teeth. 'But he's still my father. He's the thing that's been missing from my life for twenty years. The last piece in the puzzle.'

'I just don't want to see you get hurt,' Sam said.

'I won't,' she said. 'He's back now. The hurt is over.'

'So, you must sit here and wait for me,' Lena said, pulling out a chair for her father. The café was bright and noisy, the air heavy with the scent of ground coffee and frying bacon. Lena's stomach rumbled. She and Papa had left Briggsby for London that morning on the six o'clock bus. He had eaten at the bus station, but Lena had been too nervous.

'Would you like me to buy you a coffee?' she asked him.

'No, no. I need nothing. How long will you be?'

'I'll just go up and put my suitcase down and tell Natalya and Sofi that I have a surprise for them . . .' Here, she couldn't help smiling, even though she knew Papa's return wouldn't mean as much to her sister and her cousin as it did to her. 'Then I'll come and get you. We're just across the road.'

Leaving him was hard. She harboured a childish fear that he might disappear again, in a cloud of mist. 'Stay put, all right?'

'I'm not a child.'

She smiled. 'I know.' Then she turned and headed out of the warm café and into the grey London morning.

The truth was, she had no idea how Natalya would react. Surely, deep in her heart, she would have longed to see her father too? It was only natural. Natalya would warm to him; though Lena could understand Sam's suspicion of Viktor, or Anna's and Matthew's wide-eyed fear of him.

Now, as she crossed the street, she glanced over her shoulder to see if he was still sitting where she had left him. Of course he was. She took a deep breath and told herself to relax.

The holiday flat was on the second floor of a Victorian redbrick block. She knocked on the door and was immediately greeted by Sofi, who had arrived the night before, and Natalya. Hugs and laughter followed. Little Nikita sat on the floor in the sitting room, a toy truck upturned in front of him while he spun the wheels with his chubby hands. Lena took her suitcase to a bedroom, noting with pleasure that there was a third, unused, bedroom in the flat. Finally, ten minutes after her arrival, when Sofi was boiling the kettle and Natalya was helping Nikita spin wheels, Lena took a deep breath and said, 'I have a big surprise for you both. Especially you, Natalya.'

'You're pregnant again?' Sofi asked.

'How would that be a special surprise for me?' Natalya asked.

'She's pregnant and she wants you to adopt it.'

But Lena wasn't in the mood for jokes any more. 'Please, this is important. I just have to go downstairs for a minute. Wait here. On the sofa.'

Sofi switched off the kettle and, with a bemused expression, came to sit with Natalya and Nikita.

'Good. Thanks. I want everything to be perfect,' Lena said.

'This is very puzzling, Lena.'

'Everything will make sense in just a moment. Wait here.'

She dashed outside, heart pounding. He was still there. She could see his dark figure sitting very still inside the café. She waited for traffic, crossed the road. He looked up and saw her, picked up his little suitcase and met her on the street.

'All right,' she said. 'They're waiting for you.'

She noticed his hands were trembling. He was nervous too.

'Don't worry. It will be fine,' she said, grasping one of his hands and heading off while there was a gap in the traffic.

'Is this Natalya's house?'

'No, she's rented a flat up here for us this week. Her place is far grander.'

Lena had told Papa all about Natalya, and he had been surprised and proud. She had tried not to feel like the less remarkable sister: he had shown little interest in his grandchildren – not helped by the fact that they ran away every time they saw him – and she had no fancy career to brag about.

The stairs made him puff. She let him catch his breath as they stood on the welcome mat.

'Ready?'

'Yes,' he said.

Then she opened the door and led him in.

Sofi and Natalya were chatting quietly. They looked up. Natalya's jaw dropped. Sofi instinctively gathered Nikita into her arms.

'Surprise,' Lena said weakly. Her ears were ringing.

Natalya found her voice. 'What the fuck is he doing here?'

Lena bristled. 'He's back. He came to find us.'

Sofi stood. 'I'll make us all tea.'

'Natalya,' Papa said, advancing towards her. 'My daughter.'

Natalya held up her hand to stop him. 'Don't touch me.'

'Natalya, it's your father,' Lena said, her heart aching for Papa who looked bereft.

'He abandoned us, Lena. Have you forgotten that?'

'He didn't abandon us,' Lena said. 'He was taken by the KGB.'

Natalya rolled her eyes.

'There's more,' Papa said. 'I can't explain it to you now.'

'I'll tell her,' Lena said, touching his elbow. 'Later.' Lena didn't want to speak ill of Stasya in front of Sofi.

'Is he staying here with you?' Natalya said.

'If that's all right.'

Natalya stood. 'Fine with me. I'll go home.'

'Natalya –'

Papa interrupted. 'I understand,' he said. 'You need some time to consider all this.'

Natalya gave him an icy look. 'You do not understand me. I guarantee it.'

Sofi came out of the kitchen with Nikita on her hip to catch Natalya at the door. 'Natalya? Are you still fine to babysit Nikita in the morning?'

'Yes, but not here. My place. Bring him over.'

Sofi glanced at Papa. 'Yes, of course.'

Lena felt her mood sinking. They hated him. They didn't want to be near him. It wasn't his fault that he had been taken from them, kept from them for so long. Yet they were punishing him. And here he was offering his love so trustingly.

Natalya slipped out, closing the door firmly behind her. Sofi forced a smile. 'Now who would like tea?'

Lena steeled herself. Natalya didn't like it, but she would just have to get used to it. Papa was back and that was all that mattered.

CHAPTER TWENTY-NINE

Natalya was up early. She hadn't been able to sleep; yesterday's shock was still too fresh. Her father, like a resurrected corpse, shuffling into the room. Lena, child-eyed, worshipping him. Rupert had sensed her awake around three o'clock, and she'd confessed the whole business to him tearily. He had soothed her, told her that she was doing the right thing, that she was better off without him.

But was she? Was blood not more important than anything else? Should she at least give her father a chance to explain?

In any case, she could do nothing this morning. She had promised she would watch Nikita while Sofi went to a breakfast meeting with a big client. Natalya would never agree in a million years to watch Matthew and Anna, but Nikita was her kind of child: quiet, no fuss.

Rupert was dressed in casual pants and a loose shirt when he came into the kitchen. He'd put on a lot of weight this year, but Natalya tried not to notice.

'Coffee, darling?' she said.

'When does the small beast get here?'

'Nikita's not a beast. Even you would like him.'

'Doubt it. Don't get broody on me.'

Natalya shook her head. The thought of having to look after

someone else full-time, no matter how cute, horrified her. 'Don't worry about that.'

'All right, I'll have a coffee and I'll take it into my office. Don't let the little boy disturb Uncle Rupe, will you? I have a week of script outlines to finish by midday.'

Natalya set about straightening up the flat, putting dangerous or precious things out of Nikita's reach. She had bought some little board books for him, but it took an age to find the bag they were in amongst shopping bags she hadn't looked at since making her purchases. Lena and her father were on her mind, but she tried not to let those thoughts overwhelm her. She had to concentrate, be a good aunty. With a bit of luck, Viktor would do something unforgivable soon and Lena would come to her senses all on her own.

Within half an hour, Sofi was there. She looked flushed and nervous as she handed Nikita over.

'It's raining,' she said. 'A downpour. Terrible timing.'

'This is a big meeting, I take it?' Natalya said, reaching out to rub a raindrop off Sofi's forehead.

'I've taken a big order,' Sofi said. 'With Chantilly.'

'Really? That's wonderful.'

'It is, but it's eating up all my time and she wants to talk about extending the contract so I'm designing for her the following year too. I would have to drop a lot of my other clients. I'm going to have to talk to her about getting out her big chequebook.' Sofi laughed. 'I'm not great at that kind of discussion.'

Nikita sat happily in Natalya's arms. 'Ah, well. Aunty Nat will look after your boy while you take care of it. So one less thing to worry about.'

Sofi handed her a bag. 'Nappies, a drinking cup, a few biscuits and toys. His truck's in there. It's his favourite. If he gets grizzly, it will calm him down.'

'It's fine, don't worry.' She lowered her voice. 'Any news on my father this morning?'

'He was still sleeping when I left. Stayed up until midnight drinking. I've never seen anyone drink so much.'

'Where did he get the alcohol from?'

'I gave him some money.'

Natalya grimaced. 'You shouldn't give him money.'

'I know. But Lena has so little, and she would have given him her last penny.'

Natalya felt acutely Lena's vulnerability. She grasped Nikita's little hand, which was flapping about. 'You'd better go. Nikita's saying bye-bye.'

'Bye, darling,' Sofi said, kissing his cheek.

Nikita didn't struggle or cry in Natalya's arms, but sat perfectly still and content. When Sofi was gone, she took him to the sitting room. The rain beat heavily on the windows and she thought of Sofi trying to get to her meeting through the soaking streets. She appreciated fully her warm, dry flat. Nikita was not interested in the board books. He entertained himself with the lid of his nappy rash cream, while Natalya watched him. She was tempted to get Rupert after all, just so he could see that babies weren't all horrid. But before she could get up to knock on his office door, the doorbell rang.

Natalya went to the intercom. 'Yes?'

'It's Lena.'

Natalya's finger hesitated over the buzzer. She didn't want to see Viktor again. Then she remembered her earlier misgivings. It meant a lot to Lena. She buzzed them through.

It was a surprise to see that Lena had come alone.

'Papa's still sleeping,' she explained, prising off her wet shoes and leaving them at the door, 'and I thought this might be the only chance to get you alone.'

Natalya showed her through. Nikita had crawled to the bookshelf and was pulling down one of Rupert's blue books. She quickly moved him away, gave him his truck and he happily diverted his attention to that.

Lena glanced at him, then back at Natalya. She smiled. 'We need to talk.'

'We do.'

The rain was growing heavier now and it became very dark in the apartment. Natalya got up to switch on the lights.

'I think you're being very unforgiving of Papa. Wait until you've heard the whole story before you judge. He didn't abandon us.'

Natalya prepared herself to listen without prejudice. Lena repeated Papa's explanation of what had happened. The rain thundered over them as she spoke.

Natalya couldn't pinpoint at exactly which moment in the tale she realised it was ridiculously far-fetched. The little child inside her had certainly wanted to believe that her papa was an important security official for the KGB rather than an itinerant fisherman. And many people had disappeared under the old regime and wound up in Siberia. But if the idea that Stasya wouldn't pass on that he had tried to contact them was difficult to believe, then the idea that she had taken money for it was incredible. By far the most unbelievable thing, though, was Lena's gullibility.

'Lena,' Natalya said softly, when she had finished, 'do you actually believe this?'

Lena nodded. 'Of course.'

'Every word? The business about Stasya?'

'You know she can be a cross old thing. And she's poor and desperate. She takes money from Sofi.'

'She rejected Sofi's money for the first two years.'

'Which goes to show that she must be poorer now, more desperate.'

Natalya sat back, gazing at Lena, holding her tongue. Lena had been searching for her father her whole life, even if that search had more recently been buried under the pressures of family. Natalya knew that Lena had always felt there was something fundamental missing. Natalya remembered her sitting by the window of Aunt Stasya's apartment night after night, watching the street below. She had always been waiting for him to come back. Now that her wish had come true, she had to believe whatever was necessary to see her father in a good light.

Natalya knew then that she would have to get Viktor on his own, ask him some pointed questions, see if she could uncover his motivations. Because if her suspicions were proved right, she wouldn't let him play with Lena's heart this way.

'You know,' Natalya said, 'I think I'm still in shock.'

'I understand,' Lena said. 'And we must be careful what we tell Sofi. It would hurt her terribly to hear about what her mother did.'

Natalya hid her anger. 'You're right. I think I need some time alone with him. Would you mind if I took him out for a drink tonight?'

Lena smiled broadly. 'Not at all. I think that would be lovely. He's had plenty of time with me.'

'Good. I'll come by the holiday flat at around six.'

Lena's attention turned to Nikita. 'Family. It's so important, isn't it?'

'Now you sound like a greeting card.'

Lena laughed. 'I think I'm on a high.' She watched Nikita for a while, then said, 'He's not quite right, is he?'

Natalya was confused, thought she was still referring to their father. 'I don't really know.'

Lena pointed at Nikita. 'I work with children this age. All day, every day. He's not quite right.'

'Oh. What do you think is wrong?'

'He's been playing with the wheels of that truck for nearly half an hour.'

'He has a good attention span.'

'Watch this.' Lena bent down and took the truck away. Nikita sat there staring at the space where it had been without a murmur. 'Any ordinary fifteen month old would cry.' She gave the truck back, set it on its wheels. Nikita immediately turned it over and started spinning again. 'I think he might be autistic.'

Natalya was shocked. 'Surely not. He's so clever. He can speak Russian, French and English.'

'No, he can *say* Russian, French and English words. There's a difference. He's mimicking, not speaking. I've never heard him call for Mama, or point to something. He just . . . flaps.'

Natalya saw Nikita with fresh eyes now. His calmness, his concentration, his serious demeanour: not the product of a mature brain, but the product of a faulty one. At once, her heart went out to Sofi, who adored him so deeply, who thought he was so perfect.

'Sofi doesn't know, does she?'

'She has no idea.'

'You'll have to tell her.'

Lena sighed, reaching over to rub Nikita's head. 'I suppose I will.'

'Is he down?'

Sofi closed the bedroom door behind her and nodded at Lena. 'No trouble.'

'Would you like anything? Tea? A glass of wine?'

'A glass of wine. After the day I've had.'

Sofi slid onto the sofa, tucking her feet up under her. The television was on quietly, the rain still pounded outside. Natalya had taken Viktor out, which surprised Sofi greatly. She had assumed Natalya felt the same way that she did about him: mistrust bordering on loathing.

Lena returned with a glass of wine for each of them, and switched the television off. Sofi wanted to make a joke about the wine, about how they had better drink it quickly before Viktor got home and finished it off, but Lena had left her sense of humour back in Briggsby. So she sat silently, allowing herself to unwind.

Today had been one of the biggest days of her career. She had signed on for work commitments that she had no hope of honouring unless she hired two more assistants, which meant she needed to rent a workshop, maybe even a shopfront. The business was galloping beneath her and she couldn't stop it if she tried. She had to hold the reins tightly and let it go wherever it would. A lot of decisions remained to be made when she returned to France, in the three short months before Julien left for Sydney.

She turned all this over in her mind, then realised that Lena hadn't spoken for a long time either. Her cousin was staring into middle distance, chewing her lip. Sofi was worried about her. Viktor's return had filled her with manic happiness. There was only one direction her mood could go from here.

'Are you thinking about your father?' she said gently.

Lena turned, smiled. 'No, actually, I'm thinking about Nikita.'

Sofi immediately forgot Viktor, enjoying the proud glow that any mother feels when she knows that her child has been singled out as special. 'Really?'

Lena took a deep breath and ran her hands through her hair, pushing it off her face.

Sofi felt a niggle of uncertainty. 'What is it?'

'You know that I work with kids his age?'

'I thought they were older.'

'Some are. Mostly I'm in the toddler room. Sofi, Nikita's not . . . I think there must be something wrong with him.'

Sofi experienced a bolt of anger so strong that it knocked the breath out of her. Primitive and sudden. She couldn't remember feeling so furious in her life. 'Rubbish. He's a perfect darling.'

Lena didn't back down. 'I don't doubt that he's a lovely little boy, and I love him dearly. I love you dearly too and that's why I'm telling you this. You should see a paediatrician. I think Nikita is autistic.'

Sofi was speechless. Why was Lena doing this to her? Was she really so jealous of Sofi's calm, manageable little boy?

'I can see you're angry,' Lena said.

'I'm . . . I don't know what to say.'

'Then just listen.' Lena listed her evidence: Nikita's lack of affection, his indifference, his obsessive play, even his flapping – her dear little bird. 'Sofi, he is nothing like other children his age.'

'Every child is different.'

'Not that different.'

The rage bubbled up inside her again. 'Why are you doing this?' she demanded.

'Because I care about you. And Nikita.'

'How dare you put such ideas into my head? How dare you ruin everything?'

'I don't mean to –'

'I don't want to hear any more.' Sofi stood, accidentally knocking her wine glass over. Red wine splashed onto the pale blue carpet. She hurried to her room and closed the door behind her, fell onto the bed, hot-faced and teary.

She took a few deep breaths to calm down. Then stood and made her way over to Nikita's cot. He had flipped onto his tummy; his little bottom stuck up in the air as he breathed softly and rhythmically. Cold terror shook her inside as deeply hidden suspicions made their way to the surface.

Could the reason she was so angry with Lena be that her cousin was right?

The first thing Natalya had to do was fill her father with alcohol. This was not difficult. They found a table in a cramped corner of a pub at King's Cross. The noise and smoky warmth inside was a refuge from the pouring rain on the street. Autograph hunters plagued her at the bar. She signed for them, then asked for cigarettes – being in a smoky environment always made her crave – and sent them on their way. She was careful to sit with her back to the crowd, facing her father. She wasn't worried about anyone overhearing them as Papa could really only speak Russian with any success. He drank vodka, neat. She drank soda water, carefully removing the lemon. It was sugar she didn't need. They smoked together and talked about Russia, about the things she remembered from her childhood. She asked questions about her mother. It took five or six drinks before she felt his judgement was starting to get impaired. So she started asking him about his years away from his daughters.

The inconsistencies with the story Lena had related were immediate. His role with the KGB had been inflated, the number of letters he had sent every week grew, his troubles became more dramatic, his attempts to find his daughters more fraught. Finally, he related that he had paid Stasya one hundred thousand roubles for Lena's address.

Natalya pounced. 'One hundred thousand?'

He nodded solemnly, slurring over his words. 'She always hated me. I know you probably loved her, that she was a mother figure to you. But it was me she wanted, not Ivan. She was always jealous because I wasn't interested in her.'

Natalya, always the actress, hid the shuddering rage that grew inside her. How dare he come back into their lives, spreading poison between them with his careless self-serving lies, raising Lena's hopes and treating them all as though they were stupid? There was a long pause in their conversation. She butted out her cigarette, suddenly sickened by it. Her father was bleary, unfocused.

'You told Lena twenty thousand.'

His head jerked up. 'What?'

'You told Lena Stasya asked you for twenty thousand roubles.'

'I didn't want to upset her, make her think too badly of her aunty. I know she's soft. I told you the truth because you were always the strong one.'

Natalya opened her mouth to say, *Do you think I'm stupid?* But of course he did. *Everybody* did. 'How much to go away?' she said instead.

She watched as Viktor fought with his feelings. This was the moment he had been waiting for, but he hadn't expected it to come so soon. 'What do you mean?' he said. 'You can't pay me to go away. I only just found you.'

'How much?'

'I am very poor, and the hundred thousand roubles was the last of my –'

'Stop it. I know why you're here. I can see under your ribs and there's only black. Stop pretending you care because it insults me. This is really very simple. You leave Lena alone, I pay you money. Follow?'

He nodded, chastened.

'Name your price.'

'Ten thousand.'

'Roubles?'

He laughed. 'What do you think?'

Roubles were worth very little. 'Ten thousand pounds?'

'That should do it.'

She pulled her handbag up onto the table to find her chequebook, relieved that the business was over, but sick at heart for Lena. She would be mortally disappointed. Natalya wanted to kick him, not give him money. He was a wolf; he had cast a shadow over them all. With a bit of luck, he'd use the money to drink himself to death.

She handed him the cheque. 'You go now,' she said. 'Don't come back to the flat.'

'But my ticket, my passport.'

She reached into her bag, handed him the documents. 'I already thought of that.'

'My clothes?'

'You're a rich man now, buy new ones. Go away. That's the deal.'

He inspected the cheque, struggling with the English letters. The numerals seemed to satisfy him. 'I can't cash this until morning. How will I pay for a hotel tonight?'

'You won't. You can sleep on the street in the rain.'

The corner of his mouth turned up in a smile. 'You're a nasty little bitch.'

'It's in my blood.' She stood. 'Goodbye.'

He stayed put, sipping his drink, reading the cheque over and over. It was probably more money than he'd ever seen in his life. He didn't even look up as she left.

Lena woke to the sound of footsteps moving around in the sitting room. She checked her watch, which was lying on the bedside table. Somebody was up early. She doubted it was Papa. She'd gone to bed long before he came in. She couldn't wait for him to wake up so she could ask him how his evening with Natalya went. With that relationship repaired, Lena would feel a lot more positive about her future with Papa.

She rose, pulling on her robe. In the sitting room, Nikita sat on the floor next to Sofi's suitcases. It took Lena a moment to understand what was going on. She could hear Sofi in the kitchen, buttering toast. Lena picked up Nikita and went to find her.

'You're going?' she asked.

Sofi looked up. She had dark shadows under her eyes and Lena guessed that she hadn't slept. 'I think it's for the best,' she replied.

She put down her butter knife and took Nikita from Lena's arms. The gesture was possessive, defensive. Lena tried not to be offended.

'You're angry at me?' she said, wondering, guiltily, if her own anger at Stasya's deception had led to her talking to Sofi about Nikita's problems last night. She could have waited. She could have couched it more gently.

'This is not a nice situation,' Sofi said. 'But the most important thing at the moment is that I take Nikita home to Julien, and that we decide what to do about his . . . future.'

Her voice cracked, and Lena bit her lip to hold back her own tears.

'Sofi, I don't think that it's necessarily all bad. Nikita is –'

Sofi held up her hand. 'Don't talk to me again about what Nikita is or isn't. We will see somebody who is a medical expert, not a nursery worker.'

The comment stung Lena, as she assumed it was meant to.

Sofi picked up her toast, took a half-hearted bite and checked her watch. 'There's a train in twenty minutes. We'd better go.'

'This has never happened before,' Lena said, realising she sounded like a little girl. 'Winter Gathering has never ended early.'

Sofi softened. 'You and Natalya can have fun without me. Get to know your father better.'

A few minutes later she was out the door.

Lena switched on the television to wait for Papa to wake. Breakfast shows. She lay down, dozed a little. The clouds lifted outside her window. She tried to clear her mind of Sofi and her problems, her own guilt about causing them. It would be a nice day for a walk. Perhaps she could take Papa to Hyde Park. Rowing boats on the Serpentine. She frowned. Maybe all that was closed down for winter. Natalya would know. She thought about phoning her sister, but realised that if Papa was still sleeping, Natalya probably would be too.

She phoned home, spoke to Sam and the kids, had breakfast and tidied the kitchen. Showered, dressed, blow-dried her hair. Watched more television. By eleven o'clock, she felt the whole day was going to waste. She made him a coffee, knocked gently at his door. No answer.

Fear gripped her as she pushed open the door. *Please don't let him be dead; I only just got him back.* But the bed was empty. She drew the curtains. His clothes were still here, stale-smelling and strewn over the floor and furniture. But there was no sign of him. She felt uneasy, almost tripped over her feet getting to the phone to call Natalya.

It rang and rang, and then rang out. Now panic set in. They had both been killed; hit by a bus, murdered, *something*. Then there was a rattle of keys at the apartment door and Natalya was letting herself in.

'Where's Papa?' Lena gasped. 'Is he okay?'

'I'm sure he's fine.'

'Where is he?'

Natalya ushered Lena away from the door and to the little dining table. 'Sit down,' she said. 'I have something to tell you and you aren't going to like it.'

Lena sat down, feeling happiness fall away from her with a thud. 'Is he dead?'

'No.' Natalya laughed bitterly. 'He's not dead. He's alive. But he's gone.'

'Gone?' *Again?*

Natalya explained. But the explanation made no sense because Papa had searched for her for years because he loved her. Natalya was saying something completely different: that he had no doubt discovered Natalya was rich and had come looking for money. That was so typical of Natalya! To think she was so important. Papa had come to Lena first, and Natalya couldn't stand it.

'Stop, stop!' Lena said, putting her hands over her ears. 'This isn't true, not a word of it.'

'Isn't it? He took ten thousand pounds to go away.'

Lena was staggered. 'You made him leave?'

'He left willingly.'

'But you told him to!'

Natalya's words slowed, as though she were talking to a child. 'Try to understand, Lena. If he didn't want to leave, he wouldn't have taken the money.'

'He needed the money. He has nothing, and Stasya –'

'No, that is not true. He made that up.'

Lena felt as though elephants were stampeding through her head. She struggled to comprehend what had happened. Her world, just recently righted, had been tipped on its axis. By her sister.

'Lena, I know it's hard to accept, but he only came to us looking for money. Now he has what he wants, he is gone. In time you'll see we're better off that way.'

Lena couldn't bear to look at Natalya any more. Her well-kept hair and her glossy thinness. 'How tidily that all ended. I didn't even get a chance to say goodbye.'

'It's for the best. You were vulnerable. I protected you.'

'I'm not a child!'

'For God's sake, Lena. *He took the money*. He wanted ten thousand pounds more than he wanted you. I know you don't want to hear that, but it's true.'

The words hung in the air a while, and it seemed that time had stopped. Her heart denied what Natalya was saying. There was more to it. He would get in touch, he would explain. In the meantime, she didn't want to hear another word from her traitorous sister's mouth.

'I'm going home,' she managed. 'Winter Gathering is over.'

CHAPTER THIRTY

*I*n two months, Sofi and Julien had taken Nikita to six medical practitioners. Questions were asked, heads were shaken, all were reluctant to make a diagnosis. 'He's very young.' 'Bring him back in a year.' 'I'm not confident, perhaps you should see someone else.' They had been passed off, or passed up the line, so many times that Sofi began to secretly believe that there was nothing wrong with Nikita at all. A dangerous belief. Once Lena had pointed it out, the evidence was right in front of her.

This morning, they had arrived at the offices of Dr Louis Anjou, a developmental paediatrician in Paris. He was considered one of the best in the country. The call to say they had an appointment had only come the previous day. A cancellation. They had risen at five to be ready in time for the long drive. She'd been unable to eat breakfast, because of both the early hour and the serious business. She choked down half a piece of toast that felt like it still sat wedged in her gullet. Julien had managed coffee, toast, and even fried an egg, leaving the pan in the sink for their return.

After an hour of asking Sofi and Julien the same questions, of observing Nikita and interacting with him, Dr Anjou finally sat down at his desk and quietly scribbled on his notepad.

Sofi waited. The clock seemed to tick deafeningly. Julien squeezed her hand tightly and she gave him a weak smile. Still she held out hope that the doctor would declare Nikita's behaviour within the realm of normal.

The doctor dropped his pen and looked up. Sofi held her breath, concentrating very hard so she missed nothing of the French.

'It's clearly autism.'

She hadn't realised she would cry, but great hot tears spontaneously popped from her eyes. Dr Anjou patiently offered her a box of tissues. He was talking again, and Julien was asking questions, and she had lost the thread of the conversation in her distress. She gathered Nikita up, sobbing. He was indifferent to her tears. She tried to drop back into what was being said.

'It is too early to tell if his speech is impaired, but the speech repetition would indicate that it might be. He doesn't ask for things, or name things. He simply echoes what is said to him without understanding.'

Sofi interjected. 'How do you know he doesn't understand?'

The doctor turned to her patiently. 'Ask Nikita if he wants a drink.'

Sofi tried to catch Nikita's attention. 'Nikita, do you want a drink?' she said in English.

'Wan-a-dink?' he replied, mimicking her inflection.

She looked at the doctor accusingly. 'You see?'

'No, I'm afraid you don't see. All he has done is repeat what you said. If you don't give him a drink now, he won't cry, or whinge, or pull on your blouse and say Mama. Because he never wanted one.'

Sofi waited. Silence stretched out. Nikita continued to play happily with his hands. The doctor was right.

Julien touched Sofi's hair. 'It's all right, my dear. We'll work this out.'

Sofi couldn't speak, but she did manage to think how easy it was for Julien to be confident when he was going away in a month.

He turned to the doctor. 'Is there anything that can be done?'

Dr Anjou flexed forward, a gleam in his eye. 'Oh, yes. Absolutely. Many doctors will tell you it's a hopeless case, but I certainly will not. That is why I like to diagnose before two years of age, if I can. Others will hold off. By the time a child is three, it can be too late to help them. Little Nikita is a calm boy with a good brain. With early intervention, he should do very well.'

'Are you saying he can be cured?' Sofi said, new hope tingling through her body.

'No, not cured. But autism can be managed in some cases.' He scribbled again, tore off a page from his notepad. 'Here are some books that can help for a start. Make no mistake, it is extraordinarily time consuming but the results can be very encouraging.'

The doctor and Julien talked again for a few more minutes, while she held Nikita, smelling his soft hair and rocking him gently. She had an urge to grip him tightly, to stop him from falling away from her, into a place she couldn't find him. But it was too late for that. No matter how tightly she held him, she couldn't make this condition go away. The conversation was winding up, their appointment was nearing its end, and Sofi had one more question to ask.

'Dr Anjou,' she said, her voice shaking, 'will Nikita ever love me?'

She saw, from the corner of her eye, Julien turn away and pinch the bridge of his nose against tears. The doctor reached out and touched her hand.

'Every autistic child is different,' he said. 'I can't say for certain what this diagnosis will mean for Nikita and his future. But he probably loves you, even if he hasn't the ability to show it.'

Afterwards, Sofi and Julien sat inside a café at Les Halles; Nikita sat happily in Sofi's lap playing with a straw. No, not happily. Sofi had to admit she no longer knew if Nikita was happy or just in his own world. They didn't talk for a very long time. Sofi turned her options over and over in her head. When the answer came, she was surprised she hadn't thought of it before.

Finally, Julien said, 'Should I cancel Sydney?'

'No,' Sofi said immediately.

'What about your big order? If Nikita needs extra attention . . .'

'Who gives up their career, do you mean?'

'Yes. That's what I mean.'

Sofi wondered that he could still go so easily, that he didn't want to stay and be with them at this time. But then, Julien travelled. That was the nature of his work.

'Neither of us has to give up anything,' she said. 'I've had an idea.'
'What is it?'
'I'm going to Russia. I'm bringing my mother back with me.'

The renovations started in the New Year, but Natalya and Rupert were hardly ever home to be bothered by them. They would leave for the set first thing in the morning, then come home to find a wall had been knocked through, their lighting had been replaced, or new wardrobe doors had been fitted. Rupert had settled on a Japanese-inspired design, so there was rice paper and bamboo everywhere. It wasn't until the second week that Natalya saw Marcus, the cabinet-maker, again.

She wasn't needed on set, and Rupert was bustling about with the phone glued to his ear, organising meetings. Marcus showed up and started pulling apart their kitchen. Natalya stayed well away, studying her script in the bedroom. She was drawn to the door to listen, however, when she heard Rupert saying in a startled voice, 'Who are you?'

'I'm Marcus. John Pringle's son.'

'Ah. I'd thought John was coming.'

'He doesn't do it any more. Getting too old,' Marcus laughed.

Natalya winced. Rupert wouldn't like that comment: Marcus's father was the same age as him.

Rupert was at her door a few minutes later. 'Come on, we'll go out. I can't bear all this noise.'

He herded her out the door as though she were a prize cow that he didn't want anyone else to see. Marcus saw her and called out a cheery, 'Hello.' She was wise enough not to answer.

Rupert wasn't comfortable the whole week that Marcus was in their kitchen. He made excuse after excuse for them to be out of the apartment together, and even started talking about checking into a hotel for the remaining time. She caught glimpses of Marcus, his lean, hard body at work in the kitchen, but didn't speak a word to him. He probably thought she was rude. Better he thought she was rude than Rupert thought she was flirting with him.

Finally, the kitchen was finished and Marcus was gone. Natalya was relieved. Electricians moved in, new appliances appeared. Their wedding was approaching and Natalya was consumed with the preparations. Choosing from vast menus of flowers, place cards, food options and hymns. She wanted very badly to discuss her choices with Lena, but Lena wasn't taking her phone calls. She had phoned Sam three or four times, spoken to him secretly to ask if Lena was cooling off. He regretfully told her no, but that he was watching her closely. As usual, behaving like the perfect husband. Natalya had never known her sister to be so angry, and as the weeks went by she grew less and less convinced that Lena would simply cool down and then call her and everything would be right again. Damn her father. In one short visit, he had caused enormous damage.

One cool, clear March morning, four months to the day from her wedding date, Natalya had the morning off work so she could go to her second wedding-dress fitting. She was just about to leave when the door buzzed.

'Hello?'

'It's Marcus Pringle. The cabinet-maker.'

'Oh,' she said. 'Come up.'

In the few seconds it took him to arrive at the door, she should have called Rupert out of the shower. Instead, she went to the nearest mirror and checked her hair and make-up. He knocked, and she opened the door. He stood there dressed in a black T-shirt that hugged his arms and a pair of worn jeans. Not bleached and sandpapered and grated to a stylishly distressed effect in a designer's workshop, but worn against his body for years.

'Good morning,' she said, trying not to sound too bright. She heard the shower stop.

He was cool with her, no doubt because she had been rude to him in the past. He probably thought she was a spoilt princess. 'The electrician called. I have to move one of the kitchen cupboards.'

'I'll get Rupert,' she said, opening the door for him to come in and backing away. 'Go right in.' She turned, surprised at how hard her heart was thumping. It wasn't just because she found Marcus so attractive; it was because she harboured a primitive fear that Rupert could read her mind. 'Rupert! The cabinet-maker is back.' It wouldn't do to use Marcus's name; that would indicate familiarity, even intimacy.

Rupert met her in the hallway, buttoning up his shirt. 'Are you off now?' He seemed overly keen for her to leave.

'I am.'

He kissed her forehead. 'Just be careful what you eat. You can't put on an ounce between here and July the nineteenth. Not just for the dress, but for the photos.'

'I know.'

She slipped out of the apartment without even a backwards glance at Marcus.

Rupert had chosen her wedding dress: a one-off made by a young British designer near Marble Arch. She was giving it to them for free in exchange for the publicity of the *BritSoap* exclusive. It was easily the most beautiful dress Natalya had ever seen: strapless ivory silk laced with ribbons, and a fitted bell-like skirt that was beaded with seed pearls around the hem. Whenever she wore it, she felt like a goddess. She spent the hour with the designer pinning it and adjusting it gazing at her reflection in the three tall mirrors that surrounded her. When the designer let her go and she could put her own clothes back on, she felt dull and small.

She wandered back home along Oxford Street, gazing into the cheap shoe shops that Rupert would never let her shop in. She heard her name being called and didn't immediately pay attention: probably just a fan. But then she realised it was her real name – not the anglicised 'Natalie' or the confused fan's usual 'Tatiana' – so she turned. Roxanne, the wife of the director Glynn Kendrick, was waving and hurrying towards her.

'Hello!' she said, air-kissing at least three inches from each of Natalya's cheeks.

'How lovely to see you.'

'I'm shopping,' she said, lifting up hands full of bags as evidence. 'You?'

'I was at a fitting for my wedding gown.'

'Exciting!' Then Roxanne's pretty mouth turned upside down. 'We were so sorry that you couldn't take the part.'

Natalya was confused. 'Sorry?'

'Glynn was particularly. He had his heart set on it.'

She was aware that her blood was tingling, afraid of what she was about to hear. She was careful, though, not to ask outright what Roxanne was talking about in case she clammed up completely, realising she had spoken out of turn. 'He did? I didn't know that.'

'Oh, he was, I'm serious. He had to cast an American actress who's taking *forever* to nail the accent.'

The movie. She was talking about the Cold War movie that Glynn Kendrick was making, the one that he had thought about casting her in. How had this happened? She hadn't turned the part down; she hadn't even been offered it. She clenched her hands to make them stop shaking.

What had Rupert done?

Natalya faked a conciliatory smile. 'But Glynn understood why I couldn't, didn't he? He didn't take offence?'

'Of course not. A contract is a contract, and if yours with *Lonely Shores* doesn't allow long breaks, then there's not much anyone can do about it. Though,' Roxanne dropped her voice to a stage whisper, 'I did wonder why Rupert didn't try a little harder to let you go. It's his show after all.' She shrugged. 'I shouldn't say so. He probably had his reasons.'

'Oh, yes, he did. Never mind.' Natalya could barely manage to hide her fury under a polite veneer. Rupert had turned down her first serious offer of a movie role. Without even mentioning it to her.

'Hey, would you like to go and get a coffee?'

'I'm sorry, I can't. I have to dash home now. There are . . . things to . . . I need to go.' Her voice shook. She had to get away from Roxanne before she let her guard down. Before she screamed or cried or raged right here on Oxford Street.

She managed a goodbye, then hurried away, began to run down North Audley Street, nearly getting hit by a car as she crossed the road. No rational thoughts entered her mind. She just wanted to get home and shriek at Rupert. She tried to imagine what she would say to him, but words wouldn't form. Murderous fury bubbled inside her. How could he? *How could he?*

As she raced across the foyer to the stairs, she realised she was crying. She palmed the tears away, taking a deep breath. She opened the door with a bang.

'Rupert!' she shouted. 'Rupert!'

But Rupert didn't appear. Instead, Marcus stepped out of the kitchen with an alarmed expression on his face. 'Are you all right?'

Natalya tried to contain herself. She'd forgotten he was here. 'Where's Rupert?' she asked.

'He went out. I'm afraid I was making a lot of noise pulling the cupboard out.' He grasped her wrist tentatively. 'You look a mess, Natalya. What's happened? Can I help you?'

She looked down at his hand on her wrist, her heart thudding madly.

He quickly pulled away. 'Sorry,' he said.

And she thought of the perfect way to get back at Rupert. She flicked her long hair off her shoulder.

'I need you to hold me,' she breathed. It was a line from the soap, but it worked just as well in real life.

Marcus gulped once, then swept her up against his chest with his strong arms. 'I can do that.'

His lips found her ear, her cheek, her mouth. Hot pleasure sang through her. He was so hard and young and alive. Her hands scrabbled at his T-shirt, pulling it over his head. Her own buttons were popping off as he wrenched her blouse open. Skin against skin. She couldn't remember the last time she had enjoyed undressing, the last time she had enjoyed the caress of hands over her body. He picked her up and took her to the sofa, pressed his body down on top of her. Her skirt around her waist, her underwear cast on the floor, his jeans around his ankles. She closed her eyes and leaned her head back, lost all thoughts of disappointment and anger and fear and guilt in surrendering to the white-hot demands of desire.

Marcus lived in a little flat above his workshop in South London; much safer than meeting in Rupert's apartment.

Natalya was living in a dreamworld, and she did realise it, however dimly. In the evenings she sipped fine wine with Rupert while they went over wedding plans and talked to each other as though everything were normal. They took the car to work together, ate together, made love together precisely as they always had. But the moment Rupert was out – meetings for foreign sales, story-line and script meetings, business lunches, or at the solarium – Natalya was climbing into a cab and arriving at Marcus's workshop. There, he would drop everything and rush her upstairs, love her hard and sweet while he still smelled of sweat and sawdust.

Neither of them were foolish enough to talk about love. Love didn't enter into the equation. Their relationship was all about lust, the appetites of the body not the heart. The other thing she loved to do with Marcus was to eat. He was a marvellous cook, and made her buttery, garlicky, creamy pastas for lunch, complaining that she was too thin.

Too thin! She'd been bursting the seams of her wedding dress at the last fitting!

It was food, not sex, that she was indulging in when her mobile phone rang at Marcus's one spring afternoon. Her spine went cold with fear as she raced to her bag, chewing and swallowing rapidly, to answer it.

'Hello?'

'Natalya, where are you? I came home early and you're not here.'

She turned to watch Marcus, who sat shirtless at the sunny kitchen table swirling fettuccine onto his fork. 'I'm just out looking in the shops.'

'It's very quiet for the shops.'

'I've stopped for lunch.'

'Where are you? I'll come and meet you. We haven't had lunch out in a week.'

'Sorry, darling, I'm just finishing. I'll be home soon.'

He seemed to accept her at her word and Natalya knew this was a warning sign in itself. He suspected her, of course he did. He had suspected her in the past for no reason. She would have to be careful for a little while.

As she put the phone away, Marcus came up behind her, closing his hands over her breasts. 'Do you have time? Before you go home?'

'No. He's on to me.'

'Is that such a bad thing?' he said, close to her ear, his breath tickling her neck. 'You can't marry him. Not now.'

She slid out of his embrace. 'Well, I can't marry *you*.'

'I'm not asking you to. I'm just saying, you don't love him. So don't marry him.'

'I have to go,' she said, kissing his cheek. 'I'll call in again. As soon as I can.'

'I'll be here.'

She slipped out to the street and hailed a cab, thinking about Marcus's words, his simple solution. *So don't marry him.* He couldn't see. She was on a train, speeding far too fast to jump off. What she wanted didn't matter any more. A magazine had bid for the photo exclusive, a designer had provided a couture gown in exchange for publicity; every person involved with the wedding – the florist, the stationer, the gift-buyer, the caterer – had more say than she did. She couldn't stop the wedding, it had gathered too much momentum now.

'Where are you heading, madam?' the Indian taxi driver said to her as she climbed in.

Natalya cast off her sad thoughts, applied a brilliant smile. 'Mayfair,' she said, 'North Row. And you'd better be quick. Or else I'm going to be in big trouble.'

CHAPTER THIRTY-ONE

A sharp knock on her bedroom door. Lena quickly hid the bottle and the glass on the floor beside the dresser.

'Come in,' she called.

Wendy opened the door. 'Phone for you.'

'Not Natalya.' She wasn't speaking to Natalya, everybody knew that, but Wendy was likely to become starstruck if her sister phoned and do whatever she asked.

'No. Your cousin Sofi.'

Lena was surprised. She hadn't heard from Sofi since Winter Gathering. Lena, for her part, hadn't tried to contact anyone, her own wounds too raw for close examination. Her feelings for Natalya were straightforward: she was furious and blamed her for her father's departure. But her feelings for Sofi were complicated. There was guilt and shame for the way she had broached the topic of Nikita's development; but also anger and mistrust by association, because Sofi was Stasya's daughter.

She followed Wendy to the kitchen, where she picked up the phone. She glanced at the clock: 8 p.m. The children were fast asleep, Sam was at band practice. The voices and applause of Wendy's favourite game show drifted through from the sitting room.

'Hello?' she said tentatively in Russian. She always switched to Russian on the phone to Sofi or Natalya so Wendy couldn't eavesdrop.

'You were right. Thank you.'

Lena took a moment to understand. Then a keen sadness washed over her. 'About Nikita?'

'Yes.' Her cousin's voice was husky, as though she were fighting tears. 'Sorry it's taken me a while to talk to you about it. You must have been worried.'

Was she? Worried about Nikita? Or had all her energy been reserved for pitying herself? She pulled herself up to sit on the kitchen bench. The dinner dishes had been washed and left to dry, and the smell of roast chicken and potatoes lingered. It was always cold in the kitchen because there was no radiator here, so she pressed her feet on the front of the stove, hoping for some leftover warmth.

'What are you going to do?' she asked Sofi.

'I have to keep going. I love him so much, I . . . There are things you can do – intensive language development and teaching him how to be more sociable. But he'll never be normal, he'll never be in step with the world, and I might still be taking care of him when I'm eighty.' She laughed bitterly. 'You see? That's worse than having two at once.'

'What about your business?'

'I hope to go ahead with it. I need to more than ever.'

Lena paused a moment, trying to calculate the time she'd need to do both. 'Is Julien still going away?'

'Yes, he is. It's all right. I hope to have help.' Sofi's voice took on a sympathetic tone. 'Natalya told me what happened with your father.'

At mention of Natalya, Lena felt herself tense again. 'I'm sure she's only told you one side of the story.'

Sofi kept her words neutral. 'I'm very sorry if you were disappointed.'

Disappointed? How could that word possibly capture how she really felt? Rage: now there was a good word for the boiling, searing anger she felt towards Natalya. Grief: that adequately described this second loss of her father and all the inconsolable childhood sorrow that it had stirred up. Isolation: not having a single person close to you understand; having Sam say things like 'Cheer up, Lena', as though she'd lost her sunglasses, or having Wendy shrug and tell her she was probably better off without him.

But the king of all these feelings was inescapable self-loathing. She still wanted to believe that Natalya had been lying, that she'd told Papa to go away and he'd done it simply to keep the peace. That he was biding his time and would be in touch very soon. On the way home from work every day her heart pounded as she anticipated the mail, and then fell when she saw there was nothing for her. She was counting the days. She'd told herself that she wouldn't believe what Natalya had told her for one hundred days; she was giving her father one hundred days to keep her trust, to write to her and explain. Now there was less than a fortnight remaining. And she grew more and more afraid that Natalya was right: he *had* chosen money over Lena. Because she was unlovable, worthless. Hideously defective. All the same reasons he had left the first time.

'Lena?'

Lena realised she hadn't spoken for a long time. 'I'd rather not talk about it,' she said.

'I just hope you don't believe what Uncle Viktor said about Mama,' Sofi said. 'You know she would never do anything to hurt you. She loves you like a daughter.'

Lena couldn't hold her tongue. 'Sometimes people do hurtful things precisely because they love you,' she said. 'Because they think you're a baby who can't take care of yourself. And she never loved me like a daughter. Natalya and I were always very aware that you were her *real* daughter and that we came a distant second.'

Of course she regretted it as soon as she said it, and she blamed the three generous helpings of wine drunk out of a jam-jar glass in her room. Her special, secret treat on nights that Sam was at band practice.

Sofi was conciliatory. 'You're still very upset,' she said. The unspoken implication was, *You'll come round, you'll cheer up, you were always the emotional one, everything will go back to normal soon.*

Lena couldn't stand it: everybody professing to know her heart better than she knew it... There, she had already forgotten Sofi's bad news, caught up in self-pity. No wonder her father had left her.

'I have to go,' Sofi said quickly. 'Stay in touch.'

Ordinarily their phone calls ended with promises to send photographs, to phone on special occasions, affirmations of love. *Stay in touch* was very cold.

'Goodbye,' Lena said, before returning the phone to the cradle.

She slid down from the bench and approached the tapestry calendar that hung from a nail on the pantry door. Two kittens with enormous cross-stitched eyes stared back at her. She counted the days. Ten to go. And if those ten days should pass with no contact from her father?

Well, she was not too proud to contact him herself.

'You're a lazy, fat slob.'

Viktor opened one eye and trained it on the figure standing in the threshold of his room. Ulyana, dressed top to toe in new clothes, her hair freshly dyed, her fingernails tipped with gleaming white. His money had bought back some of her youthful beauty and here she was calling him a lazy slob. 'What the fuck?' he muttered. 'Let me sleep.'

'Get a job.'

'I don't need a job, I'm rich.'

'You won't be for long at this rate.'

'There's always more.'

Ulyana slammed the bedroom door shut. He heard her footsteps retreating as she headed out to work. She was just jealous. He was on holiday – a long, long holiday – and she had to work every day. Well, working was for fools.

Certainly, he could have spent his money another way. Taken Ulyana to Odessa for a holiday by the Black Sea. Bought a car or some new furniture. But to be able to walk up to his boss, tell her that she was a frigid bitch with a face like a hatchet... that was value for money.

He was tired. He needed a break.

Ulyana had been horrified at first, when he'd come home from England with all that money. 'But they'll want something from you,' she said. 'They'll want to stay in contact, be part of your life.'

'That's the beauty of it. They gave me money to go away.'

But it wasn't the entire truth. It was Natalya who wanted him to go away. Lena was a different matter, and it was Lena to whom his thoughts too often turned.

Viktor flopped over on his back and stared at the ceiling, cursing himself for the one note of regret and shame that wouldn't go away. Her soft eyes, her trusting affection. More than that, there was something about her that was familiar to him. A way of holding her mouth that he could feel in his own jaw, a quickness to laughter that he recognised from his own youth. He closed his eyes and tried to chase sleep. Damn Ulyana! Why did she have to wake him up? He banished his thoughts. Too late for regrets. Sentiment was for men less desperate than himself.

Lena decided to call Papa from a phone box. She didn't want Sam and Wendy to ask what she was doing, who she was calling; she didn't want the kids running about shouting and giggling in the background.

It was raining lightly when she left the nursery. All day she had been anticipating this moment, and her hands shook as she unfolded the small piece of paper with Papa's address and phone number written down on it in his own loopy handwriting. She'd asked him to write it down, that first evening he had arrived in Briggsby, when she'd been afraid he would disappear before morning. She placed the piece of paper on top of the phone, fed in some coins and dialled. Her heart thudded; she had rehearsed her first line over and over in her head. 'Hello, Papa, it's Lena. No matter what Natalya has said to you, you must talk to me and tell me the truth.'

Except the call wasn't going through. The phone didn't ring at the other end. She hung up and tried again, with the same result. From memory, she scribbled down Aunt Stasya's number below Papa's, counted the digits.

Papa's was shorter. There was one digit missing.

The familiar fear of her own inadequacy and unlovability rolled over her. Had he simply missed a digit by mistake when writing it down, or had he deliberately given her a false number because he didn't want to remain in contact with her? What was she to do now? Write a letter and send it off to this address, only to wait another hundred days for a reply? If it didn't come, would she assume again that it had been misdirected? Or would she finally accept that he didn't want to hear from her?

She looked at the piece of paper. Stasya's number. Of course! Papa surely must have left his address and phone number with her. All those years he had tried to find his daughters and she had refused to help; he must have left her with contact details.

Only . . . if Natalya and Sofi were right and that was just a story Papa made up; if he'd never really tried to find his daughters until he'd discovered somehow that one of them was rich; if he'd planned to target Lena particularly because he knew she'd be the softer touch . . .

Lena felt as though her ribs were caving in. Until Papa's arrival just before Christmas, she had been getting along without him. Perhaps she had even accepted, finally, that she would never see him again. For him to return and then disappear once more seemed unbearably cruel.

She leaned her head on the wall of the phone box. Her breath fogged against the glass. The rain had intensified and was running in rivulets down the panes. She steeled herself and phoned Stasya.

This time the line connected and her aunt answered the phone.

'Aunt Stasya?'

'Natalya?'

'No, it's Lena.'

There was a brief silence. Then Stasya said slowly, 'Lena, I hadn't expected to hear from you.'

Of course. Natalya had told Sofi about Papa's story, and Sofi had passed it on.

'Look,' Lena said, 'you and I don't agree on something important, and I presume you did what you did for good reasons –'

Stasya's voice became sharp, and with that sharpness Lena was reminded that she was the child in this relationship. 'I did nothing, Lena. He came, I gave him your address. I hadn't seen him for twenty years. He didn't know that his brother was dead, and nor did he care. Whatever nonsense he's told you is for his own benefit, because in the end that is all he cares about. There was honey on his tongue but ice in his heart.'

Lena gathered herself. She was a grown woman now, with children of her own. She wouldn't be spoken to this way. 'You may think what you like, Aunt Stasya,' she said. 'I just want you to give me his phone number or address or both. I'll make up my own mind about what to do with them.'

'I don't have them.'

Lena was staggered. The *liar*. How could she profess innocence about her part in this drama when she was lying again, right this moment?

'That isn't true. You must have them.'

'I don't. I didn't want them. I didn't want to see him or hear from him again. Why would I have asked for his phone number?'

'I realise you're doing this to protect me –'

'Oh, hush, you silly girl. He came to me out of nowhere, he was here for five minutes while I gave him your address – which I very much regret now, I might add – and then he was gone. There wasn't time for pleasantries and exchanges of numbers. Now, you can believe his ridiculous story if you choose, but I urge you to think about the many long years that I looked after you. He was not there.'

'He came as soon as he could!'

'Lena, I'm going to hang up now. I will not have this argument with you. I can't help you.'

Her voice grew desperate. 'If he comes again, or calls or –'

'Goodbye. I hope you come to your senses.' Stasya hung up.

'Damn!' Lena kicked the wall. Through her anger, she began to feel it. The horrible realisation that Stasya was telling the truth. Hearing her voice had conjured memories in Lena's mind: Stasya was warm, soft, practical but always caring, soothing scraped knees and the cruel taunts of school bullies alike, full of little wisdoms and complicated superstitions. Remembering such things made it almost impossible to continue to believe Papa's story. And much easier to believe Natalya's.

He wanted ten thousand pounds more than he wanted you.

She slipped out into the rain, turning her face up to it, letting it mingle with her tears.

CHAPTER THIRTY-TWO

Natalya was almost dozing in the car when a soft voice said to her, 'Excuse me, Miss Chernoff? You're home.'

Natalya roused, looked up. Streetlamps glowed in the dark. The city was almost quiet, just the faint hum of faraway traffic. It must be after midnight. The day had gone on and on. At the moment, Natalya's character was embroiled in a feud between two families. Tatiana was central to everything that was going to happen on *Lonely Shores* for the next six weeks, which meant long days of filming. She found herself wondering if Rupert was keeping her busy on purpose, so he could justify turning down the movie role. They still hadn't spoken about it. Natalya didn't want to bring it up because she was afraid she would sound weak or pathetic. She much preferred to go on pretending to be Rupert's perfectly behaved fiancée, while misbehaving badly with Marcus behind his back.

She thanked the driver and made her way up to the front door of the building, yawning vastly. Five hours' sleep, then back on set. It was cruel.

Upstairs, she was surprised to find the lights still on. Rupert was dozing into his chest in an armchair. The television flickered in front of him. She paused for a moment to watch him. Asleep, soft-faced, cheeks sagging under the weight of years. She could see that he was older than her father. Her stomach went cold. She couldn't marry him. But nor could she escape him.

She went to him, leaned over and shook him gently. 'Rupert?'

He sat up, shook his head. Glanced at the clock. 'You're very late.' Always, that note of suspicion. Even when he had decided on the scripts, he had organised the car, he was intimately acquainted with what went on at the set most days.

She perched on the arm of his chair. 'There was a lot of work to do.'

He reached up and stroked her cheek gently. 'You look tired, my dear.'

'So do you.'

'I was watching a movie.' He reached for the remote, switched the television off. 'Now I won't know how it ended.'

She laughed lightly, but couldn't help thinking that falling asleep in front of the television was something old people did.

'Natalya, I have to tell you something. I have to go to New York for a week. Without you.'

'When?'

'Thursday morning. I'm leaving at ten. You'll be on set. I have an American cable network interested in *Lonely Shores*. It's a big deal. You don't mind if I go without you?'

Natalya's mind was on fire with the possibilities. Rupert away for a week? Over the weekend? Marcus could move in for two days and make love to her in every room. In Rupert's bed, in Rupert's shower, on Rupert's desk. Her legs tingled just thinking about it. Marcus leaving his gorgeous impression on all of Rupert's things.

She pretended to pout. 'Don't go to any fashion shows without me.'

'I can't promise that.' He stood and stretched, his robe gaping to reveal his hairy belly. 'Come on, let's go to bed.'

She followed him obediently, allowed him to do what he wanted with her. Afterwards, he kissed her cheek and said, 'I love you,' before flopping over on his side to fall asleep.

'I love you too,' she murmured in the dark. Despite the late hour and her deep weariness, she lay awake a long time. Did she love him? Perhaps she did, although she sometimes hated him too. The wedding was eight weeks away now and despite her misgivings she knew she would go through with it. So he had turned her down for a movie? She was already living a life of glamour and luxury without Hollywood. Rupert took care of her. The nonsense with Marcus was a fling. She had to end it. While Rupert was away she would get it all out of her system; and then she would say goodbye to Marcus and prepare herself to become Rupert's dutiful wife forever.

Lena woke, head aching, and sat up with a start. The digital clock by the bed said it was eleven, and Sam wasn't in bed yet. He'd had a band meeting but should have been home by now. She rubbed her temples. Too much wine tonight. She'd started with a glass with Wendy over dinner. A second before the kids went to bed. A third, a fourth, and . . . a fifth? In her own room, while Sam was out. Or was it more? She'd managed to empty a bottle alone. It was cheap wine too, the type that left a salty aftertaste and was most likely to induce a headache.

She climbed out of bed, trying to fight the uneasy feelings about Sam's absence. Her threadbare robe was hung over the end of the bed. She slipped it on and opened the bedroom door. Immediately, she was aware of lights on elsewhere in the house, Sam's voice. Ah, so he was up late talking with Wendy. But she couldn't hear Wendy's voice. Just Sam's. Curious, she crept down the corridor and paused near the doorway to the sitting room.

'I know . . . I'll have to talk to her . . . Seems to be, but who can tell?'

Who was he talking to quietly on the phone this late at night? She drew closer to the kitchen, banged her shin on the coffee table. The noise alerted him to her presence. He said, 'I have to go. Bye.'

A rush of panicked jealousy. He was having an affair. He had to be. Why else would he hang up so quickly? Why else would he emerge from the kitchen and greet her cheerfully but nervously?

'Lena, you're up.'

'Who were you talking to?'

'Nobody important. Just band stuff. Let's go to bed.' He slid his arm around her and guided her towards the bedroom.

Sleep eluded her. She couldn't shake the conviction that he was lying to her, and that made her feel as though she were standing on a sand dune that was quickly eroding beneath her feet. She tossed and turned for a long time, then finally it occurred to her that if Sam had placed the call – which she couldn't be sure about, of course – all she had to do was press the redial button on the phone and she would know who he had been talking to. But now it was one in the morning, an impolite time to call anyone. Especially somebody who was not a mistress. She fought with her reservations for a little longer, then decided that she would get no sleep unless she did it right away. So she quietly rose and went to the kitchen.

Lifted the receiver.

Pressed the redial button. It beeped softly in the dark.

A long series of rings. Nobody was going to answer, it was too late. But then an answering machine clicked into life. A man's voice. 'Hello, you have reached the residence of Rupert Palmer and Natalie Chernoff . . .'

Lena's legs wobbled underneath her. *Natalya*. She dropped the receiver into its cradle and lowered herself to the kitchen floor. Why was Sam making late-night phone calls to her sister? She didn't know what to do. Wake him up and confront him? She racked her brain, but could not think of a single good reason that Sam would be talking to Natalya so privately and nervously. There was only one conclusion to draw, and the thought of it made her weak.

She got to her feet, made her way down the corridor and back to the bedroom.

'Sam?' Her voice broke and she started to cry.

He sat up, bleary and confused, and his arms went around her immediately. 'Hey, hey. What's wrong?'

'Why were you talking to Natalya?'

His body went stiff. 'What?'

'Are you having an affair with her?'

Sam sighed, pulling her close. 'No, no. Oh, Lena, don't think that for a second. I'd never do that to you.' He stroked her hair.

Her relief was tempered by suspicious puzzlement. 'Then why were you talking to her?'

'You wouldn't talk to her. Every time she called, I had to tell her you wouldn't come to the phone. She was worried about you, she asked me to call her every now and again to tell her how you're going.'

Lena's heart tensed. No, they weren't having an affair, but still it was a betrayal of sorts. Keeping secrets with her sister.

Sam sat back and looked at her directly. 'To be honest, Lena, I phoned her tonight because you're frightening me a little right now.'

'What do you mean?'

'You're miserable all the time, you drink too much . . . I've seen the empty bottles, I'm not stupid. Ever since that man showed up here –'

'My father?' she said, bristling.

Sam's voice grew warm. 'Well, when has he ever been a father to you apart from in a biological sense? Natalya told me about how he offloaded the two of you for practically every minute of your childhood. *I'm* a father: I live in the same house as my kids, I put them to bed every night, I make sure they eat their peas and brush their teeth. That's the basic requirement. Any man who doesn't meet that has no right to call himself a father.'

Tears pricked Lena's eyes.

'He ruined you. You were doing great, you were happy. Then he came along.'

'But don't you see? It wasn't fresh unhappiness. It was the old unhappiness, stirred up again. I always felt it, but it was buried.'

'Yes, and he caused that too.'

'We can't be sure . . . his explanation . . .'

'Was very far-fetched, full of inconsistencies and opportunities to brag.'

Lena hung her head. She had started to realise this on her own, but her embarrassment at being so foolish kept her from accepting it completely.

'Lena, you aren't yourself. I phoned Natalya this evening to talk about you, about what can be done. And I think the first thing that you need to do is talk to her, mend that bridge. I don't want you to lose something so precious as your sister's love.'

'All right,' Lena said, too weary to protest any further. 'I'll call her tomorrow. But Sam, don't keep secrets from me.'

'I'm sorry.'

She wanted to say, 'Especially secrets with my sister,' but she didn't.

Aunt Stasya had always said that to name one's deepest fear would be very, very bad luck.

The sun was shining and it matched Natalya's mood. She felt light, bright, she couldn't stop smiling.

She and Marcus lay in bed – Rupert's bed in Rupert's apartment – with the sun streaming in the window, eating a box of Swiss chocolates. She had woken up next to him this morning, for the first time ever. While he was cooking her a traditional English breakfast, with bacon and eggs he had brought with him for the purpose, the phone had rung. Lena, wanting to put their argument behind them. Natalya's relief was so great that she only realised then how tense she had been. Not speaking to Lena for months? It had never happened before. They affirmed their love for each other and talked about catching up in person soon. If matters still felt a little strained at the end of the phone call, that was only to be expected. It would take time. At least they were talking.

After breakfast, she and Marcus went straight back to bed, where they stayed. Dozing, making love, eating. She felt as though every need of her body was finally being fulfilled. She also knew, as did Marcus, that it couldn't continue. It was the end of their affair, but a very pleasing way to end it.

The phone rang just before twelve. She asked Marcus to be quiet in case it was Rupert and got up to answer it.

'Hello?'

'Natalya, darling. How are you?'

'I'm fine. The weather here is beautiful. How's New York?'

'Ah, very grey and overcast today. And my meetings aren't going so well.'

They fell to chatting, she lied about what she was doing today – promised to learn lines and go for a long jog – and then the call was over and she was back in Marcus's arms. Losing herself once again in pleasure.

Only what was that sound from within the apartment? She froze, listening hard.

'What is it?' asked Marcus.

'That sounds like the door.'

Then the distinct sound of the door closing, keys being dropped onto the kitchen bench.

'There's someone in the apartment,' Marcus said.

Natalya rose, reaching for her clothes, but it was too late. The bedroom door was flung open. Rupert stood there. 'Surprise.'

Her brain could not comprehend it. Rupert was in New York. She had just spoken to him. So how could he be standing here in front of her, while she and her lover were naked and the bed was covered with chocolate wrappers?

Marcus was scrabbling for his clothes, but Rupert wasn't interested in him, only Natalya. He threw her dress at her. 'Get dressed, you little whore,' he said.

'How . . . ?'

'I called you from the cab.'

Realisation dawned. The whole thing was a set-up. He was not stupid. He knew she was cheating. Perhaps the trip to New York was genuine, but he had lied about when he'd return, to catch her out on purpose.

'You'd better go,' she said to Marcus, not sure what else to say.

'Don't worry,' he replied, 'I'm going.'

Rupert stood silent and still as Marcus gathered his things and left; as Natalya slipped the dress over her head, tensed her knees so they didn't shake. Her stomach was hollow.

'How very insulting,' Rupert said at last, in a surprisingly reasonable tone. 'The son of one of my old school friends. Did you choose him on purpose to be cruel to me?'

Natalya didn't know what to say, so she said nothing.

The first blow was a huge shock. He stepped forward, backhanded her hard enough to knock her onto the bed among the warm, twisted sheets. She scrabbled backwards, away from him, nursing her jaw. 'Rupert!'

'You think you don't deserve it?'

He marched around the bed and pulled her up by her wrist, threw her on the floor and kicked her in the back. A horrific thud of pain. Her mind was white with fear, she struggled to get away, but he pinned her to the ground with his foot.

'Are you listening?' he said through gritted teeth.

She nodded, her hair stuck to her face by tears.

'I will go out for twenty minutes. When I return, you will be gone. You will not tell anyone about this. You will show up for work as usual on Monday. I will call off the wedding and, as far as the world knows, it will be because I went cold on you. We will never speak to each other again. Is all that clear?'

Again, she nodded. He took his foot off her back and strode away. The door to the apartment closed. He was gone. She looked at the clock. Twenty minutes. One warning was enough.

She picked herself up off the floor, ignoring the pain in her back. Pulled down her suitcases and frantically began to pack. Whatever she could fit, whatever she couldn't bear to be without. She left a mile of dresses and shoes. Grabbed photo albums and CDs. Remembered to call a cab. Went back to packing. Toothbrush. Make-up. Time had run out, she had to go. Ran down to the street. The sun was still shining. It was a perfect spring day.

The cab was waiting. 'Where to?' the driver asked.

She hadn't even thought about it. But she could see Rupert's dark figure rounding the corner, on his way back to the apartment. Her back sang in pain. 'Away,' she gasped. 'Just get me away from here.'

Natalya had booked into a hotel at Haysbridge-on-Sea, within walking distance of the *Lonely Shores* set. There was no chance of anonymity at the hotel, so she made up a story about renovations in London and having to stay a little while locally. In fact, she didn't know how long she would stay. At least a week, until she could find somewhere else.

As she sat in make-up that morning, she dreaded seeing Rupert. But he didn't arrive. She checked her schedule and made her way over to number twenty-seven for a scene in which Tatiana was confronted by Meg Bradley. Tatiana and Meg Bradley had periodic confrontations and they always rated well.

Natalya was waiting on set when Dan Ellison, the first-unit director, arrived carrying a sheaf of papers. 'New script,' he said.

Natalya was used to this by now. She skimmed the pages. Her lines were exactly the same, so she skimmed forward. At the end of the scene, her eyes began to read properly and her heart jumped.

TATIANA leaves, slamming the door. MEG slumps to the sofa, crying. There is a noise of screeching tyres, then shouting. TREVOR runs in, screaming for MEG to call an ambulance. TREVOR: It's Tatiana! She's been hit by Dad's car!

Clutching the script in her fist, Natalya approached Dan. 'What is this?'

He turned, smiled and shrugged. 'I just take orders from the big guy.'

'Rupert did this?' Of course he did. 'Does Tatiana die?'

'Yes.'

'Is there a death scene? On the road? In a hospital?' Her voice was growing desperate now. He couldn't do this to her. She was under contract until January 2000: more than eighteen months away.

'Nope. You walk out the door and that's it.'

That's it.

Dan lowered his voice and leaned towards her. 'Don't worry. You're still under contract so you'll still get paid.'

It was the closest thing to sympathy she'd ever had from Dan. 'Why is he doing this to me?'

'He said you'd know.'

Then the lighting director interrupted and Dan wandered off with him, leaving Natalya alone.

She slumped against the doorjamb. Had she really expected Rupert wouldn't take it out on her this way? Dan was right: he had to honour the contract. But then, so did she. She couldn't accept any other work without Rupert's express permission. Which she knew he'd never give her.

'Right, Tatiana, we're ready,' Dan said.

Natalya dragged herself up on set, put in a terrible performance. It didn't matter. Dan declared it was a take. Natalya stood by the camera operator and watched the actor playing Trevor, Tatiana's ex-husband, run in shouting that Tatiana had been hit by a car. That was it. Her swan song in third person. Then the lights on the set were all switched off and people began moving to film something else, somewhere else. In the whirl of sound and movement, Natalya walked down to the street then out the gates into anonymity.

Nobody said goodbye.

CHAPTER THIRTY-THREE

Sofi felt strange being back in St Petersburg, back on her mother's street, after five years away. The city had changed in many ways, but in fundamental ways it had stayed the same: its grubby grandeur, its uneven footpaths and its barely heeded road rules. The apartment building in which she had grown up was rust-stained around the windows, its plaster crumbling. And yet a shining new security door had recently been fitted. She was rearranging Nikita on her hip, trying to find the right doorbell to press, when a very thin woman coming the other way opened the door for her.

The lift, as always, was out of order. She picked up her suitcase and started up the stairs. Out of breath, she paused at the top, then made her way down the corridor. The lights had recently been replaced and illuminated graffiti-tagged walls. Outside Mama's door, she put down her suitcase and knocked.

The door opened, Mama was waiting. 'My dear Sofi! And your beautiful little boy.'

Sofi set Nikita down and launched herself into Mama's arms. It had been an age since she'd seen her or felt her warm embrace, and the comfort it brought her was measureless. Eventually, she stood back. Nikita was very still, looking into the corner of the room.

Stasya kneeled before him. 'Do you have a hug for your Babushka?'

'Babushka,' Nikita said earnestly, not making the slightest move to hug her.

'Ah, listen! What a beautiful word.'

Sofi smiled weakly, helped her mother up. She hadn't aged a day since Sofi had left, the strong jaw and bright eyes untouched by time. Sofi hadn't told her anything about Nikita yet, nor the reason for her visit. She glanced around the room: it was spotless and smelled of furniture polish. She realised Mama had spent a lot of effort cleaning and tidying for her arrival and it made her sad. She wasn't a stranger to impress.

'Let's have tea,' Mama said, going to the corner of the sitting room that had been converted into a kitchenette. 'Would Nikita like a drink of milk?'

Nikita took a few uncertain steps into the room. He had spotted Mama's pedestal fan. He stopped in front of it, watching the blades turn around and around.

'I'm sure he probably would. Can I help?'

'No, no. You're my guest. Sit down. I must say, I'm so delighted to have you back, even if it is only for a few days.'

Mama returned with a tray. Tea, milk and biscuits. She called for Nikita to come and fetch a biscuit, but he wasn't interested. They fell to talking, catching up. Still Sofi didn't reveal to Mama what was wrong with Nikita. She wanted to see if Mama would notice for herself that something was amiss. Mama complained bitterly about Uncle Viktor and Lena, talked about her job at the bakery, the string of unpleasant boarders she'd had to put up with until deciding to brave paying the rent alone, thanked Sofi again and again for sending money. And all the while she glanced repeatedly at Nikita, occasionally tried to encourage him to interact with her. Sofi sat back and listened and watched.

Finally, after an hour and a half, when Nikita had taken down all the coasters from Mama's coffee table and arranged them in a perfect circle on the floor, Mama turned to Sofi and said, 'He's very quiet.'

'He is.'

'Nikita?' she tried in English. 'Come to Babushka?'

Nikita didn't look around. Sofi stood and fetched him, deposited him in Mama's lap. 'There's a beautiful boy,' Mama said, back in Russian now.

'Beautiful boy.'

'My word! He's speaking Russian already?'

'No. He's just repeating what he's heard.'

Mama frowned. 'All right, Sofi. You'd better tell me. There's something wrong with the child, isn't there?'

'Yes,' Sofi admitted. Her voice shook. Every time she had to tell it anew, the pain rolled over her again. 'He's been diagnosed with autism.'

Mama nodded, her face not showing a trace of sadness. 'Ah, well. He'll be a lot of hard work then?'

'I don't know. Every child is different. But we have a doctor who has given us a million things to do to help him adjust to the world.' Sofi leaned forward, grasped Mama's hand. Her words came out all in a rush. 'Mama, I want you to come back to France with me.'

Mama shook her head immediately. 'What's this nonsense?'

'My business is growing, Julien is away until November, Nikita needs somebody to look after him. I can't do it all.' Sofi bit her lip, holding back tears. 'Mama, I need you. I need you so much right now and I can't . . .' Her voice squeaked off into a whisper.

'Oh, dear,' Mama said, her own eyes filling with tears.

'I can't go forward without you there. I'll be crushed.'

Mama gently set Nikita down and folded Sofi in her arms. For the first time since the diagnosis, Sofi allowed herself to sob. Her face grew hot and tears ran down her cheeks and dripped off her chin. Mama said, 'Hush,' over and over, until finally Sofi started to calm.

'Will you come, Mama?' Sofi said.

'It's been a long time since I've been needed, Sofi,' she replied. 'Of course I'll come.'

The spare room, which had once been Sofi's workshop, was now converted back into a bedroom, with new curtains and a bedspread to match. Sofi lowered her mother's suitcase to the floor and opened the curtains with her free hand. It was late afternoon, Nikita was asleep on her shoulder. They had been travelling all day and Sofi was exhausted too. Mama took it all in her stride.

'It's blue,' Sofi said, 'your favourite colour.'

'You were very sure that I'd come,' Mama said, sitting on the bed and easing off her shoes.

Sofi smiled. 'I hadn't let myself consider the possibility that you wouldn't.'

She was glad to be home, with the familiar smells and sounds. Even better to be here with Mama. Rattling around with only Nikita for company had been a strain. Nikita roused, rubbed his eyes. Sofi kissed his soft cheek.

'Could I leave you here for half an hour while I run down to the workshop?' she asked Mama. 'I haven't been here for nearly a week and I'd like to check in.'

'So I'm on duty already?'

'Yes, I'm afraid so. I hope you don't mind. I have rather a tight deadline.'

Mama stood and gently took Nikita into her arms. 'Of course I don't mind. I'm grateful to be here with my daughter and grandson, grateful for my bed and board.'

'And the weekly wage,' Sofi said sternly.

'I won't take it.'

Sofi didn't argue; they'd been arguing about it for days already. She would simply set up a bank account in her mother's name and start depositing money. 'You'll have to find your way around the kitchen. He'll be hungry by now.'

'Then I'll make him *blini*.' Mama had been feeding Nikita up on Russian food, which he seemed enthusiastic about. 'You go, I'll take care of things here.'

It was a strange feeling to walk out of the house and down to the workshop alone. The last few weeks, she had brought Nikita with her. She'd give him a box of beads and he would line them up with intense focus for an hour or so in the corner of the room while she did some work. The whole time, she'd felt terribly guilty. She should be with him, one on one, taking him through his speech exercises, honing his adaptive skills, teaching him the social cues and responses that he hadn't a hope of picking up alone. Now, Mama would do all those things. Mama would take him to his appointments in Tours and Paris on the train. Mama would make his lunches and sit with him while he munched noisily. And Nikita wouldn't miss Sofi at all.

The streets of the village were soaked in afternoon sunshine. Spring was here, the air was scented with sharp, sweet smells. Swallows, back from their winter migration, darted overhead and nestled in windowsills and roof beams. She passed her neighbour and exchanged pleasantries, which shocked her back into thinking in French. Mama would have to learn French too. Was Sofi asking too much of her? Then she thought of the dim apartment back in St Petersburg, and compared it to the vibrant spring sunshine, and put the thought out of her head.

She arrived at the shop, at the southern end of Rue Henri Proust, and stood in the door recess to find her key. It was a poorly kept building, with crumbling windowsills and peeling paint on the doors. But inside it was spacious and well lit.

'Sofi, you are back!' squealed Francette, leaping from her seat to hug her. The other two women also greeted her, but not as warmly. Francette was a sweet girl, full of life and very clever. She had unofficially taken over the role of workshop manager and Sofi relied upon her to keep up stock and ship and bill orders.

The workshop was arranged with four huge tables in the centre of the room, upon which were pinned out half-finished necklaces and bracelets, cuffs, earrings, anklets and rings. There was ample room to grow, with vast yardage of unused space and another room at the back. The floor was made of unfinished wood boards that creaked when anyone walked on them. Two huge windows let in natural light, but every desk had a halogen lamp to work by. In the corner by the stained sink, Sofi had set up a refrigerator, a table and chairs, a coffee machine. One of the women had brought in a radio from home, and soft classical music played. At the moment, her staff were in the process of making seventy-four versions of the same bracelet: angel skin coral and dark green tourmaline, woven together with yards of fine sterling silver wire. She picked one up to examine it. How she loved tourmaline, its innumerable colours. Egyptian legend said that the stone had journeyed through rainbows.

'Do we have any silver shells?' she asked Francette.

'Yes, about one hundred.'

'That would look nice on here, don't you think? With the coral and the sea green?'

'Show me.'

Sofi lost herself in work, trying the silver shells in different positions, unwinding wire and winding it back again. She barely noticed her two new workers pack up their things and head home. It was only when Francette placed a thin hand on Sofi's shoulder that she looked up.

'Sofi? I'm sorry, it's after seven. I'll have to go.'

'Oh. Of course. I am so very sorry. I lost myself.' She thought about Mama alone with Nikita. 'I'll have to go too.'

'Are you coming in tomorrow morning?' Francette asked.

'Yes. I'll be in every day from now on. I have a lot of work to do.' She smiled at Francette. 'So you can have the morning off. I've kept you here too long today.'

'I don't mind. I'll be here.'

They walked out to the street together, chatting until the junction of Rue Traversière where they parted. Sofi hurried home, an old childhood fear of her mother's disapproval beating in her chest.

But she needn't have worried. Mama had fed and bathed Nikita and put him to bed, cleaned the kitchen, and left a plate of *blini* in the oven for Sofi. Sofi was speechless with gratitude, then realised this was exactly the service she'd been providing Julien for years and he'd never once been speechless.

They sat at the table together while Sofi ate. 'You mustn't cook for me every night,' she said to Mama.

'I like to cook.'

'I'll get fat,' Sofi said, pointing her fork at the lump of sour cream on her plate.

'You're too thin.'

Sofi laughed, thinking about the roll around her belly that had stayed after Nikita's birth. 'Only my mother would say that.' She finished her meal, changed the subject. 'I'm sorry again about being so late tonight.'

Mama considered her in the harsh light of the kitchen. 'Don't be sorry for my sake, Sofi. But don't miss too many of Nikita's bedtimes, will you?'

Sofi felt chastened. She hadn't even thought about Nikita missing her; only the inconvenience to her mother. 'He doesn't notice if I'm not here,' she said guardedly.

'How do you know? Just because he doesn't express it doesn't mean he doesn't miss you.'

'Mama, it's not like that. Autistic children don't . . .' She couldn't bring herself to finish the sentence, distressed by the thought that always circled just out of consciousness. *He doesn't love you, he'll never love you.*

Mama shifted her chair closer to Sofi, took her hand gently. 'Now you listen to me, Sofia Ivanovna Chernova, all children love their mothers. It's as much a part of their biology as breathing. Don't ever doubt that he loves you. And one day, you will see I am right. You will realise that he's been showing his love all along, in some way that only he understands. So by all means throw yourself into your work. But make sure you are here enough for him to show you. Understand?'

Sofi nodded tearily.

'I'm proud of you.' Mama looked away, her voice gruff. 'Your papa would have been proud of you.' She rose and took Sofi's empty plate to the sink.

Sofi let herself cry: for Papa's loss, for Julien's distance, for Nikita's disability, for her mother's life of sacrifices and hardship. But then she palmed the tears from her face and took a deep breath. No time for crying now. Her business was about to climb the ladder to new heights. There was work to be done.

Christmas lights strung around the fireplace twinkled, and the air was filled with the smell of roasted meat and gravy. Sofi returned from putting Nikita to bed and paused in the doorway to the dining room. Winter Gathering this year was bursting at the seams. Their usual dining table was too small, so she'd bought a big round one for the occasion. Closest to the entrance of the room was Julien, whom Mama had come to adore. Mama sat next to him, laughing at one of his jokes. Beside her, Anna and Matthew, up far too late and wild with excitement. Stasya had made sure that they called her Babushka too, and seemed to delight in their company. Next was Lena, her face flushed from champagne as she talked to Sam, who had just turned thirty but still looked like a teenager with his long curls and easy grin. Then her own empty seat. And rounding off the circle, at Julien's elbow, was Natalya, actually eating something. Music played, champagne flowed. It looked like such a bright, happy scene. But there were shadows lurking beneath.

Lena and Stasya had avoided speaking to each other. This made Sofi cross, because Stasya had certainly never done anything wrong and Lena should apologise. Anna and Matthew were spirited and noisy, and sometimes Sofi spoke sharply to them. She wasn't sure if her impatience was driven by the twinge of jealousy she felt seeing them both behaving so perfectly normally – smiling and talking, as children should, Matthew constantly reaching out for Lena to hold her hand or stroke her hair – or by the fact that Lena barely seemed to notice this blessing. Natalya was still being paid handsomely, but hadn't worked in months and was battling Rupert's company to be freed from contract. It was all she talked about, and that morning Julien had chided her gently for her self-pity, sending Natalya into a sulky mood that still hadn't lifted. And finally, the easiness between Lena and Natalya seemed to have suffered greatly. They were both trying admirably to restore it, but things were complicated by Sam who could not talk to Natalya without making Lena painfully tense. Her voice would suddenly become too loud and shrill, her laughter forced, her hands would reach for him to display too obvious affection.

Sofi slid into her seat next to Julien. He took her hand, but was still caught up in his conversation with Mama. Natalya avoided Sofi's eyes; perhaps Sofi was guilty by association of Julien's crime. Sofi sipped her champagne, eyes turned towards the dark outside the window, the wild flurry of snow. Yes, it was normal for them to bicker, to hold resentments. But this Winter Gathering felt different. Their relationship was like a sturdy piece of pottery. Over the years, there had been chips but no significant damage. Last year, with Viktor's return, it had broken. Certainly, they had repaired it, but the fissure line remained.

Sofi feared that from now on it would be forever weakened.

IV

CHAPTER THIRTY-FOUR
2000

Natalya was happy to leave behind the distinction of being the highest paid unemployed person she knew.

For more than a year and a half, she had been unable to accept any acting work, not even an interview or photo shoot, so tied up was she in Rupert's contract. For the first six months, when offers had repeatedly come in, she'd pleaded and begged with Rupert – via his office, never in person; she was too frightened of him for that – but he'd remained firm.

'Mr Palmer intends to honour the contract,' a string of secretaries and underlings had repeated to her.

After the first six months, the offers stopped coming.

She hired a lawyer, who went over her contract with her and explained everything. Within the document were clauses that essentially meant the end of her career if she left Rupert. The only good thing about it was the annuity that Sofi had told her to insist on: one-quarter of her salary for her entire stint on *Lonely Shores* had been put aside in a special account for her, to become available on the termination of the contract.

So now she was trying to decide what to do with both her money and her freedom. That was how she'd ended up in the office of *Gentlemen's Club* magazine, in a baby-blue waiting room with soft white sofas, while piped saxophone music played and naked women gazed at her seductively from glass-framed posters on the walls.

Back in the first few months, after Tatiana disappeared without warning from British television screens and the gossip columns had speculated madly about the split from Rupert, six different men's magazines had contacted her to bare all for them. She had turned them down, along with dozens of offers for commercials and at least three offers for small parts in good-quality television dramas. The one that had hurt most to reject was the offer from a new cosmetics company to be the face of their product.

In the early days, she'd thought she could simply wait out the contract then pick up where she'd left off. She moved into a beautiful one-bedroom apartment between High Street Kensington and Notting Hill, with immaculate white paint and huge bay windows, and tried not to feel too frustrated with the wait. If anything, all the speculation and attention was thrilling. She had become the ultimate mysterious femme fatale. Dumped from the show, responsible for the wedding scandal of the year, and followed by photographers if she dared to step out shopping.

But then the next celebrity scandal, the next bright young thing, the next new star on *Lonely Shores* – Rupert had been very clever about it – had driven her out of the gossip columns and into obscurity. She tried to maintain friendships with her old castmates, but had to admit she had done a poor job of befriending them when Rupert was on the scene, and so they slipped away from her very easily. Marcus had been terrified to take her calls, so she had left him alone too. The phone stopped ringing. She tried to tell herself that nobody was offering her work because they knew she would turn them down. She refused to believe that she was washed-up.

She spent her time shopping, travelling, dating pretty but disposable young men, visiting Sofi or Lena, and keeping herself beautiful. She tried to read, but became bored in the middle of most books. She toyed with the idea of writing something – a memoir, perhaps – but, despite the expensive laptop computer she bought for the purpose, couldn't get started. She spent a lot of time searching for her own name on the internet, then snapping the computer shut if she saw a derogatory comment. She thought about taking acting lessons, but decided it was beneath her. Indolence became her way of life, and time ceased to be marked by days and weeks. She was always slightly bored and tired, and knew that doing nothing of value was eroding her soul.

When the contract ran out, that very day she began the process of finding more work. One by one, she phoned the people who had wanted her eighteen months ago. One by one, they turned her down; some dared to ask who she was. Only *Gentlemen's Club* had expressed an interest in meeting her.

As she sat in the waiting room, looking around at all the bare flesh, misgivings gnawed at her. Whether or not nude photographs were 'tasteful' had nothing to do with poses and lighting and very much to do with how badly the model needed money or publicity. Had she stripped for the magazine back at the start, it would have been a triumph. Thumbing her nose at Rupert, riding the wave of intense interest, displaying her glorious beauty so that all men wanted her and all women envied her. Doing it now, after her star had waned, smacked of desperation.

'Natalie?'

She looked up. A well-dressed man in his early forties, with close-cropped dark hair, was approaching. She rose and shook his hand firmly. 'Ted, is it?' She had spoken to him on the phone. He was the senior editor.

'An absolute pleasure to meet you. I was quite a fan in your heyday. Come in. I have my head photographer with me.'

Natalya didn't like the word 'heyday', but feigned brightness.

He led her to a meeting room. Piles of magazines covered the table, and a silver-haired man with a long ponytail waited for them. 'This is Carlo.'

They exchanged greetings and settled.

'Thank you for seeing me,' Natalya said, launching into her carefully rehearsed opening lines. 'I'm finally out of contract and I think a fabulous photo spread in a quality magazine would be a way of signalling to the world that I'm back. You once asked me to pose for you, and I wondered if that offer still stood.' There, her voice hadn't shaken with nerves. She sounded in control, rational.

'Ah, well, no,' Ted said. 'I'll be straight with you on that. When we asked you, the circumstances were very different. Carlo?'

Natalya's heart sank.

'I have no doubt that you would photograph beautifully,' Carlo said, assessing her coolly, as though she were a pretty object and not a person.

'You see, we have two types of models in the *Club*,' Ted continued. 'Celebrities, as you are . . . or were. And anonymous girls who are really just . . . well, chosen for their bodies.'

'And you don't have the right kind of body, really,' Carlo said, pressing his hands onto his chest. 'Do you see what I mean?'

'But you are right. A spread would certainly signal you were back. Problem is, you aren't back, are you? You're not working yet? No new shows coming up? A movie?'

She shook her head.

'If that were the case, we would certainly be interested. We'd be offended if we weren't the first magazine you called.'

Carlo's mobile phone rang and he excused himself and scurried out of the room, leaving the door open. Beyond the threshold, she could hear the receptionists chatting, footsteps in the corridors, loud laughter somewhere. She felt mortified by offering her bare skin to them and being rebuffed in such practical terms.

'So you're saying to me that you're interested,' she said, 'but only if I have something else to promote.'

'Yes, precisely.' Ted smiled. 'You are certainly very beautiful still. How old are you now? Thirty-four?'

'Thirty-one,' she said, offended. It took a few extra hours in the gym each week, a few stinging jabs of a needle to her forehead, but she was still easily as beautiful as she'd ever been.

'I don't want you to think I'm turning you down because you're not beautiful,' he continued. 'Think of it as me protecting you. It would do you no good. The gossip columns would be cruel, they'd say you were washed-up and desperate. You would be embarrassed.'

Natalya told herself not to cry. She managed to say, 'Thank you,' though wasn't sure why she should thank him when she felt so old, unattractive and stupid in his company.

He reached for her hand, smiled his brilliant smile. 'There, there. Would you like me to take you out for a drink?'

She was shocked, searched his face. He was well-groomed, powerful, wealthy. Alarms went off in her head. She withdrew her hand. 'No,' she said, mustering her dignity.

He shrugged slightly, nonchalant. 'Well, then, if there's nothing else?'

'Goodbye,' she said, rising before she could be dismissed.

She walked home, turning the impossible situation over in her mind. She had to build a profile to get work, but nobody wanted to interview or photograph her if she wasn't working. An agent, that was what she needed, a star-maker. Natalya wasn't ready to give up yet.

As Lena bundled Grandad's sheets off the bed and spread out smooth ones that smelled of laundry softener, she remembered a childhood game that Natalya and she had argued over. Natalya was the princess – again – and Lena was the servant. Again. She always hated being the servant and yet she seemed to wind up in the role more than her sister ever did. Sofi managed to avoid it too, usually electing to be 'Assistant to the Queen's Philosopher' or some other far-fetched title. In her childhood, Lena had tightened her little fists and promised to herself that she would show them all. That she would never be a servant. Why, then, had her life been so full of changing other people's bed linen and wiping other children's bottoms?

She plumped the pillows and sat them up tidily, then went to the window to help Grandad out of the chair.

'Come on, back to bed.'

'I can manage.'

He couldn't. His age had brought new illnesses: arthritis that made his joints ache, skin ulcers that plagued his legs and back, high blood pressure that necessitated a bewildering array of tablets. His lungs hadn't worsened though, and he often spoke of his last joy in life being able to breathe a little fresh air through the window in the afternoon. Before he demanded it be shut in case he 'caught his death' from the strong sea wind.

She settled him back in bed with a newspaper and his magnifying glass, and made to leave.

'Wait, Lena,' he said.

She stopped, turned to him.

He indicated the chair. 'Stay a while?'

Lena thought about the pile of laundry she had to do. Saturday was washing day; though it needn't have been if Sam would just remember to do it during the week while she was at work. Then she sighed and slid into the chair, leaning her body forward onto his bed. 'What's on your mind?' she said, taking his hand.

'You haven't told anyone, have you? About my money?'

'Of course not,' Lena said. 'You asked me not to.'

Though she had thought about it from time to time. When Wendy bought a new sofa on a no-repayments-for-three-years deal. When Becky, who was home for Sam's birthday, confessed that she was going to wait until Grandad died before enrolling in university because it would be easier if she didn't have to work as well as study. When Sam asked him for three hundred pounds to buy a new guitar; he was refused and borrowed the money from Tony, much to Lena's despair. But Grandad had asked her to keep the secret and so she had.

Grandad pouted. 'She's been talking about me going somewhere else. Making me "more comfortable", she says.'

'I know. She's mentioned it to me too.'

Grandad was a lot of work. But, in Lena's opinion, he didn't need to be sent elsewhere. Wendy was getting tired or lazy or both, that was all. Lena felt very strongly that old people belonged at home, with their families. She hoped that one day, when she was old and infirm, Matthew and Anna would feel that way too.

'But don't worry, she won't. I won't let her.'

He squeezed her hand. His fingers had been worn down to smooth by the years. 'God bless you, Lena.' Tears sprang to his eyes and he glanced away. He gathered his composure and said, 'I'm not afraid to die, but I am terrified of what happens right before it.'

'No more morbid talk. It's bad luck.' She patted his hand and moved to rise, but once again he stopped her.

'He didn't deserve you,' he said. 'That drunkard that turned up here claiming to be your father.'

Lena's chest tightened. 'He was my father. *Is* my father.'

'He blew in and blew back out fast enough,' Grandad said. 'Should have realised what a good thing he had going with you for his daughter.'

'Hush, Grandad, I don't want to talk about it.'

'I want to talk about it. I also want to talk about the smell of alcohol on your breath when you come to turn my light out at night.'

Now she was growing annoyed. She wasn't in the mood for a lecture. 'Most people have a drink or two in the evening.'

'Not every evening. And they stop before the bottle is finished.'

Lena shook her head. He couldn't possibly know how much she was drinking. She was functioning perfectly well. 'I'm afraid you're not making much sense to me, Grandad.'

'No. You're afraid that I *am* making sense.'

Lena fell silent, feeling ashamed and exposed.

'Are things going badly for you, girl?' he asked in his husky, breathless tone.

She sighed. 'Not badly. Just . . . not brilliantly. I feel like I've been stuck in the same place forever: working just to survive, relying on my sister and cousin for their charity – I'd never leave Briggsby otherwise. I'd just stay here watching Sam spend money like there's . . .' She trailed off, shrugged. 'Grandad, in all the stories you've told me about your youth, you've never once mentioned love.'

'I've told you about Anna, Wendy's mum.'

'Not much. Did you love her?'

'Of course.'

'Did you love her foolishly?' Lena laid her head on her arms. 'Or am I the only fool?'

'Love is foolish by nature,' Grandad said, stroking her hair. He gently lifted her chin so she was looking at him. 'Make me a promise?'

'What?'

'Promise.'

'I can't promise until I know what it is.'

'It's the one thing that will make me happy.'

Lena had to laugh. 'Well, how can I say no?'

His white eyebrows drew down sternly. 'Stop drinking. For one month.'

She closed her eyes. Weariness suffused her body. She was prevented from answering by the sounds of an approaching squabble.

'Mummy will be cross with you.'

'Don't tell tales!'

The children burst into the room. A familiar tableau: Matthew's bottom lip trembling, Anna's eyes blazing with indignant fire. Matthew ran to Lena and launched himself into her arms, crying about Anna turning the video off while he was watching it. Anna stood proudly by, her fair curls escaping from the neat plait Sam had imposed on them that morning. Lena was jolted out of self-pity, and rose to take them back to the sitting room where they couldn't disturb Grandad.

'Lena,' he called as she was about to pass through the door. 'Are you going to promise me or not?'

The thought of getting through today without a drink made her skin prickle, let alone a whole month. But, underneath it all, she knew he was right. Perhaps she had even been waiting for someone to show that they cared enough to stop her.

'All right,' she said. 'I promise.'

Sam was out with the band. The children were asleep, Grandad too. Wendy was watching *Heartbeat*. And Lena itched to drink.

The first day, she had been fine. She had even bragged to Grandad that it would be easy. The second day, she had been irritable, but then that wasn't unusual with two small children always around. But today, the third day, had been hellish.

She had expected nausea, trembling, headaches, but had suffered none of these. Instead, an acute anxiety had worked its way into her body. Even though it was just a normal day, her body was sending shots of adrenaline through her for no good reason. Her mind went on strange tangents of morbid imagination: restless fantasies in which Sam borrowed more money from Tony without telling her, or one of the children became sick and needed an operation they could never afford, or the nursery discovered she had a drinking problem and fired her. She was panic-stricken in her bedroom, despite being safe and warm.

And she knew that if she just unscrewed the top on one of those bottles of nasty red wine she had stashed with her old clothes under the bed, she could make the feeling go away. Just one little glass . . . it was foolish to stop suddenly. She could wean off slowly . . .

She locked the door and crouched to pull out the old suitcase. Unzipped it and opened it. There they were, three bottles of the cheapest wine she had been able to find, nestled amongst Matthew's and Anna's old baby clothes.

Lena reached for the bottle. The back of her knuckle brushed the soft material of a tiny romper suit. Guilt made her pause, pick it up. It was one the first things Wendy had bought for Matthew; pale blue with fine white stripes. She noticed with sick regret that a large stain of red wine was spread over one of the little legs.

Had she really hidden alcohol among baby clothes? The idea of it seemed almost sacrilegious; as though she had defiled something beautiful. Three days without alcohol allowed her the clarity of mind to see this. She thought of Grandad, of the promise she'd made.

Lena took the three bottles to the bathroom and carefully poured them one by one into the sink. Then searched under the vanity for bleach to scrub away the stains and the smell. Her heart was hammering.

Wendy peered around the doorway. 'Lena?'

'Mould,' she muttered, without looking up.

'Want a cuppa?'

Lena knew she was too anxious to sit on the couch and gossip with Wendy. She forced a smile. 'Thanks, but I'm going to bed now.'

Wendy's mouth turned down at the corners, a habitual gesture that was starting to make permanent marks on her pretty face. 'Another time, then.'

Lena washed her hands, went back to bed and climbed in. The anxiety rattled through her. She reached for the little stained romper suit and clutched it between her shaking fingers as though it were a rope to safety, while she was tossed about on the wild, open sea.

CHAPTER THIRTY-FIVE

*I*t was the worst possible time for the phone to ring. Sofi was already running late. Julien was already short with her. He didn't like flying, so insisted on arriving at the airport hugely early so he could sit in a bar and take a few stiff whiskies for his nerves.

Sofi thought about not answering the phone, but Mama was out with Nikita and she would hate to miss an important call.

'It's Natalya.'

'Hello! I'm so sorry, can I call you back tonight or tomorrow? I'm just leaving to drive Julien to the airport.'

Natalya, as always, proceeded as though she hadn't heard. 'I'll be quick. I finally picked up that annuity from my contract, so now I've got a lump sum of money that I don't know what to do with. You're good at those things.'

She certainly was. The money that she'd invested right at the start, that she had earned from Natalya, had continued to grow sufficiently to pay for all of Nikita's treatment so far. 'Invest it,' she said. 'Find a good broker.'

'Do you know one? In London?'

'No, I . . .'

Julien was gesturing to her to get off the phone.

'Which stocks are doing well now? Do you know?' Natalya continued. 'I'm not working, so I'd like ones that earn a lot of money.'

Sofi knew Natalya well enough to realise that she was embarrassed to ask a broker, who would explain things too quickly and whom she wouldn't understand. She trusted Sofi to help her. 'Can this not wait, Natalya? You don't want to rush into it.'

The familiar impatience in Natalya's voice. 'I won't rush into it. Just give me something to go on. I'll research it, just like you would. I'll be very rational.'

'All right. I've had some very high yields lately with technology stocks. Internet companies. Have a look at those.'

'Anything else?'

'Diversify,' Sofi said, then, for emphasis, repeated the word in Russian. 'Eggs in different baskets, all right?'

'But should I –'

'I'm sorry, Natalya, I must go. Call me tomorrow and we'll discuss it properly.'

Julien was waiting at the front door. The car, a shining yellow Citroën Berlingo van that she had bought for her business, was packed and waiting.

'Do hurry, Sofi.'

'Stop worrying,' she said.

He held on to his reply until they were in the car, belted in. 'It's easy for you to tell me to stop worrying. Not so easy for me. Understand?'

'Well, if you don't like planes, stop going away on them.' She hadn't meant for her tone to be so sharp, and her pulse quickened. She didn't like to argue.

He fell silent as she drove. She pulled out onto Route de Tours and they were on their way. Finally, he said, 'If you don't like me going away, the time to tell me is before I leave to catch the plane.'

She didn't answer. This discussion was too complicated to have now. But then, she thought wryly, when would they have it if she kept putting it off?

'Sofi,' he said, more gently, 'when I told you I was going to Canada, you did not say it troubled you.'

'I wouldn't, would I?' Sofi replied. 'You would have gone anyway, but you would have felt guilty and we would have been at odds. It was simpler to say nothing.'

'I am surprised. I thought we understood each other.'

Sofi considered this. Julien was away at least three months of every year, but this year was by far the worst. He would be in Canada until May, home for summer, then off again to Beijing until Christmas. To him, it was all a great adventure. He was living a grand life of travel and acclaim, with a family who supported him fully waiting at home. To Sofi, it was a constant struggle. Readjusting to him being around, finding comfort in his presence only to lose it again, wondering continually why being away from her wasn't so painful that it made him stay. He seemed no more interested in Nikita's welfare than he was interested in the welfare of their cat, Masha. As long as the boy was fine, he seemed happy. Grateful, of course, for all of Mama's help, but puzzled by the little breakthroughs.

Sofi recalled the occasion, just after Nikita's third birthday, when Mama had taught him how to ask for a drink directly. His usual method was to wait by the fridge, patting it rhythmically with his right hand. But Mama held firm, saying 'Ask properly' over and over, beyond the point where Nikita was red-faced with tears and Sofi would have given in to him. Finally, quietly, Nikita took a shuddering breath and said, 'Drink.' Sofi had been over the moon, sweeping Nikita into her arms, phoning Lena and Natalya, talking too fast. Julien had smiled and ruffled his son's fair hair without a word, before returning to his studio to paint.

Of course, Sofi knew that the long hours Julien spent in his studio, the absences, the lack of involvement in Nikita's development, were his way of protecting himself. If he didn't talk about Nikita's condition, if he wasn't there to see how it played out on a daily basis, then perhaps he could pretend it wasn't happening. Sofi couldn't blame him: she was tempted to do the same. As her business grew and grew – she employed eighteen staff now, and Francette was opening a shop for her in Paris in April – she could very easily be away from home from early in the morning until late at night. Thoughts of a second baby were put on the back burner while she dealt with the work at hand. But Mama knew precisely when and how much guilt to apply to get her to stay in and take time with Nikita, even if he didn't seem to notice she was there for most of it.

'We do understand each other,' she muttered to Julien, switching on the car's heating. 'I'm sorry.'

When she arrived home, the sky had grown dark and cold. The light over the front door glowed, illuminating a flurry of raindrops carried on the wind. Sofi hurried inside. Mama was in the sitting room, watching television.

'He's still awake,' she said. 'If you want to kiss him goodnight.'

Sofi slipped out of her shoes and went to Nikita's room. By the glow of the nightlight, she could see him curled on his side, opening and closing his hands in front of his face.

'Nikita?' she said, sitting on the bed next to him.

He didn't look up, studying his hands. He did it when he was tired, watching them until he fell asleep. She often wondered whether he closed his eyes or stilled his hands first.

'Goodnight, darling,' she said, leaning over to kiss him.

'Goodnight.'

Sofi gasped, wondering if she'd heard properly. He wasn't mimicking her: he would have said, 'Goodnight, darling,' if he was.

'What did you say?' she asked.

No answer. Hands opening and closing.

She smiled, kissing his cheek again. 'My clever boy,' she said, and went to join Mama.

'He said goodnight,' Sofi said, in Russian.

'I know. I taught him. He just got the hang of it today. I hoped he might surprise you with it.' Mama turned off the television.

'Don't turn it off for my sake.'

'It's in French. I'm tired of French.'

It was difficult for Mama, the multitude of languages spoken in their house. Mostly Russian when Julien was away; French in public and to Nikita; sometimes English when Julien was around, though that was a habit on the wane. But Mama never complained, was never embarrassed if she couldn't understand or said the wrong word. She just got on with things. It was a quality that Sofi admired very much.

'Did Julien get away on time?' Mama asked, with a knowing smile on her face.

'Of course. He was drunk when he got on the plane, though.'

Mama shook her head. 'He who drinks to the bottom lives without mind. He should find another way to settle himself.'

Sofi sat on the sofa, stretching out her legs. 'He only does it when he flies. You know that. He's the picture of moderation the rest of the time.'

'Your Uncle Viktor drank. Ivan always hated it. I was pleased not to have a drunk for a husband.'

Sofi smiled to herself, thinking of the Thursday nights when her father would drink with his friends, away from Stasya's eyes, while the girls waited outside on the street. She shook her head. 'His drinking is the least of my worries.'

Mama's voice became gentle. 'It's hard for you, isn't it? The separations?'

'Yes,' Sofi said, surprising herself by starting to cry.

'There. Shh.' Mama was next to her, stroking her hair.

'I love him so much, Mama, but I don't feel as though he loves me.'

'He does.'

'Then why does he go away?'

'Tell the truth, did you know he was this way when you married him?'

Sofi nodded, mournfully. 'I suppose I did. I met him when he was away from home. Twice.'

'There you are. Black dogs can't be washed white.'

Sofi allowed her mother to cuddle her, taking comfort in her softness and her careworn practicality.

'Sometimes it helps to count your blessings, Sofi. It's got me through the hard times. Your career is doing so well. You live in a beautiful place. You have plenty of money.'

'But neither my husband nor son can show they love me,' Sofi added. 'I'd trade all of the other things for that. What kind of bad luck is that, Mama? Did I look into a broken mirror when I was little?'

'Don't say such things,' Stasya said, pretending to spit three times. 'Don't talk about bad luck. You haven't earned bad luck. You've done nothing bad. Get it out of your head.'

You've done nothing bad. But she had, hadn't she? She and her cousins had played with Roy Creedy's heart, they had taken his money. And all of it at Sofi's insistence. It was such a shameful piece of her past that she couldn't bear to think about it. Mama didn't know, and Sofi would certainly never tell Julien. So it lingered at the back of things; a secret from another time, when she was a different Sofi.

Sofi was not normally superstitious but, tired and overwrought, the idea seized her. She had created so much bad luck with her actions that her son was disabled and her husband couldn't love her. Her skin froze over. But then she shook herself, reason and clarity returning.

'You're right, Mama,' she said. 'It doesn't pay to think of such things.'

Natalya let herself into her apartment in high spirits. Finally, things seemed to be moving along. After four weeks of meetings with a string of entertainment agents, she had secured the services of Leida Frost, who represented a slate of big-name actors and models. Leida was certain she could find work for Natalya, but only if she was prepared to work for less money and in some unexpected places.

'You have to put your trust in me,' Leida had said. 'It may seem a roundabout route, but I can make you a star again if you do what I say.'

Natalya agreed readily. Money wasn't an issue just yet. She'd invested in line with Sofi's advice, and she expected that would keep her going for a while. Working again would get her out, keep her busy and – maybe – she would meet Someone. She didn't want to be desperate, she was choosy, but she really longed to have a man in her life.

She dropped her bag on the floor and admired her new French manicure: a present to herself to celebrate. The phone rang and she picked it up, holding her left hand at arm's length. Was her pinkie fingernail painted straight? It had looked it at the salon.

'Hello?' she said.

'Natalya. It's your father.'

Viktor. His voice, his words, were so unexpected that she nearly dropped the phone.

'How did you get this number?' she demanded.

'Your husband gave it to me. Rupert.'

Of course he did. 'He's not my husband. What do you want?'

'I've run out of money.'

She sighed. She should have suspected that this would happen. 'I don't care,' she said. 'Leave me alone.'

She hung up. Stood by the kitchen bench, drumming her fingernails. The phone rang again, as she knew it would.

'I still have Lena's phone number too, you know,' he said, before she had a chance to say anything.

And he had her. The last time their father had shown up, it had plunged Lena into a deep depression and threatened to poison the sisters' relationship forever. Natalya knew she couldn't let that happen again. She sighed, hated giving in to him. 'The same deal as last time?'

'Yes,' he said, his gruff voice weak with relief. 'The same.'

'But this time, you won't contact me again.'

Of course she had stipulated that last time too. He would run out of money. He would contact her again. And as long as she wanted to protect Lena, she would continue to pay him. She knew it and, now, he did too.

'I promise,' he said.

She made the arrangements with him, knowing all the time that his promise was worth nothing.

CHAPTER THIRTY-SIX

Spring was two days old, but winter hadn't really let go of the streets of Paris yet. The light was fading from the sky as Sofi walked, arms aching from carrying a box of champagne, towards the shop. Her shop. Anastasia Designs now had a boutique at Village Saint-Paul, in the Marais quarter. The cobbled streets were only accessible under stone archways stained with lichen and centuries. Her narrow shop was flanked by an antique store and a patisserie, both of which were closed for the evening and in darkness. By contrast, the light shone through her windows, illuminating a small but animated crowd and displays of her jewellery.

She pushed the door open. The bell rang. Francette looked up and the gathered crowd began to applaud.

Sofi, flushed with excitement and embarrassment, put the box of champagne on the glass counter. 'I'm sorry to be late,' she said. 'My little boy doesn't like hotels much.'

It had been a mistake to bring Nikita to Paris, even with Mama to help. One of the first aspects of his treatment was to set up an iron-clad schedule so that Nikita's life was utterly predictable. He hadn't been away from home at suppertime since then. At the hotel, he'd refused to eat, petulantly turned a bowl of food over and splashed his hands in it, sending warm soup everywhere, including on the crisp white dress that Sofi had bought for the party. Now she was in black. Not that it mattered what clothes she wore, so long as she was accessorised in her own jewellery.

The champagne started flowing, and Sofi dipped in and out of conversations around the room. She was stupidly flattered that so many people had come to the opening. Her staff and their partners, boutique owners who stocked her wares, Rosemary Simons from Chantilly who had always been a great champion of her work. The notable omissions were all family. Mama and Nikita; Julien; her cousins . . . Lena couldn't get away from work, though she'd sent a lovely card. And Sofi hadn't asked Natalya. Childish, she supposed. But Natalya had never shown any interest in Anastasia Designs, especially at a time when her interest could have made a great difference. She didn't ask because she didn't want to be rejected again.

The evening deepened, everyone had too much champagne. Finally, people began drifting away, to make their way back to Richelieu or their hotels or to dinner. Only Francette and Sofi were left, cleaning up glasses and champagne corks, making the store neat for tomorrow's opening.

'It was a pity Julien couldn't be here,' Francette said as she ran a broom over the floor. In her voice was a veiled accusation. Francette had known Julien since she was a child, so Sofi didn't mind the familiarity.

'Canada is a long way to come.'

'I can't imagine you missing something this important of his.'

'I've missed half-a-dozen of his exhibitions, actually.'

'You know what I mean. Aren't you terribly disappointed?' She raised her hands defensively, dropping the broom. She looked very pretty tonight, with her black hair tied up on the top of her head. 'Don't get cross with me.'

Sofi laughed, handing her the broom again. 'Just keep sweeping.'

They worked in silence for a while.

'Do you think anyone will come to my shop tomorrow, Francette?' Sofi asked as she cleaned the display glass with window cleaner.

'I'm certain they will. If not the first day, then sometime soon.' She smiled at Sofi. 'Don't worry about it.'

'I don't worry about anything if you're taking care of it,' Sofi said.

Francette had proved herself invaluable. Every aspect of Sofi's business bore traces of Francette's calm intellect and eye for detail: the jewellery-making, the accounts management, the customer service. She had begged to be given the opportunity to open the Paris store and, although Francette was only twenty-two, Sofi had agreed happily. Sofi and her team would make jewellery at the workshop in Richelieu. Once a fortnight, she would drive stock up to Paris. Francette would take care of all the orders from there, including the big ones for the chain stores. In effect, Sofi could get back to doing what she loved most: designing and making pieces.

She had often wondered if eventually she would run out of ideas. If there were only so many ways she could weave gems and silver together before she repeated herself. But the opposite was the case: the more she created, the more she could create. She spent hours each week researching jewellery from different countries and periods, becoming inflamed by ideas and going into a frenzy of designing. Sometimes she ended up with a disaster: a piece of jewellery that was such a mish-mash of varying ideas that it looked as though it had been drawn by a three year old. Other times, she ended up with a piece that she could make three hundred of and sell all over Europe. Art was a risk. Julien always said that.

Francette was standing by the door, a fuzzy woollen hat on her head and her leather bag over her shoulder. 'Time to go?' she asked.

'Wait a minute,' Sofi said. 'I need to speak with you.'

Francette nodded, and sat on the leather-covered bench by the door. Sofi sat next to her.

'I really appreciate you uprooting yourself and coming to Paris to run my shop.'

'It's the best of both worlds. Working for you and being in Paris. I couldn't have stayed in Richelieu forever. I needed to get out of the village.'

'Have you found somewhere nice to live?'

'Yes, I'm sharing with a couple of girls at Montparnasse. It's a very small flat, but it's nice. An adventure.'

Sofi thought about the flat that she and her cousins had shared when they came to London, all crammed in the one bedroom. That had been an adventure, indeed.

'It's important, isn't it, when you're young, to have such an adventure,' Francette continued. 'You must have felt the same, coming from Russia.'

'I did,' she said, suddenly feeling old. 'Francette, you are much more than a shopkeeper. I'd like to promote you and give you a pay rise too.'

Francette fell silent, waiting.

'I think you should be assistant director of Anastasia Designs. I'll double your salary.'

'You're too generous.'

'No, you're too generous. With your time and your care. It's nice to be able to rely on you. Nobody wise in business keeps all the work for themselves.' She patted Francette's knee. 'Congratulations.'

They locked up the shop and stepped into the cold night air. Sofi could hear music, distant and faint. The sound of traffic on the road that ran along the Seine. She bade Francette farewell and made her way back to the hotel. Francette was right: she was terribly disappointed that Julien couldn't make it. She had asked him to come home a month early, but he had held firm, all the while telling her how proud he was of her, how it was a wonderful achievement. But didn't he realise his actions did not agree with his words?

She shook her head. It was just the champagne high fading away, making her gloomy. Tomorrow she would head home with Nikita and Mama, and get back to work. Work seemed to solve everything.

Leida had told her that she'd be working for less, but Natalya hadn't thought she meant working for nothing.

'Trust me on this one,' her agent had said, new white-blonde streaks in her hair catching the light in her immaculate office. 'Besides, don't you want to cheer up sick children?'

The children's hospital just outside Haysbridge-on-Sea was having a fundraising day and had invited the cast of *Lonely Shores*. When Leida got wind that nobody from the cast had agreed to come, she'd thought it a perfect opportunity for Natalya to gain some publicity for herself. Also on the bill were a pop starlet, a television handyman and a local storyteller who wore an armchair costume.

'The children won't even know who I am!' Natalya had protested.

'Even if they don't, they'll see that you're glamorous and beautiful, and the press that come for the others will snap you too. I'll get one of my gossip-columnist friends to cover the event. Imagine: *Lonely Shores* snub, only Tatiana shows up.' Leida had gone off into her familiar cackle, very pleased with herself.

And so Natalya spent the day drawing faces on balloons, signing autographs for children who barely recognised her, flirting with admiring fathers, making hot dogs while wearing a green plastic apron, and smiling and smiling and smiling. Even though she had tomato sauce under her fingernails.

The next morning, she was eager to see if any of the photos she had posed for had been published. She collected the papers and the mail, made coffee, and headed back to bed. Could life get any better? Laura Ashley sheets, a lie-in while the sun dropped a weak beam on her bed, strong coffee, and a career on the rise again. She hoped. Nervously, she began to leaf through.

There! Page eighteen, next to the entertainment guide. A gloriously large photograph of herself standing at the bedside of a little boy who smiled weakly. She looked sympathetic and serene. The headline read: NATALIE CHERNOFF OUTCLASSES *LONELY SHORES* CAST. She laughed out loud. Leida had been right; it had all been worth it.

She went through the other newspapers and found nothing, but didn't mind. In her mail was a letter from her investment company and she slit it open eagerly. Her first quarterly statement. What a great morning! She was excited to see how much money she had made.

At first she didn't quite understand. Was the figure at the bottom of the page her income for the quarter? It was rather a lot. But then she looked again. No. This was what was left of her money. And it was only a little over half of what she'd started with.

She sat upright, heart thudding. How could this be? How could she lose so much money in such a short time? Sofi had never raised that possibility.

She jumped out of bed and went straight to the phone to call the investment company, racking her brains to remember the name of the man who had taken her money. Barry? The secretary had never heard of a Barry; did she mean Gary Moffatt?

'Yes, that was him. I need to speak to him urgently.'

'I'm afraid he's on annual leave until the end of next week. I can take a message –'

'No. You listen to me. I opened my statement this morning and nearly half of my money is gone. How do you explain that?'

The secretary's voice grew firm, almost angry. 'I'm sorry, Miss Chernoff, but Gary isn't here. I can put you through to our director, but you should read the terms and conditions letter that would have been given to you at –'

'How is it possible?' Natalya raged. Of course she hadn't read the terms and conditions letter; she wouldn't have understood it anyway.

'You are not the only investor to have lost money in the dotcom crash,' the secretary said archly. 'Would you like to speak to our director?'

Dotcom crash? What the hell did that mean? Natalya knew there was no point speaking to anyone else. They would use more technical terms and she wouldn't understand them. She needed to speak with Sofi.

'I want all my money out,' she said to the secretary. 'As quickly as possible.'

'Fine, I'll send you the forms. Is there anything else I can help you with today?'

Natalya hung up on her overly polite voice and dialled Sofi's number instead. She had to go via Aunt Stasya who gave her the workshop number. But Sofi had stepped out of the workshop. Natalya left her number and hung up, by now growing more and more angry and confused. She tried very hard to understand. She didn't watch the news or financial markets; was there a chance that something significant and terrible had happened without her even knowing it? She wanted to turn on her computer and search online for information, but then the phone line would be tied up when Sofi rang. So instead she paced the flat, hoping that there had been some dreadful mistake.

When the phone rang, she pounced on it. 'Hello?'

'Natalya. Mireille said you sounded upset.'

'I am upset. Half my money is gone.'

There was a short silence. Then Sofi said, 'Ah, I see. You did put eggs in different baskets? Like I said?'

'I invested in two companies.'

'Two internet companies?' Sofi said with alarm.

'Yes. Like you said.' Natalya was aware that her pulse was thudding in her throat. 'Isn't that what you said?' She went over the conversation in her head, remembering now that she'd been supposed to talk to Sofi again before doing anything. But she'd been riding such a wave of excitement that she'd forgotten. And the investment company had fulfilled her instructions. They'd offered advice, but she hadn't understood or listened. She had simply done what Sofi had told her to do.

Sofi's voice grew patient, and the patience irritated Natalya.

'High growth always means high risk,' she said. 'The dotcoms were in what they call a stock market bubble. They went too high. I've lost some money too.'

'Some? Nearly half?'

'That's what I meant by different baskets. Spreading your money across a lot of share types. Natalya, I told you not to do anything without talking to me properly.'

'You didn't warn me that this could happen.'

'I don't know what to say, Natalya. I feel terrible that my advice has led to you losing money, but I'm certain I told you to speak to me again, or to ask a broker for advice.'

'What am I going to do? I'm not working, I'm living off my savings. I can't afford to lose that money. How can I get it back? I don't even really understand where it's gone.' She checked herself, aware that she sounded frantic and stupid. 'Is there any way to get it back?' she said in a small voice.

'No. It's gone. If you invest it wisely, it will grow back over time but –'

'I'm going to put it in a bank account,' she replied hotly. 'Where it can't get lost.'

'I would advise –'

'Your advice didn't help much last time,' Natalya said, aware that she was speaking more sharply than she should. She tried to force herself to be calm. 'Sorry,' she said. 'You didn't deserve that.'

'No. I didn't.'

She recovered, changed the topic so that Sofi didn't hate her forever. 'How is the shop going?'

'Brilliantly. You should come over to Paris to see it. We could meet for lunch.'

'I won't be travelling to Paris any time soon,' Natalya said glumly. She didn't have the money to throw around any more. She would have to draw up a budget. And talk to Leida about some engagements that paid her not in publicity but in money.

She finished the conversation and went back to bed, gazing over and over at the statement. It wasn't fair. Sofi should have known something like this would happen and warned her. Even though she knew it was irrational, she couldn't help blaming Sofi, who hadn't lost half her money, who wasn't lonely, and whose life seemed to be working so much better than Natalya's.

Wendy's house never seemed so small as when it was filled with six year olds. Originally, the twins' birthday party was planned for the park, but a rain squall had blown in off the sea and now there were sixteen small people shrieking and playing through the sitting room and kitchen. Lena, stuck in the kitchen cutting up fruit, glanced over to see Sam, with a cone-shaped purple hat on his head, at the centre of a lively pass-the-parcel game. Wendy and Grandad were holed away in their respective bedrooms. Lena couldn't blame them.

It was long past the time that Sam and Lena should move out. Years and years of living with their children behind a curtain in their bedroom had taken its toll on their privacy – making love was becoming rare – so Lena had asked if the children could move into the dining room. That accomplished, Wendy had doubled their rent. Lena fantasised about a place of their own, something small but private, on the outskirts of town. Sam was reluctant. Having Wendy on hand to babysit was too convenient. The car had died and they needed to save for another so Tony didn't have to pick Sam up for band practice all the time. But Lena had her reasons for staying too. She was worried about Grandad, and what might happen to him if she wasn't there. So things continued as they always had, and Lena wondered if her children would be teenagers before she got out of Wendy's house. The first six years had gone in a blur; no doubt the next six would as well.

The phone rang just as she was pulling the cake out of the refrigerator. She ignored it. It rang out. She poked six candles into the blue side for Matthew, and six onto the pink side for Anna. The phone started ringing again. The caller was insistent and she wondered if it was urgent. She held off lighting the candles and picked it up.

'Hello?'

'It's Tony. Is Sam there?'

She had come to loathe Tony, as much for his seldom-met promises as for the fact that he loaned Sam money without blinking, then pressured him to pay it back quickly. 'He's in the middle of his children's birthday party, can it wait?'

'No. Urgent.'

Lena sighed, rested the phone on the bench. 'Sam,' she called. 'It's Tony. He says it's urgent.'

They swapped places. She entered the fray, led the game of pin-the-tail-on-the-donkey. Got stabbed in the hand by a hyperactive boy with a skinhead haircut. Sam was finally off the phone. He looked bewildered.

'What's wrong?'

'Nothing,' he said. 'We'll talk later.'

Lena was curious, but Anna had started demanding cake, so she returned to the kitchen and lit the candles.

She watched Sam smiling and taking photos of the children. A familiar fear had ignited in her heart: he'd borrowed more money, Tony was pressuring him to repay it. No, surely he hadn't; she had asked him not to. Where would they get more money from? They'd already sold their car for parts, getting a lousy forty pounds for it, which had disappeared immediately on new school uniforms for Matthew, who was growing taller by the second. She told herself to be calm, not to spoil the birthday party with her worrying. Wait and see what Sam said. It was terrible to doubt her husband so much.

The party wound up, and the rain cleared. Anna and Matthew went to their room to play with their new toys, while Sam and Lena cleared away the mess. Finally, in the late afternoon, they asked Wendy to watch the children and got away for a walk.

The sun was low in the sky, the clouds had shredded apart and were moving on, but the streets were wet and they picked their way over puddles on the way down to the pier. All the benches were wet, so they came to a stop at the end of the pier, leaning on the sodden wooden rail.

'So,' she said, 'what did Tony want?'

Sam smiled weakly. 'He's left the band.'

Guiltily, unexpectedly, Lena felt a huge wave of hope. 'I'm sorry to hear that.' She paused a moment, watching Sam as he looked out to sea. The wind tangled his long hair. She felt such an ache of love for him that it took her breath away. At length, she tested the waters. 'But you can find someone to replace him, can't you?'

Sam shook his head. 'Lena, I think it's time to admit that it's over.'

'Really?'

He turned to face her, his back against the railing. 'I'll be thirty-three this year. I've been trying to break into this business for ten years. I've got nowhere. The band had a total of eight gigs in the last twelve months, we've sold thirty CDs. It's time to face facts. I'm never going to be a pop star. I'm never going to buy you a mansion and a flash car. I've wasted all our time, all our money, on a stupid dream.'

'It isn't stupid.'

'It is. It *was*.' He shoved his hands in his pockets. 'It's over.'

'Are you certain?'

He drew his eyebrows together. 'How can you *not* be certain? Do you think I should keep going? Because if you do, I will. I'd do anything for you.'

Lena was completely unable to speak. So much hung on what she said next that it was almost impossible to go on breathing. Two seagulls landed on the railing nearby, their feathers ruffled by the wind, their black eyes implacable: as though they knew the answers to everything but weren't telling. She found her voice, wanting the moment to be over quickly. 'No. I don't think you should keep going.'

'You see? You've probably been thinking that for a long time, haven't you? Wishing I'd quit the band and get a full-time job so we can have a car again and a place of our own. Am I right?'

'Sometimes I have,' she said guardedly. 'But I would have supported your dream until the day I died.'

'Not very wise,' he said with a shrug. 'Neither of us have been very wise. We're parents, for God's sake. We have children to consider.'

Lena didn't point out that she had never stopped considering her children. Instead, she said, 'I'm sorry, Sam. I would do anything to take away the sadness you're feeling right now.' She brightened. 'Maybe you can find another job that involves music. Teaching guitar?'

He laughed bitterly. 'I can barely play it myself. I don't know the notes I use. It's all done on instinct, figuring it out. I can't teach that.'

'Working in a music shop?'

He shrugged. 'There isn't one in Briggsby.'

'We can move, we can –'

'It's not worth it. I've got a job here, they'll give me more hours. I'll just have to get used to it. You've been slaving away in the nursery for years. Didn't you once want to be an actress? You got used to it. I can too.'

Lena put her arms around his waist and held him close, her ear pressed against his heart. She couldn't bear to see him so unhappy; it made her want to cry. But, at the same time, she was so relieved that she could hardly keep herself from smiling.

Sofi woke up in the grey morning light and stretched her back uncomfortably. It had been a long time since she'd slept on a mattress on the floor. Lena was still asleep next to her, her long hair spread out untidily on the pillow. Sofi rose and moved as quietly as she could to the kitchen to switch on Natalya's coffee machine. Lena heard her and woke up.

'What time is it?' she said blearily.

'Eight.'

She laughed. 'I haven't slept in this late in six and a half years.'

Winter Gathering at Natalya's this year was like a sleepover party. No husbands or children, just the three of them crammed into Natalya's London apartment. They had taken turns making breakfast, and this morning it was Sofi's turn. Natalya emerged from her room, looking gorgeously dishevelled in a silk dressing-gown, and they sat at the kitchen bench having tea and tomato and parsley omelettes for breakfast, and planning what they'd do with their day.

'We haven't been shopping yet,' Sofi said. She was keen to get out and see the stores where her jewellery was for sale. Admittedly, so that Natalya might finally take her seriously.

'I'll come along and look,' Lena said. 'No spare money for shopping.'

'I'm the same,' Natalya said, pouting.

Sofi felt mingled irritation and guilt. Irritation because it was unfair of Natalya to compare her situation – living in a glamorous London flat – with Lena's situation, which was one of constant financial struggle. This year, Sofi had paid for Lena's train to London, and made sure that she was always on hand to pay for lunches and takeaway coffees while they were out. But she also felt guilty because she hadn't taken the time to explain to Natalya how the stock market worked, that she had forgotten about Natalya's enquiry and never called her back to check on her. Natalya still had a lot of money, but the crash had wiped out her ability to spend without thinking.

Lena, hiding her jealousy well if she felt it, put her hand softly on Natalya's shoulder. 'I'm sure you'll be working again soon.'

'I've been offered work, but Leida won't let me take it. Nightclub appearances, an independent film.'

'That script in the bathroom?' Lena said, alarmed. 'It's practically pornography.'

'You don't want to do nightclub appearances,' Sofi said. 'You'll look desperate and washed-up.'

'I *am* desperate and washed-up,' Natalya said, sipping her black coffee. 'No point in pretending I'm not.' She turned to Lena. 'Tell Sam to hurry up and get famous, then I can make my comeback in one of his video clips.'

Lena hedged, her face flushed, then finally admitted that Sam had given the band away. As she spoke about how depressed and lost he had seemed lately, and Natalya moaned about losing her money and never working again, and Sofi thought about her distant marriage and her son's condition, the superstitious fear returned to her. Had they somehow brought this on themselves? The idea gripped her fiercely, even though it went against everything she ordinarily believed. Perhaps it was having Mama around all the time, with her dozens of little superstitions; or perhaps it was the natural result of having a child who wasn't healthy and normal. Her rationality was being stripped back, exposing a primitive and fearful heart. She became aware of a pause in the conversation and looked up to see that Natalya and Lena were both watching her. She had been asked a question.

But instead of answering it, she said, 'I think that what we did to Roy Creedy is coming back to haunt us.'

Lena went pale. 'What do you mean?'

'Bad luck. We created bad luck. We led him on and broke his heart, stole his most precious things. What if our bad luck is due to that?'

Natalya sniffed. 'Don't be ridiculous.'

But Lena seized on the idea. 'Yes, and I'm the most to blame so I've profited the least from what we did. I wrote the letters, I made him fall in love.'

'No, *I'm* the most to blame,' Sofi said emphatically, relieved and frightened at the same time to have her feelings validated. 'I started it all. It was my idea, and I brought this bad luck on all of us. But me especially.'

Natalya spread her hands, looking incredulous. 'Have you two lost your minds? Sofi, you don't even believe in bad luck. And as for who is most to blame, please remember that it was me who broke into his bedroom, stole his jewellery and his car keys. I don't feel guilty, I don't blame my bad luck on it, and I'd do it again.'

Lena looked uncertain. 'Is there anything we could do to make things right?' she said.

'We could send him money,' Sofi said. 'I mean, I would do it. Neither of you can at the moment. And write a letter of apology.'

Natalya was already shaking her head. 'No, no, no. The past is the past. Absolutely not.'

'I think it's a good idea,' Lena said. 'Two against one, you're outvoted, Natalya.'

Natalya's eyes began to glitter with anger. 'No. He could be dangerous, and if he wanted to hurt somebody it would be me. Not either of you, despite how guilty you feel. Me. We should never, ever make contact with him, no matter if it is with money or apologies. I absolutely will not allow it.'

Sofi recognised that Natalya's extreme resistance would not be worn down, so she put her hands up in the air. Her rationality was returning. 'All right.'

'We're going to give up that easily?' asked Lena, and Sofi felt guilty for having given her hope.

'Natalya's right. We blame ourselves, but he would blame her. She has the final say.'

'Well, I've had the most bad luck, so I think I should have the final say,' Lena said.

Sofi wondered how she could feel she'd had the most bad luck when she had a husband who clearly adored her and two healthy, normal children.

'Subject closed,' said Natalya. 'If anyone says another word, I'm leaving the room.'

Lena fell silent, pushing her food around her plate with her fork.

Sofi regretted bringing it up and causing an argument, but the fear still brewed inside her, and she superstitiously wondered what terrible thing might befall them next.

CHAPTER THIRTY-SEVEN

Sofi had heard of a 'buzz' but never expected to find herself at the centre of one. It seemed that role should belong to somebody much more glamorous than herself. She owed much to Francette, who had an extraordinary ability to connect with the right people at the right time. And, of course, much was due to the shop, which had been discovered by a number of models, fashion designers and style mavens. Sofi's jewellery had been borrowed to complement couture and ready-to-wear in half-a-dozen fashion shows, culminating in a fashion spread in French *Elle*. The intense interest quickly spread across the channel, and *Vogue* magazine in England had run a feature article on Sofi, her village, her shop and her work. The press was calling her a 'new' designer, which amused Sofi as the shop in Paris had been open for a year, and she'd designed professionally for nearly seven years before that. But the strongest of all recommendations were word-of-mouth, and it became increasingly common to see photographs of the most fashion-conscious celebrities wearing an Anastasia cuff or choker as they turned up at red-carpet functions. Sofi had received more than a dozen special orders for one-off pieces, which she had been asked to design and make with her own hands.

She was no longer a small operation; she employed thirty-one staff at two locations. And so it was time to make a decision about what to do next. To this end, she now sat under the awning outside a café on Boulevard Saint-Germain with Francette, and Miranda and Bryan Ackroyd, the head creative team of Ackroyd Advertising. They specialised in fashion and beauty, and had designed ads for dozens of English and European magazines.

It was spring, the sky was clear blue and the sun was warm. This was the Paris that people dreamed of: the faint music of an accordion playing somewhere on a street corner, the mingled smells of croissants baking, passing cigarette smoke and cut lilies from the nearby flower market. Miranda and Bryan carefully outlined their ideas for an advertising campaign, first across the fashion magazines and then filtering down to the women's glossies. The cost was astronomical, but Francette held firmly that it would be worth it. Sofi listened, evaluated, scaled the spread of the campaign down, then was convinced to scale it back up, while they drank endless cups of coffee and Miranda Ackroyd chain-smoked. The tiny table filled rapidly with empty cups. Finally, talk turned to the kind of model they would hire for the campaign.

'Miranda and I feel very strongly,' Bryan said, stirring three sugars into his sixth cup of coffee, 'that you should not hire an anonymous model for each ad. You want coherence, and you want somebody who can be the public face of the product. We want to hire someone exclusively, so she can't advertise other jewellery or fashion over the course of the contract, and we want her to be already well known, and preferably not a model. Someone with personality, with a life outside the photographs.'

'Like a movie star?' Sofi asked.

Miranda hedged. 'Well, we don't really have the budget for a movie star, not a big one in any case. We want to find somebody who's just on the verge of making it. Perhaps somebody who's done a few small roles, is touted as the Next Big Thing. Young, fresh, beautiful. Like the jewellery. We'll cast for it.'

'But it adds extra expense,' Bryan said. 'An exclusive deal always does. We'd want to lock her into a two- or three-year contract.'

Sofi turned to Francette, who nodded slightly.

'Two years,' Sofi said. 'Keep the costs down. I'm not rich.'

She was lying. She was rich, but she was also frugal and didn't like to be swept away by this silver-tongued pair who persuaded people for a living.

Business was concluded shortly after two o'clock, when Sofi was buzzing with caffeine and hunger. It was a beautiful day, so she and Francette decided to walk back to the shop, across the bridge and the Ile de la Cité, then along the quay with the Seine glittering beside them. The air felt light and fresh. They bought crepes from a vendor and discussed the advertising campaign, the business, their sales figures. Deep inside Sofi was a little mournful girl, wanting to get away from all this grown-up business and back to threading beads on string. She knew it was time to return to Richelieu and her workshop, and leave business up to Francette.

'You know, Francette,' Sofi said, turning to her young companion, 'could I put you in charge of this advertising campaign?'

'If you like.'

'I should promote you again . . .'

'I don't think you can without making me owner of the company,' she laughed. The sun caught a reddish tint in her dark hair. 'I'm very flattered though.'

'Another pay rise then. Do some research, work out how much other people in your position are paid. I just want to go home and make jewellery. You take care of the business. Hire someone new to run the shop if you like.'

Francette, ever practical, nodded. 'All right, then. I'll send you the figures to approve. You go home and do what you love.'

Once a fortnight Natalya met with Leida Frost, her agent, at the immaculate office on Shaftesbury Avenue. They went over what offers, if any, had come in, what castings she might be suitable for, and Leida always assured her that the next big thing was just around the corner.

That corner had been promised for a long time now.

Natalya had worked, but it had not been the work she'd imagined. She'd done a highly paid television advertising campaign for a furniture company in Sweden, where they were years behind on *Lonely Shores* and Tatiana had only just left. She'd done bit parts in television dramas, always carefully selected so that she looked like a guest star, not a desperado who would take any part. Her characters always seemed to be murder victims or seductresses, and were rare enough that she had begun to doubt Leida's plan. She thought that if she just took everything that was offered, she would hammer her way back into the public consciousness by sheer volume of appearances. Leida had a vision for a long-term career of credible roles. But Natalya knew, at thirty-three, that her biggest drawcard – her beauty – had a use-by date.

She stepped out of the lift and crossed the foyer, saying hello to Alannah, Leida's long-suffering assistant. Leida was out from behind her desk in a moment to grasp Natalya's hand. 'Something's come in,' she said. 'I'm excited.'

Natalya's pulse picked up. 'Really?'

Leida led her to an armchair, sat opposite with a folder tucked under her arm.

'Has somebody big asked for me?' Natalya said, desperate for good news.

'No. Nobody's asked for you. But a casting call has come across my desk that . . . your real name is Chernova, right?'

'Yes.' Now she was puzzled.

'Then you must be related to this person?' Leida flipped open the folder and slid it onto the coffee table between them.

Natalya leaned close. An article cut out of a magazine. Sofi, at home in Richelieu. 'That's my cousin,' she said, surprised.

'You act like you don't know about this,' Leida said. 'She's one of the hottest jewellery designers in Europe at the moment.'

'Sofi?'

Natalya knew that her cousin's business was doing well, but had thought she was mass-producing five-quid bracelets for a chain store. Was she so out of touch with the fashion world? Well, when was the last time she'd been to a show? She didn't dare turn up at fashion week in case she was seated in the back row. But why hadn't Sofi told her? Natalya winced, remembering half-a-dozen reasons why: occasions when she had turned down wearing her jewellery.

'That's marvellous. I'm very proud of her,' Natalya said. 'But what does it have to do with me?'

'The advertising company is looking for an exclusive deal. The face of Anastasia. A massive campaign across twelve countries. Can you imagine anyone better for it than you? Native Russian, the designer's cousin, beautiful and already a little bit famous? It's a shoo-in, dear. You get on with your cousin, I take it?'

'We're very close.'

Was that still true? Gone were the days when they'd phone each other on a whim. Apart from Winter Gathering, she spoke to Sofi only rarely. The disaster with her money had made her resentful and embarrassed to talk to her cousin. But they still loved each other of course. They were still family.

'A contract like this is *perfect* for you. A high-profile advertising deal, your face in all the glossies. My dear, nothing says "I'm back and you can take me seriously" like a high-profile sponsorship deal. Can you call her? Tell her you want it?'

'I . . .' Natalya couldn't answer with certainty. 'Perhaps we should just let them know we're interested, let her call me. I don't want to be pushy.'

'Now's the time to be pushy, Natalie,' Leida said sternly.

Natalya nodded. 'Send my portfolio to the advertisers, and I'll call Sofi and tell her I want it.'

A sense of conviction grew inside her. Of course Sofi would give it to her. She was made for it. Though she did wonder why Sofi hadn't called her directly to ask . . . She pushed her doubts aside.

'I must say, Natalie, I'm excited,' Leida said.

'So am I.'

Lena hadn't had a day off sick in over two years, but there was no way she could get out of bed this morning. Especially not to face a dozen small children. It was probably one of them who had given her this cold. Mothers, keen to drop their children at the nursery so they didn't miss a day of work, would dose them up with medicine so they remained dry-nosed until morning tea time. After which they would pass their colds on to everyone else in the nursery.

So she called in sick. Sam got dressed and headed off to the greengrocer, Wendy backed her car out into the street and took off to do the weekly shopping, and Lena dozed in bed. Her head felt heavy and she was slightly feverish, and she just wanted to sleep and sleep and sleep.

A faint voice woke her around ten. She roused, listening.

'Lena? Lena?' It was Grandad, calling to her weakly.

She threw back the covers and hurried to his room. Her head was like a block of wood and she was still in her threadbare nightie.

'Grandad? What's wrong?'

'I don't feel right.'

She drew closer to the bed, saw that he was very pale. 'What do you mean?'

'I'm scared, Lena, I think this is it.'

Still she was having trouble understanding his meaning. He grasped her hand desperately. It was icy cold.

'I think I'm dying,' he said.

Hot adrenaline rushed through her. She began to pull away. 'I'll call an ambulance.'

'No, no,' he said, tightening his grip so hard that it crushed her fingers. 'Don't leave. Not for a second. I don't want to be alone.'

'Are you in pain? What do you feel?'

'I feel . . . cold. Cold creeping over me. I feel like a clockwork toy that's winding down.'

Lena sat with him, holding his hand and stroking his wrinkled brow. 'There, there. Maybe it's nothing.'

'No, no. I'm dying.' His breath caught. She tried to move away to get his oxygen mask, but again he pulled her back. 'Don't . . . leave me.'

'Your oxygen –'

'No . . . use . . . now . . .'

He slumped, eyelids fluttering, breathing laboured. She didn't know what to do, but felt very keenly that she should do *something*. She wanted to tell him goodbye, that she loved him, that she was forever grateful that he had cared enough about her to convince her to stop drinking. But she wasn't even sure if he could hear or understand her any more, so instead she began to sing to him. '*Bayushki bayu*', an old Russian lullaby that Aunt Stasya had sung to Sofi every night when they were children. It was all she could think of. Her little voice, lonely in the dim room.

She remembered back to when she had first met him, when he had seemed to be a terrifying old man full of long-winded stories and stern glares. She could never have predicted that he would come to mean so much to her, and her voice nearly cracked as she contemplated the hole his passing would leave in her life. Love, it seemed, had crept up on her. And now it was creeping away.

His eyes flew open, panicked. He gasped, struggled to talk.

'Shh,' she said, 'don't speak. It has all been said.'

'No,' he managed. 'I made . . . the right . . . choice.'

She didn't know what he meant, but she said, 'That's good. You take no regrets into the next world, then.'

'No. I don't.' He tried to smile, but it looked more like a baring of teeth.

She picked up the lullaby. He closed his eyes, took a deep breath. And stopped.

Lena began to shake. Hot tears fell. 'Goodbye, Grandad,' she said. 'Goodbye.'

Lena sat on the floor of the kids' bedroom, trying to sort out which toys to throw away and which ones to keep and pack for their move. In the two months since Grandad's death, the house had felt curiously cold, the kids had been sombre, Wendy had been speechless with her grief and guilt. Lena was so pleased to be leaving: away from the sadness and from Wendy's sharp edges. But she was also sad to be bidding a final farewell to the house where the old man had lived, and had loved her as her own father couldn't.

Anna, as always, was doing her best to complicate matters by crowding her, snatching toys out of the rubbish bag.

'Not him!' she protested, waving a ragged teddy by one leg. 'I still play with him.'

'Rubbish, Anna. I haven't seen you play with him for years. It's a baby toy. You're seven.'

Anna pressed it against herself, shaking her head. Lena had never met anyone as stubborn as her daughter. She terrorised poor little Matthew, who was made of much more delicate material. But Lena had learnt how to choose her battles carefully. 'All right, you can keep that teddy if you find five other baby toys to throw away.'

Anna began to plough through the other toys crammed into the cupboard, helpfully offering up two of Matthew's favourites. Matthew started crying, Sam lost his temper and roared at them both, Lena kept her head down and packed. Removalists were coming at seven the following morning and this was taking much longer than she'd thought.

With a full suitcase of old toys, she invited Matthew to come in the car with her to the local recycling station.

'Get us some lunch on the way home,' Sam suggested. 'What about hot dogs from Morrie's?'

Lena wanted to point out that now they were moving out, they couldn't afford to buy lunch at Morrie's, but it was too late as the children were shouting and jumping up and down with excitement. She took the car keys and her son and left.

When she returned thirty minutes later, Wendy was in the room talking in a harsh whisper to Sam, who was sitting on the bottom bunk with a lap full of children's books. He looked dazed. Lena's skin prickled. Something was amiss.

'Lunch,' she said brightly.

Wendy turned, her eyes as cold as stone.

'Is everything all right?'

Wendy took a deep breath. Her face was dark red. 'No. Everything is *not* all right.'

Matthew, frightened by Wendy's temper, clung to Lena's side. Lena glanced at Sam, who looked guilty.

'Mum's had some interesting news,' he said.

Wendy raised her finger to point at Lena and her hand shook slightly. 'I've just come from the solicitor's office. My father's solicitor. He changed his will in June this year, it seems. Named a certain Lena Chernova-Tait as his sole heir.'

Lena shook her head. 'Wendy . . .'

'Don't speak to me. All this time you were in there, undermining me. Well, you got what you wanted. Are you happy?'

Lena fell silent, stroking Matthew's back. She was touched that Grandad had left what little he had to her, but didn't he realise how much trouble it would create? Though, Lena admitted, she was to blame a little. She still hadn't told Wendy or Sam that Grandad actually had no great fortune, even when Wendy had gone into a frenzy of speculation about how much it would be and what she might be able to buy with it. Lena, cruelly she knew, had almost enjoyed the idea that soon Wendy would hear from the solicitor and be terribly disappointed. But Lena had also been protecting herself. If she told them now, they would know that she had kept it from them for years.

Wendy dissolved into tears. 'How could you? How could you?'

Sam stood, banging his head on the bunk. 'Mum, calm down. We'll give you some too. We'll help you out.'

Lena turned to him, realisation suddenly upon her. Sam thought she was rich. He was already spending that money in his head: the band was back, they had a new car, maybe even a house with a recording studio underneath. She had to tell him before he went too far.

'Stop,' she blurted. 'Both of you stop. There is no money.'

Wendy and Sam stared at her.

'Wendy, has the solicitor told you what Grandad was worth?'

'Not yet. He's organised a search of assets. Dad didn't list everything.'

Lena took a deep breath. 'Grandad told me that all he had was a little money in his cheque account. That he never had much, that he let you believe he did so that you wouldn't put him in a home. I think it will be a couple of hundred pounds at most.'

Wendy's mouth opened and closed, a fish drowning in air.

Sam said, 'When did he tell you this?'

'About five years ago,' she admitted softly. 'I'm sorry. He asked me to keep it a secret.'

'You shouldn't keep secrets,' Anna piped up, always glad for a chance to wag her finger at a grown-up. 'Not if they can hurt people.'

Sam rounded up Anna and Matthew and told them to go outside and play. Once they were gone, Wendy – pale and shaking – turned on Lena.

'You knew for five years that he had no money? And you let me go on believing he did?'

Sam, who had suffered a very quick rise and fall of his hopes, joined with his mother. 'Lena, I can't believe you didn't at least tell me.'

'I made a promise to an old man,' Lena said.

'But think of the damage you've done!' Wendy shouted. 'You've treated me like a fool for all this time, listening to me making plans for the future and knowing they'd never come true. Did you have a good laugh at me?'

'There's nothing funny about this situation,' Lena replied, hands held up in front of her. 'I'm not laughing.'

Sam ran a hand through his hair. 'You should have told us, Lena,' he said. 'You should have told us.'

'I made a promise.'

'You made a promise to me too. On the day we were married. As husband and wife, there should be no secrets between us.'

Now Lena became irritated, thinking of the half-dozen occasions Sam had borrowed money and she had only found out later. Both Wendy and Sam were calling her morality into question, but the real issue was how disappointed and embarrassed they felt about missing out on the money.

She held up the plastic bag with the hot dogs. 'There's nothing more I can say. I did what I thought was right. I'm going outside to eat lunch with the children.'

It was much later that night before Sam spoke another word to her. They were getting into bed and she, superstitious of them sleeping all night on their resentment, asked him if he could forgive her.

He sighed and flopped back on his pillow. 'Of course, Lena. You were so good to Grandad, perhaps better than he deserved. I can't fault you on that. But... in that half-hour, when I thought we were rich... God, Lena, it was like I was free. And now, after feeling that, I realise how trapped I actually am.' He put both his hands over his face and she suspected he might be trying to hide tears.

'I'm sorry. If I'd known Grandad was going to leave me his money, I would have warned you in advance. So you weren't so disappointed.'

He removed his hands. 'But don't you see? All that doesn't matter: Grandad and Mum and you, who said what and when, all that business. It's just a stupid family tiff that will blow over. The problem is, I *felt* it, Lena. I felt the freedom, and now I'll never have it but I'll always know what I'm missing. Forever.'

She wanted to say, 'You might have that freedom, one day.' But it wasn't true. And, besides, her throat was aching too much to say anything.

CHAPTER THIRTY-EIGHT

Winter Gathering at Sofi's had officially become the family gathering. Sofi paid for everyone – even Natalya, who was crying poor – to come, and put them all up in a holiday house just outside the walls of the village. The weather was mild this year, with pale blue skies and white sunshine, and every morning so far they had all gone out walking in the chateau parklands: Sofi, Julien, Nikita, Lena, Sam, Anna, Matthew and Natalya. Mama stayed home with her feet up, doing her cross-stitch. Lena's son was a dream with Nikita, trying to involve him in games, spinning the roundabout for him, teaching him a clapping song. Anna, in full make-up courtesy of Natalya, was less patient with this strange, silent little boy who couldn't meet her eye.

They stopped near the entrance to the pool, which was closed for winter, and Julien and Sam began kicking a soccer ball around, teasing Matthew and Anna to try to take it from them. Much shouting and cross-channel rivalry followed. Nikita stood at the outside of the game, clutching his fingers rhythmically. All the work with Mama was paying off very, very slowly. Nikita was five now, but still seemed no closer to understanding the world. He grew frustrated and cranky if he was out of his routine, called Julien, Stasya and Sofi 'Mama' interchangeably, was fascinated and bewildered at the same time by other children, and his vocabulary for communicating was extremely limited. But then, from time to time, there would be a glimmer of *something* and Sofi's heart would soar. He would finally catch on to a simple turn-taking game, or he would put a doll in its toy bed, or he would simply smile or laugh at Sofi if she made an amusing noise. She had no illusions: there was no cure for him. But every day she felt they were one step closer to getting him used to the world.

Sofi, Lena and Natalya sat on a bench to watch them play.

'I wish you wouldn't put make-up on her, Natalya,' Lena said. 'She's only a little girl.'

'And little girls love make-up,' Natalya responded. 'She begged me.'

At that moment, Matthew fell over and landed face first in the grass. Before he had even opened his mouth to howl, Lena was on her feet and running towards him.

Now would be the moment for Natalya to turn to Sofi with one of her usual offhand, behind-Lena's-back comments: 'She babies him'. But there was no easiness between them at the moment; Sofi could barely meet her eye comfortably.

It was all the fault of the stupid advertising campaign that she'd agreed to. Never in a million years had she thought that Natalya would want the job; she'd not shown a moment's interest in Sofi's jewellery since she'd started work on television. So her phone call had come as a shock. Sofi had immediately said she loved the idea, of course. Natalya was beautiful and, more importantly, Russian. She promised to run it past the other people involved. But Sofi hadn't reckoned on the resistance she met: from Francette, first, but especially from the advertising company.

'She won't work, especially not in England,' Miranda Ackroyd had said, blowing an elegant stream of smoke in the air.

'But why not?' Sofi asked.

Miranda struck the reasons off on her fingers, dusting ash everywhere. 'Too old, too trashy. All wrong.' She smiled briefly. 'Sorry for saying. You did ask.'

And so now a huge dilemma lay at Sofi's feet. She had asked for time to consider, delaying the campaign for months. Francette kept the pressure up: they had to advertise *now*, while the buzz was happening. Miranda and Bryan sent her a constant stream of emails – photographs of beautiful young actresses – no doubt imagining a potentially lucrative ad campaign slipping out of their grasp. But that was the problem, wasn't it? If she was going to spend that much money, then she couldn't use the wrong model. If Natalya really was just a washed-up sexpot in the English public's imagination, then Sofi simply couldn't choose her. It would be a terrible business decision.

Natalya had pretended to understand the delay in making the decision, but it hadn't stopped her from asking a million questions since she'd been here in Richelieu. Who else was in the running? How many countries would the ads be in? Which magazines? For how long? Sofi had tried to feign only a vague knowledge, hoping Natalya would infer that it wasn't her decision to make. But, of course, it was. It was her company; she had the final say.

Thankfully, Lena returned, saving them from making conversation. Matthew, who had two grazed elbows, sat in her lap snivelling. Lena stroked his hair. Then Nikita walked up, prised open Matthew's hand and dumped in it a few shreds of grass.

Sofi's heart stopped. He was trying to cheer Matthew up, trying to give him a present.

Matthew, bless him, patted Nikita's head and said, 'Thank you.'

Sofi gathered Nikita up and pressed him close. 'Oh, you darling boy,' she said. Nikita allowed himself to be held, as detached and silent as usual. All her worries about Natalya and her business melted away, lost in the beautiful moment with her son.

January came and went. Francette had finally had enough.

'Sofi,' she said over the phone, her voice sharp, 'if you do not decide *today* about the ad, you will miss the spring editions of the fashion magazines. You must move ahead with this.'

They had found the face of Anastasia: a twenty-two-year-old actress who'd had a small part in a surprise hit movie. Offers were being thrown at her; they had to pin her down as soon as possible.

'But my cousin . . .' Sofi started.

'You told me that your cousin once said she wouldn't wear an Anastasia necklace made by you with a Chanel dress. Now the Chanel people are asking for your jewellery for their next catwalk show.'

Sofi winced.

'Please, Sofi, it's make-or-break time.'

'All right,' Sofi said, eyes fluttering closed. 'All right, no Natalya. Go ahead with the actress.'

'Good. You've made the right decision.'

'Have I?'

'For your business.'

It was little comfort.

'Can you please help me with a favour, Francette? Can you call Natalya directly and tell her? So she doesn't hear it through her agent?'

'Why don't you call her?'

Good question.

'I simply can't. Best if she thinks the decision was made without me.'

Though Natalya wasn't a fool. She would know that Sofi had given in, that she had let her down at precisely the moment when Natalya needed her help most.

Neatly packed boxes waited just inside the front door. Natalya was moving out. The rent on her Kensington flat was eating through her savings too quickly. She'd found another flat – small but still beautifully decorated – at Finchley. It was cheaper, and she didn't really need to be walking distance from the shops any more considering she hadn't the money to go shopping.

It wasn't that she was broke. Money ticked in from her various scraps of work and she still had a lot in the bank. It was just that she was used to a huge income, being able to buy things without thinking about it. Maintaining her appearance was a major expense that she couldn't cut back on, especially now she was growing older. So moving was her only option. She told herself that once her career was flourishing again, she could find somewhere else. But it seemed that a flourishing career was more unlikely by the moment. Even Leida Frost seemed to have lost faith: their meetings were now every two months instead of every two weeks. Still she tried to push Natalya into poorly paid jobs because they were the 'right kind' of exposure. Her latest was to encourage Natalya to work for a Russian director who had asked for her. Low-budget art movie, shot in St Petersburg. The fee was a pittance and she simply *couldn't go back*. It would be like giving up, returning home with her tail between her legs. Leida didn't understand, grew cross with her. But then Leida went home to her penthouse flat at Butlers Wharf. It was Natalya who had to live with these decisions.

The removalists wouldn't be here for another hour. Natalya had bought a magazine to cheer herself up, so she sat on the sofa with her feet up and began to read. Five pages in, she saw it. The Anastasia campaign. Two full pages with a fold-out. A young actress – what was her name? Was it Olivia something? Natalya had seen her movie and thought her very bland – was dressed in a black satin gown, reclining on a red chaise. Every part of her body was covered in Sofi's jewellery, down to two gorgeously delicate ankle bracelets resting on her bare feet. She looked amazing, like a star. Natalya's stomach rolled: she was nauseous with envy. She slapped the magazine shut and threw it across the bare floor. She closed her eyes, holding in the tears. *Not fair, not fair.* Sofi could have made her the star, but had chosen not to.

The doorbell rang, the removalists were early. She threw herself into helping them, just to push the dark thoughts away. They were surprised, but didn't complain, as she lugged boxes down the stairs and into their truck. Finally, she watched them drive off, and went back upstairs to get her handbag, lock up the little flat for the last time.

Just as she was switching off the last light, the phone rang. She scooped it up, distracted.

'Hello? Natalya?'

A Russian man. She couldn't place him at first, wondered if it were the Russian director making a direct plea for her to work for him.

'Yes?' she said warily.

'It's your father.'

The pressures finally caught up with her. She began to laugh, a huge cackling laugh that made tears run down her cheeks. 'You want money again already?' she said. 'Oh, that is funny.'

'It's been two years,' he said. 'Ten thousand pounds doesn't go far. You'd better double it this time.'

She felt reckless. 'I don't have it,' she said, still laughing. 'I don't have any spare money to give you. So go away, don't call me again. It's over.'

'Well, it isn't over if I contact Lena.'

Natalya sobered up. 'Leave her alone. I have no money. I am not lying to you. I'm all washed-up, Papa. I haven't been a star in more than three years. I lost most of my money in the stock market. I'm just today moving to a tiny flat in the middle of fucking nowhere.' And it all could have been so different. If Sofi hadn't given her bad advice; if Sofi had given her the ad campaign. Then an idea glimmered into her head. 'Call Sofi,' she said. 'She'll give you money.'

'Sofi? Why would she give me money?'

'The same reason I did. To keep you away from Lena.' She pressed on, knowing she was doing the wrong thing but unable to stop herself. 'Have you got a pen?' she asked. 'I'll give you her number.'

Lena couldn't get used to the frantic morning pace at their new flat. Without Wendy to help find shoes or plait Anna's hair, she and Sam really struggled to get both children ready for school on time. Then it was all into the car and Lena dropped them off in turn: Sam at the greengrocer, Anna and Matthew at school, and finally herself at the nursery. They had also relied on Wendy to pick the kids up from school, but now Lena had negotiated her break to be at mid-afternoon so she could race to the school, race them home, then come back to work to finish the day without having had lunch. Despite all this, she did not regret one little bit moving out of Wendy's house. For the first time, it felt as though she and Sam were grown-ups. Their new flat was very clean and uncluttered, not as close to the sea so sheltered from the harshest of the gales, and there was a park at the end of the street.

Sam didn't share her happiness about their new situation.

'As long as we were living with Mum,' he had said on the first evening, when Lena had cautiously opened a bottle of champagne and poured herself one small glass, 'I could pretend it was temporary, something I was doing in the meantime. But this . . . this is real and permanent. This is my life.'

Lena tried to have patience with Sam's melancholy, trusting it would eventually fade away. But it had been nearly six months since their move, since Lena had inherited four hundred and twenty-eight pounds from Grandad and watched it disappear in less than a week on a second-hand car with so much rust that it flaked off spontaneously if the doors were slammed. And still Sam wallowed in his misery and self-pity.

This morning, she scooped up the post on the way out the door, ensured the children were buckled in, started the car to warm up the engine, then waited for Sam who was cleaning his teeth and locking up the house. He was taking ages, as usual, so she leafed through the letters, tensed, as she always was, for an unexpected bill. In the middle of the pile she found a letter from the solicitor who had dealt with Grandad's will. A legal bill, it had to be, one she hadn't anticipated. She picked it open, scanned it quickly.

Then stopped. Went back and read carefully.

After Grandad's death, the solicitor had said that he was still searching for assets, but agreed with Lena that he would be unlikely to find any. They were both wrong. A house and land at Little Ayton, on the edge of the moors, had been found in Grandad's name. Lena's heart stopped beating, her ears rang. Then the car door opened and Sam slid in. On instinct, she hid the letter in her handbag and forced a smile. 'All ready?' she said.

'Are you sick?' he replied. 'You look very pale.'

'I . . . ah . . . I feel a bit strange,' she said, putting the car in gear.

'It's those kids you work with,' he grumbled.

On the drive, she tried very hard not to get excited. Perhaps she had read incorrectly. She didn't understand legal terms. She just needed to get to a phone and call the solicitor, ask him what the letter meant. She was in a daze as she dropped Sam off, kissed the kids goodbye at the school gate, then drove straight home to call in sick at work. She had to wait half an hour for the solicitor to phone her back, during which time she cleaned the kitchen savagely, alternating between hope and despair. Finally, the phone rang.

'Hello?'

'Mrs Chernova-Tait?'

'Yes?' Heart thudding.

'How may I help you?'

'The letter you sent. The house. Is it . . .' She couldn't bring herself to ask, fearing the letdown so keenly.

'Yes, it's yours. Your grandfather was very secretive about his assets. We had to go through rather a lot of correspondence to find it.'

Grandad's dying comment about having made the right decision suddenly made sense. He meant changing his will in favour of Lena. Lena, who had stood by him and helped him and loved him even when she thought there was nothing to be inherited from him.

'It has taken many weeks of work. I'm afraid there will be a substantial bill.'

But Lena didn't hear the bad news, only the good. 'May I go to see it?' she asked.

'You certainly may. I'll leave a package at the front desk for you, paperwork and keys and so on. But, please, keep your expectations low. I would imagine it is in poor repair. You will probably find it more practical to sell the property.'

And so she found herself on a drive out through the moors, heart in her throat. The wild fields were choked with heather that hadn't yet flowered. Fast-moving clouds scudded over the sun, dappling the ground with shadows. Then, behind the soft peak of Roseberry Topping, she found the little village. She stopped to ask for directions and buy a takeaway coffee, and continued down a winding country lane that bumped and shook her rusty little car. She found an unmarked front fence between two numbers that might be her new neighbours, and reversed onto the shoulder of the road.

Her hands were shaking as she let herself out of the car. A low stone wall grown over with lichen and vines, the thatched roof and two chimneys of an old farmhouse. The front gate was hanging off its hinges. She walked up the overgrown path. The house – *my house* – was made of grey stone. White windowsills peeled, glass panes were missing. She found the front door and slid in the key.

Inside, puddles and spider webs. The kitchen was a crumbling mess. The fireplace was black. Three tiny bedrooms waited off the narrow hallway. Part of the ceiling was missing, and swallows had nested in the roof beams. The bathroom was black with mould and smelled as though an animal had died in here. 'Poor repair' didn't even begin to describe the house. And yet . . . Lena allowed herself to imagine it fixed and painted and decorated. Photographs of the children in frames on the walls of the hallway. A new stove in the kitchen, the floor tiles cleaned, a wooden table for Anna and Matthew to do their homework while she cooked . . .

Of course, repairs of that nature took money. They had no money.

She let herself out the kitchen door and the view stopped her. Rolling away from her, green fields bordered by ancient hedgerows, an old stone barn – was that hers too? – clusters of trees, neighbouring gardens tight on the verge of flowering, cows moving slowly in the distance, all spread out under shifting sunlight. She stood for what seemed like an age gazing at that view; enjoying the feeling of owning a piece of the world, a piece of forever.

Sadly, she had to admit it would never be possible for them to fix the house up and live in it. They would have to borrow a lot of money. Even if a bank gave them the money, and she doubted this very strongly, they would have to hope to find jobs nearby and labour under the debt for life. Sam was hopeless with money; they had trouble managing rent. A mortgage might very well finish them off.

Would she sell it then? She'd need money for the legal fees. But the thought made her feel desperate. She knew what would happen if Sam suddenly had access to a lump sum of money. He would spend it. All of it. He would buy a brand new car, something impractical. He would want to rent a big place, live off the money. He would want to enjoy himself, because he felt that life had given him too few things to enjoy. God forbid, maybe he would even quit work and start talking about the band again. It would all be gone in a few years and they'd be right back where they started. She hated to admit these things about her husband, whom she loved as ardently now as she had on the day they'd married, but it was true. It was the reason she had hidden the letter that morning. Perhaps a stronger woman might have been able to manage him; but how could she tell him the money was hers, that he couldn't touch it, when it had come from his own grandfather?

But there was a third option. They had children. If she just kept quiet about the property, let it sit there as it had for years, it would continue to grow in value. Perhaps when Matthew and Anna were adults, they would have good jobs that paid well, and they could fix up the house and live in it, or knock it down and sell the land. They could decide for themselves. She indulged a brief fantasy about Anna in the house with two little children of her own – cooking and homework – and far fewer cares than Lena had had to experience. She smiled, blinking away tears. Her decision was made.

She locked up the house, making a promise to come back when she could and board the windows properly, perhaps call someone to fix the hole in the roof so it was at least weathertight. As she drove home, she decided to call Sofi. She was clever with things like business and property, she would know what to do. And, most importantly of all, she could keep a secret.

CHAPTER THIRTY-NINE

With Nikita's hand in hers, Sofi walked to the postbox. It was important when Nikita was moving, especially if they were in the car but even when he was walking, to keep his mind occupied. Otherwise he drifted into a dead-eyed daze. So she had told him to find as many round objects as he could with his eyes. His powers of observation were extraordinary, she had to admit, as he found circles everywhere from designs on bumper stickers to elaborate cornicing on the tops of buildings. She slid the letter into the slot. Money for Lena. Her cousin had called with a story of inheriting a run-down farmhouse, of wanting to keep it a secret so her children could have it one day. Sofi had gently offered her the money for legal bills and roof repairs, and Lena had grown completely tongue-tied with gratitude, babbling about paying it back when she could.

'No, it's a gift,' Sofi said. 'Not for you, but for Matthew and Anna.'

Within that perspective, Lena had been freed to say a breathless yes.

Sofi and Nikita walked home amongst the growing shadows. This time they found square things, but Nikita was becoming tired. It was as though the world was too much for him to process, as though he was convinced he had to assess every sensory impression from every perspective before he could move on. She picked him up and told him to close his eyes if the world bothered him, but she could see over her shoulder that he was gazing back the way they had come, glazed.

At home, Julien was cooking. This meant he'd had a bad day in the studio. Mama was good for him, refusing to let him sink under the weight of his artistic crises. She would give him a broom or a frying pan and tell him to join her in the real world for a while, do something physical or practical. And so he was laughing with her in the kitchen, while garlic fried in butter and Ella Fitzgerald sang on the stereo. It would be too much for Nikita, so she took him to his quiet bedroom and put a Baby Einstein video on for him – he had never grown out of baby videos – while she went to share a glass of wine with her husband.

He made her try his creamy basil sauce, accidentally dripping it down her chin then kissing it off. The phone rang and Mama went to answer it.

'Bad day?' she said, sipping her wine.

'Terrible,' he laughed. 'Thank God for your mother.'

Sofi tried not to feel inadequate. All those years, she had simply let him be when he was having trouble painting. She had been in awe of him, terrified of interrupting his creative flow. But Mama had figured him out in no time. It made her wonder if there were other ways she was mismanaging Julien. Perhaps she should be more demanding, order him to stay home, insist that he told her he loved her every day. Perhaps she should tell him about the yearning that was growing again, deep in her heart, for a second child. But she had barely acknowledged it herself yet. Afraid that wanting another child would somehow signal to Nikita that he wasn't enough, that his defectiveness had left her with a hole that could only be filled by trying again. Afraid that her bad luck would come down just as heavily on a second child.

Her thoughts were interrupted by Mama speaking harshly in Russian. 'No, you cannot talk to her.'

Sofi turned, Mama was about to hang up the phone. She dashed over and seized it, covering the receiver. 'Who is it?'

'Your Uncle Viktor,' Stasya said, her voice shaking.

Sofi was puzzled, angry. 'What does he want?'

'Just hang up.'

Sofi waved her off gently, held the phone to her ear. 'How did you get this number?' she asked.

'Natalya gave it to me.'

Sofi shouldn't have been surprised. She hadn't spoken to Natalya since the model had been chosen for the Anastasia campaign. They were avoiding each other. But she'd known that Natalya would be angry.

'I see. And what do you want?'

'I want money. To stay away from Lena.'

'I'm afraid I won't give in to blackmail, Uncle Viktor. The answer is no.'

He hadn't been expecting this. She wondered how many times Natalya had paid him off. 'I'll call Lena,' he spluttered. 'I'll come to see her again. You'll regret this.'

'No, you won't,' she said. 'You have no desire to see her, none of us have anything to offer you any more. I'm confident you'll stay away.'

Was she confident? Not really, but she wasn't going to go down this path with him. He deserved nothing; she would give him what he deserved.

'Goodbye,' she said, and hung up, tensed for the phone to ring again. It didn't. Perhaps he'd already known he was defeated before he rang.

Mama scowled at her. 'You shouldn't have even spoken to him.'

'Don't worry, Mama,' she said. 'I have a feeling we won't hear from him again. He's done with us.'

Natalya hadn't been wined and dined for a very long time, and she enjoyed it far too much. She sat in Browns restaurant at Covent Garden, sipping wine and picking at her ravioli – entree size – while the man across the table told her how much he loved her. He wasn't a boyfriend, though, sadly. The most Natalya seemed to manage was four dates before her partner revealed he was vain, or lecherous, or empty. Perhaps she was making terrible choices. Her loneliness had crept up on her, and fuelled her anxiety about getting older and still being unemployed.

But the man across the table was a director. Arnold Grassman, a forty-something independently wealthy filmmaker who was shooting a horror/sci-fi film called *Skin Crawlers* and wanted her for the lead female role.

'It's your beauty that makes you perfect for it,' he was saying. 'You're so queenly, so noble. And these disgusting creatures are so slimy and foul.' He said 'foul' so passionately that spittle jumped from his lips and landed on the table. He wiped it away with his fist. 'I may not be a big name yet in filmmaking, Natalie, but I have deep pockets. I'm willing to pay you a lot of money for this role because I am *that* convinced you are the right person for it. You are my drawcard.'

She had her doubts of course. The movie required her to run around in her underwear for most of the second half, blasting away at aliens with a shotgun, before being eviscerated by a large tentacle. Grassman had made two other movies, which had gone straight to video. But one could never tell in this business who would make the next high-camp hit, become the hippest darling on the scene. Leida had warned her away sternly. 'He has no credibility. Maxim Levitsky still wants you; he just won the Un Certain Regard award at Cannes. Can't you just meet with him?'

But Maxim Levitsky had no money and worked in St Petersburg. Arnold Grassman was a billionaire and was filming right here in London. And so Natalya had set up this meeting without Leida's knowledge.

Natalya tried not to look excited when the talk turned to money. 'Well, Arnold, if your offer is generous I'd like to see a draft of a contract. Then I'll be in a better position to say yes firmly.'

He fumbled through an overexcited thank you, promising to load her contract with little extras. She regarded him across the table, marvelling that this bumbling, overgrown boy was so wealthy and powerful. She smiled graciously, sipped her wine again, then couldn't resist asking him, 'Arnold, for an independent filmmaker, you say you have quite a large budget. How is that so?'

'Oh, I don't skimp,' he said, puffing up proudly. 'Especially not on my leading ladies.' He laughed self-consciously, appeared to deflate as he loaded up his fork with pasta. 'I own a mining machinery company,' he said. 'I inherited it when I turned twenty-one. We're the largest manufacturer of mining machinery in England.' He shrugged. 'I was never much interested in mining machinery, Natalie. I always wanted to make sci-fi movies.'

She pushed her plate away, tossed her hair over her shoulder. 'When can I expect to see the contract then?' she said. How long would she have to wait to find out what he was offering? He could be all bluster and no substance for all she knew. Maybe he thought 'a lot of money' could be counted in five figures. She could do another Swedish commercial if she wanted five figures.

'I'll start working on it this afternoon. But . . . I don't want to insult you with my offer.'

Here it comes. The dashing of her hopes was imminent. He was about to suggest a profit-sharing deal. A week's wage on *Lonely Shores*.

'So, could you tell me,' he said, clearing his throat, 'if one million pounds would be enough?'

Natalya's voice was stuck.

'It's not, is it?' he said mournfully. 'I'm afraid I haven't worked with any big stars before so –'

'Up-front?' she said.

'The day we start filming. First of July. It's a twelve-week shoot.'

'Deal.' She realised she'd spoken too quickly. Smiled and tried to feign languor in her limbs. 'It's a deal, Arnold, and it will be a pleasure working with you.'

Sofi gave all of her staff four weeks off over Christmas, but she loved the day in January when they all came back and production cranked into life once more. She made sure she was the first person at the workshop – which now covered two floors – turning on the lights, the heating and the radio, putting fresh milk in the refrigerator and pouring fresh coffee beans into the grinder. She walked around all the work tables, inspecting them one by one. Half-finished pieces were pinned to all of them. Her own hand-drawn designs in blue pencil on sheets of cream paper covered the walls. There was no smell of glue because Anastasia Designs still didn't use glue; everything was set using hand-woven silver. Though Sofi had been asked to make a budget line of jewellery; she'd said no, of course.

The door opened and Elita came in: one of her newest employees. She was fifty, had been out of the workforce raising her five children for twenty years. Nobody else would give her a job, but Sofi had. She needed no experience, just nimble fingers and a willing brain. Sofi sat with her and they worked together for half an hour on an amethyst and pearl cuff. The others arrived, the room filled up with warmth and chatter. She liked her staff to be happy, so they wandered about drinking coffee, helped each other, talked about their personal lives while they wound and wove patterns of silver. Sofi sat amongst them as often as she could, hand-making jewellery as she had always loved to do. She had a little office on the upper floor for designing and paperwork, but she spent a lot of time there staring out the window down onto the village's cobbled streets, its pale seventeenth-century buildings, the variety of locals who ambled past – nobody ever rushed in Richelieu – coming back from the markets with full baskets, on their way to coffee shops, or simply walking for pleasure. Village life agreed with Sofi. She had given Francette the power to make more and more decisions, freeing herself up. Francette was ambitious. She had two of the big New York department stores interested in Anastasia, but Sofi was reluctant to cross the Atlantic. If the company grew any larger, she feared she would lose control of its quality.

Gabriel, a lanky and obviously gay teenager who did finishings and findings for her, asked how her holidays had been. She told him about Briggsby, her cousins, the grey ocean, the long cliff walks, and it sounded happy, even idyllic. She couldn't tell him about how tense

Lena had become, trying to hide a house from her husband. Nor about Natalya bragging constantly that she'd made a million dollars for a blockbuster film, no doubt in the hope that Sofi would regret not employing her for the Anastasia campaign. Sofi's relationship with Natalya, she admitted, would need time to recover. When Sofi had got her alone, had demanded to know why she had put Viktor in touch, Natalya had tearily apologised.

'I didn't have any money to give him,' she said, 'but I knew you would and you care about Lena just as much, so . . . I hope you didn't give him too much.'

'I didn't give him anything.'

Her head snapped up. 'What?'

'You should never submit to blackmail. I knew he wouldn't contact Lena; he doesn't really want anything to do with her, he certainly doesn't want the bother or the expense of coming all this way. And I was right. He hasn't even phoned her.'

Then Lena had come in and they'd fallen silent. It had been a Winter Gathering of secrets for Sofi. As well as keeping talk of Viktor out of Lena's ears, Lena had been keen that Natalya not know about her inheritance. Sofi and Lena had managed to get away early one morning to see the little farmhouse.

'It's watertight now, thanks to your money,' Lena had said, clearing away cobwebs from the kitchen windows. 'I thought I might come up here sometime, if I can disappear without Sam seeing me, and paint the front door or clean up the bathroom. Just for fun.'

Sofi could see the place needed more than a bit of painting and cleaning. And yet it had much more charm than the sterile little flat Lena was living in. Quietly, she had taken Lena's hand and said, 'Please, let me loan you the money to fix the place up and move into it.'

'Oh, no, I couldn't. It would be too much. Everything inside needs replacing: all the cupboards, the bath, the toilet, the stove. The plaster is a mess, it will have to be chiselled off. I think one of the walls has to be knocked down and rebuilt, and the entire roof will have to be rethatched. Not to mention the wiring, the plumbing . . .'

Lena chewed the inside of her mouth. 'I could never take that kind of generosity, and I don't know if we could ever pay it back.'

Sofi fell silent, deciding to bide her time. She would work on Lena over the coming years, and she would eventually win. It became very important to her too that Lena not tell Sam about the house, or anyone else.

Sofi roused herself from her reverie, aware that Gabriel was still talking about his holiday at his mother's house in Languedoc. She was just about to ask him a question when the door to the workshop opened and Julien walked in.

He hurried over to Sofi and caught her wrist. She immediately assumed something was wrong with Nikita and her skin iced over. 'What is it?'

'I've had great news,' he said.

Sofi relaxed, laughing at herself. 'Come up to my office.'

She led him up the worn stone stairs and into her office, closing the door behind her. In here, she had an antique wooden desk and three of Julien's paintings on the wall. She sat at her desk and Julien went to the window, perched on the sill.

'Well?' she asked.

'I've been awarded a fellowship to go to Brazil for a year.'

Sofi's smile froze on her face. This was 'great news'? Julien had been home for two years in a row, and she had thought that perhaps his globe-trotting days were over.

'Say something?' he said, laughing nervously.

'I didn't even know you were applying for another fellowship.'

'I . . . there was no point in upsetting you if I wasn't sure I'd get it.'

'So, you did know it would upset me?'

'A little, perhaps. But I thought you might be excited too.' He clasped her hands. 'Come with me, Sofi. You can still design over there. Francette runs your business.'

'Nikita has his appointments.'

'Your mother can stay here with him.'

Sofi was amazed that he could suggest such a thing: leaving Nikita behind for a year! But then, *he* did it all the time. Went away, left them as though it didn't hurt him.

'I'm not due to leave until June. We have plenty of time to make a decision.'

Sofi took a deep breath. 'Julien, I don't want you to go.'

He looked at her as though she had just spoken Swahili. 'I'm sorry?'

'I think you should stay here, with your family. With me.' Already her voice was growing weak. How dare she stand in the way of his art? Then she chastised herself, reminded herself that it was time he heard the truth of her heart. 'I don't like it when you're away. It feels as though you abandon us, as though you can't stand to be around us.'

Julien's eyes were soft. 'Oh, my dear. No. No.'

'And Nikita?'

'I love him, I'm mad about him. My little boy. But he doesn't mind if I go. You know that.'

'If you love us, how can you be away?'

'Because when I'm away I am painting. I feel nothing else. Surrounded by a language I don't speak, people I don't know.' His voice grew serious. 'And I *need* it, Sofi. I need to be in that place, where all the practicalities of the world cease to exist, and it's simply me and the colours and shapes. I will die if I don't have it.'

'But you need the real world too,' she said, realising she sounded petulant. 'You told me that once.'

'I have been here for two years now. It's time to get away. Please do not ask me to stay, because if you ask, I will have to say yes.'

What choice did she have? 'All right,' she said. 'Go. But . . .'

'But?' he said, tilting his head. 'What else is there, Sofi?'

'Before you go . . .' Did she really want to say this? Did she really *want* this? 'Before you go, can we talk about trying for another baby?'

An expression of horror crossed his face. Sofi's heart fell.

'No. Oh, Sofi. Not again.'

In the wake of his refusal, she suddenly felt the full surge of maternal longing. 'Why not?'

He slumped against the desk. 'Because if it goes wrong again, I couldn't bear it.'

'It might not . . .'

'You have met some of the other families. Many with more than one child affected.' Julien, as always, could not bring himself to say the word 'autism'.

Sofi sighed. 'What if I insisted?'

'I would still say no.'

'What if I tricked you?'

His eyebrows drew down angrily. 'Do you want me to be away for longer? More often?'

Sofi was taken aback. 'I didn't realise your precious art could be used to threaten me.'

He glared at her a moment, then softened. He was not a man for arguing. 'Sofi, don't do this. We have a nice life, good careers, a solid marriage. You see only what's missing, and forget to count what is there.' He took her hand and placed it over his heart. 'If we had another child and that child was the same as Nikita, this heart would not be able to stand the strain. Can you understand that? It is too great a risk to take.'

Sofi dropped her head. He was articulating one of her greatest fears, also. She was too easily convinced; perhaps the urge wasn't as strong as she'd thought.

'I really should get back to work,' she said.

'So I can tell the fellowship organisers I accept?'

'Yes, of course you can.'

The evening after Julien went away, Sofi lay down on the sofa next to Mama and cried. Mama soothed her, stroked her hair and her hot face with her cool hands. Sofi felt empty in every sense. Her heart was empty, but most importantly her womb was empty. Julien had refused to be talked around. There would be no second baby.

At length, Sofi had gazed up at Mama and told her the awful superstition she had been harbouring, that she had brought terrible bad luck on herself.

'This is just nonsense, Sofi,' Mama replied. 'What have you done to invite bad luck?'

And so Sofi had confessed it all: the scam, Roy Creedy, the theft. Knowing that Mama would be angry and disappointed, and yet needing to unburden her guilty heart. Mama's hands went still, then withdrew. Sofi sat up, took a deep breath.

'Mama? Do you hate me now?'

Mama shook her head. 'I don't hate you. You are my child. But it was a terrible thing you did.'

'I suggested to Lena and Natalya that we contact him, offer to pay him back his money. But Natalya won't hear of it. She thinks he would be dangerous.'

'Then don't deliberately put yourself in the path of danger.'

'But the bad luck, Mama?'

Mama considered her in the warm glow of the lamplight. 'You don't believe in bad luck.'

'Perhaps I do. Deep down.' She took Mama's hand. 'Can you forgive me, Mama? If you could forgive me, I know I wouldn't feel this way. As though I'd done something so wicked that it had stained me forever.'

'I'm sure I can forgive you.' Mama smiled tightly. 'A mother's anger is like the spring snow: no matter how much falls, it melts away quickly. And it was a long time ago.'

'Ten years. A lot has happened.'

Mama's voice regained its warmth. 'Sofi, you must not look back over those ten years and see only bad luck.'

'I know. I know.'

'It is a fool who sees only dirt on her palm when she has a handful of gold dust.'

Sofi turned this over in her mind, thinking of her cousins. Lena, who had two perfectly healthy children. Natalya, who had beauty and wealth. All three of them, jealous of what the others had. And her ideas about bad luck now seemed to be ridiculous, misguided.

'Thank you, Mama,' Sofi said. 'I know you don't like what I did, but I am still glad I told you.'

CHAPTER FORTY

The time when Lena felt most acutely sorry that Wendy wasn't around was when she needed quick babysitting. Not that she could leave them with Wendy this morning anyway, as Wendy would ask too many questions. Where was she going? How long would she be? It was Saturday. Sam was at work, and she'd hastily organised a thatcher to come to the farmhouse and quote on replacing the roof. It was madness, really. She wouldn't be able to afford it. And yet she simply had to know how much it would be, so that she could convince herself decisively. So she reluctantly took Matthew and Anna to the flat next door to theirs.

Jillian, the single mother who lived there, was delightful. Friendly, warm, always wanting to help. It was her daughter, twelve-year-old Izzy, who was the problem. She was insolent, precocious, boy mad, and Anna's hero. Jillian was, of course, blind to her daughter's flaws.

'Sorry, Jillian, something's come up. I shouldn't be more than two hours,' Lena said, pushing the children ahead of her into the flat.

'Oh, I'd love to have them! Anna and Izzy get on so well. Come in, come in, kids. Take your time, Lena.'

Then she was away, driving the now-familiar route out to Little Ayton.

Lena had been unable to stay away from the farmhouse. She had painted the front door red, had scrubbed the mould off the bathroom tiles, cleaned all the floors. None of it made the place more habitable but she liked to do it anyway. It had meant a lot more secrecy than she'd originally intended; sneaking off, hiding letters, making vague excuses. But Sam didn't seem to notice. He finally seemed to be coming out of the dark pit he'd fallen into in the wake of the band's demise. He'd started playing guitar again, and talked about trying to get some solo gigs at the Briggsby Arms. 'They can pull the plug on that jukebox,' he joked. Dreams of being a pop star were gone forever. Buried beside her dreams of being a movie star.

She pulled up outside the farmhouse and made her way up to the front door. She was early, had fifteen minutes to wait for the thatcher. She sat in the long grass at the top of the hill, gazing down towards the fields. In the year since she'd inherited the house, this view had become imprinted on her imagination. She often saw it as she was drifting off to sleep at night, and had begun to wonder – superstitiously – if the house were calling her in some way, if she were meant to live here and it was only stubborn pride that was stopping her from borrowing Sofi's money, renovating and moving in. Sofi had made it clear the loan would be interest-free and could be paid back whenever it suited. In other words, it was all but a gift. But how could she take such a gift? She had already got this house for nothing. Was she still little Lena whom everybody else had to take care of?

She had to admit, though, that the idea seemed less outrageous as time passed. Perhaps, one day . . .

The sound of tyres pulling onto the shoulder roused her. She rose, and walked around the house to meet the thatcher.

Only it wasn't the thatcher. It was Sam.

Adrenaline flushed through her. 'Sam!' she squawked.

'What the hell are you doing here?' he asked, striding up to her. 'How did you . . . ?'

'I followed you. You were acting strangely all morning. You've been acting strangely for months. I borrowed a mate's car, waited for you to leave. Who were you expecting? Are you having an affair?'

Lena tried to calm him down, knowing it was fruitless. 'No, no. I'm not having an affair. I'd never betray you like that.' But she had betrayed him, hadn't she? She'd kept something enormously important secret from him, because it was so precious she couldn't trust him with it.

'Then what are you doing here? Whose house is this?'

Lena watched as the thatcher's van pulled up. She dropped her voice. 'I'll explain everything. Just a moment.'

'Don't walk away from me.'

'Do you want everyone in the world to know our problems?' Lena hissed, shaking off his hand. 'Wait here.'

She walked over to greet the thatcher, made small talk as though everything were normal. All the while her blood was flushing with heat. The thatcher went to his van for his ladder and she returned to Sam, who was glaring at her unforgivingly.

'Walk with me,' she said.

'Lena?'

'It's my house, Sam. Mine. Grandad left it to me.'

He froze. 'Then you were lying about him having nothing?'

'No. No, I wasn't. That's what he told me. The house came six months later.'

Sam was doing calculations in his head. 'You've owned a house for a year, and you didn't tell me?'

'Walk with me,' she said again, urging him forward, down the gentle slope and into the overgrown field. The smell of cut grass and damp earth hung in the air. As best she could, she told him the whole story, knowing all the time that no matter how she worded it he would be angry. He listened, tight-lipped, to her excuses. Finally, he stopped, turned to her, his eyes as cold as stones.

'You're angry, aren't you?' she managed.

'You could say that.'

'I hope you understand just a little why –'

'I understand. You did it because you think I'm useless, or stupid, or both.'

'No, no, Sam. I just wanted to –'

'You can keep your damned house. I don't want it. I certainly never want to live in it.'

'Sam, don't be like that. We should talk about it. We should –'

But he wouldn't let her finish a sentence. 'I won't talk about this again. You want to keep this secret? Have it your way. Pretend I don't know. It's easier for both of us that way.'

He stalked off, up the hill and towards his friend's car. Helpless, she watched him go. Perhaps he just needed to be alone, to cool off. But she had to admit that if she were in his situation, she would be anything but cool. She sat in the field, looking up at the pale blue sky, wondering how she could ever have made such a mess of things.

Natalya had hoped for a West End premiere. She had hoped for a stroll down a red carpet, for a loaned designer gown and diamonds, for a sea of photographers. Instead, *Skin Crawlers* was opening at the Oak Street Twin Cinema in Shepherds Bush. The carpet was burnished yellow, the gown was recycled Dior by Galliano, but the jewellery was a handmade one-off from Sofi, an apology for not being able to make it in person. There were six photographers, which Natalya knew was better than none. And, given Arnold Grassman's last two films had gone straight to video, a cinematic release was better than nothing also. It had been picked up by a small distributor – they were hoping good reviews would drive it into other cinemas, that it would be a sleeper hit. Certainly, Arnold hadn't skimped on production costs, and a pre-release buzz about the film had been generated by Arnold's surprising inclusion on a website's Britain's Eligible Bachelors list.

So why the niggling doubt? Was it because Natalya was intimately acquainted with the script, which was both improbable and very poorly written?

The cinema was full as she made her entrance. Applause surrounded her. She waved and smiled, was shown to her seat next to her leading man, an actor so far known only for his role as a superhero in a cleaning products commercial. No doubt his hopes were just as high as hers. She glanced around the cinema for familiar faces. There was Arnold, looking slightly stiff but pleased with himself. Two of her old castmates from *Lonely Shores*. Lovely of them to come. And there were Lena and Sam. She gave a little wave. Sam waved back but Lena hadn't seen her. They were staying overnight at a hotel nearby.

She turned to view the other side of the cinema. Her heart froze. Rupert. His arm around a young, beautiful woman. What the hell was he doing here?

Natalya closed her eyes, groaning inwardly. He was here to see her fail.

The lights dimmed, the crowd hushed. The movie began.

She made her first appearance on screen. A whip-thin, glamorous astrophysicist – this drew laughter from the audience. Natalya clutched the arms of her seat. Laughter was all right. A movie could still be a hit if it was over-the-top, ridiculous. She looked wonderful on screen. Perhaps it would all work out.

What she hadn't counted on was boredom.

The first ten minutes of the film worked, even if they were laughably improbable. But from there on, it became a confused mess, with overly long scenes that seemed to go nowhere. People began to shift in their seats. And with boredom came impatience. The ridiculous plot twists were no longer camp and hilarious; they were irritating. One loud-voiced man down the front began to wisecrack between the actors' lines, drawing ripples of laughter. Natalya sank lower and lower in her seat.

Forty-five minutes in, the first person left. Then another. And another. It became an avalanche. They left for many reasons. Some, simply because they were bored. Some, because they felt insulted. But most probably left because it was fun to do: to walk out on a stinker of a film. On screen, her character had just lost her dress and picked up a shotgun. But it was too late. Nobody cared about her toned stomach – all those sit-ups, gone to waste – they were caught up in the moment, in showing just how little they cared for Arnold Grassman's millions.

Natalya longed for a way to leave the cinema without being seen. She knew Rupert was still there, watching her. She knew that if she looked towards Lena she might see a sympathetic eye, but she couldn't look anywhere but straight in front of her. The dashing of her hopes was painful. Leida had been right. But she hadn't listened and Leida had dropped her from her books. Natalya had a million pounds, but this was surely the final nail in the coffin of her career.

After the credits rolled and the three-dozen or so people remaining applauded especially loud out of pity, Natalya waited in her seat for everyone to leave. When the cinema was nearly empty, she looked up to see Lena and Sam edging between seats. They sat with her, one on either side.

'It was great, Natalya,' Sam said.

'You looked beautiful,' Lena added.

'Thanks,' she replied numbly. 'I don't think many people shared your opinion.'

Arnold Grassman stopped by. 'Thank you, Natalya. I couldn't have asked for a more perfect leading lady.'

'Arnold, they hated it!' she wailed.

He shrugged. 'It's my first cinematic release. A small step. And a very big tax write-off.'

Natalya burned up. *A tax write-off*? Her career was in tatters and he was calling it a tax write-off? She shot out of her seat, pushed past him awkwardly. 'I have to go,' she blurted.

'Natalya?' Lena said. 'You don't want to go out for dinner?'

'No,' she called behind her as she dashed out onto the street.

Damn the weather for being mild and fine, not pouring with rain. Damn the streetlights for shining brightly, not flickering. Damn the people that she passed who called out after her, 'Are you all right, luv?' instead of brushing past anonymously and coldly. Life was nothing like a movie. She had forgotten her script, messed up her lines and lost sight of the happy ending. She ran home to hide.

Natalya woke early, went down to the street to buy the papers. Most hadn't bothered to review *Skin Crawlers*, but the two reviews she found – both accompanied by huge photographs of her – were brutal. She turned on the computer, connected to the internet and searched for more reviews. *A flop. A stinker. An embarrassment. Natalie Chernoff is perfectly cast as a mindless sexpot.* She opened her email. One from Rupert: *Congratulations, it was the worst film I've ever seen.*

So she cried. Great, heaving sobs of self-pity that seemed to go on and on. She was washed-up, she was lonely, she was growing older with every second that ticked past. In a few weeks she would be thirty-five! Her instincts were telling her to get away. Away from London and the scene that she was so desperately trying to battle her way back into. She swallowed her tears and reached for the phone, called Lena and Sam's hotel room.

'Natalya?' her sister said. 'I've been worried about you.'

'It's all fallen apart,' she sobbed. 'Can I come home with you?'

At first Natalya had only intended to stay a few days, to clear her head and decide what to do next. But then the flat across the street from Lena and Sam became vacant, and she took it as a sign: she was meant to stay. She signed a lease, giving herself six months away from London to think about her career – what was left of it – and spend some time with family.

She had been so long in London, where she could live in a flat for years and never know the names of the people next door, that she was charmed and comforted by having someone she loved close, by being able to stop and talk to neighbours in the street, by seeing friendly faces everywhere. It was like the fictional world on *Lonely Shores*, though a great deal uglier. She had never realised that such relationships really existed in the world. Lena's neighbour Jillian was overly friendly if a little starstruck; the staff at Lena's nursery included her in their coffee mornings; Sam came over whenever she needed a washer changed or a loose tile fixed. She found she could get through most days with a smile on her face, though alone at night the shadows circled again. But if she had to be lost at this time in her life, it was nice to be near her sister.

She was so wrapped up in her own problems, it took her more than a month to realise that all wasn't well with Lena and Sam. Ordinarily, they were very affectionate with each other. Natalya couldn't count the times she had ached with envy seeing their ease with each other: the casual warm cuddles, the shameless kisses, the way they always held hands. But lately she hadn't seen any evidence of that closeness at all. She took Lena aside and asked her about it, but Lena – in her usual fashion – wouldn't admit anything was wrong.

'We're just busy,' she said. 'Two jobs, two children . . .'

Was that a veiled criticism of Natalya's long, ambling days? Anna and Matthew weren't the incomprehensible, noisy terrors they had been when little. In fact, she was starting to enjoy their company. She offered on the spot to have the children over three afternoons a week. She bought two buckets of Lego to keep Matthew happy, and Anna was content to play among her dresses and make-up. Perhaps if Lena and Sam had a bit of time to themselves, they could resolve the issue, whatever it was.

But as the weeks drew out, Natalya noticed that the coolness between them intensified. So she determined to ask Sam instead.

It was a Sunday morning in the middle of summer. The sky was blue and cloudless, and the breeze off the ocean was fresh and mild. The leaves on the plane trees that lined the footpath caught the sun, making the dingy grey street look almost pretty. Natalya knocked on Lena's door and waited. In time, Matthew opened it.

'Hi, Aunty Nat,' he said. 'You want Mum?'

'Actually, I need your father. I want to move my television unit and I'm afraid I'm not strong enough.' She mimed a limp body-builder's pose. 'Do you think you could ask him to come over?'

Matthew disappeared into the house, leaving Natalya waiting at the door. A few moments later, Sam emerged, buttoning up his shirt. He wore jeans and his feet were bare, his long curls messy.

'Sorry, I was still in my pyjamas,' he said.

'I didn't realise it was so early.'

'It's not,' he laughed. 'I'm just lazy. Come on.'

They crossed the road together, and Natalya let him move her rented furniture around for ten minutes before finally offering to make tea.

'Why don't you come back with me?' he said. 'Lena would like tea too.'

'I... look, Sam. I'll be honest.' She felt embarrassed all of a sudden. 'I'm worried about you and Lena. Something's not right and she won't tell me...'

'She won't?' His eyebrows shot up. 'She hasn't said anything about the farmhouse?'

'Farmhouse?'

Sam sat on the back of the sofa, shaking his head, laughing. 'Well, it's not just me she's keeping secrets from then.'

'I don't understand.'

'Just over a year ago, Lena inherited an old farmhouse from my grandfather.'

'She did?' Lena had inherited property?

'Despite the fact that it came from my grandfather, and despite the fact that I'm her husband, she didn't tell me until I caught her out a couple of months ago.' He couldn't hide the bitterness in his voice.

'But... why didn't she tell you?' *Why didn't she tell me?*

'She told Sofi,' Sam said.

Natalya was surprised by how hurt she was. Lena had told Sofi, but not her own sister?

'What possible reason could she have to keep it from us?' Natalya said. 'The two people closest to her?'

'There's something in Lena I don't understand,' he said. 'She judges people, puts them in boxes. Decides who she can and can't trust on instinct, not reason. She thought I'd want to sell the house and spend all the money, as though I'm an unreliable teenager rather than a grown man.'

'What's she going to do with the house?' Natalya asked. 'Live in it? Sell it?'

'I don't know and I don't care.' His tone became brittle. 'She's made it clear that I'm outside that decision, and I have no desire to be part of it if I'm not welcome.'

Natalya gazed at him, knowing she should say something to defend Lena, but allowing her own anger to hold her tongue. 'Why didn't she tell *me*, though?' she asked.

'Because you and I kind of have a history, Natalya,' he said softly, and for some reason the words stirred feelings inside her that should never have been stirred. 'After Viktor came, when you used to call to check on her. She probably thought if you knew, you'd pass it on to me.'

Natalya looked away, chewing her lip.

'Would you have told me?' he asked. 'Would you have trusted me to act responsibly?'

She met his eyes again. He looked bereft, a little boy. In truth, if Lena had asked her to keep something secret she would have complied. But Sam needed some affirmation of his trustworthiness, so she nodded. 'Of course. I would have called you immediately.' As soon as she said the words, she knew that she had said them for the wrong reasons. Not to affirm Sam, but to tie him a little closer to her. She chastised herself, uncomfortable with the sick feeling of guilt. She forced a bright tone. 'Let's go to your place for tea, stop all this miserable talk. You and Lena are solid as a rock, it will all blow over.'

Sam shrugged. 'I hope you're right.'

CHAPTER FORTY-ONE

'She's here, she's here!' Much squealing and giggling greeted Lena on her arrival home from work.

Natalya stopped her in the hallway as children fled into bedrooms. 'You have to come into the sitting room. Close your eyes.'

Lena allowed herself to be led, smiling, but wishing she could just take her time, drop her bag, make a cup of tea before the show started.

She sat on the sofa. The coffee table had been moved out of the way. Natalya hit the button on the CD player and thumping music burst into life. 'Welcome to Briggsby Fashion Week,' Natalya intoned. 'Meet your first model, Matthew.'

The bedroom door creaked open. Nobody came out. Natalya leaned her head around the corner. 'Matthew!' she called.

And there he was, in his own design – four T-shirts layered on top of each other and Sam's belt wrapped around his skinny middle – strutting up the runway and into the sitting room. Lena had to laugh despite herself.

The school holidays seemed to be dragging on forever. Every afternoon, Lena came home from work to two hot-faced, over-tired nine year olds who had spent the day with Sam, or Natalya, or Wendy. Trying to get Matthew and Anna calmed down before bed was impossible. The long days exhausted her, and she yearned for the start of school when life could resume its normal rhythms. Maybe then, things with Sam could go back to normal too.

Having Natalya around had been terrible timing. Just when she and Sam needed to talk about the farmhouse – the secret which he saw as a betrayal – Natalya had turned up on their sofa. No privacy. They'd had to pretend the issue didn't exist. By the time Natalya had moved out, a hard shell had formed over Sam's feelings. His protestations that he didn't want to discuss it became more and more passionate, until she'd had no choice but to stop talking about it.

Matthew turned and strutted back down the corridor.

'Please welcome our fantastic ready-to-wear designers and models, Anna and Izzy!' Natalya announced.

Lena hadn't known Izzy was here. Natalya didn't share Lena's dislike of the child, probably because Izzy was obsessed with celebrities and fashion much like Natalya was. The two girls came down the corridor and Lena cringed. Natalya had dressed them in her clothes – rolled, tucked and pinned to make them fit – and made them up with heavy eyeshadow and lipstick. She had taught them the loose-hipped walk, the bored-sexy gaze. Izzy had mastered it, slinking into the sitting room and posing over her shoulder like a centrefold. Anna, much younger but in awe of her friend, tried to pull the same pose. Lena squirmed in her seat. She didn't want to ruin their fun, but . . .

Then Izzy turned, put her hands on Anna's hips and rubbed her body suggestively on her, flicking her tongue in Anna's ear. No doubt she had seen it in a music video and thought it was great fun, but Lena couldn't hold back her anger.

'Hey, stop!' she said, leaping to her feet and gently pulling the girls apart. 'Natalya, they're just little girls.'

Natalya's eyes opened wide. She was puzzled. 'It's only a bit of fun.'

Izzy rolled her eyes – an expression Lena had seen at least a hundred times – and mimed a huge yawn. Lena ignored her. This was the problem with Natalya: she loved to look after the children, but she was a hopeless parental figure. She lacked judgement.

'Come on, Anna,' Lena said. 'Go and wash all that make-up off.'

'But the fashion show isn't finished yet,' Anna protested.

'Your mum is *sooo* boring,' Izzy said to Anna.

'Hey!' Lena said. 'That's enough, miss. You can go home.'

'You *are* boring!' Anna shouted. 'Why can't you be more like Aunty Nat? She's cool.'

Natalya moved to the CD player to turn it off. In the wake of the loud music, Lena could hear her blood pumping angrily. 'Anna, go to your room.'

Matthew hovered uncertainly nearby, still in his fashion outfit. 'Mum?'

'It's all right, Matthew, you're not in trouble.'

Anna gave her brother a glare that terrified Lena, a presage of teenage conflict yet to come. But Anna was only nine. Lena rounded on Izzy. 'I said, go home.'

Izzy flounced off towards the door, Anna flounced off towards her bedroom. Matthew stood in the threshold, still sure that somehow he must be in trouble. Lena took his arm and pushed him gently towards the sofa. 'Put the telly on, darling. I need to talk to Aunty Nat.'

Lena led Natalya to the kitchen, where she filled the kettle and put it on the stove. 'Tea?'

'Just get it out. You're angry at me, aren't you?'

Lena sighed, leaning against the kitchen bench. 'Not angry so much as . . . bewildered. They're little girls.'

'It was Izzy's idea.'

'There's something not right with that child. I don't like Anna playing with her. I don't want her to grow up too soon. Could I ask you not to get Anna too interested in things like make-up and fashion?'

'She's a girl, she's naturally interested in it. We were.'

'It's different now. Everything is so sexualised.' Lena could see that Natalya was offended, but pushed ahead anyway. 'Can you be more like a grown-up, and less like one of them?'

'Are you saying I'm childish?'

'No. You're just not very parent-ish.' Lena laughed, trying to defuse the tension.

Natalya raised her hands. 'You don't want me to babysit any more?'

'I didn't say that.'

'You don't trust me though?'

'I do.' Lena had the distinct feeling that a different grievance was being aired now, but she wasn't sure what it was. 'Why would you say that?'

'Because you didn't tell me about your farmhouse. You told Sofi, but not me.'

Lena took a moment to comprehend. 'How did you . . . ?'

'Sam told me.'

Sam had been speaking about their problems with Natalya? She felt cold inside.

'Why would you tell Sofi something so important and not me?'

Lena tried to focus on the issue at hand. 'You have to understand. It was a secret. The more people I spoke to about it, the harder it would be to keep it from Sam.'

'But Sofi?'

'I needed her advice.'

'Ah. Because Sofi is the smart one and I'm the dumb one.'

Lena bristled; somehow Natalya had become the victim in this argument. 'Not everything is about you, Natalya,' she said. 'My financial situation, the state of my marriage, they aren't your concerns. You shouldn't have spoken to Sam. I didn't want to talk about it, so you should have let things be.'

'I wanted to help.'

She softened. 'I know, but you must think about what might happen if you help. Dressing Anna up like a pole-dancer doesn't help me. Taking Sam aside to discuss my problems doesn't help me.'

She remembered the months after her father's brief visit and his sudden departure, and wondered how many phone calls had passed between Natalya and Sam without her knowledge.

The kettle began to whistle. 'Would you like tea?' Lena said again.

'No.' Natalya straightened her back. 'I should go home.'

Lena sat at the kitchen bench after she'd left, sipping her tea, listening to the muted sounds of cartoon guns going off in the sitting room. Her first quiet moment alone that day. She went over the argument with Natalya in her mind. Why did it bother her so much? They were sisters, they argued, they made up, they moved on. Just because Sam was involved . . . she should be glad that her sister and husband got on well.

Surely there was nothing to feel so worried about.

Natalya was making her bed, the bedroom window open wide to let in a breeze against the stuffy morning heat, when somebody knocked at her door. It was Sam and the kids.

'Hi, Natalya,' he said. 'We're going for a drive down to Scarborough, to the beach. The kids want to know if you'd like to come.'

'Please come,' Anna said.

'Where's Lena?'

'At work,' Sam said. 'I've got the day off. Beautiful weather.'

Natalya felt guilty, but told herself not to read too much into the invitation. The kids loved her, why not go? 'All right, then,' she said. 'Let me just get changed.'

She raced to her bedroom, pulled on shorts and a T-shirt, found her bikini – last time she'd worn it was in Spain; was it even possible to get a tan in England? – and slipped on a pair of cotton espadrilles. She glanced at herself quickly in the mirror, then looked away. What she looked like didn't matter. It was a family day out.

Anna and Matthew took a hand each as they crossed the road. They were loud and excited, grew more so as the car took off, backfiring twice before smoothly joining traffic.

Sam was quiet, the twins were raucous, and a hundred rounds of I Spy passed the time, growing more and more silly until Matthew spied 'a fart' and Sam roared that that was enough. Natalya thought he was being a little harsh: they were only children after all, and she could easily remember the hot flush of silliness that she and Lena and Sofi had enjoyed at that age. But then, Sam had to live with them. Natalya just blew in and blew out when she felt like it.

Sam found a car park on the crowded Esplanade, and they walked through the gardens to the beach. The sand was teeming with beach chairs, children, sandcastles and sunbathing mums. Anna and Matthew stripped down to their bathers in seconds and ran off to splash and paddle in the shallows. Alone with Sam, Natalya grew shy at the idea of slipping into her bikini, so she sat on the sand with her sunglasses on and watched the children. Sam took off his shirt and commenced construction of a sandcastle. The weather was warm and mild, the continuous roll of the sea soothed her. She avoided looking at Sam's lean back and square shoulders, but forgave herself the desire to.

'You're very good at that,' she said, when Sam had built two turrets and a crenellated rampart.

'Lots of practice when I was a kid,' he said. 'We came here every day in summer. No sand at Briggsby. I'd find a pretty girl on the beach and be too shy to talk to her, so I'd build a castle for her and see if she noticed me.'

'Did they ever notice you?'

'Once or twice. But then I'd get tongue-tied and not talk to them. Run away.' He laughed.

'Well, that's a beautiful castle. Don't run away.'

He smiled. 'When would you like to move in, Your Majesty?'

'As soon as I can,' she said, faking a queenly voice. 'I'm living in a one-bedroom flat in a dingy town and . . .' She trailed off, realising the joke wouldn't be funny to Sam, who had no option of leaving Briggsby and living in a nicer place.

He sat back on the sand, his gaze going out to sea. Anna and Matthew were crocodile walking in the shallows. Then Sam turned to her and said, 'Natalya, what's it like to be rich and famous?'

'I . . . well, I'm hardly famous any more and –'

'What's it like to do what you're really passionate about, and have people love you for it and pay you loads of money?'

Nobody loved her for *Skin Crawlers*, that was why she was here in the first place. But then Natalya remembered Sam's band, his abandoned dreams. At least she'd tasted success. 'It's great,' she admitted. 'It's the best feeling in the world.'

He nodded. 'I thought so. It's not fair, is it? Some of us have charmed lives, and some of us just struggle on. Only one chance in the lottery; if you lose you lose.'

'You think I have a charmed life?' Natalya said. 'Because I can assure you, it doesn't feel that way from the inside.'

'But no matter which way you look at it, you're a famous actress who's rich.' He spread his hands. 'Dream come true. Me, I work at a greengrocer's. They offered me a promotion last week, to store manager. I turned it down because that would have been admitting I'm stuck there for the long term. But I'm stuck anyway, aren't I?'

'You could do something else.'

'I could. More of the same. Rubbish jobs. I asked the local pub if I could sing for them one night a week. They said no. I never told Lena.' He sighed. 'She was right: I would have made her sell the farmhouse, I would have spent the money unwisely. The first thing I thought was, we could have gone on a holiday, taken the kids to Disneyland.' He looked so defeated, so sad-eyed.

'I'm sorry, Sam,' she said.

He held her gaze a moment past comfort, then said, 'I expect I'll get over it. I expect life will continue on, as it always has, and nothing will change.' He returned to building his sandcastle while the summer breeze tugged his hair in the sunshine. 'And I'll just get used to it.'

Autumn came, and Natalya knew she would have to move on soon. It wasn't just Briggsby's relentless showers and gales, its long grey streets, drab shops and resigned dissatisfaction. It was what was happening between her and Sam.

On the surface, things continued as they always had. She and Lena talked, laughed, fought occasionally. Natalya had dinner with the family, played with the children. Lena and Sam hadn't regained their warm physicality, but they seemed to be getting on well enough. Beneath the surface, matters were far more complicated. Every time she was alone with Sam, talk turned too quickly to his marriage, its misunderstandings, Lena's impatience with him. He told her that she understood him, that Lena was being too abrupt with him, had failed to see his heart. She caught Sam looking at her but she resisted his gazes. He had grown attracted to her, and she knew that she had to get away before the situation grew worse.

And yet it was so flattering to have a good man, a gorgeous man, a man who had seemed indifferent to her for years, grow interested in her. Her lonely heart was weak.

On the first of October, Natalya gave notice that she would be breaking her lease at the end of the month. She would go back to London, back to Leida Frost, or maybe somebody better, and try again. Put Sam's liquid eyes out of her mind.

It was a dismal day, as usual. Grey skies, grey sea, grey houses. Rain threatened but didn't fall. Natalya was pacing her flat, waiting for Leida to return her call. She had to impress upon her that she was ready to do whatever Leida said, that she'd learnt her lesson. When the phone rang she pounced and said, 'Leida, I know you're angry at me, but you must hear me out.'

'It's Lena.'

'Oh.'

'You were expecting your agent?'

'I . . . I'm going back to London.'

'Really? When?' Was she imagining it or did Lena sound relieved.

'End of the month,' she said, trying not to be offended. 'Why did you ring? Why didn't you just come over?'

'I'm at work. I need a big favour, and I need it right now. Can you help?'

Lena explained that a tradesman had visited the farmhouse that morning to quote on cutting out some wood rot, and rather than returning the key to her as agreed, he had left it under the mat.

'I know it's ridiculous, but I don't want anyone to let themselves in. I've been cleaning it up a bit. I don't want graffiti on the walls. I won't get a chance today, and I can't ask Sam. Can you go up there and collect the key for me?'

Natalya had to admit she was curious to see this house that had created so many problems for Lena. But what if Leida phoned while she was out?

Who was she kidding? Leida wasn't going to call her any time soon. She'd make her suffer first, for weeks if she could.

'Of course,' Natalya said.

'See if Sam will loan you the car. Don't tell him why, please. He's sensitive about the farmhouse.'

So Natalya crossed the road and knocked on the door. Sam answered, his eagerness to see her carefully shielded.

'I need to borrow your car,' she said.

'Sure. Where are you off to?'

Don't tell him why, please. 'Lena has asked me to go to the farmhouse for her and fetch the key.'

'Why didn't she ask me?'

Natalya shrugged. 'She doesn't want to make you angry, I suppose. Or hurt your feelings.'

'Do you know where it is?'

'She gave me directions.'

Sam grabbed his jacket from the hook near the door. 'I'll take you.'

'But Lena –'

'Doesn't need to know,' he finished for her. 'Come on.'

The leaves were ripening to red and brown; the rich, dark colours stood out against the grey skies. Out across the moors, mist clung to hollows. Natalya and Sam didn't speak, and the long silence began to frighten her. They were doing something wrong, she felt it in her bones. Though she wasn't sure precisely *why* it was more wrong than Lena asking Natalya to go alone and not tell Sam about it. The music on the radio buzzed in and out, thanks to the broken antenna on the back of the car. Voices talking, an interview with a pop star who had a strong northern accent. Natalya strained to hear who it was, but Sam snapped it off. They pulled up outside a run-down farmhouse. Natalya was immediately disappointed.

'This is it?'

'Yes.' Sam unbuckled his seatbelt and climbed out of the car. Natalya followed.

'I see now,' she said. 'You couldn't live here.'

'It would fall down on our heads.' He led her up to the front door, lifted the mat and retrieved the key. 'Want to go inside and have a look?' he asked.

Natalya wrapped her cardigan closer around her. 'Yes.'

Inside smelled mouldy. It was clean, but in poor repair. Cupboard doors hung askew or were missing altogether. The benches sagged, one of the walls was bowed. The tiles were cracked and lifting, and the plaster on the ceiling was flaking.

'Good lord,' Natalya said. 'Why on earth is she keeping it? It needs to be knocked down.'

'She wants to keep it for the kids.'

'It will fall down before they're old enough to own it,' she said, moving down the hallway to look into the bedrooms.

'I think she's imagining it can be repaired. That's why she gets tradesmen out here, giving her quotes that she never uses. I found them in a drawer, dozens of them. Kitchen quotes, bathroom quotes, painting, plastering, thatching. It would cost less to buy a new house.' He shrugged. 'I can't say anything about it to her. But you understand, don't you?'

Natalya stopped, turned to look at him. The intensity was unguarded now. She felt a pang of guilt. She said, 'Sam, I'm leaving at the end of the month.'

His expression softened, his shoulders dropped. 'You are?'

'You need to work things out with Lena. I'm just in the way.'

'No, no. You've made things easier. Talking to you has really helped me. You were there when I didn't know who to turn to.' He looked away, probably realising he sounded too passionate. 'I will miss you.'

'And I'll miss you.' She moved towards him. 'I know that Lena lied to you, didn't trust you, but you mustn't let this problem become a stepping stone to bigger problems.'

She patted his arm, and a spark of electricity flew between them. His gaze fixed on her fingers. It was as though she were frozen. She told herself to move, get her hands off him, get as far away as possible. But then he had caught her fingers in his own and tugged her towards him. In slow motion, it seemed, he reached out to touch her hair. His fingers twined around a strand.

'Sam, no . . .' she said. Or perhaps she only thought it. He pulled her hair gently, leaning in to kiss her.

No, no, no. She was shaking her head, but somehow his lips were on hers and her body was pressed up against him. Everything seemed to blur as desire and guilt swept through her in waves. Gorgeous Sam, who she'd always admired – coveted – was kissing her. His touch was so firm, so infused with passion and knowing. Who had ever touched her like this? Not Rupert, with his sour heart. Not Marcus, who barely knew her. Not one of the dozen fly-by-night boyfriends since, who admired her beauty but didn't care to understand her soul. Her hands went to his back, under his shirt, curious to feel his smooth skin. She felt she might pass out, turned her face away for air. His lips moved quickly down her neck, his fingers picked at her buttons. Their clothes were falling on the floor. There was nowhere to lie, so she hooked her leg over his hip, helped him inside her.

Then it was too late. She had done it. She hadn't stopped when she could have. She clung to him, her face pressed into his arm and tried to hold back tears. He pushed hard against her at first, then sagged, stopped.

'I can't,' he said.

'It's too late,' she replied.

He was pulling away from her, dressing himself, and the blur of desire was gone. Now she saw the situation for what it really was. This was not a grand passion, denied for years and suddenly bursting into inevitable life. She was just an ageing, out-of-work soap star fumbling with her sister's husband in a mouldy old house. As her shaking fingers struggled with her buttons, she let her tears fall.

'I'm sorry, I'm so sorry,' Sam said.

'We are the worst people in the world,' she said. 'I hate myself.'

'No, it was my fault. I started it. I –'

'Take me back,' she said. 'I never want to see this place again.'

Natalya found herself at Heathrow airport, with four suitcases on a trolley. It was late afternoon, and she stood uncertainly in the middle of the throng. London was not far enough away from what she had done. Besides, she was kidding herself if she thought Leida Frost would take her on again after the *Skin Crawlers* disaster. And so she stood, waiting for inspiration about where to go.

A group of young men walked past. Students perhaps. They were speaking Russian. It created a sudden and acute ache of homesickness.

And so it was decided. She could move again, her feet were no longer frozen to the spot. She would find a flight to St Petersburg. She was going home.

CHAPTER FORTY-TWO

The key to the farmhouse was waiting for Lena inside a white envelope on the kitchen bench when she got home from work. She discreetly put it back in her bedside drawer and got on with making dinner, getting the kids ready for bed, ironing clothes, tidying up. She knew she ought to go across the road to thank Natalya, but she didn't want to arouse Sam's suspicions. He was very quiet, withdrawn. She wondered if he was angry with her for something. At around nine, she said she was going to slip over to Natalya's briefly and he didn't protest.

But Lena could see from her front door that all the lights were off at Natalya's. It was unusual for her sister to go to bed so early, but she shrugged it off and went back inside.

The next day, Natalya was out in the afternoon. Her lights weren't on again in the evening. And Lena began to suspect something was wrong.

She waited until morning and went across the road again. Knocked furiously. No answer. A pit opened up in her stomach. Natalya hadn't been home for two days. She'd left no note, hadn't phoned . . . what if something terrible had happened to her?

She raced home to call the police.

Sam was making sandwiches for the kids' lunchboxes. He glanced up as she came in. 'What's wrong? You look pale.'

'Natalya. She hasn't been home for two days.'

Sam feigned a shrug, but Lena could see the tension in his body. 'She's probably gone down to London for an audition or something.'

'She would have told me. She would have phoned by now.'

'You know Natalya, always wrapped up in –'

'No, Sam. She would have told me if she was going away. She could be dead over there. Or dying. Or . . . I don't know.' She reached for the phone. 'I'm going to call the police.'

Sam's hand shot out and took the phone from her fingers, hung it up gently.

'What are you doing?'

'I know where Natalya is.'

'You . . . ? What?'

'Just calm down.'

'What are you talking about?'

'We'll talk once the kids are gone.'

'No, talk now. You're frightening me.' Lena didn't like this. She had failed to notice some important piece of evidence about the world; a bad situation had crept up on her. She went to the threshold of the kitchen, checked on the kids. Matthew was watching television; Anna was trying to make a yoyo walk the dog. 'Now, Sam,' she said, returning to him and dropping her voice low.

Sam closed his eyes, looked like he wanted to die. Lena's heart went cold. He didn't have to say anything, she knew. She *knew*.

'No, Sam, no,' she said softly, tears brimming.

'I'm sorry,' he breathed. 'I'm sorry. It was just once and it was a disaster. I'm sorry.'

Lena's whole body sagged. Her arms, her legs, her chest were all made of lead. She leaned on the kitchen bench, head drooping. It had happened, just as she always knew it would. Its inevitability made it no less painful. Any hope of sorting things out with Sam, of regaining their warmth and closeness, had disappeared. Natalya – her *sister* – had erased her future. Now there were just long, empty years ahead of her, either without Sam, or with a Sam she could never trust again.

'Lena, I want us to be together. I was wrong. I did the wrong thing.' Sam was crying and, impossibly, she felt sorry for him. 'Can you forgive me? It's like I've been in a stupid dream and . . . the farmhouse, that stuff doesn't matter. Maybe because I felt betrayed, I wanted to pay you back, but I was wrong. I was an idiot. Can you forgive me?'

A surge of anger. 'Are you comparing my secret about the farmhouse with you having sex with my sister?' She had spoken too loud. The children would hear.

'I . . .' Sam looked bewildered, and she had to look away. She didn't want to feel sorry for him, not now. 'Betrayals,' he managed. 'Secrets.'

'You cheated on me,' she said, 'and not just with anyone, with Natalya.'

'But it was meaningless, it was –'

'It means *everything*. It means that even you, in the end, thought she was more beautiful than me.' Now tears gave way to sobs.

Matthew stood uncertainly in the kitchen doorway. 'Mum? Dad?'

'It's all right, Matt,' Sam said, shooing him away.

'Mum's crying,' he said.

'Leave us be!' Sam shouted.

'Don't shout at him,' Lena said, going to Matthew and gathering him in her arms. 'You are the one who deserves to be shouted at. You pig. You *pig*.' Her fury terrified her, it was beyond her control. 'You have ruined everything. Don't you see? You have to go. I can't forgive you. You did the one thing that is unforgivable.'

Now Anna was there, watching them fight, her eyes like saucers.

Sam opened his mouth to speak, but Lena shut him down. 'Go. Leave.'

'Mum, no,' Anna said. 'Daddy, don't go.' Matthew was crying. Lena almost gave in. Almost.

'I said go,' she repeated, standing firm amongst the whirl of hysterical feelings. She forced her voice to be even, quiet. 'Our marriage is over.'

'Sofi?' A little voice on the other end of the phone.

'Lena? Are you all right? You sound like you've been crying.' Sofi took the phone to the sitting room and sat on the sofa. Stasya and Nikita were playing a turn-taking game with blocks.

'Sam slept with Natalya,' Lena said. 'I've kicked him out.'

The revelation seemed to knock her body sideways. 'No. He didn't. *She* didn't, surely.' Sofi wanted to race over to England, to hold Lena and comfort her. This was the cruellest blow imaginable to Lena and, no doubt, she would blame herself in some way. Decide that she was not lovable enough to keep Sam from straying. How could Natalya have done it? What madness had possessed her?

'Have you heard from Natalya?' Lena asked. 'I don't know where she is.'

'No, I haven't.' No doubt Natalya was ashamed of her actions, hiding from Sofi and Lena.

'She won't contact me, I know. But she will eventually contact you. She's supposed to be hosting Winter Gathering this year. Tell her I'd rather eat poison than see her. Can you tell her that?'

'Lena, why don't you and the kids come here? Take a few weeks off work, come to France. I'll look after you.'

'No, no. The kids have school, I'd lose my job. I'll just keep going. I'll ask my next-door neighbour to help. I'll manage.'

'Promise you won't sell the farmhouse,' Sofi said. 'If things get that bad, you call me. Understand?'

'I will.' Lena's voice shook, and she took a deep breath. 'But make sure you pass my message on to Natalya. It's very important to me.'

'I'll make sure she knows how angry you are,' Sofi said.

'I think about them together and it kills me, Sofi,' she said in a defeated tone that made Sofi's heart ache. 'It kills me.'

'I know,' Sofi said. 'I'm so sorry, Lena. You didn't deserve this.'

Lena sighed. 'Perhaps I did,' she replied. 'The curse of Roy Creedy.'

'You mustn't think that,' Sofi said. But the primitive fear stirred again and she realised she was bracing herself against further bad luck. What could happen next?

On Christmas night, Lena went to check on the children and found Anna climbing out her bedroom window.

'What are you doing?' she asked, pulling her daughter's skinny arm gently so that she stood in front of her.

'Running away. I want to live with Daddy.'

Lena glanced at Matthew, who had screwed his eyes shut to pretend he was asleep and avoid trouble.

'Well, you can't live with Daddy. You have to live here with me.'

'Why?'

'Because I'm your mother.'

It had been a long, trying day. Wendy had forced them all to come to Christmas lunch. 'For the sake of the children, let's put aside our differences and have a lovely celebration,' she had said. But then she'd changed the rules as soon as Lena had arrived. She was cold to her, rude when nobody was listening, threatened to call solicitors to look into Grandad's will. Sam pretended to be Super-Dad with the children. He had spent way too much money on them, spoiled them. He was living rent-free with Wendy so perhaps he could afford to. Or perhaps he had put it all on a credit card, and would find another hard-working wife to pay it back for him one day.

The thought made her ache. Sam with somebody else. And yet she couldn't take him back.

Now, as she stood here trying to stop her daughter from running away, she thought that perhaps she should dump the kids on Sam. Anna, at least, who had sided with her father from the first day. But no, siblings belonged together. She knew that from her own childhood.

Thoughts of Natalya made her stomach churn. The most ridiculous thing of all was that she missed her sister. Not the cheating, vain

Natalya who had devastated her marriage; but the Natalya who was full of life, strong and protective, affectionate and funny.

'Anna, you must stay here with me. I –'

'Anna!' A voice, outside the window. Lena leaned out to see Izzy waiting.

'It was her idea,' Anna muttered.

Of course it was. 'Go home, Izzy. Anna's not running away tonight.'

Lena knew she should talk to Jillian, ask her to speak sternly to Izzy about influencing Anna, who was so much younger than her. But Lena was stuck in a bind with her neighbour. She didn't want to offend her, because she watched the twins five afternoons a week after school.

Finally, she had Anna back in her pyjamas and settled in bed. Lena sat on the edge of the bed, stroking her daughter's hair. But Anna's mouth had adopted an insolent pout, her eyes were fiery.

'Please, Anna,' Lena said. 'I love you, darling. I don't want to fight with you.'

'I know why you and Daddy split up,' she said in a snaky tone. 'And I wish that he had married Aunty Nat, because she would make a better mum than you.'

Lena reeled, but she kept her voice even. 'I'm sorry you feel that way,' she said. 'But I'm your mother, and you will just have to accept that.'

Anna flipped over on her side, turning her back to Lena. Lena kissed Matthew goodnight and went to the sitting room – always so much tidier now that Sam wasn't here – and eyed the bottle of red wine that Sam's sister, Becky, had given her for Christmas. It had been a long time since she had sworn off drinking at Grandad's behest. But tonight, more than any night, she felt the need to take the edge off her feelings. She uncorked the bottle, filled a glass. Then sat back to drink it, and to cry a little more.

Sofi paced the shop, glancing out the front window. 'He's late,' she said to Francette. 'Not a good sign.'

She had reluctantly come to Paris to meet with an American businessman, Jack Merryweather, who was passionately keen about introducing Anastasia Designs to the US market. Sofi had said no to him half-a-dozen times already, via Francette. But Francette was convinced it was a good idea, so had arranged for them to meet in person.

'He's not late,' Francette said. 'You were early.'

'I just don't feel –'

'Then stop feeling and start thinking instead,' Francette said, good-naturedly. 'Anastasia could be a truly global business.'

'But if the company gets too big . . .' Sofi didn't bother finishing; they had been over it a hundred times before. She continued pacing. The door of the shop opened, right on time.

Jack Merryweather glanced from Francette to Sofi. 'Hello,' he said in a strong American accent, fixing his gaze on Sofi and extending his hand. 'You must be Sofi.'

'I am. This is Francette. I believe you've spoken with her a number of times.'

'I have, but it's always been you I've actually wanted.' He was a slight man with dark hair and eyes, not the big, brash American she'd been expecting. Sofi guessed he was not much older than herself. He smiled brilliantly, sending deep lines arrowing from his eyes. 'Can I take you for a coffee, Sofi?'

She picked up her bag. Better to get it over with quickly. 'Let's go.'

She didn't want to be led too far from the shop, so suggested a café just around the corner, with wrought-iron tables spilling out onto the cobbled square. They ordered and sat down, and Jack began a long, almost breathless account of how highly he thought of her jewellery and her business model. She tried to be wary, but his openness was very disarming.

'I know you've been reluctant to meet with me, Sofi, but if you'll just hear me out and think about my proposal, I'd be real grateful.'

'All right. Go ahead.'

'I don't want to import your jewellery. Anastasia trades on its boutique appeal: everything is handmade, Sofi Chernova is there overseeing it all. Hell, she might have even *made* the piece you're looking at. The US market is big, you'd have to reconfigure your business model to keep up.'

'Precisely,' Sofi said, surprised to hear this clear summation from him of all people.

'I want to franchise the name Anastasia and set up a workshop in the States. We would very clearly mark the business Anastasia New York, and replicate the business model you have here in France. We work from your designs in the US for the US market, and market the pieces appropriately as non-authentic alternatives to the French originals.'

'Cheap knock-offs?'

He shook his head emphatically. 'Not at all. Sofi, you know that's not what I'm suggesting. If I wanted to set up a company that made cheap knock-offs, I wouldn't have come to you first.'

Sofi admitted she knew that. Plenty of other companies had already done so, making jewellery that resembled hers for sale in the cheap chains and pharmacies; necklaces that the glass fell out of the moment it was brought home.

'By far the most important part of my offer is the extremely generous franchise fee I'm willing to pay. I want to give you five hundred thousand US dollars, followed by an ongoing licence fee of thirty per cent, scaling down to twenty per cent over the first five years of the business as it learns to stand on its own. Then we renegotiate. You lose nothing, you gain . . .' He shrugged. 'It's money for nothing, Sofi.'

'Only my designs?'

'Absolutely.'

'No glue?'

He feigned horror.

'I would have to be satisfied that the jewellery was made to very high standards.'

'Then be my guest, come to New York and see for yourself.' He put his hand over his heart. 'You have my personal guarantee that

I am as committed to quality as you are. In time, you will come to trust me. I look forward to earning that trust.'

Sofi sat back in her chair and considered his offer. She was already wealthy, perhaps it would be easy to leave things as they were. But then, a niggle of ambition teased her. Her jewellery, her designs, being worn all over the globe. She glanced up to see that Jack had tilted his head, was studying her left hand where it sat on the side of her coffee cup. With a flush of heat, she realised he was seeing if she wore a wedding ring. Embarrassed, she withdrew her hands into her lap.

He snapped to attention, blustering to cover the awkwardness. 'Women in the States want your jewellery, Sofi,' he said. 'They see it in the European magazines, they know they're missing out.'

She was stupidly flattered by his interest, both in her business and herself. It was not a good time to make a decision. 'Thank you, Jack. I will consider everything you've said today, and I'll have Francette contact you.' She stood, extending her hand for him to shake.

He remained seated, shook her hand firmly, and she strode off towards the store.

'How did it go?' Francette asked.

'Give it twenty-four hours,' Sofi said, 'then phone him and ask him to send a contract over to our lawyers.'

Francette clapped her hands together. 'Hallelujah,' she said. 'I knew you'd like him.'

Yes, thought Sofi, *a little too much*.

CHAPTER FORTY-THREE

Sofi stood at the window of her hotel room, on the thirty-fourth floor of the Four Seasons in New York, and gazed down at the view: the dark square of the park hemmed on all sides by bristling buildings alive with light. She had been here for nearly two weeks now and hadn't yet got tired of that view. She knew, now, why Julien liked so much to be away from home. No commitments, no responsibilities. Just her and the big city; waking up every morning and deciding what she wanted to do, with no thought for anyone else's wishes. Her breath fogged the window and she stood back, smoothed her skirt.

She was going out for dinner. A business dinner. It shouldn't make her so nervous. But it was with Jack Merryweather, and Jack Merryweather made her nervous.

On her first day, he had taken her to the little shop in the East Village that he had rented and introduced her to the American staff. She looked at their work, had to admit that it was easily the equivalent of the jewellery made in France. She'd been back to the shop three times since then, in between wandering in museums and art galleries, and never seen any evidence of a drop in standards. Her fears were allayed.

Jack had met her for lunch, for coffee. He had phoned every morning to suggest places for her to go and things for her to do. He had worked his way under her defences to the degree that she grew melancholy on days she didn't see him, inferring coolness where there wasn't any. She was a married woman; why did she expect him to behave like a love-struck suitor? She thought of Julien, his inscrutability, his distracted gaze. Jack was entirely the opposite: all passion and directness.

There, why was she comparing her husband to another man? It wasn't right, she had to stop. And yet the thought of saying goodbye to Jack in three days made her feel restless and sad, as though she were missing out on something everybody else was enjoying.

A gentle knock at the door. Sofi clasped her hands together, rested her forehead on them a moment. Then she straightened and went to the door.

'Hello, Jack,' she said.

'You look great,' he said with a broad smile. 'Let's go.'

They left the hotel and made their way down East Fifty-Seventh Street to Bergdorf's, then along Fifth Avenue. It had rained earlier and the streets were slick, the million lights of Manhattan caught in puddles. They got to Saks and crossed the road to the Rockefeller Center, where a skating rink had been installed for the winter. They stopped for a while to watch the skaters. Sofi stole glances at Jack, the lights of leftover Christmas stars and angels shining on his face. He caught her looking and she glanced away.

He put his arm around her shoulder. 'Did you go ice-skating when you were a kid?'

'Sometimes. Near my grandmother's place at Izhevsk there was a lake that froze over every winter. She had ice skates that were too big for me, so I packed them with rolled-up underpants to make them tight.'

She remembered skating, fast and breathless, in the still cold air, while Natalya and Lena waited on land, calling and calling to her to finish, to come back so that they could have a turn. It made her think of Winter Gathering, how they had missed it for the first time in nearly a decade. Natalya had phoned her just before Christmas, from St Petersburg.

'I know I've done the wrong thing,' she'd said. 'There's nothing you can say to me that I haven't already said to myself.'

But Sofi had said it anyway, had voiced her anger and disappointment. Natalya was dismayed to hear that Lena and Sam had split. Sofi guessed that she had been crying at the end of the phone conversation. Good. Natalya deserved to feel bad.

'Come on,' Jack said, guiding her away. 'The place I'm taking you gets real crowded after eight.'

They continued down Fifth Avenue, while traffic barked and fumed around them. He took her into a restaurant on West Forty-Seventh Street, a bar and grill with 1940s-inspired decor. It was already teeming with people. Swing music and loud laughter. They were shown to a table and ordered drinks, but Sofi despaired of being able to converse with Jack over the noise.

'So we've passed Bergdorf's and Saks,' he said, raising his voice. 'We can go walking a little further later and swing past Macy's and Bloomingdale's if you like. I'm hoping to have your jewellery in all of them in time for summer.'

Sofi shrugged out of her coat and hung it on the back of the chair. 'It's like a dream,' she said. 'I mean, it really was a dream. Me, and my cousins, in Leningrad. Dreaming about the west, about America.'

'Then why did you go to Europe?'

Guilt and shame prickled just under her skin. Since she had been in New York, she had thought about contacting Roy Creedy. She could meet with him, give him back his money, tell him she was sorry . . . But ultimately she was too afraid. Natalya's voice echoed in her mind: *He could be dangerous*. She simply had to let go of these thoughts of bad luck. Right now, she was in a beautiful city, rich, successful, creatively satisfied. And sitting across from a passionate man with a gorgeous smile and an interesting face. Though she knew she shouldn't take too much pleasure in the last blessing; Julien certainly wouldn't approve. But then, Julien wasn't around, was he?

Sofi realised she hadn't answered Jack's question. 'Visa problems,' she said. 'It was easier to go to London.'

'And France?'

'I met my husband in London,' she said, quietly, reluctantly. They'd not spoken about Julien more than in passing. 'I went to Richelieu to marry him. Have you ever been married, Jack?'

'Yes, I was. It didn't work out.'

'Why?'

'I think I set my sights too high. I'm searching for a heart of gold . . . you know, like the Neil Young song?'

Sofi nodded, though she wasn't sure which song he meant.

'Somebody creative and smart, but good and kind too.' Now he couldn't meet her eye, and she was lifted and dumped by a wave of longing for him. He changed the topic. 'You've got a little boy, haven't you?'

'Nikita,' she said. 'He's seven.'

'I bet he's a handful.'

Sofi had to laugh. 'You could say that. But not in the usual sense. He has autism.' She wondered if Jack now conjured a picture of Nikita as an intellectually slow child who raged and needed constant attention. Nothing like the real Nikita with his skinny shoulders and faraway gaze, hunched over his drawing books drawing the same picture over and over – car, car, car; or washing machine, washing machine, washing machine – all rendered in perfect proportion and three-dimensional detail. 'He's a beautiful boy,' she said. 'But not here in the world with us.'

They continued to talk over the noise, skirting around the edges of personal details. Sofi drank three glasses of wine, which was a lot for her, and felt light-headed. Her throat was sore from raising her voice, and she just wanted to get Jack somewhere quiet so she could keep talking to him, and not have to say goodnight and then goodbye.

'Come back to the hotel with me,' she said boldly. 'I have a wonderful view from my window, and there's a bottle of champagne in the refrigerator. We could toast the opening of Anastasia New York.'

'I'd like that,' he said.

In the time they'd been inside the warm restaurant, the temperature had dropped and Sofi felt the familiar crackling cold in the air that told her snow was on its way. She thrust her hands deep inside her coat pockets as she walked along beside Jack. She didn't feel real; she felt like a character in a movie. Surely the real Sofi Chernova would not invite a man back to her hotel room? And yet here they were, climbing into the lift together, unlocking her hotel room door . . .

The phone was ringing. Sofi checked her watch; it was almost ten o'clock. Who was ringing now? She picked it up.

'Hello?'

'Sofi, it's me.' Mama, and she sounded frantic.

Sofi's blood went cold. 'What is it? What's happened?'

'Nikita's gone missing.'

'What? How?'

'I don't know. I got up to have a drink of water and I noticed his door was ajar, and he wasn't in his room. I ran around the whole town in the dark trying to find him, but I couldn't and now . . . I've been trying to phone for an hour. I'm so sorry, Sofi, I'm so sorry.'

'I'm coming home,' she said, feeling acutely the vast distance between her and her son. 'Keep looking. Wake up the neighbours.' She tried to fight the images that crowded her head. Nikita had no sense or judgement in traffic, he couldn't swim, he was easily disoriented and it panicked him. Was he frightened? Cold? God, it would be less than ten degrees in Richelieu at the moment . . . 'I'll be there as soon as I can, Mama. Please find him. Please find my boy.'

She hung up and turned. She had almost forgotten Jack was there. Any feelings of longing or desire had evaporated into mist.

'Is everything okay?'

'My baby,' she said, bursting into tears. 'My baby's gone missing. I have to get home.'

'Hey, it's okay. He'll be okay,' he said soothingly.

Her panicked brain couldn't cope with what to do next. 'I should pack. I need to get to the airport.'

'Don't pack. I'll do it. I'll ship your stuff back to you. Let me take care of everything. Just grab your passport and your purse and go. You'll feel better once you're moving.'

She reeled. She had so far to travel. And all the while the world stretched off in infinite directions away from Nikita.

Thirteen hours of travel; a long, slow nightmare.

Sofi had called at each stop: Frankfurt; Paris. Mama was out looking, but had installed Yvette, their elderly neighbour, at her house to answer the phone. No, they hadn't found him yet. Yes, the police were helping. No, she didn't know if anyone had called Julien. Yes, the whole village was looking. Come home as soon as you can.

She hadn't slept, couldn't sleep. She was jetlagged and dazed. Francette had picked her up from the airport and roared home to Richelieu along the A10. Dark closed in. Sofi had been on planes for the entire short stretch of daylight in Richelieu. Nikita was still out there, and it was night-time again.

Mama met them at home. The house looked too bright, ablaze with lights. People she didn't know crowded her sitting room. Asking questions. Where did he like to go? Did he have friends?

Mama shooed them away. 'Leave her be, can't you see she's tired? I already answered those questions.'

'I just want to go out and look,' Sofi said to Mama. 'I can't wait here.'

'You should sleep. Everyone else is out looking.'

'I can't rest until I find him,' Sofi said, suddenly aware of the tears on her cheeks.

'I'll come with you.'

Out of the warm, bright house and back into the cold, dark street. Sofi didn't speak, hesitated. *Which way?* He could be anywhere. Anywhere. Where was her maternal intuition? Why couldn't she just call him in her mind and locate him? Was that silence a horrible confirmation of his death?

She took a deep breath. 'Someone would see him in the village. He must be in the parklands.'

'There are police searching the parklands.'

'I want to go there.'

Mama nodded. 'All right.'

Every step felt as though it shuddered through her body. She felt swollen-headed and hot, precisely as though she had a raging fever. The playground was empty and ghostly in the dark. They crossed the canal and headed towards the dark woods that separated the village from the farmlands beyond. Torch beams darted around in the dark. Sofi's heart squeezed tight at the sight of all the water. One wrong step . . .

She began to call. 'Nikita? Nikita, it's Mama!'

At the edge of the woods, at the sight of the trees crowding in infinite patterns, her knees gave way. Fatigue and emotional exhaustion overwhelmed her. Mama took her elbow and helped her sit on the ground.

A tall, beefy man approached. 'This is the child's mother?' he asked.

'Yes,' Mama said. 'Sofi, this is Inspector Girard. He's in charge here.'

He crouched in front of her. Night and torchlight made sinister shadows on his face. 'Madame,' he said, 'there is nothing for you to do here. You should go home and rest. I promise you that I will look for your Nikita as though he were my own son.'

His words pricked at her memory. 'Oh, God. Julien! Has anyone called Julien?'

Mama shook her head. 'I didn't even think of it.'

Inspector Girard helped her up. 'There, you have already found yourself a task more suited to your abilities. Call the child's father. Perhaps he can give you some comfort.'

Sofi began to stumble back the way she had come, lost in a dazed bad dream. Her stomach ached with hunger, and her senses were confused. Mama led her back across the canal, back towards the playground. The squeak of playground equipment caught her attention.

She looked up. Her blood surged. There was a child standing by the roundabout. Still as a statue.

'Mama?' she said, jaw trembling.

'Oh, my God.'

Then Sofi was screaming his name. 'Nikita, Nikita!' She ran for him. He looked up calmly, allowed himself to be crushed in a hug. Sofi stood back to check his face and arms for scratches or bruises. He wore only his flannel pyjamas and his hands and feet were icy.

He looked at her and said, 'Roundabout, Mama?'

Sofi glanced behind her, realised he wanted her to spin the roundabout for him. 'Is that why you came out here?' she asked.

Voices were approaching, torch beams bobbing.

'Roundabout, Mama?'

She spun the roundabout. He watched it dreamily. She glanced around; a crowd gathered, shouting, cheering.

'How did you not find him, Mama?' Sofi asked. 'You must have come here surely?'

'Of course I did, it was the first place I came. He must have hidden on purpose. From me, from everyone.'

'But why?'

'Because he wanted you.' Mama looked at her in the dark, her eyes very serious. 'Sofi, I think he missed you.'

Hot tears spilled down her cheeks.

'I told you one day he'd show he loved you,' Mama said, touching her hair. 'It looks like I was right.'

CHAPTER FORTY-FOUR

Natalya hesitated in front of Maxim Levitsky's apartment block on the Petrograd side of the Neva River. The building was late nineteenth-century style moderne, made of stone and finished with wrought iron, narrow arched windows with decorative wooden frames, and a carved relief of flowers over the locked front entrance. Dusk had closed in very early, and powdery snow drifted over her. Maxim Levitsky didn't want to meet her. At least, that's what his secretary had told her. Repeatedly. But Natalya thought she knew better. Maxim Levitsky had pursued her for more than a year, and she had asked Leida to turn him down over and over again. He couldn't have gone cold that easily. Though, if he had seen *Skin Crawlers* . . .

Natalya straightened her back. It didn't do to doubt herself. She had his address thanks to Tolya – her old friend from her younger years, who was still racketeering very successfully. She approached the front door and pressed the doorbell. Then waited.

'Yes?' The voice crackled through the intercom.

'Maxim Levitsky?'

'Who wants to know?'

He sounded wary. Of course he was wary. He was a movie director with a growing profile; no doubt many desperate actors threw themselves at him. Just as she was doing now.

'It's Natalie Chernoff,' she said, falling back to her anglicised stage name. 'I'd like to meet you.'

No more words. The buzzer went, she pushed the door open and was inside the building.

She found his apartment on the third floor. Stopped for a moment to catch her breath and straighten her hair, then knocked.

He opened the door and peered out at her. He had hair as black as coal, and eyes to match, a three-day growth and a smell of tobacco. Natalya was surprised to notice he was not much older than her, and attractive in an intense, dishevelled way. He wore a long-sleeved blue shirt and loose jeans.

'Why did you come? My secretary told you I wouldn't meet you.'

'I didn't believe her,' Natalya said.

He opened the door wide, unsmiling. 'Come in,' he said.

She followed him inside a messy apartment. Books and papers littered every surface. He moved a pile of scripts to make a space for her on the battered leather sofa. 'You want a drink?' he said, not waiting for an answer before disappearing into a small kitchen to pour two unevenly matched glasses of vodka. She glanced around the room quickly. On the sideboard, there was a large framed photograph of a smiling blonde woman with two little dark-haired girls. There could be no doubt they were his daughters; they looked exactly like him. He returned and offered her a glass.

'My wife and daughters,' he said. 'We are no longer together, much to my regret.'

'I'm sorry,' she said, thinking of Lena and feeling the pinch of remorse again. 'The little girls are beautiful.'

'The oldest one is very clever,' he said. 'But has a temper . . .' He shook his head, laughing. 'Don't start me talking of my children. I will let down my guard.'

'Is that a bad thing?'

He still hadn't sat. He scowled at her. 'I wasn't good enough for you, Natalie. I wasn't good enough for a long time. Then you made a very bad film and nobody liked it or you. And now you are here. So I assume I am your director of last resort. Is that right?'

Natalya was mortified. It was exactly right. Arriving back in St Petersburg had been the unhappiest time of her life. She had thought she would find comfort in home, but the nostalgic familiarity merely served to remind her that she had failed. She hadn't become a movie star, an American princess. Certainly she had enough money for the moment, but it wouldn't last forever. Her career highlights were all behind her. And she had brought with her a burden of guilt and shame so immense that some mornings she could not get out of bed because of its weight. The only thing she had clung to was that there was a director here, a credible one, who had once wanted to work with her. So she had tracked him down, she had found him, but she hadn't anticipated that he would see right through her in the first sixty seconds of their acquaintance.

'No, no,' she said. 'I couldn't work with you before because I wanted to stay in London. Now I'm home, it made sense to meet with you.'

Maxim sat, finally. He gulped his drink, rubbed the back of his hand over his bristly chin. 'I had a part for you, Natalie. I shelved the project when you said no. I could see nobody else playing it.'

She glowed. 'Really?' she said. 'And please, call me Natalya.'

'Well, Natalya, then you made that terrible film, and became even more perfect for it.'

'Really?' she said again, this time warily. 'What kind of part?'

He scooped the script off the top of a pile and thrust it into her hands. The title was written in a plain font on the front: *A Home in the Soul*.

'Lilya is a fading beauty, approaching forty,' he explained. 'In her youth she was a great seductress; now she does not like that she hasn't that power any longer. She tries frantically to regain her sexual power, does not see that her conquests now prove nothing but her reckless desperation. She succumbs, slowly, slowly, to a crippling melancholy. Then she meets Arkady, a man dying of a brain illness. And through their love she is redeemed.' He moved his hands apart in a flourish, slopping his vodka on the carpet.

Natalya was horrified. 'And I'm perfect for this part?'

'Yes.'

'Perfect for the part of a desperate, sad old slut?'

'Yes.'

'I'm only thirty-five.'

'Did it take long to get there? Do you think you'll never be forty?' His voice grew warm. 'Let me ask you, Natalya, did shooting puppets in a G-string make you a star? Did anybody say, "Now, there is an actor who has touched my heart"?'

Natalya didn't answer.

'I didn't think so. People speak of credibility as though it is lost once and forever. In this business, that is not so. If you make a good film now, you can earn it back. This is a good film and, whether you like it or not, you are perfect for it. Be brave.'

She stood, putting her untouched drink aside and offering him the script. 'I think it was a mistake to come to see you.'

He shrugged. 'At least take the script with you.'

'I don't think so.'

But he folded his arms and shook his head. 'Take it and read it. If you agree, we can start filming in April. I'll move another project.'

Out on the snowy street, she allowed herself to cry. She found a warm café behind Trinity Square, ordered a strong coffee and worried the edge of the script with her fingertips. She could see out the front windows to the Trinity Bridge, lights gleaming in the dark. The snow continued lightly, powdering windowsills and melting on car tyres. She took a sip of coffee and began to read.

How she hated the part of Lilya. How she hated being offered the role of a woman who was everything Natalya feared she had become. How she despised the way Maxim Levitsky had seemed to uncover her soul and put it in this script, even though he had never met her. And yet, as she turned page after page, she found her heart pulled into the story. She realised this was the first script she had read that had touched her. Why had nobody ever offered her a part before that was emotionally meaningful? She had played sluts and corpses, women who had existed merely to sleep with or kill. Often both at once.

Be brave.

She stood, the script still unfinished, and hurried back out into the snow. A woman leaving Maxim's building held the door open for her, and Natalya raced up the stairs to knock. Snow hung in her long curls and her nose was moist from the cold. He opened the door. This time, his blue shirt was unbuttoned and she could see the dark hair on his chest. A surge of desire surprised her.

'You again? I was about to have a bath.'

'I love it,' she said, thrusting the script towards him. 'I love it, I want it.'

He took her arm and pulled her inside. For one alarmed moment, she thought he was going to kiss her, but he didn't. She was surprisingly disappointed. He closed the door behind them and turned to her. 'Are you certain? Don't waste my time.'

'I'm certain. It's beautiful. You're a genius.'

He smiled, fully and brightly. It made him look wolfish. 'I know,' he said. 'Would you like to stay and have something to eat with me? We can talk some more.'

'Yes,' she said, trying not to sound breathless. 'I'd like that very much.'

Matthew and Anna's tenth birthday party was held at the park on the foreshore two blocks from Wendy's apartment. Matthew and Anna were in different classes at school now, and had very different sets of friends, so they had been limited to four guests each. Matthew and his group were huddled around Matthew's new Game Boy at one side of the picnic shelter; Anna and her group – including the dratted Izzy – had taken the other side of the shelter to put on glittery lipstick and chat on pretend mobile phones. Izzy, thankfully, looked bored. At nearly fourteen, she would be interested in Anna only so much longer. Girls of her own age, not to mention boys, would soon be infinitely more appealing.

That left Lena standing at the picnic table in the middle of the shelter, with Sam, Wendy, Sam's sister, Becky, and her partner, Sue. Lena took comfort in the fact that Wendy and Becky were arguing over something; for a change, she wasn't the focus of Wendy's cold stares. Still, she had nothing to say to them, least of all Sam who was sullen and silent.

'Ah, damn,' Wendy said as she tried unsuccessfully for the third time to get the candles on the cake alight. 'Too much wind here. Sam, move back over this way and block it.'

Sam did as he was told. Lena hung back. Wendy had organised the party and made the cake. Lena didn't have time with work and managing the children. Or was it that she didn't have the energy? It didn't matter. Wendy had taken charge and for that she was grateful. She sipped at the glass of orange juice in her hand and longed for a large splash of vodka in it. Being near Sam was almost unbearable. Her eyes wanted to feast on him, her hands wanted to reach for him. He was open and affectionate with the children, and she knew they would be morose and sulky when they got home because he wasn't coming with them. A million times since they had separated she had asked herself why she didn't just invite him back. It was natural, they were meant to be together. But then she'd remember what he'd done and her heart would harden again.

After the cake, Becky and Sue wandered off for a walk along the cliff path, and Wendy headed away from the children – at Lena's request – to smoke a cigarette. This left Sam and Lena sitting together at the picnic bench, surrounded by the sounds of the children shouting and laughing, the ocean thundering. The sun was high and full in the sky, illuminating the white clouds until they dazzled. Sam said nothing for a long time, then finally he spoke.

'Are you all right?'

She glanced at him over her shoulder. The wind caught his long curls and she ached to smooth them back into place. 'I'm managing. You?'

'Same.' He tried a smile. 'I'd be better if we were together.'

'You should have thought of that before,' she said sharply.

'Hey, hey,' he said, palms up, 'I don't want to fight. I just want to talk.'

Her instinct was to unload upon him a heap of recriminations. She fought it, forced a pleasant voice. 'All right. We can talk.'

'Anna wants to come and live with me.'

Lena sighed. 'I know.'

'You think it's a bad idea?'

Right now, she thought it was a marvellous idea. Anna was difficult, stubborn, seemed to be on a collision course with early puberty.

'I won't separate them,' she said. 'When I was little, all I had was my sister...' She trailed off, blinking back sudden tears.

Sam said nothing.

'Do *you* think it's a bad idea?' Lena continued.

'Yes. I'd rather they stayed together. And Matthew wouldn't leave you in a fit. A real mummy's boy, that one.' Sam laughed softly. 'Just like I was.'

'So we're united on this one? Anna stays with me?'

'Absolutely. Though she's not going to want to hear it.'

Lena felt a pang of sadness. She and Sam were a good couple: like-minded, great parents. Why, why, a million times *why* had he done the only unforgivable thing? The answers that sprang to her mind were acutely painful. She was missing some vital ingredient – beauty or goodness or an ineffable inner light – and that was why people couldn't love her enough. That was why they abandoned her, or overlooked her, or betrayed her. The thought created a physical pain in her guts, a raw feeling that she knew a couple of glasses of wine could wash away.

Matthew ran up then and showed her his racing car going around a loop on the Game Boy. She admired it, ruffling his hair, then he was off again.

'Ten years,' Sam said. 'It's flown.'

Lena didn't answer. She remembered being in the hospital, waking up with Sam there looking so young and scared and hopeful all at once; how madly, stupidly in love they had been. Now they sat a metre apart, afraid to say the wrong thing to each other, brimming with resentments. There had been no talk of divorce yet – the word made her stomach clench – but what other path was there for them? Tears, never far away, pricked at her eyes. She blinked them back.

Wendy returned, reeking of cigarette smoke. 'Looks like a storm coming,' she said, indicating the gathering dark clouds over the sea. 'We'd best pack up.'

It took the kids hours to come down from their birthday high. Sofi rang to wish them happy birthday at six, and they were still too excited to talk for more than a few moments. Lena sent them out to play on the footpath and watched them from the kitchen window while she talked to Sofi. Matthew was tightrope-walking along the low fence outside their building, while Anna tickled his knees with a stick.

'You sound exhausted,' Sofi said.

'What person with children isn't?' Lena replied.

Working full-time and then coming home to single-handedly manage the children was draining her. Added to that, coping with the rent on one income meant a tight budget that made her anxious and that the children constantly complained about. Sam helped out, of course, but the responsibility fell hardest on her shoulders. She didn't want to sell the farmhouse, but it would make things so much easier. If only she were brave enough to ask Sofi to loan her the money to fix the farmhouse so she could live there with the kids, get a part-time job that didn't tax her so much. Away from grey Briggsby, away from the nursery.

'But I expect I'll manage,' she went on.

'You need a break. How about coming to France after Christmas? It's my turn this year.'

Lena bristled. Winter Gathering. Sofi wanted to pretend nothing had happened, get the three of them together again. Every time they spoke she mentioned it. Obviously, she was in touch with Natalya; obviously Natalya wanted to repair their relationship. Lena wouldn't bend on this issue.

'No, absolutely not,' she said hotly. 'I won't see her. I won't speak to her ever again.'

Sofi's voice was conciliatory. 'All right. I'm sorry if I've made you angry.'

After the phone call, after getting the wound-up children bathed and in bed, Lena pulled a chair under the sitting-room window and watched the soft twilight deepen slowly to night. She swirled the wine in her glass, thinking about Sofi and her attempts to get her to forgive her sister. Didn't she see? In one cruel blow, she had lost her sister and her husband. It would almost have been better if they'd died; she could have mourned them and got on with life. This way, there was always the temptation that she could reconcile, forgive them, and let them know that she was weak and would accept any kind of bad treatment. Then what was there to stop them doing it again? She would wonder for the rest of her life, any time they were both out of her direct line of vision, if they were betraying her. Saying to each other, 'She's forgiven us once, she'll forgive us again.'

Lena clenched her free hand, driving her fingernails into her palm. She gulped her drink, trying to wash away the pain.

Sofi was lighting candles when she heard the knock at the door. Julien was early. She quickly finished with the candles, hit the light switch and surveyed the dining room. There, perfect for a romantic dinner. Nikita was in bed and Mama had offered to stay in her room, giving Sofi and Julien some space. They hadn't seen each other in a year; it was an important night.

She hurried to the door, flung it open. 'Did you forget your key?' she said.

He stepped forward, caught her in his arms and held her tightly. He smelled different, perhaps he was using a different soap or shampoo. She sank into him and was so grateful that she hadn't let the madness with Jack Merryweather go any further. She had given strict instructions that Francette deal with Jack from now on, so those complicated feelings wouldn't arise again.

Finally, he stood back, sniffing the air. 'Sofi? Are you cooking?'

'Dinner for two,' she said. 'Come in.'

All through dinner, she couldn't take her eyes off him. He didn't seem real. Even though she had spoken to him at least once a week on the phone, his physical presence was unfamiliar to her. The distance had made strangers of them, but the process of becoming close again was sweet. Sofi realised that as much as she hated their separations, this aspect of their relationship had brought a distinctive colour to their lives. Finally, slowly and warmly, they moved to their bedroom to make love. His homecoming was complete. He was once again here with her, and she would enjoy it as much as she could until the next inevitable separation.

'It was a shame my plane came in so late,' he said as they lay there afterwards, limbs tangled together. 'I would have liked to see Nikita before he went to bed.'

'It will be a nice surprise for him in the morning. He's done some drawings for you.'

Nikita's art was nothing like Julien's. Nikita's were images copied down exactly, no imagination or artist's perspective. But they were very good, and he could spend hours on them. Since the awful day he had run away, Sofi had scaled back her work to spend more time with him. They sat at the dining table every afternoon drawing together. He still was not an affectionate child, sometimes barely seemed to notice she was there. But she detected that he was more relaxed, didn't cling quite so tightly to his routines or play so obsessively with his toys.

Julien rolled onto his side. 'I have been thinking about your problem, with your cousins,' he said.

'You have?' Sofi was never sure if the chatter she made on the phone to him ever actually sank in. She often felt at the end of their conversations, that she had blathered about trivial rubbish the whole time.

'I have a solution. Natalya will come but Lena won't. Until Lena comes, they can never reconcile. Am I right?'

'Yes, that's right. And Lena's too angry or too proud or . . . something. But I would love so much to have them both here, and give them some time to sort it all out.'

'It's very simple. You tell Lena that if she comes, you will pay for her farmhouse to be made livable. She won't say no.'

Sofi recoiled. 'That feels wrong.'

'Why? Does not the end justify the means?'

She shook her head. 'Besides, I don't think it will work,' she said. 'Lena wouldn't accept that kind of generosity – it's too much.'

'When did you last ask her? Before she split with her husband and became a single mother? You are so wealthy now, you have forgotten the way deprivation wears people down.' Julien stroked her hair. 'Try it. You may be surprised.'

Sofi gazed up at the ceiling in the dark, turning the idea over in her mind. She would never miss the money, that was for certain. And it could represent for Lena a chance to take happiness in both hands: a house of her own to live in, and a reconciliation with her sister. She vowed to ring her the next day; and every day after that if she refused. This time she wouldn't take no for an answer.

Damp autumn had closed in on St Petersburg. Gold and red leaves languished in puddles all up and down the uneven footpath of Nevsky Prospekt and Natalya tried vainly to keep her new boots dry as she hurried to the Tsvyet restaurant. Finally, finally, Maxim had asked her out. Throughout the entire film shoot, he had kept her at arm's length. At first she'd thought it was a game he was playing, to make her want him even more. But she soon caught on that Maxim did not play games. One more thing to admire about him, along with his intensity, his focus, and his black, black eyes. She made every excuse to be near him, talk to him, brush against him. Despite all of her efforts, he was simply, bafflingly, not interested in her.

But then the shoot had wrapped and he had softened towards her. On the last day of filming she had approached him boldly and said, 'I don't like to think this is the last time I'll see you.'

'Let me take you to dinner then,' he had said, almost nonchalantly. Her heart had flipped over in her chest, and that was the first inkling she had that her obsession with Maxim might be love.

Then how had she managed to be running so late? Perhaps she was trying too hard to look perfect. She had changed three times. Then the rain had slowed her down on the way to the metro and she had missed the train. She hoped Maxim wouldn't read into her lateness any signs of indifference. She was desperate to impress him.

She took a breath outside the restaurant, glancing through the front window to see if she could spot him. She realised immediately she was overdressed. Maxim had told her that Tsvyet was his favourite restaurant, so she'd assumed it would be up-market, dimly lit, with starched tablecloths. Rather it was full of large work parties, harried mothers trying to control small children, elderly middle-class women in their best beige shoes. She looked down at her Torrente checked jacket and skirt, her knee-high suede Prada boots; even the little bracelet Sofi had sent to cheer her up – blue amazonite for hope – was a designer piece that couldn't fail to attract attention. She sighed. Pushed the door open and went in.

She scanned the room for Maxim, but couldn't see him. A second later, he was at her shoulder. She turned. His hair was wet.

'Natalya, I'm sorry to be late,' he said.

'I only just arrived myself.' She glanced around for a waiter. 'Do we have reservations?'

He laughed. 'No, we find a table, then we go up to the bar to order. I'm sorry if you're used to doing things differently.'

Very differently. Every date she'd been on since her time with Rupert had been about the best table in the best restaurant, waitstaff scurrying about trying to please her. And always across the table from her was some overgroomed, empty-headed, pretty boy. Maxim wore faded jeans and scuffed Doc Martens boots. She noticed, as they sat, that his white shirt was missing a button. The food was stodgy, the wine was cheap, and yet Natalya couldn't remember having such an enjoyable dinner date since . . . Actually, she couldn't remember one at all.

After dinner and a sticky dessert that she never should have eaten, Maxim suggested they take a walk.

'Where to?' she asked.

'To my place,' he replied. 'If that's what you'd like.'

Natalya's blood fluttered. 'Ah, yes. I would.'

The rain had weakened to drizzle as they took their time past the Hermitage, the Marble Palace and the wild Summer Gardens. The river smelled sour and ancient. They crossed the Trinity Bridge; the spire of the Peter and Paul cathedral pierced the night sky. As they walked, they talked about the film, their work, their lives. The cold dampness barely registered on Natalya, who felt herself falling and falling. Maxim took her hand and the desire that shot through her was so acute that she almost had to catch her breath. It was just his hand, around hers; and yet it was the sexiest touch she had ever felt.

His bedroom was just as messy as the rest of his apartment. No concession had been made for her arrival. He threw books off the covers and onto the floor, and laid her down among the sheets – they smelled like him, musty and masculine – and undressed her slowly, all the while kissing her as though he were waking her up from a long sleep of unhappiness. Their bodies, when they came together, felt like two parts of the same whole, finding each other at last.

Maxim wasn't interested in lying in bed afterwards, making promises of love. Instead, he kissed her neck and asked if she wanted coffee. Then he left her to dress alone in the dim room.

She joined him in the kitchen, slid her arms around his bare chest while he poured coffee.

'You are wonderful,' she said.

'Careful, Natalya, I don't want to burn you.'

She pulled away, hoisted herself up on the kitchen bench. He handed her coffee, then stood between her knees, stroking her right thigh with his free hand. Warm shivers.

'Why do you still wear your wedding ring?' she asked.

'Because I am still married,' he answered.

Did she detect anger in his tone? 'I'm sorry,' she said, 'I didn't mean to offend you.'

'You haven't.'

She wanted very much to ask him when he intended to divorce, how long he had been separated, if his wife had found somebody else. To ask him if his heart was actually free to love her. But she didn't. She was afraid of the answer.

After eight days of torrential rain, Lena had been certain that the roof of the farmhouse would have leaked. But it seemed the interim repairs had held up well. The sun was shining now on the autumn fields, and Matthew and Anna were racing to the barn and back while Lena checked every room. And found no puddles.

It was more than a concern about leaks that had brought her here. Sofi would not let her be, filling her head with promises and fantasies.

'It's very simple, Lena,' she said. 'I will give you the money. Because I love you, because I want you and your beautiful children to live somewhere nice. The only repayment I ask of you is that you come to Winter Gathering here in Richelieu, and you talk to Natalya. You don't have to be friends with her, you just have to talk to her.'

But it wasn't simple. Nothing about it was simple. No doubt Sofi thought her offer was kind, but Lena felt as though it were blackmail. Asking her to choose between her children's future and her own stubborn desire to stay angry at Natalya forever. Of course she should say yes.

Why, then, was it *so hard* to say yes?

Anna came in, breathless and flushed, a little girl again instead of the hostile pre-teen Lena had become used to. 'I beat Matthew!' she shouted.

Matthew came in after her. 'No, you didn't!'

'Yes, I did!'

They argued for a few moments, then Anna turned to Lena and said, 'This place smells funny.'

Lena had never brought them to the farmhouse before. In fact, she hadn't been out here herself for months. Only once since the split with Sam.

'It needs fixing up. Would you like to live here if we fixed it up?' Her heart thudded. Why had she said that?

'No way!' Anna said.

'It wouldn't smell funny any more. We'd put a new kitchen in, and you and Matthew could have a bedroom each.'

'Cool! That would be totally amazing!' Matthew shrieked, running off and calling behind him about getting the best room. Anna was off after him, leaving Lena in the kitchen.

She made up her mind.

CHAPTER FORTY-FIVE

It was a tense drive home from Paris for Sofi. And not just because she was driving Julien's monstrous V6 Peugeot on icy roads. It was the ice inside the car that was the problem.

It had been a long day. Natalya had flown in first, at ten that morning. Sofi picked her up, showed her the shop, then took her for an expensive lunch at Baracane just near the Bastille. Natalya had been full of chatter about her new boyfriend and Sofi had been amazed that she hadn't even mentioned Lena, Sam, the betrayal. Finally, Sofi had asked, impatiently, 'What are you going to say to Lena?'

Natalya shrugged. 'What can I say? I'll tell her I'm sorry and that I still love her.'

'I don't think Lena is going to be won over that easily,' Sofi said, frowning. 'What you did was –'

'Yes, yes, I *know*,' Natalya said. 'Don't lecture me, Sofi. It's very tiresome to always be the person in the wrong.'

Sofi backed off. Her own relationship with Natalya had never really recovered from the Anastasia campaign. She bundled Natalya into the car and back out to the airport to meet Lena's three o'clock arrival. At Sofi's urging, Natalya waited in the car.

Lena looked sallow and too thin, as though she'd aged ten years since the last time Sofi saw her.

'Is she here yet?' Lena asked, eyes darting about.

'She's waiting in the car. Take a deep breath.'

Lena hitched her bag over her shoulder. 'I'm not nervous.' This was a lie; anyone could see that. 'She should be nervous.'

When they returned to the car, Natalya had climbed into the back seat, letting Lena have the front. Lena, silent as the grave, buckled her seatbelt and kept her eyes to the front. Natalya tried a brave, 'Hello, Lena.' But was greeted with nothing.

Sofi put the car in gear. She was used to her little van. This car was Julien's Christmas present from her. The silence continued for nearly half an hour, despite Sofi's attempts to get a conversation started. She glanced at Lena, whose dismal face hid nothing. She placed a hand over her wrist, rubbed her gently, then returned her hand to the wheel. Natalya saw the gesture and finally said something.

'Lena, I'm sorry and I still love you.'

Lena remained silent.

'Lena?'

Sofi tensed. Would she have to remind Lena that part of their deal involved her speaking to her sister?

'Lena, if you just –'

'Your apology is not accepted,' Lena snapped, eyes still glued on the road.

Natalya began to cry. 'I didn't mean to hurt you so badly. I'd do anything to make it up to you.'

'The only thing that would make it right would be if you could go back in time and not have sex with my husband. Can you do that, Natalya?'

Now it was Natalya's turn to be silent.

'I didn't think so.'

Neither of them spoke the rest of the way home. Sofi turned up the radio and concentrated on the road.

At home, Natalya made small talk with Julien and was much more at ease than poor Lena. Sofi took her aside to show her to her room. Mama had gone away to Paris with a friend from St Petersburg, so Sofi had cleared it out for Lena's things.

'Here, a room by yourself,' she said, closing the door behind them.

'Thanks. I wouldn't have been able to share.'

'I understand.' Sofi smiled at her. 'You're very brave to come.'

'Then why do I feel like such a fool?'

Sofi reached into the pocket of her pants and pulled out a folded slip of paper, a cheque. 'You're not a fool. You've been hurt badly. I don't think you're a fool. Here.'

Lena unfolded it and her eyes glistened. It was probably more money than she'd seen in her life. 'That's more than I asked for.'

'To cover emergencies.' Sofi pulled her tight. 'I just want you to be as happy as I am.'

She regretted it as soon as she said it. It wasn't money that had made her happy, but finally making peace with what life had given her. Finding a way to love Julien on his terms, spending more time with Nikita. Money could certainly not buy back Lena's happiness.

'I wish it were that easy,' Lena sniffed.

'You will get through this. Just give Natalya a chance. I know you're angry, but no matter how angry you are, the past can't be undone. Forgiveness is very healing.'

Lena shrugged her off. 'I'll talk to her,' she said. 'But as for forgiveness . . .'

'Just try,' Sofi said, but Lena had already turned away to unpack her things.

By dinner on the second night, it had all fallen apart. Lena knew she was handling the situation badly, but was powerless to stop herself from being hostile towards Natalya. If her sister spoke, she snapped. Everything Natalya said provided Lena with an opportunity to vent some of her feelings, unspoken for too long in the year of silence between them. Sofi had done an admirable job of umpiring, but even she was starting to get worn down by the constant tension.

On the third day, Sofi was called into work late in the afternoon – an emergency involving a lost order – and Julien had discreetly taken Nikita and gone for a drive. For the first time, Lena and Natalya were alone.

Despite the cold, Lena sat on the back terrace watching the weak sun make long shadows, hoping that Natalya wouldn't come out. Of course, she did.

'Can we discuss it?' Natalya said.

Lena remembered the cheque and shrugged. 'If we must.'

'Yes, we must,' Natalya replied, sitting down. 'Do you want to go inside where it's warm?'

'No.' Cold rain began to mist down, but Lena wouldn't budge. 'I want to stay out here.'

'All right,' Natalya said slowly. 'You've made it really clear to me how you feel, and I'm almost certain I can imagine it.'

'Never in a million years,' Lena laughed. 'You've never been able to see life outside your little bubble.'

'I have said that I'm sorry so many times, Lena,' Natalya said. 'What else can I do?'

If only there *were* something she could do. Lena felt herself stuck in the helpless moment. Forever. She might as well be dead.

She stood. 'I need a drink.'

'You're drinking again? I thought you gave that up.'

Lena rounded on her. 'Don't you *dare* to take the moral high ground.'

'I'm not, I'm just saying –'

'Don't say it. I agreed to talk to you about how guilty and wrong the things *you* do are. Leave what I do out of this.'

Natalya followed her into the house. 'I'm sorry, I'm sorry.'

'You keep saying that.'

Lena uncorked a bottle of red wine in the kitchen and poured herself a glass. She didn't offer Natalya one, and Natalya didn't ask.

'It's true, I am sorry. And I love you. Do you love me?'

What a question. Lena blocked off the feelings that arose, afraid they would unseat her, undercut her resolve. 'Don't ask me that.'

'I'm your sister.'

'That's what makes what you did unforgivable.'

Around and around they went: Natalya trying to open a line of dialogue, Lena shutting it down with recriminations. Lena was agitated, drank too fast. Within half an hour, the bottle was half-empty. She began to speak recklessly, argue in circles.

Finally, Natalya had had enough. 'I can't talk to you when you're like this,' she said. 'I'll try again in the morning when you're sober.'

'I am sober.'

Natalya walked away.

'You can't win this by walking away!' Lena shrieked, catching her in the hallway.

'This isn't about winning anything,' Natalya said. 'Or is it for you? Is this just sibling rivalry? I've finally done something so bad that you *win*?'

Lena was midway through a stream of abuse when the front door opened. Julien and Nikita stood there. She became aware of how her voice must have sounded from outside. A harpy, swearing in Russian. Natalya flounced up the stairs, leaving Lena straining against tears.

Julien offered up a basket of groceries. 'Dinner?'

Lena sniffed, blinked, composed herself. 'Sofi's not back yet.'

Julien frowned. 'She's lost track of time again. I usually go to pick her up. She forgets otherwise. I'll phone her.'

'No, I'll go and get her,' Lena said, already heading for the door. 'I need to cool off a little.'

Julien smiled weakly. 'Yes, it certainly sounded that way.'

Lena nodded fast, lips pressed together. 'I'm sorry.'

Nikita stood between them, looking from one to the other.

'Oh, Lena, would you mind taking Nikita with you? He likes the walk to pick up his mama, and it would keep him out of the way while I cook.'

Lena forced a smile, holding out her hand. 'Of course. Come on, Nikita. Let's go fetch Mama.'

Nikita was still in his coat and hat. Lena grabbed a coat and an umbrella by the door, and headed out into the drizzly cold. She held Nikita's hand and pulled him along gently. She wasn't in the mood for ambling. She was in the mood for stomping and shouting, and Julien had probably known that when he'd urged her to take Nikita with her. Give her something else to focus on. Part of her was grateful that he cared, but another part was just angry. Angry at everyone for thinking they knew what was good for her. It had been that way her whole life. Weak Lena, scared Lena, Lena the victim. She realised that this was more than half the reason she couldn't forgive Natalya: to show her sister that she had strength, mettle, the moral centre that Natalya lacked.

There. She had admitted it. Natalya was right. This was about finally winning. Shame washed through her.

A second later she realised Nikita's hand wasn't in her own any more.

She turned around, disoriented. He'd pulled away to look at something, a poster in a shop window on the other side of the road: a tractor pulling a cart with a cartoon cow in the back.

'Nikita!' she called, beckoning, shaking her head to clear it. Perhaps she had drunk too much.

He turned and began to run towards her. Only he wasn't Anna or Matthew; he didn't know how to look for traffic or judge speed and distance . . .

The howl of tyres against the road. Nikita froze as headlights bore down on him. Lena screamed and closed her eyes so she wouldn't see.

When she opened them again, Nikita was at least five metres from where she'd last seen him. She began to run, her heart thudding wildly. This wasn't real, it couldn't be real. She would wake soon in her own bed, with her own mundane problems, and it wouldn't be her fault that Nikita was lying sprawled and motionless on the road while the woman who'd been driving the car leaned over him screaming, 'Ambulance, ambulance!'

Lena skidded in the wet, fell to her knees next to Nikita. Footsteps around her. Traffic stopping. Any moment now she would wake from this dream, she just knew it. Her hands shook madly as she felt for the pulse at his soft throat. There! He was alive.

'Nikita, Nikita, talk to me. Say something. Mama's coming, darling. Wake up.'

But his arm flopped around like a rag doll's. Voices shouting French words surrounded her. She looked at her hands. They were covered in blood. Still, she hadn't woken. The nightmare went on and on.

V

CHAPTER FORTY-SIX

Roy Creedy was not happy.

But what was happiness? The world had been turned on its head. All his old ideas were rendered meaningless by the news he'd had today. The only thing that stopped him from slipping into the void of madness was this search. And so he didn't think, he didn't feel; he just searched. Overturning books, emptying shoeboxes, shaking out folder after folder from his filing cabinet. The house was littered with debris: he had to find that letter.

In the bedroom, despair caught him. He wouldn't cry; no self-respecting man would. Instead, he sat back heavily, striking his spine against the knobs on the dresser. The pain bit into him, and he told himself this was nothing, *nothing* compared with what he might go through at the end.

When the doctor had said 'cancer' – in a deep, serious voice that made him sound like an actor in a movie – Roy's stomach had disappeared, his heart falling through to his feet. A million questions and answers followed: the possibility of treatment, of remission, the worst-case scenario of not seeing out the year. All laid out 'for you to think about'. And then the doctor had given him advice: 'Put your affairs in order, but don't succumb to negativity.'

At the time, Roy had only heard the first half of the sentence. *Put your affairs in order.* And instead of thinking about wills and trust funds for his ungrateful nieces and nephews, he had thought about those bitches again. About how he'd never got them back.

So the search for the letter had started. The letter that the sister had written, the naive apology that had done nothing but throw fuel on the flames. He wanted to search it again for a clue to their whereabouts, go hunt them down one by one and make them feel as scared as he was now . . .

Roy slumped forward. He had burnt the letter; he knew it. This search was born of desperate and delusional hope, of a desire to avoid the problem right in front of him. He had burnt all of their letters. They were proof of his foolishness and had to be removed from the world. The same reason he had never tracked the women down – in case somebody found out what a dick, what a brainless loser, he'd been. He felt his embarrassment acutely. The same embarrassment he'd felt through all the tests – why did they have to stick things up his butt? – and through the doctor's explanations of the operations that might save his life. He'd wanted to shout, 'I'd rather die!' But now, he wasn't so sure.

The second half of the doctor's advice came to him. *Don't succumb to negativity.* So what should he do? Cling to hatred, to fantasies of revenge? Or cling to life?

Roy Creedy put his head in his hands and, sick with shame, cried his heart out.

As Sofi walked from the sunny car park into the quiet and bright linoleum-floored building, she decided she didn't mind it too much for Nikita's new home. Better than the nightmarishly sterile intensive-care unit in Tours, or the neurological wing with its muffled noises of suffering. The St Colette nursing facility was homey, with bright curtains and wide beds. More importantly, it was in Loudun, only twenty minutes from home. Sofi could finally settle again. No more waking up and not knowing where she was: home, hotel or hospital? She would be back in her own life for the most part.

But the thought also filled her with terrible sadness. Nikita's move to this nursing facility meant that he hadn't got better. He wasn't going to die, but there was little more that anyone could do now but hope for him to come back to consciousness.

Sofi spoke to a soft-voiced woman at the nurses' station, and was led to a buttercup yellow room with cartoon frogs on the curtains and bedspread. There lay Nikita, much as he had been since the accident – impossibly little and still – tucked into his new bed as though he were sleeping. As though he didn't have tubes and monitors surrounding him, invading him.

'Hello, darling,' Sofi said, touching his hand as she pulled a seat up next to the bed. He twitched, his eyes moved behind his lids, he made a little groaning sound. All of it could have been due to Sofi's touch, or it could have been a random response. There was no way of knowing. In the past sixteen weeks, Sofi had learnt a lot. By far the biggest surprise was that comatose patients were not necessarily quiet. Her previous experience – when Papa had been in the hospital, so still and silent – had left her unprepared. In the intensive-care unit, the amount of noise – groaning and muttering – that Nikita made frightened her. She had remained poised by his bedside, flexed towards him, waiting for those sounds to become coherent. A nurse had kindly told her that dealing with a loved one in a coma was not a sprint but a marathon. Sofi hadn't listened, had stayed awake for three days straight, poised and waiting. Meanwhile, the walls of the room crept in, the endless stream of medical language in French jangled in her mind, the pain of seeing her son covered in abrasions and so utterly helpless tore her up. By the third day, Julien asked the nurses to intervene. They had all but forced her to take two sleeping pills and, still sitting in the chair beside Nikita's bed, she had succumbed to six hours of dreamless slumber.

After that, she had learnt to pace herself.

She remembered the first sixteen weeks of Nikita's life so differently. It had gone quickly, in an eye-blink. One moment she had been holding a tiny, impossibly soft bundle of wriggling arms and legs; the next, a white-skinned, chubby boy had been sitting on her hip, his goggle eyes blinking at any bright object. The sixteen weeks since the accident had moved infinitely slower. Day piled on top of day, week on top of week, ponderously. No change, no change. Doctors and nurses tried to comfort her, using words like 'oculovestibular reflex' and 'flexion withdrawal', while flushing icy water into his ears or torturing him with needles. The prognosis, she was told, was a better-than-average chance that he would wake up one day. But the words of one nurse, in the first week, continued to haunt her. 'The longer the coma continues, the less likely he is to recover.'

Sixteen weeks. And now this move to a nursing facility. Wasn't it a tacit acknowledgement that nothing was expected to change? Ever?

Sofi sighed, leaning forward on the bed to stroke Nikita's hand gently. She still wasn't sure whom she was the most angry with. Lena, for being drunk and careless with her precious child. Julien, for forcing Lena to take Nikita with her that night. Or Natalya, for not stopping them heading out the door together. Julien had protested of course: he hadn't known Lena was drunk. Natalya, too, had been quick to absolve herself of blame: she was upstairs, she didn't know Lena had taken him. Only Lena had said she was sorry. Over and over again, tears coursing down her face, until Sofi had screamed at Julien to get her cousin away from her, to put her on a train and send her back to England.

'It should be her!' Sofi had shouted, refusing to talk to Lena directly. 'She should be the one lying here half-dead. I can't bear to see her alive and well, get her out of my sight!'

But most of all, Sofi blamed herself. She never worked in the last week of December. Her workshop was closed. But then came the frantic call from Francette – a special order that somebody had commissioned as a birthday present was missing. She'd gone to work, found it, prepared to ship it, had been distracted by a design that came to her mind and – guiltily alone in the workshop – she'd sat down to draw. Night closed in, she forgot everything and kept drawing.

Then someone had been calling her and calling her from the street. She hadn't heard for a long time, as she'd locked the workshop so nobody could come in. She hadn't arrived at Nikita's side until he was already in the back of an ambulance, being comforted by strangers.

'You are Nikita's mother?'

Sofi was roused from her unpleasant memories. The bright room at St Colette's came back into focus. She turned to see a tall, thin woman with a hard face. She was in her mid-fifties, and wore a white coat.

'Sofi Chernova,' Sofi said.

'I'm Doctor Pelletier,' the woman replied. 'I will be taking charge of Nikita's recovery.'

Sofi was too weary to stand, to shake hands or exchange pleasant conversation. She had met so many doctors and nurses; she could hardly keep track of them all. The doctor pulled up a spare chair and sat next to her.

'I imagine you have been feeling helpless, as though there is nothing you can do.'

Sofi considered the doctor. 'Of course.'

'There is something you can do. Something that we all do here. We speak as much as possible and within Nikita's earshot of his recovery. We do not use negative language, nor dire warnings. I believe Nikita will come to consciousness again. From now on, that is all we say. Do you understand?'

Sofi nodded slowly. 'I think so.'

'Don't sit here silently in tears. Talk to him, tell him what you will do when he's better. Never let doubt tinge your voice. He will hear it.'

Sofi was sceptical. Even conscious, Nikita was unable to pick the nuances of people's speech. She voiced her doubts, but the doctor held firm.

'I have worked with dozens of patients like Nikita,' she said. 'I know it is not a suggestion you would ordinarily expect from a medical professional . . .' She set her chin high, a parody of the highbrow doctor who knew everything. She had such a harsh face that Sofi had to laugh. '. . . but I promise you, positive language *always* makes a difference. Especially in children, who are often psychologically distressed by hospitals and care facilities.'

'Even an autistic child?'

'There is only one way to find out, Sofi. I know you will be willing to try.'

Then the doctor was on her way again, leaving Sofi in the sunny room, watching her little boy's eyelashes lying softly on his cheeks. The urge to cry swelled inside her, but she fought it. Instead, she forced a smile into her voice. 'Did you hear that, Nikita?' she said. 'The doctor thinks you will be well again soon. Then I can take you to the park to watch the roundabout. The sun will shine on your hair, the gardens will smell like roses . . .' She trailed off, uncertain what else to say. 'I know you'll get better,' she finished, hoping she sounded more confident than she felt. 'I'm here waiting for you when you do.'

Sofi sat back, watching his chest rise and fall rhythmically. She knew that even if Nikita did wake up, there was no way of assessing until then whether he had permanent brain damage. She could remember a time, so far in the past now, when she had cried because her child wasn't normal: he didn't communicate properly, didn't do things the way other children did. How could she have been so ungrateful? Because now Nikita had truly fallen out of the world, and she would give anything to have him back, exactly as he had always been.

There were always a few moments on waking when the horrors couldn't find Lena. But then it would all rush back to her, weighing her down, making her want to close her eyes and sleep forever. The inescapable guilt that had plagued her for months. While her own beloved, healthy children slept in the next room, Sofi's son was lost to a coma from which he was increasingly unlikely to wake. All because she was so wrapped up in her own feelings, had no self-control, had forgotten how vulnerable the boy was. Over and over again she went through the events of that evening in her mind, but always she arrived at the same destination. Nikita was injured, possibly fatally, and it was her fault.

And, horribly, life went on. She had a job to hold down, children to care for. Somehow she managed to get through it, not giving her best to her job, or her family, always relying on a few drinks in the evening to numb the pain then waking up the next morning feeling bloated, sick, guilty because the very thing that had caused the problem in the first place – her drinking – was the only thing that could soothe the pain. She had heard somewhere that the first step in recovering from an addiction was recognising she had a problem. Lena *knew* she had a problem, she hated it, but was helpless to fix it.

Somehow, she climbed out of bed. She pulled some clothes off the floor to dress herself, thumbed at a stain and then went for clean clothes from the wardrobe instead. None. She would have to sponge the stain off. She passed her dressing table mirror. Stuck into the frame – along with an old picture of herself with Sam and the children – was Sofi's cheque for the renovations. Never cashed. How could she cash it? Sofi hated her, had probably cancelled the cheque the moment she thought of it. Even if she hadn't, Lena couldn't take money from her at a time like this. So it was pinned there, a constant reminder to herself of just how comprehensively she had squandered her opportunities.

Matthew was already up, watching cartoons and slopping milk out of his cereal bowl onto the sofa.

'Clean that up,' she muttered.

He didn't hear.

She put the kettle on the hob, reached for the instant coffee. The mornings killed her. She was always tired, hungover, and yet there were lunches to be made and packed, shoes and clean uniforms to be located, two slow-footed children to get into the car, which had to be started four times before running. Six times on a cold morning.

She started buttering bread, glanced at the clock. 'Matthew, can you get Anna up?'

Matthew came to stand next to her, gazing at her solemnly.

'Come on,' she said, 'we're running late.'

'Anna's not here.'

Lena tried hard to focus. Not here? Was she away on camp and Lena had forgotten? She had already had two blackouts... was this evidence of a third? Her gut clenched with stress and all she could think of was how badly she needed a drink. 'What do you mean she's not here? Where is she?'

Matthew flushed pink. 'She climbed out the window last night after you put her to bed. With Izzy.'

'She's run away?' Frantic now, she dropped the butter knife. 'Why didn't you tell me?'

'Because I knew she'd go to Dad's. I knew that you'd want to go over there. And I didn't want you to drive... you know...'

'What do you mean?'

'I didn't want to have to get in the car with you if you're drunk,' he blurted. 'We had a safety class at school. They told us about drink driving. And that's like what happened to Nikita, isn't it? You were drunk.'

Lena felt as though the floor were dissolving underneath her. She would be a fool to think that Anna and Matthew hadn't gleaned details of what was wrong: she had sobbed the whole story to Sam while the children were in the next room. But to hear it said in such an ungarnished fashion by her own son: *You were drunk last night, I didn't want you to have a car accident with me too...*

But then she shook herself. Anna was out there somewhere. If she'd arrived at Wendy's place, surely Sam would have phoned.

'You should always tell me,' she said, shaking his shoulder roughly. 'Anything could have happened to her.'

Matthew lowered his head, gazed up at her accusingly. She never used to be rough with him. No matter how tough things got, she was always soft with Matthew, because Matthew was a soft boy. Everything had changed.

She picked up the phone and hastily hit Sam's number.

Anna answered.

'What the hell are you doing there?' Lena demanded.

'I'm going to live with Daddy.'

'Well, you can't. When I get hold of you, miss, I will –'

There was a rustle, the sound of the phone changing hands, then Sam was on the line.

'Lena?' His voice was always tender, whatever the circumstances. She suspected he still loved her, though lately he had been dating the music teacher from the twins' school, Miss Burton.

'Why on earth didn't you ring me?' she said. 'I wake up to find my daughter's missing and –'

'That's exactly the problem, though, isn't it?' Sam said. 'You didn't know she was missing until you woke up. Anna said she made a lot of noise on purpose, just to see if you'd come after her. You didn't hear a thing.'

'I was watching television.'

'Lena, I know what you were doing.'

A hard fist of anger. 'Oh, *everyone* knows what's wrong with me. If my husband hadn't betrayed me with my own sister, perhaps I wouldn't need a drink or two in the evening.'

He refused to be baited. 'Anyway, she's safe and well, here with me.'

Lena tried to relax. It was pointless to argue this again; they went round and round like a rowboat with only one oar. At least Anna was all right. 'You'd better bring her home. She'll be late for school.'

'Actually, Lena, Anna doesn't want to come back to live with you, and I would like her to stay with me.'

Lena was confused and frightened all at once. 'What do you mean? We agreed she should stay with me, we wouldn't split the kids up.'

'A lot has happened in the year since I said that,' he replied. 'Things have changed. *You* have changed.' His voice became very slow and patient, and she knew that he was preparing to say something she didn't like. 'I think Matthew should come here too.'

'No.' Her answer was a reflex.

'You said yourself, they should be together.'

'Matthew wouldn't leave me.'

Sam sighed. 'Then ask him. It should be his decision.'

'We're the grown-ups here,' Lena said.

'No, Lena, you're not acting like a grown-up. You're not responsible. You drink too much, despite what happened to Nikita. I won't let you put my children at risk the same way. Ask Matthew. I'll stand by his decision.' And the phone clicked.

She hung up the receiver, frustrated and desperate, and turned to saucer-eyed Matthew. She decided directness was the best approach. 'Do you want to go and live with your father?' she said.

'Is Anna staying there?'

'Yes.'

He gulped hard. She knew she was defeated. But would he have the courage to say it? To her face?

'You'd be lonely, Mum.'

'Don't worry about me. Would you be happier living with Dad and Gran?'

Cautiously, he nodded. 'I love you, Mum,' he said, 'but it's so sad around here.'

She closed her eyes, pressed her face into her hands.

'Mum? Are you crying?'

'No,' she said, uncovering her face. 'I'm just tired, Matthew. It might be good if Dad looked after you for a while. Give me a little rest.'

By the end of the week, her children had moved out.

CHAPTER FORTY-SEVEN

Viktor would have let the phone ring until it rung out, but Ulyana's voice came from the bathroom, 'Answer it, you lazy pig. It could be my mother.'

All the more reason *not* to answer it, but her mother was sick and he didn't want to upset Ulyana further. Already she was angry with him that he had lost another job. Five in a year. This time, a good job as a groundsman at the local school. They hadn't taken happily to finding a bottle of vodka behind the power tools in the shed. He'd tried to deny it was his, but his breath had probably given him away. It always did.

'Hello,' he said in what he hoped was a hostile tone.

'Viktor Chernov?' An unfamiliar male voice.

'Yes.'

'I have your number from the phone book.' Very, *very* bad Russian. 'I hope you can help.'

'You English?' Viktor said, switching languages. He hadn't practised his English for years, but it was still better than this man's Russian.

'Oh, you speak English? That's good. Look, I'm trying to track down Natalya, Lena or Sofi Chernova. Are any of those names familiar to you?'

'Why you want them?'

'I'm an old friend.'

'I know them. I am Lena and Natalya's father, Sofi's uncle.'

'Do you have phone numbers? Addresses?'

Viktor's neck prickled. Why should he believe this man was an 'old friend'? Natalya and Sofi were both rich and well known. Maybe he just wanted money. After all, Viktor could understand that.

He was silent for long enough to prompt the man to say, 'I'm willing to pay you.'

'For phone numbers and addresses?' Viktor kept his voice cool, but his pulse had quickened.

'Yes.'

'You pay good? Ten thousand dollars.'

'I . . . No. I'll pay you five thousand dollars.'

'No, ten.'

'Goodbye then, Mr –'

'Yes, yes. Five thousand dollars.' Viktor kicked himself; he shouldn't have given in. 'You send me money, and when I have money you call again and I give you addresses.'

'I'll give you one half when you give me the addresses, and the other when I'm sure somebody lives at them.'

Viktor marvelled that somebody would pay that much money for some addresses. This man must want to find the girls very badly. Why? He almost changed his mind, but the money was too great a persuasion.

'Okay, is deal.'

'All right then, Mr Chernov. You tell me where to send the cheque.'

Viktor gave him all the details, and then, worried that the man would change his mind, decided to get his phone number to ring and prompt him if he hadn't heard from him in a fortnight.

'And who is your name?' he asked, taking out a pen to write it down.

'It's Creedy,' the man said. 'Roy Creedy.'

It should have been an idyllic day out. April sunshine, green returning to the lime groves, the grassed banks of the silent Krestovka River on Kamenny Island, a picnic blanket, Maxim . . . The problem was – or rather, the problems were – his two daughters, Katria and Varinka.

Katria was nine and Varinka was six, and neither of them had expected Natalya to come on the picnic. Natalya could understand how irritated they were: she hadn't expected them either.

'Katria, over here. We'll put the rug under this tree,' Maxim said, directing his children as imperiously as he directed his actors.

Katria obeyed, laying out the rug. Varinka, who was much smaller, tried to help but ended up scrunching the corner. A squabble ensued, just as Maxim's mobile phone rang. He walked off a short distance to answer it.

'Girls, girls,' Natalya said, sensing an adult needed to intervene. 'Don't fight. Can't we just smooth the rug out again?'

'You're not my mama,' Katria said.

Varinka, sparked into the same defiance by her sister's example, held her little nose in the air and said, 'You're not *my* mama either.'

Now united, they began to play a game together, laying out the plastic containers one by one on the picnic rug. 'These pickles are not my mama, this cheese is not my mama, these *verniki* are not my mama,' and so on, all the while giving her sly looks. Natalya pretended to ignore them, dropped her handbag and sat down. Maxim returned, snapping his mobile phone shut. The girls quickly ended their game.

'Everything well, darling?' she asked, as he sat with them.

He smiled. 'Natalya, you are a lover of fine things. I suppose you would like to go to the French Riviera next month?'

'Cannes?' she blurted, heart in her mouth.

Somehow he was calm. 'The Festival Selection Committee has put *A Home in the Soul* into competition.'

Natalya squealed, hugging him. She ignored the girls' petulant little faces. She was going to Cannes; a film in which she starred was in competition! Every critic who had called her a sexpot, had said she couldn't act, had said she was washed-up . . . even Rupert . . . they would all have to eat their words. She held Maxim so tight that he complained, but she didn't care. She loved him, loved him to the stars and back. He had made her into a movie star.

Finally, she let him go. 'Don't pretend not to be excited.'

'I'm not surprised. I knew it would get in.' He wagged a finger at her. 'You didn't trust me.'

He had been offered a small international distribution deal; hadn't taken it as it would have made him ineligible for Cannes.

'I always trusted you!' she said. 'I just got a little nervous . . . if you hadn't been selected.'

'Something else would have come up. It's a beautiful film, Natalya. And you are beautiful in it.'

She hugged him again, her head full of fantasies of rubbing shoulders with A-list Hollywood stars, what offers might come her way next, what kind of dress she'd wear to the premiere . . . She'd had her eye on a gold and cream Valentino gown; what a perfect excuse to buy it. But the real world soon intruded.

'Varinka, you're walking on Natalya's handbag,' Maxim growled. 'Get off.'

If Natalya hoped for any favouritism from Maxim, even on a day like today, she was to be disappointed. Even though he spoke sharply and impatiently to his daughters, he clearly adored them. The film festival forgotten, at least for the present, he invited them to sing a song for her, recite poetry, display their grasp of foreign languages – Katria could speak English almost as well as Natalya could. They happily showed off, smiling at her and using her name sweetly as though the you're-not-my-mama game had never happened. Natalya had to admire their naughtiness; it was just the kind of thing she would have done as a child.

After they had eaten, Natalya and Maxim sipped white wine while the girls ran around chasing each other. Their shouts and giggles turned her mind to Nikita, lying still and pale in hospital. She had only just recovered from the shock and the guilt; she blamed herself for making Lena so angry, for storming off instead of staying to sort it out. Thinking of Nikita again made her sad, so she pushed him out of her mind. She didn't want to be sad on such a beautiful day.

She watched Maxim for a while, as he watched his daughters. His black hair had flopped over one eye, but she resisted the urge to push it back. Little gestures like that made him impatient with her. 'Just leave me be,' he would rumble. He'd said it when she sewed all the missing buttons back on his clothes, when she'd bought him a woven Roberto Cavalli shirt, when she'd surreptitiously slipped some Molton Brown men's skincare products onto his bathroom shelf. 'Leave me be, Natalya. I am as I am.'

And she would kiss him and tell him she loved him and he would grumble that he loved her too . . . only he never used the word 'love'.

Now, in the park, Natalya sat up and wriggled to be close to him, bending down to kiss his ear. 'I love you,' she said.

'Me too,' he said.

That was the best she ever got. But then, Maxim was not good at expressing his feelings. He could write magnificent scripts, direct emotionally wrenching scenes, but was not able or not willing to discuss his heart with Natalya. Any prompting from her was met with the same response. *Just leave me be.*

She was content to infer his love from the small scraps he threw her way. He was endlessly kind and patient, he never made her feel ugly or fat as Rupert had, he treated her as though she were clever and talented. That was enough.

Almost enough.

'Aren't they beautiful?' Maxim said, smiling at his daughters as Katria piggy-backed Varinka along the path next to the river.

Stupid, childish jealousy made her say what she shouldn't. 'They played a nasty game at my expense when you were on the phone, though,' she said.

Maxim turned, eyed her sharply. Immediately, she regretted speaking.

'What do you mean?'

'It was just childish fun.' She explained what they had done and Maxim frowned.

'Where would they have got the idea that I was going to replace their mother with you?' he said.

Natalya didn't like the emphasis on the last word, *you*. Was it so unthinkable that he might be in love with her, might marry her one day?

'You know children. They get ideas in their heads,' she said lamely.

'I'll have to talk with them.' He turned his black eyes on her. 'Natalya, would you mind? I have to drop the girls home soon. I'll need some time alone with them to discuss this . . .'

It took a moment for his hint to sink in. 'Oh. You want me to go?'

'I'll call you this evening, take you out to dinner to make up for it. To celebrate.' He smiled, that wolfish smile that always melted away her misgivings. 'I knew you'd understand.'

Uncertainly, Natalya picked up her handbag. She knew how little girls, especially selfish ones, worked. Katria and Varinka would see her go and they would think they had won. She very badly didn't want them to think they had won. But in that moment it was dazzlingly apparent that they *had* won. That Maxim had sent a strong message to both them and Natalya about who was the most important.

'Of course I understand,' she purred, as she leaned over to kiss his stubbly cheek. 'Tell the girls I said goodbye.' She stood, hoping to make it across the park and onto the path before the girls saw her leaving. No such luck.

'Goodbye, Natalya!' they called sweetly, waving coyly with both hands. 'Goodbye, goodbye.'

'That's enough, girls,' Maxim grumbled.

Natalya had taken criticism from far more important people than two smug little black-haired girls and survived. Head high, she made her way through the wide parklands and back to the metro. She was a movie star.

Natalya had finally arrived where she always knew she should be. Standing in the arched doorway to the balcony of her hotel room at the Intercontinental Carlton in Cannes, gazing out over the palms on

La Croisette to the water, while shopping bags littered the enormous bed behind her.

So why was she feeling down?

She glanced at her new Chopard watch. She didn't need a new watch, and yet when she'd walked past the shop and seen two movie stars and a supermodel inside, she'd had to go in. To buy something, to show them she was one of them. Nobody had recognised her. Perhaps they hadn't been at last night's screening of *A Home in the Soul*, where the audience had given the film a standing ovation. She and Maxim had come back after the screening to drink champagne and search the internet, finding web logs and online reviews as they were uploaded. *A triumph. Shattering, yet ultimately life-affirming. Levitsky joins the ranks of the masters. Deeply moving.* Nobody said anything bad. So far, it had been universal acclaim. Maxim was ecstatic.

But Natalya felt the opposite of that.

It was partly Maxim's fault. He had been distressed by the lack of lines on her face. After all, she had done everything in her power to avoid or remove them. So she had been made up and lit harshly. In the cinema last night, she couldn't bear to look at her face on screen: the tiny lines around her mouth from years of smoking, the crow's feet, the almost imperceptible sag of her neck. She looked every one of her thirty-seven years; an absolute shock to her, as she only saw her twenty-four-year-old self in the mirror. While the rest of the audience had been swept up in the raw emotion of the film, all she could think about was how hideous she looked when she cried and how nobody in Hollywood was going to cast her in glamorous, young parts.

And then the reviews had compounded her self-loathing. *Natalie Chernoff is perfect as the femme fatale past her prime. Her fading beauty is mesmerising. The role she was always meant to play: a brave and riveting performance of a woman coming to terms with losing her looks.*

Past her prime? Fading beauty? Losing her looks? It was a nightmare. She had to go on smiling, charming, pretending that she was that brave actress. But she wasn't. She wanted to be thought of as young, beautiful and sexy. That was that.

Voicing her doubts to Maxim had been the wrong thing to do.

'You are so vain, Natalya,' he said. 'You served the film, the film is the king. Don't bring your pettiness to me.'

Natalya sighed, turned her back on the view and sat at the dressing table mirror. There. Not a single line in sight. Forehead as smooth as a newly peeled boiled egg.

The door opened and Maxim came in, kicked off his shoes and left them in the entranceway. They had taken different routes this morning. He wanted to see the old town, the museum. She had wanted to see famous people on yachts, spend money on the waterfront boulevard. Natalya was willing to make concessions, to accompany him, but he had said he needed some time alone.

'Looking at yourself in the mirror again, Natalya?' he asked, shoving the shopping bags off the bed and sprawling across it.

She rose, embarrassed. 'I only just sat down.'

He beckoned her over, pulled her down to sit next to him. 'What were you looking for? Your face from your twenties? It's gone, you know.'

'Do you think I'm beautiful?'

'I do.'

She lay down next to him, curled up against his side. He stroked her hair.

'Do you love me?' she asked.

'I do. I do.'

She relaxed against him. Perhaps she was never going to be a glamorous Hollywood A-list leading lady. And, with Maxim in her life, perhaps that was all right.

The tearoom at the St Colette nursing facility was all too familiar to Sofi now. After the drive from Richelieu, between wheat fields rimmed with wild daisies and poppies, she – and Julien or Stasya too, if they came – would head straight for the tearoom to make strong instant coffee. Then, leaving all their worries and doubts about Nikita's recovery behind, they went to visit with him. And still nothing changed.

Today was the first of June, the first day of summer. Nikita's coma had now extended over three seasons. The winter of nightmares, the spring of anger . . . was this to be the summer of acceptance? Although she fought against the idea, she grew weary.

Julien was with her, stirring three sticks of sugar into his soupy coffee. He had been quiet this morning on the drive out. He hadn't been in his studio for a few days, was stuck somewhere between an idea and its expression. Sofi knew that place herself; since the accident, she'd spent only a few hours here and there at the workshop.

She walked over, rubbed his shoulder. 'Are you all right?'

He turned, smiled weakly. Took a deep breath as if to speak, then thought better of it. Stirred his coffee furiously. Sofi felt her skin go cold. Something was amiss.

'Julien? What is it?'

'A residency,' he squeaked. 'Los Angeles.'

She gaped at him. He had applied for another residency? He was thinking of accepting it? But perhaps she had misunderstood.

'You want to go to Los Angeles?'

'It's what I do,' he said defensively. 'I go away, I paint.'

'Our son is lying in a hospital bed, in a coma.'

'Sofi, that's exactly the point. Nothing is changing. We come here every day –'

'*I* come here every day. You only come two or three times a week.'

'Nonetheless, our lives must go on at some point. We don't know how long Nikita will be like this.' His voice dropped to a whisper. 'The child won't miss me.'

Sofi understood him; she was even envious of the blind spot that allowed him to run away from his troubles and never realise he was doing it. But this time she wasn't going to let him run away.

'No, Julien,' she said. 'I absolutely won't allow it.'

'Well, Sofi,' he said gently, 'can you stop me?'

She considered him under the bright lights of the tearoom. The last ten years had etched themselves on his face, thinned his hair, and yet he was still the same old Julien: slippery, unable to be pinned down, avoiding emotional responsibility. She had had enough.

'If you go to Los Angeles, you will come back to an empty house.'

His eyes rounded. 'You'd leave me?'

'I would. I know just how hard it is to see Nikita lying there, and not having the slightest hint about when or if he'll ever come back to us. But running away from the problem doesn't make it go away. You can't go, I won't let you.'

He fell silent, regarding her. She almost wavered, but told herself to hold firm.

To her surprise, he started to laugh. 'Oh, Sofi,' he said, 'that feels good.'

She tried not to smile, concerned that this might be the start of a cruel joke. 'What do you mean?'

'You've taken the decision out of my hands.' He spread his hands apart as though to demonstrate. 'It's a relief.'

'I don't understand,' she said honestly. 'This can't simply be about me finally laying down the law.'

'No, no. I haven't told you everything.' He shook his head. 'I haven't painted a thing, Sofi. Not since the accident. I put brushstrokes on the canvas, but they're all meaningless.'

He hadn't painted? But he spent hours locked in his studio . . . though, now she thought about it, she hadn't seen a finished canvas in a very long time. There had been too many other things on her mind for her to notice.

'When the residency came up, I thought that perhaps it would be the one thing that could get me painting again. But you have made everything so clear. Now, this moment, is not for painting; it's simply for being human. Artists are humans first, after all.' He reached for her hand. 'Can you forgive me, Sofi, for not knowing what I want?'

Sofi sighed, squeezed his fingers. 'I would run away too, if I could,' she said. 'Anything to stop feeling this pain, this anger.' Her voice dropped. 'This guilt.'

'I'm more guilty than you. I should never have let him go out without me.'

'I should have been home.' Her stomach clenched. 'Lena shouldn't have taken him.'

'You're never going to forgive her, are you?' he asked.

'No,' she replied. 'Never.'

At that moment, a nurse that Sofi hadn't seen before bustled into the tearoom. 'Excuse me, but are you the parents of Nikita Blanchard?'

The pit of Sofi's stomach hollowed. Bad news; it had to be.

'Yes,' she said, clenching her styrofoam cup too hard and slopping hot coffee onto her hand. 'What's happened?'

'One of the other nurses was making his bed. Your boy reached up and pushed her hand away.'

It took a few seconds to sink in that the nurse didn't have bad news. That, in fact, she had good news. Very good news.

'Come,' the nurse said. 'Doctor Pelletier is with him now.'

Sofi's vision seemed to have turned bright around the edges. She nearly tripped over her own feet on the way to Nikita's room. Two doctors and three nurses surrounded him. More poking. Sofi wanted to shoo them all away, put her arms around Nikita and see if he would hug her in return.

But, of course, he rarely did that even before the accident.

Instead, she held back, half-listened to the medical jargon being passed between them all. She didn't even realise that Julien was holding her hand until he dropped it to put his thumbnail to his teeth.

Doctor Pelletier turned, saw her. 'Ah, Sofi. This is very good news.'

'Has he done it again?'

'No. Unfortunately no, we haven't been able to replicate the response. But that means little. What does matter is that he made a deliberate movement.'

Julien sounded disappointed. 'One movement? That's all?'

Doctor Pelletier quickly cleared the room, sat on the edge of Nikita's bed and addressed them slowly. 'Comatose people don't just suddenly wake up,' she said. 'It's rather like a chicken hatching from an egg. A little crack appears, he'll struggle against it for a while, have a rest, then another crack and so on. What we have seen here today is that first crack.'

It was all Sofi could do to stop herself from sobbing with happiness. 'Is it certain, then, that he will recover?'

'Nothing is certain,' Doctor Pelletier said quietly. 'But the prognosis has improved dramatically.' She patted Nikita's knee under the blanket. 'He is doing beautifully. Take heart.'

Sofi tried to be cautious, but her blood was singing. The first day of summer. The summer of Nikita's recovery.

CHAPTER FORTY-EIGHT

Viktor had to remove every trace of her. Traitor, whore, *liar*.

It had been two days since Ulyana had left him for another man. Man! The fat toad she'd run off with was hardly a man. A eunuch, somebody she would be able to control happily. That was it, in the end, wasn't it? Viktor was too much of a man for her. He puffed up his chest, continued swiping her toiletries off the bathroom shelves and into a black garbage bag. Activity made him feel better. The two days lying in bed, attempting to drink himself into oblivion, hadn't worked. He was still alive. So, instead, he had to erase her.

He went to the bedroom. Anticipating his temper, she had packed quickly and left a note. *When you have cooled down*, it said, *I will contact you about picking up the rest of my things.*

Ha! There would be nothing left to collect. He pulled out scarves and socks and moth-eaten coats. They gathered in a heap on the floor. The sight of one of her sleeves, hanging limp and forlorn from the pile, made him catch his breath.

'Ulyana,' he said mournfully. He had loved her. Loved her so hard. Without her, he was vapour, he would drift, disappear.

'Bitch!' he said, stamping on the sleeve. He swore all the way to the sitting room, where he found her latest pile of magazines.

They would make a nice fire. He gathered up armfuls to take to the incinerator. Dropped half-a-dozen. Swore again.

Then saw his daughter, Natalya.

Curious, he put down his load and picked her up. She was in a Russian magazine: she had made a Russian movie that was in contention for a prize. Viktor thought about the man who had wanted to find Natalya and Lena. In the few months since he had received his first instalment of money, he had been tense. Waiting for repercussions. None had come. He had spent the money on a car, been too cocky to insure it, then wrapped it around a tree while driving home drunk one evening. He had walked away unscathed. Ulyana had been in the passenger seat, had broken her hand and six ribs. That had been the beginning of the end, really.

Viktor sat back with the magazine, staring at the photograph. His daughters were so beautiful. Their mother had been pretty enough, but the girls far outstripped her. Proudly, he took the credit for their strong faces, their dark hair.

Now, then. He was getting sentimental. He wondered about Lena, remembered how badly he had hurt her, and found himself finally able to understand her situation. Ulyana had abandoned him, but at least she had left a note. Viktor had abandoned Lena twice, without any further contact. And then he had sold her out to the American man who had sounded far too serious and passionate to be 'just a friend' as he'd claimed.

'Mr Chernov,' Roy Creedy had said, after Viktor had dictated the last of the phone numbers to him, 'you have made a dying man *very* happy.'

Viktor hadn't asked for clarification, keen to get Creedy's furtive voice off the line.

Well, at least Natalya's address and phone number would be wrong. And who was to say if Lena and Sofi had moved on too? Maybe Creedy would never find the girls.

And yet he couldn't shake the feeling that he'd done something terribly wrong.

Especially to Lena.

Lena picked up the post on her way out the door to work. Sam had taken the car with the children, so she had to leave much earlier these days. So far, the weather had been mild and pleasant. Once autumn and winter came, she was unlikely to enjoy the walks any more.

There was one letter, addressed to her at Wendy's house. That address had been crossed out and replaced in Wendy's neat handwriting. Wendy always redirected letters rather than calling and letting Lena come and pick them up. And maybe see her children. At the moment they were out of her life for twelve days in every fortnight. Of course she couldn't have them during the week and disrupt their schooling. And she could understand Sam wanting to spend some time with them on the weekend. After all, it was exactly the same arrangement when they had lived with her. But two days were simply not enough. They had slipped out of familiarity with each other. They were becoming strangers.

Lena had never imagined, eleven years ago when the children were born, that she could bear to be without them for such long periods of time. And yet she had fallen into numb acceptance. She kept their bedroom door shut, so she wouldn't see the few things they had left behind and pine for them.

She flipped the letter over. No return address. Curious, she unpicked it. A single folded sheet, written in very bad English.

Lena. What I do to you is not right. I am sorry and you will forgive me. You want to talk to me and here is number. Viktor your papa.

Lena didn't know how to feel. The edge of a promise. He had apologised, he wanted to talk to her. But then the wariness crept in. If he wanted to get back into their lives, to ask Natalya for more money, this was precisely what he would say. She screwed the letter up and tossed it on the bench; was about to do the same with the envelope when she realised there was something else in it. She tipped it up.

He had enclosed an old black-and-white photograph. Papa as a young man, with two little girls. Natalya, about four and already standing tall and proud. And Lena, a chubby-faced toddler who hung back, afraid of the photographer. But was this him really reaching out to her, or just a cruel manipulation?

Carefully, she put the photograph aside; she was already late for work.

The day dragged. She nearly raced home at lunchtime to phone him, then restrained herself, called herself a fool. The image from the photograph came back to her. How his hand encircled her waist so easily and casually, how she clung to the sleeve of his jacket. She couldn't concentrate on tasks, forgot a child's nappy: he wet himself all over his mother's business suit when she arrived. Finally, Lena escaped for the day and returned home to her dilemma.

She found the letter, smoothed it out. Laid it on the coffee table with a bottle of wine as a paperweight. Then started drinking the bottle.

Around nine, she knew she should eat something, so she microwaved some fish fingers.

Around ten, she finished the bottle and opened the next.

At eleven, she went to the phone.

It rang and rang. She knew he wouldn't answer. It probably wasn't even a real number. Then she realised it was much later in Moscow than here, and was about to hang up when he answered.

'Hello,' he said gruffly.

'Papa, it's me,' she slurred in Russian. 'It's Lena.'

'Ah, you got my letter.'

'Did you mean it?'

She heard him shift, a lighter flicking. He was having a cigarette at two in the morning. 'Yes, I meant it,' he said, but he sounded cautious, diffident. 'I did you wrong.'

The ferocity of her tears surprised her. 'You did,' she cried. 'You did.' Her sobs were loud in the dim room. He was perfectly silent, and after a few moments she thought he had hung up. 'Hello?' she said, a note of fear in her voice.

'I'm still here,' he said. 'I can't make you better. I can't be your father the way you want me to be. I'm sorry.'

'Why did you leave me?'

A pause, the sound of smoke being exhaled. 'Which time?' he said. His voice was small, distant. The hum of the refrigerator springing into life almost drowned it out.

'The first time.'

'I fell in love. She didn't want to be a stepmother. I thought you were young enough to forget me. You were better off with Ivan and Stasya.'

'Didn't you love me?' Her heart was thudding wildly; her face was hot and damp.

'Perhaps I didn't,' he said. 'I remember being proud of you and Natalya when you were little. But as you got older . . . I didn't understand you. It was easier to leave you with other people. And Ulyana came along and made the decision for me.'

'I loved you,' she whispered.

'I didn't deserve any love,' he replied. 'I didn't want it. It made me feel suffocated. I could only imagine myself getting older and unhappier with such a responsibility. And look, I'm old and unhappy anyway.'

He fell silent. The clock above the television ticked loudly. Lena wiped her nose with the back of her hand.

'Can you forgive me?' he said at last.

'No,' she said with a sigh. 'I don't think I can.'

'No?' He was clearly surprised.

'My heart is a stone, Papa. A year ago, two years . . . maybe. But I am gasping under the weight of my misery and it all goes back to you, doesn't it? Telling me you'd be home for my birthday and then never coming back. I could have been something different, I could have lived a happy life. But you ruined me. You made me so defective that even my husband . . .' She was stumbling over words as much with passion as with drunkenness, and told herself not to divulge too much to him. He didn't deserve the confidence. 'So this time, I get to end it, not you. This time, you go because I tell you to. You leave my life because I want you to.' And before he could do it first, she hung up.

The phone rang again within thirty seconds. She picked it up.

He said, 'I have to tell you something.'

'I don't want to hear it,' she said, and hung up again.

Again, it started ringing. This time she let it ring out. Standing in the kitchen, exhaling sharply. She felt slightly dizzy, dissociated from herself. As though watching herself from up near the ceiling. Finally, after ten minutes, he didn't try to call again. It was over.

It was finally over.

CHAPTER FORTY-NINE

It irked Natalya that Maxim hadn't let her move in with him yet. They had been dating for eight months, she was absolutely sure of her feelings. Why was he taking so long to commit to her? It had taken him six months even to give her a front door key. Prior to that, she'd had to ring the buzzer outside to be admitted. Like a door-to-door salesman. Finally, she'd complained about it. 'I shouldn't have to stand out on the street and wait,' she'd said. 'It's embarrassing. If anyone recognised me . . .' She'd not been able to finish the sentence, knowing how sceptical Maxim was of fame and its trappings. But what she meant was a famous actress shouldn't have to wait on the street to be buzzed through, in case passers-by thought she wasn't that famous after all. Within a week, he'd had a key cut for her, the key that she was using on a hot St Petersburg afternoon to let herself into the cool stone foyer of the building.

She climbed the stairs, and gently knocked once before opening the door. She was confronted by the noise of Katria and Varinka. A petite blonde woman sat on the sofa. Maxim was nowhere in sight.

'Oh,' Natalya said, guessing immediately that this was Maxim's wife. 'Is Maxim here?'

The blonde woman rose, brushed pale hair off her face. Natalya realised she had been crying and her heart went cold. Was something wrong with Maxim?

'He's here,' the woman said. 'I'm sorry I'm in such a state. You must be Natalya. I'm Orlenda. Maxim is just getting changed. Maxim!'

Natalya felt as though she were on a set, but didn't know her lines. What was going on? Maxim emerged, dressed in black. He glanced at Natalya and an expression of irritation crossed his brow.

'Ah, damn. I forgot you were coming, Natalya.'

Katria and Varinka were chasing each other around the room, trying to hit each other with pillows. Maxim roared at them so loudly that even Natalya was terrified.

'Can't you see your mother is upset?' he growled.

The girls put the pillows down, waited quietly.

'Maxim?' Natalya said.

He approached her, guided her gently towards the door.

'Orlenda's father has died,' he explained. 'We are just going to the funeral.'

'I'm . . . I'm sorry,' she managed.

Orlenda blew her nose noisily into a tissue.

'It's all right, we were expecting it. He has been sick for a very long time.' He opened the door and she had no choice but to step through it. 'I will be back by nine. Meet me for dinner?'

'Of course,' Natalya said, even though she wanted to demand how much contact he kept with his wife; why his father-in-law's death should be a matter for him to mourn.

'Tsvyet?'

'At nine. Yes.'

Then she was standing outside a closed door and he had returned to his family.

Out on the street, the unforgiving humidity wilted her. She couldn't bear to go home to her stuffy flat, so she spent her time cruising the air-conditioned shops, buying things she didn't need, smiling and signing autographs for the few that recognised her. But only ten per cent of her mind was focused on the moment. The rest was constructing elaborate imaginings: Orlenda and Maxim. She all pale and trembling at the funeral, he supporting her with his strong arms. *No!* The thought of him touching somebody else was like hot needles in her gut. But the imaginings continued to unfold. Orlenda had known her name; that meant Maxim had told it to her. But Maxim had never mentioned Orlenda by name, only ever called her 'my wife' or 'the girls' mother'. She'd thought this namelessness was a sign that he was dismissive of her; now she saw that he had been protecting Orlenda. Keeping her special. And he mentioned that Orlenda's father had been sick for a long time. Had he been comforting her the whole time? With his firm hands and his rumbling voice? Before she could stop it, she imagined them in bed together, and wanted to cry. Those caresses belonged to her! The taste of his skin, the hard muscularity of his thighs, the frantic thumping of his pulse . . .

She gasped out loud. Two women in the Versace boutique turned to look at her. She put her head down and scurried out of the shop. She found herself ducking down a side street, scrabbling for a tissue in her handbag. Not because she felt sorry for herself – even though she did – but because she finally, *finally* understood how Lena must have felt. The business with Sam had been so brief, so bungled, and so long ago that Natalya barely remembered it. She was guilty and ashamed by it, couldn't really understand why she had done it. But it was a small blip in the background of her life. For Lena, it was a mountain of unbearable feelings.

Damn. If she'd left Sam alone, Lena wouldn't have been so angry nor drunk so much that night. And Sofi wouldn't be living by Nikita's bedside in a hospital. Very clearly, everything bad had been all Natalya's fault. And here she was, shopping for designer accessories, swanning about at film festivals, swept up in her love for Maxim, as though that tragedy at the centre of Lena's and Sofi's lives had nothing to do with her. With trembling hands, she pulled out her mobile phone and dialled Lena's number.

No answer. Of course, she was probably at work. She tried Sofi. Again, no answer. She was probably at the hospital. Sighing, Natalya put her phone away. She still had three hours with nothing to do before Maxim met her. Three hours alone with her painful thoughts.

He was late. Maxim was often late, and Natalya had always put it down to his disorganised nature. Now she wondered if his lateness meant he had been with his wife.

'I'm sorry,' he said, kissing her cheek gently and sitting opposite her.

His eyes were very soft this evening. It made her skin prickle with suspicion.

'How did everything go?' she asked.

'It was very sad. Orlenda lost her mother when she was a teenager; she and her father were very close.'

Again, that sharp feeling. Maxim had never asked about her family. 'I see,' she said.

Maxim ran his hand through his hair, making it stick up at the front. 'Natalya, you are a lovely woman. Very talented, and very beautiful.'

Natalya froze; she could hear the 'but' before he said it.

'But I can't continue in this relationship with you.'

And then she unfroze, and the world was falling away from her feet. 'Why not?'

His words came out all in a rush, a surge of passion and tenderness that she barely recognised in him. 'I'm still in love with my wife. I always have been. We have our problems, but I feel older and wiser now. She's willing to give me another chance, and there is nothing in the world I want more than to be with her and the girls. A proper family.'

Natalya knew she should try to look unaffected, regal, disdainful even. But she couldn't.

'Have you been sleeping with her?' she asked in a gaspy, jealous voice.

'Only three or four times since I've been with you,' he answered candidly.

So the imaginings had been real. The thought hit her with blunt force. 'Did you ever love me?'

'I did, in a way. If the timing had been different, maybe there would have been a future for us . . . It's impossible to say. I enjoyed our time together.'

'Enjoyed? You make it sound so casual. I love you, Maxim. I love you until my heart wants to burst with it, and you . . .' She trailed off, aware that she was shouting, that people were looking. She couldn't believe he had brought her to this ugly 'family' restaurant to break it off with her. She gathered herself. 'I suppose there's nothing I can do to change your mind?'

He shook his head, looking sorrowful but relieved.

She stood. 'Then I will go.'

'I am sorry, Natalya.'

Out onto the dusky street. Mosquitoes and midges, prickling perspiration. It was time to leave St Petersburg. Back to London? She had status now, would probably be able to entice Leida into representing her again. Or should she go to Los Angeles, finally try to crack Hollywood? But she couldn't bear the thought of working with a broken heart, pretending that everything was all right when everything was falling apart. No, she needed to be with people who loved her. Her veins ached at the knowledge that Lena wouldn't welcome her now. Natalya had foolishly ruined that relationship. But Sofi might take her in. Sofi might even need Natalya as much as Natalya needed her.

She sighed, weary at the thought of another move. Why couldn't she settle any place?

Resigned and heartbroken, she made her way back to her apartment to start packing.

It hadn't quite been the summer of recovery that Sofi had hoped for. The watching and waiting had become acutely painful now Nikita was showing signs of coming back to her. Arm movements, some deliberate, some involuntary. A shaking of the head from time to time. Mumbles that sounded like words if she listened closely enough. Then long periods of nothing. Somehow, she managed to keep going. Up every morning at six, a long phone call to Francette who was managing the business, then dressed and out the door to make a brief appearance at the workshop. She liked to be in the car on the way to see Nikita by ten thirty. Mama held the house together, keeping it tidy, making sure she and Julien ate. The summer days were long, the waiting was wearing her down. Every little sign of recovery made her heart soar; every day that passed with Nikita silent and still made it plunge again.

She was pulling on her shoes near the front door, wondering if today would be an up day or a down day, when there was a loud, fast knock.

Curious, she rose and opened the door.

'Surprise!' Natalya. With suitcases.

'Natalya?' Sofi was caught between delight and wariness.

Natalya didn't give her a chance to waver; she dropped the cases and gathered Sofi into a hug. 'You don't mind if I stay a little while? I want to help out.'

Sofi knew it was more than altruism that had brought Natalya to her door, but saved her questions for later. 'It's wonderful to see you,' she said, standing back. 'I'm just about to go out to visit Nikita. Would you like to come?'

Natalya hesitated momentarily. Perhaps she had been expecting an offer of tea. Then she said, 'Of course. I'll just drop my suitcases off.'

Mama, drawn by the voices, appeared in the hallway. 'Natalya. How lovely to see you, dear.'

Natalya raced down the hall, stooping to give Mama a hug. 'Aunt Stasya. I know you've been doing a wonderful job looking after Sofi, but I am here to help.'

Mama made a face over Natalya's shoulder and Sofi stifled a laugh.

'Leave your bags there,' Mama said. 'I'll take them up later. I'll have to get the room freshened up for you.'

As Sofi and Natalya buckled themselves into the car and took off towards Loudun, Natalya made vapid chatter, apologised a dozen times for turning up unannounced, even tried to make conversation about the weather. Sofi was far more interested in what wasn't being said.

'Natalya,' she said finally, 'why didn't you call first?'

Natalya was silent for a few moments. Then she said, in a little voice, 'I was worried that you would say, no, don't come.'

Sofi mused on this. Would she have said it? Perhaps. She was deep inside her cave, didn't want to be coaxed out of it. Natalya's arrival would certainly make it hard to hide away. 'I'm glad you came,' she said gently. 'But you're running away from something, aren't you?'

Natalya sagged slightly, letting her guard down. 'Everything was going really well, the movie had wonderful reviews – it's coming out in England next month, in America just after Christmas – but then Maxim dumped me.'

'Maxim? The director?'

'I was in love with him.'

She sounded so forlorn; Sofi couldn't remember Natalya ever sounding so young and lost.

'Ah. I'm sorry.'

Natalya forced a bright tone. 'Oh, I'll get over it, I suppose. And anyway, my problems are trivial.' As if she had just realised the truth of this statement while speaking it, she grew solemn. 'How is Nikita?'

Sofi told Natalya about the signs of recovery, the endless hours at the hospital, the waiting. 'It's as though I'm continually holding my breath,' she said. 'And everything bad that comes with not breathing is happening. Feeling dizzy, and trapped . . .' She trailed off, unable to translate her feelings into words. Her whole being, her life and whatever lay beyond it, were hanging dependent on what Nikita might, or might not, do today.

'I'm so sorry, Sofi,' Natalya said, extending her cool hand to rub Sofi's wrist. 'I can't even imagine.' Then, hesitantly, she said, 'Have you spoken to Lena?'

Sofi generally tried not to think about Lena. She knew that Mama had phoned her several times in the month after the accident, to give her progress reports. But Sofi had asked her not to.

'She is like a daughter to me,' Mama had protested.

'She nearly killed your grandson.'

'She is suffering horribly.'

'She deserves to suffer. Why call her? There's nothing to tell her. Nothing changes. When you call her it makes me feel that you care more about her feelings than mine.'

Sofi wasn't proud of her behaviour back then, but how else was she to act under the circumstances? She knew exactly how unforgiving Lena would be if their situations were reversed.

'Sofi?'

Sofi realised that she still hadn't answered Natalya's question. 'No. I haven't spoken to her. Have you?'

'No.'

Silence drew out.

'It's sad, isn't it?' Natalya said.

'What's that?'

'We used to be so close. And now . . . she could be dead for all we know.'

Sofi tried to laugh at Natalya's hyperbole, but she sounded brittle. 'Don't worry,' she said. 'Sam would have contacted us if she were dead.'

'Yes, and then how would you feel? If Sam phoned you and said she was dead?'

Now Sofi grew irritated. 'Natalya, this is just childish. Lena's not dead.'

'No, but you'd hate it, wouldn't you? If she died and you were still at odds with her.' Natalya shrugged. 'I'd hate it.'

'My priority is not Lena, her feelings, whether or not she's dead and whether or not I'd care about it,' Sofi said patiently. 'My priority is being there for Nikita, in case he wakes up. I haven't the energy for anything else.'

At St Colette's Natalya hid her discomfort well. Sofi had clear memories of the forty days her father had spent in hospital before his death, how Natalya had been bored, sad and naughty all at once. But here, after Sofi explained that talking to Nikita was important, Natalya was brilliant. She held Nikita's hand and chatted for hours, told him about how movies were made and even promised him a trip to Disneyland when he woke up. Nikita showed no signs of improvement that day, but Sofi didn't leave the hospital with a heavy heart. Her cousin's presence had lifted her spirits, and she was ultimately glad that Natalya had come.

Late that night, as Sofi was making her way to bed, she heard stifled crying from Natalya's room. Softly, she knocked and let herself in.

Natalya turned, her face a mess of tears. The curtains were parted on the near-full moon, and the soft glow of a lamp illuminated the tidy room. Sofi closed the door behind her and went to sit on the bed next to her cousin. She pulled Natalya's head down on her shoulder and listened to her cry for a while.

'It's not fair,' Natalya sniffed. 'I loved him, Sofi. I really loved him. The first time in my life I've loved anybody.'

Her bony back heaved with sobs and Sofi patted her gently. 'Sh, sh.'

'I'm supposed to be trying to find work, but my heart is broken and I just want to hide from the world.'

'You can hide here for a while. As long as you need to.'

Natalya withdrew, sitting back to look at Sofi. 'I'm so selfish. I promised myself I wouldn't bother you with my problems.'

'It's all right. We all hurt.' Sofi stood and fetched the box of tissues from the dresser.

Natalya blew her nose. 'Lena hurts too,' she said.

Sofi didn't answer. She would wait for a better time, lay down some rules. If Natalya wanted to stay, she would have to promise not to mention Lena. The anger and sadness were too much to bear when she already had so much weighing on her heart.

CHAPTER FIFTY

Lena woke with a sore back, a sore neck, a sore head.

She sat up, remembering where she was. On a quilt, on the floor of the farmhouse. Beside her, an empty bottle of vodka and a hardened pool of wax that had once been a candle. The boards on the windows admitted no light, but she could hear birds chirping so she knew it was morning. She rose, longing for clean running water. Shuffled to the kitchen and out the door into the garden.

Here she sat, on a dew-damp fence rail, gazing down at the morning sunlight on the fields. Her fields. But not for much longer.

Managing alone was tough. Sam was no longer giving her money to help with the kids, so rent and utilities were eating up most of her salary. She couldn't move to a smaller place, as she needed somewhere for the kids to stay. Sam hadn't asked for any money from her yet, but it was only fair that she contributed. And he had hinted very heavily that Matthew might need braces.

And, of course, it was terribly expensive having a drinking problem.

So she had finally come to accept that it would be easier to sell the farmhouse. She could buy a car, have enough to pay the rent and get Matthew's teeth fixed, maybe even buy the kids a computer . . . She saw her farmhouse dissolve in her imagination, turn to sand and get swept away on the wind.

Yesterday afternoon, she had packed a shopping bag with some essentials and taken two buses out here. The nearest bus stop was a half-hour walk away, and she'd arrived breathless and sweating at around four o'clock. She started drinking right here, on the fence, then moved inside as the night closed in. A goodbye to the only piece of property she was ever likely to own; but more importantly, a goodbye to a long-cherished fantasy. A realtor was coming at eight to list the property.

Lena sat on the fence until her backside went numb. She heard tyres pull onto the shoulder and assumed the realtor was there early. But when she looked around, she saw Sam approaching. Puzzled, she stood. He had a tray with two paper cups in it. Coffee! Exactly what she needed.

'What are you doing here?' she asked when he was close enough to hear.

The sun caught his hair. 'Bringing you coffee.'

He sat on the fence next to her, offering her a cup. She sipped it gratefully. The coffee was only just warm, but the bitter taste of it helped peel off the fog.

'How did you know I was here?'

'I didn't. I tried you at home, but there was no answer. I was going to offer to drive you up here for the appointment. Anna told me about it. I figured you must have come up last night. To say goodbye.'

Lena felt tears prick her eyes. She glanced away so he wouldn't see them.

'Anyway,' he said gruffly, embarrassed, 'I knew you'd need a lift home.'

'Thanks, Sam,' she said, two unexceptional words that hid a million unexpressed ones. 'How are the kids getting to school?'

'Anna's determined to walk. So Mum said she'd follow her about a block behind with Matthew.' Sam laughed. 'She's so independent.'

'She had to be,' Lena said. 'Matthew was so needy. Poor Anna always had to rely on herself.' She turned to Sam. 'Do you think we're all products of our childhoods?'

'I don't know. Probably.'

'My father called me about a month ago.'

The fierce spark in his eye told her that even though they were no longer together, his protective instinct towards her was still strong. 'What did he want?'

'Believe it or not, he wanted to tell me he was sorry.'

'No, I don't believe it,' he said.

'I think he was genuine. He asked me to forgive him. I didn't.' She laughed, self-consciously. 'I suppose you'd know all about that.'

Sam frowned. 'I hope you don't rate my one little mistake alongside deliberate abandonment and manipulation.'

Lena opened her mouth to say, 'You had sex with my sister, that's not a little mistake.' But she didn't. They had covered that ground to the point of nausea.

His voice became gentle. 'Have you heard about Nikita?'

Lena shook her head. Stasya had promised to phone if there was any change. 'I haven't heard,' she said. 'He must still be in a coma.'

'I know you feel guilty, but drinking doesn't solve anything.'

She rolled her eyes, letting herself down from the fence. 'Here we go. Another lecture.'

He put his hands up, a gesture of surrender. 'I'm not lecturing you, I'm just pointing out the evidence. Because of your drinking, you caused an accident, you lost the love of your cousin, you lost your children, and now you've lost your house.' He pointed his thumb back over his shoulder.

She glanced at the house, thinking about how she had tried to hide it from Sam so it didn't get sold and consumed in daily living. And yet that was precisely what had happened anyway. Her betrayal caused his betrayal, his betrayal caused her to drink again, her drinking caused Nikita's accident, Nikita's accident caused all the misery since. Dominoes, falling onto each other. She just needed one thing, one *good* thing, to happen to her, to stop the inevitable collapse. But she couldn't see where it would come from.

The realtor arrived on the dot of eight, looked through the house with a wrinkled nose, glanced over the fields, and suggested a starting price far lower than Lena had hoped for. She signed the papers, and as she drove away with Sam, the realtor was hammering a For Sale sign into the soft earth outside the front fence.

As she gazed out the window, Lena cried softly, wiping her nose on her sleeve.

'There are tissues in the glove box,' Sam said.

Lena squirmed. She'd hoped that he hadn't seen her crying. She opened the glove box and found a packet of condoms.

'Oh,' she said.

Sam glanced at her, nearly swerved the car, returned his eyes to the road. 'Sorry,' he said, flushing. 'Judy and I –'

'Judy?'

'Miss Burton,' he laughed. 'Because she teaches the kids I can't really have her stay over, so . . . we only have the car.'

Lena's acute jealousy was tempered by the small satisfaction that Sam and his new girlfriend were forced to fumble in the car for pleasure. She swallowed a laugh, watching his profile for a few moments. She had no right to be jealous: she had kicked him out, she had refused to take him back.

'Sam,' she said, 'do you want a divorce?'

'Do you?'

'I'm asking you. You're seeing somebody else . . .'

'I don't want to marry her. Divorce is expensive. Let's just leave it for now.'

She was surprised by her relief, and wondered if that one good thing had just happened today after all.

The light was dying out of the sky as Sofi and Julien pulled up outside their house. Julien had driven most of the way with one hand on the steering wheel, the other clutching Sofi's fingers. A reverent awe had settled over them, they were quiet and still.

Sofi turned to Julien. He smiled at her, shaking his head. Tears in his eyes.

'Sometimes I wish it was just the two of us,' she said, thinking about Stasya and Natalya waiting for them inside with champagne and eager questions.

The call had come at eight that morning. Sofi had planned to give herself a rare day off. Natalya had been pressuring her to go up to Paris, do some shopping together. It was the last thing Sofi felt like, but she acknowledged that getting out and having some fun with her cousin would probably be healthy. But before she was even dressed Doctor Pelletier had called, urging them to come out to St Colette's as soon as possible. Almost breathlessly, the doctor had explained that Nikita had opened his eyes, tracked the nurse briefly, then fallen back into his sleep.

'I am very hopeful,' Doctor Pelletier said. 'Very, *very* hopeful.'

They raced out to St Colette's. Sofi's heart was thumping. They were climbing out of the car before she realised she wasn't wearing shoes. At Nikita's bedside, Doctor Pelletier greeted them. Her harsh face had been transformed by a smile. 'He's awake.'

Sofi pushed nurses out of the way. Nikita lay very still, his eyes open and looking at the ceiling.

'Can he see anything? Is he in there?' Sofi felt the cold fear that her child was brain damaged. But then, almost before she finished the sentence, his eyes had met hers. She waggled her fingers, he watched them. 'Nikita?' she said. 'It's Mama.'

'It's Mama,' he repeated in a gravelly little voice, and she had never been more glad to hear his sweet echo. The staff gathered around the bed cheered.

After twenty minutes of silent consciousness, he had lapsed back again. The doctor explained this was quite normal, that it could take weeks before he was fully conscious. But all signs pointed to an imminent recovery.

Recovery! It hadn't come in summer, as she had hoped. Autumn fell outside the windows of his bright room, but it *had* come. The relief was intense, sacred.

Sofi opened the car door, planted her bare feet on the ground. The front door of the house burst open and Natalya was running down to greet her, Mama close behind. Sofi tried to explain the situation but suddenly found she was speechless, so Julien took over. Mama sobbed so hard that Sofi was afraid she would break in two. Natalya, by contrast, danced about like a teenager.

'Shall we go in?' Julien said. 'It's getting cold out here.'

'Yes, and we're going to drink masses of champagne,' Natalya said. 'Aunt Stasya and I went out and bought six bottles.'

Soon, neighbours and some of her more senior employees had been contacted and invited too. Sofi enjoyed the impromptu party, but was longing for solitude. To sit and think. She had been living under the pressure of waiting so long that she felt she didn't know herself any more. It was close to midnight when the last reveller left, when Mama had fallen asleep on the sofa, when a very drunk Natalya had offered to clean everything up and urged them off to bed.

'Are you sure, Natalya?' Sofi asked, guilty about the mess, but far too tired to do anything about it herself.

'I'm so sure.' She grasped Sofi's hand softly. 'I'm very happy for you.'

'I'm happy too,' Sofi said, and realised she hadn't said it for months and months. It felt so good she said it again. 'I'm very happy.'

Natalya's hand grew firmer. 'I'm just drunk enough to ask you this,' she said. 'Can I call Lena and tell her?'

The usual irritation Sofi would have felt at the mention of her cousin's name was curiously absent. 'I . . . I suppose you can. Yes. Call her. But I'm not ready to speak to her yet.'

Natalya raised her perfectly shaped eyebrows. 'Well, she might not be ready to speak to me either.'

Julien was waiting for Sofi in their bedroom. She went to him, felt firm in his embrace. He held her for a long time, minutes dissolving into one another. Two heartbeats, their breathing almost in sync.

'Sofi,' he said at last, 'it's been an age since we made love.'

Her head spun. Champagne, relief, love. 'Yes, yes,' she said, her whole body primed to affirm life. He gently went to work on her buttons. She closed her eyes and took deep breaths, and found her lungs were bigger than she'd remembered. His caresses set her skin on fire. She couldn't recall the last time he had touched her like that, she had been so caught up in the aftermath of the accident.

He laid her down on the bed. 'You have never looked more beautiful, my dear,' he said. 'Happiness suits you.'

She smiled. He was right. Happiness suited her very well.

Self-recriminations and worries about money kept Lena awake. An offer on the farmhouse had come, but it was a pittance. The realtor thought she should take it, that it was the best offer she would get. And yet the small sum was a good reason not to sell. To hang on to it for as long as she could. She had slept on the decision for a week, the realtor growing increasingly impatient with her, her debts mounting up . . . Finally, they had withdrawn their offer and she had immediately regretted not saying yes.

Somehow she must have drifted to sleep, because the phone's shrill ring in the dark startled her awake.

Bad news. One of the kids.

But then she realised that both her children were here, with her. It was a Friday night. Still, she hurried to the phone, dreading what news she would hear.

'Hello?' she said breathlessly.

'Lena.'

'Natalya.' Lena's first instinct was anger; she fought it off, superstitious still that it was bad news. 'What is it?'

'I'm here at Sofi's. I wanted you to know that Nikita has started to regain consciousness.'

Everything went bright. Lena dropped the phone on the bench, slid to the ground and gathered her knees to her chest to sob. A second later Matthew was at the threshold of the kitchen.

'Mum, are you all right?'

'I'm fine, I'm fine,' she said, palming away her tears. 'It's good news about Nikita.'

Tinny and far away, Natalya was saying her name over and over. She climbed to her feet and picked up the phone again. 'I'm sorry, Natalya. I'm a little overwhelmed.'

Matthew came to her, snuggled under her arm.

'There is a long way to go yet,' Natalya explained. 'But they're expecting a full recovery. I know it's late, and I know you probably don't want to talk to me, but I thought you'd want to know right away.'

'It's the news not the messenger I'm interested in,' Lena said. 'I . . . I'm pleased you called.'

'You are?'

Lena nodded her head tearily, then realised her sister couldn't see her. 'I am,' she managed. Then she ventured, 'Can I talk to Sofi?'

'Ah. No. She's, ah . . .'

'She doesn't want to speak to me?'

'Not yet. I'm sure she will. Give her time.' Natalya took a brave breath. 'And I'll give you time too, Lena. But I'm going to be up in London from next month, and I would really . . . really like to see you if . . .'

Lena didn't know how to answer. Her heart was stubborn; she'd lost her husband – perhaps even her children – because of Natalya. And yet relief had softened her. She had read in a magazine about Natalya's Russian film, about the acclaim it had received. In amongst the bitterness, she had felt proud of her sister. Had longed to tell her how proud she felt.

'Maybe,' she said. 'You can call me. When you get to London. I'll see how I feel.'

'I'm sorry, you know.'

'I know. I know you are,' Lena said. 'But no matter how many times you say it, I still hurt. I still hurt so much.' She sniffed, gathered herself. 'I have to go. Matthew's popped out of bed.'

'Lena, I –'

'Goodbye, Natalya.'

She firmly placed the receiver back in its cradle. She didn't want to talk to Natalya any longer, not while she was so weak with relief. She might forgive her sister, then regret it forever after.

CHAPTER FIFTY-ONE

Natalya had returned to London in style, and she loved it. The pleasure of being made up in her Mayfair suite at Claridge's Hotel while a television crew set up lights around the plum-coloured sofas; of people solicitously offering her tea, coffee, chilled water; but most of all, the pleasure of knowing she was doing this for Maxim, for his art. He had declined to come to England – his English was terrible; she assumed he was too proud – and had asked her with extreme tenderness if she would do this favour for him. She'd agreed, pierced by her loneliness; longing for his warm arms and his hard body. Life seemed so uncertain without him. This meant she would still be part of his life, that he would be grateful for her hard work on the promotion of the film. Though, Natalya admitted, she would have been very happy to be fawned over and to talk about herself for two days under any circumstances.

'I think we're ready to go, Natalie.' This was the perky young journalist from the off-beat cable movie show. All television interviews were taking place in the morning, leaving the afternoon for newspapers and magazines, and tomorrow for radio.

Natalya waited while they checked the light, took some test footage, relit the room and tried again. Finally, the questions started. Nothing new. A lot of talk about how brave she was, how Lilya was so different from her previous roles. Natalya tossed her hair and played the part of the serious actress for whom the trappings of beauty and glamour were trivial and stood in the way of real art. But she didn't mean it.

Offers had started to drift into Leida Frost's office for her. Leida was clearly delighted with them – serious parts in serious television and art movies – but Natalya was anything but delighted. A bag lady who was secretly a millionaire; a mother whose teenage son was kidnapped by the Russian mafia; a lawyer who had spent too long on her career and embarked on a heartbreaking adoption journey because her biological clock had ticked its last tock. How on earth, at thirty-seven, had she managed to attract menopausal roles? Some actresses might relish it: these were meaty parts. But Natalya wanted a romantic comedy, or an erotic thriller. Not these drab, worthy movies.

The day wore on. As each new journalist arrived she feigned weariness with the process, only to perk up as soon as the camera was running. Somebody asked her for her lunch order. She chose the most expensive thing on the menu then didn't touch it. The lights were packed away and the print journalists came, one by one. Natalya answered the same questions in the afternoon. Finally, the last appointment of the day arrived.

Her media manager, a blonde girl who looked about nineteen, approached Natalya with a concerned look on her face. 'There's someone here who's not on our schedule. Ted Aston from *Gentlemen's Club*.'

'It's fine, I invited him,' Natalya said. 'You can go now if you like.'

The girl's face was doubtful, but she sent Ted through.

Natalya invited him to sit opposite her, and she made small talk while the room emptied. When they were finally alone, she said, 'You told me to call you if I had something new to promote.'

'I'm glad you did,' he replied, sitting back with a languid smile. 'But are you sure you want to do this?'

'I'm absolutely sure. I want everyone to know I'm not a fading beauty. I want your magazine to show that I'm in full bloom.'

'I would love to do that, Natalie.' He spread his hands. 'In fact, I look forward very much to seeing what you have to offer us.'

His easy charm, his beautiful dress sense, impressed themselves on her. She found herself suddenly tongue-tied. 'Please, my name is Natalya,' she said. 'Only people who don't know me call me Natalie.'

'Well, Natalya.' He hitched back one perfectly pressed shirt cuff, peered at his Rolex watch. 'It's five o'clock. Why don't we go and have a drink and discuss this in more detail?'

She smiled. 'I would love to do that, Ted.'

Lena shredded a napkin between her fingers as she waited. The local café: neutral ground. She regretted inviting Natalya to meet her here now. Somebody would spot them, tell Sam. She was keen for Sam never to lay eyes on Natalya again.

She had no idea why she'd agreed to meet her sister. She had nothing more to say to her that hadn't already been said. But the months of suffering, her own awful guilty crime, had worn away her resolve to stay angry forever. There was no harm, surely, in talking. At the very least, she might get details of Nikita's recovery. She needed them desperately, to lift the dark shadow.

The coffee grinder barked into noisy life, and Lena looked up to see her sister arriving. Tall, thin, impossibly glossy. Heads turned to see her, faces perplexed: she looked familiar to them, but not familiar enough for them to jump out of their seats, greet her and ask for her autograph. Not like the old days when she was on *Lonely Shores*. And still Lena felt intimidated by her presence, felt dull and worn by comparison.

Natalya approached, stood uncertainly. Lena nodded towards the chair. Wanted to cry for the times when she would have leapt up for an embrace.

Natalya slid the chair out and sat. 'Thanks for seeing me.'

'Thanks for coming all this way.'

'Have you ordered anything?'

Lena shook her head. She wouldn't tell Natalya that on her budget even a seventy-pence coffee was out of the question. 'I don't feel like anything.'

'Rubbish,' Natalya said with a snort. 'Coffee and cake. I'll buy it.'

Natalya managed to call a waitress over, even though the rule was to order at the counter, and flapped money at her ostentatiously. While they waited for their morning tea to arrive, Natalya filled Lena in on Nikita's recovery up until she had left for London. It was Saturday, the café was filling up. Lena wished for a less conspicuous table. A less conspicuous sister.

'So,' Natalya said, leaning forward on her elbows and fixing her big blue eyes on Lena. 'I've been thinking. We should try to do Winter Gathering this year.'

Lena blinked. 'Are you out of your mind?'

'It's not so crazy.'

'Sofi doesn't want to see me. I don't want to see you.'

'You're seeing me now.'

Lena bit back her retort. 'No. Winter Gathering is in the past, we were all different then.'

'No, we are all still the same. Same hearts, same memories, same history.' Natalya paused for dramatic effect; one of her most annoying habits. As though all of life were a television soap and she was the star. 'If you forgive me, I know that Sofi could forgive you.'

Lena shook her head. 'How can you say that? You don't know that.'

'Sofi is an open book. Now that Nikita is getting better, she has no reason to set her heart against you any longer. If she saw that you could be forgiving, she would follow suit. I just know it.'

Lena's throat was blocked with unexpressed emotion. 'No,' she managed, 'I can't do it.'

'But why not?' Natalya's voice gave away her irritation, even if her brow stayed impossibly smooth.

'Because if I forgave you, I'd also have to forgive Sam.'

'Is that such a bad thing?'

'Yes, yes, it is.' Lena said. 'If Sam is forgivable, then why on earth did I separate from him and bring upon myself all this misery? He won't come back now.'

Would she have to face the rest of her life – lonely, alienated from her children – knowing that she'd thrown it all away on some trivial, pardonable misdemeanour? Natalya didn't realise: for Lena's life to make sense, she had to go on refusing to forgive.

'Do you want him back?' Natalya said. 'Do you still love him?'

Lena refused to answer, wanting to guard her heart from her sister. 'I could try to explain, but you'd never understand.'

Natalya pouted, offended. 'How do you know I wouldn't?'

'Because everything always goes in your favour. And everything always goes against me.'

Natalya grew solemn. 'Do you truly believe that?'

'I do.'

'Then you'd never understand me either,' she said. She stood, pushed away her untouched food. 'It was a mistake to come to see you.'

A small part of Lena wanted to drag her back, beg her not to leave. But she kept her hands very still on the tabletop. 'I tried to tell you that on the phone,' she snapped.

Natalya rolled her eyes; the same expression of impatience she had used with Lena since they were children. 'I'll see you another time, then. When you're not so stubborn and self-important.'

'When you're not so vain and careless.'

Natalya walked out. Lena became aware that other customers were stealing glances at her. She kept her head down, quietly finishing her coffee and trying not to cry. A moment had passed her by, a moment when everything could have changed. But her situation was impossible; nobody in the world would envy her. Everything was already and forever ruined. No matter how she tried, she couldn't imagine what could put it right.

CHAPTER FIFTY-TWO

He'd been watching for days, organising his materials, organising his thoughts. Time to act. Nobody knew better than he did how precious time was. If he had to leave the world, then it was very important not to leave it with regrets.

At first she hadn't been at the address, and he'd thought about going to Russia, hunting down Chernov and taking revenge on him instead. But he'd told himself to bide his time; wait and watch. Sure enough, she'd come by to pick up her children. Her misery-stricken face so like her sister's and yet not quite as heavenly. He'd followed her home at a distance, decided to wait until he was sure the kids were gone. They would get in the way. He needed time alone with her.

She'd just dropped them off again this morning. Bravely kept a smiling face on until she was round the corner, then burst into tears and cried all the way to the grocery store.

Well, he'd soon give her something to cry about.

After walking two blocks with her shopping bags, Lena was exhausted. The bags were sadly limp and empty – money was tight – but her hands were freezing and so the bags cut red grooves into her palms. She let herself into the house and slid the bags on the kitchen bench. Paused a moment to catch her breath. The vodka bottle by the microwave caught her eye. She poured a large helping and drank it while she put the shopping away.

A knock at the door. She hid the glass behind the toaster and went to answer it.

The man looked vaguely familiar, though a baseball cap put his face in shadow.

'Yes?' she said warily.

'You're Lena, aren't you?'

An American accent, and suddenly it fell into place. Memory was on her in a rush: a photograph of a man standing proudly in front of a red car. *Creedy*. She moved to slam the door.

He shouldered it, pushing it open all the way. His voice was firm. 'Come on now, open up. You owe it to me to talk to me.' He barged past her and strode into her house. 'I'm not going to hurt you. That's all in the past.'

Her head swam. She took a deep breath, forcing her thoughts into order. *Just talk to him, explain everything, then make him go away.* It had been more than ten years; if he'd wanted to take revenge he would have done it before now. Perhaps he just wanted money. That was all right; Sofi would give it to him. She had said so before.

Lena pointed to the sofa, stammering, 'Please, sit down.'

He did as she asked, whipping off his baseball cap. He was like a character from one of her childhood's dark fairy tales; sinister, not quite real. She calculated he must be in his sixties, but he looked lined and grey, a hundred years old. She hovered, unable to sit, not sure what to do. If only she could ring Sofi . . .

'Well,' he said, 'you're almost as pretty as your sister.'

'What do you want?' she gasped.

To her surprise, he smiled. 'Lena, I'm dying. I need your help to put some old matters to rest.'

He was dying? That explained the way he looked. Disarmed by his reasonable tone, she sat down. Her hands shook; she needed that glass of vodka.

'Would you like a drink?' she said hopefully.

'I can't drink. I'm too sick.'

'I'm sorry,' she said in a rush. 'I'm so sorry about . . . that business. We were young and foolish.'

He waved her words away. 'I didn't come for an apology. Apologies mean nothing.'

Perched on the edge of her seat, she clasped her hands in front of her and focused all her attention on him. She realised her heart was beating arrhythmically, tried to will it to slow and calm.

'When you girls pulled your scam on me, I was ready to murder you all,' he said. 'But I was so ashamed of being taken for a ride that I didn't tell anyone.'

At the mention of murder, Lena's pulse spiked. 'Sofi will pay you back,' she said. 'She's told me before she wants to.'

'I didn't care about the money,' he said impatiently. 'It was my pride. I tried not to think about you all for a long time. Then God decided to give me cancer. Prostate cancer. Cancer of the prick.' He laughed loudly. 'When I first found out, I decided I'd ring every Chernov and Chernova in Russia looking for you girls. Your father gave me your address.'

Lena swallowed hard. Impossibly, she despised her father more deeply than before.

'Then I had some treatment and things didn't look so bad. Looked like I might get better. I was so happy, I almost became forgiving.' He laughed again. 'But it came back, the cancer. It could be pretty much anywhere now. I don't have long to live, they say. I feel fine, but it's eating away at me inside, slowly. I got maybe six months, maybe three. Maybe I'll still be around next Christmas. I have to die, though. We all have to die, I guess.' He shrugged.

Lena sat silently, hoping that this was all he wanted to say. Knowing it wouldn't be.

'I could have stayed home, had some more chemo. But I didn't feel much like it. Die on your feet, don't live on your knees. Not when you've got important business to take care of.' He rubbed his hands over his face.

'What do you want from me?' she said.

He leaned back, folded his arms behind his head. 'You know, when I first got sick I asked myself, what was the one thing I regretted?

And it was clear as day. I regretted being too embarrassed to pay you three back. I thought the idea of Natalya getting old and ugly in a jail cell might satisfy me, so I called a lawyer, but he said I had insufficient evidence.' He emphasised the last two words by drawing quotation marks in the air with his fingers. 'I'd burnt all the letters you wrote me, my car never turned up anywhere to fingerprint...' He flexed forward, his mouth trembling with sudden anger. 'Then I thought of something I'd like much better.'

Her blood cooled dramatically. 'What is it?' she managed.

He smiled, cruelly. 'Don't worry. You were the nice one. That's why I'm here. Your letters were genuine; you took the time to know me. I told you things that... I never told anybody else. And you cared for me too, didn't you? That's why you apologised?'

'In a way,' she whispered, frightened.

'It's the other two hard-hearted bitches I can't get out of my mind. But I can't decide which I hate the most: Sofi for thinking it all up, or Natalya for wrecking my judgement with her goddamn perfect...' He trailed off; shook his head as if to clear it. 'So, you have to decide. Who is the most to blame?'

Something very bad was going to happen. 'Why are you asking me that?'

'Because one of them has to die.'

A rush of heat. 'No. No, it was so long ago and –'

'Pick one. Sofi or Natalya.'

Lena leapt off the sofa and dashed towards the door. He intercepted her. He had suffered a long illness, but she was sick too: awash with poison, her muscles wasting. He easily overpowered her, fought her to the ground, pinning her on her back and sitting astride her tummy. From inside his shirt he pulled out a hunting knife, which he poked into the soft skin under her chin.

'All right, you made me do this,' he said. 'I didn't want to get heavy with you, but there is no escaping from this, do you understand? I've been here for two weeks. I've been watching that house where you don't live any more. I know the two children are yours, and I know the route your little girl takes to school every day. This is going to go *my way*. You don't know where I'll be, who I'll be watching. If I see police turn up here, or even your ex-husband, I'm going to get you good. I'm dying, Lena. I don't have anything to lose. You want to risk disobeying me? You want to risk calling the police and wondering what's going to happen to those pretty children of yours in the time it takes for them to arrive? Or are you going to do what I say?'

Lena groaned with fear.

'Is that a yes?'

'Yes,' she managed.

'So, pick which one it's going to be.'

'Me,' she said. 'Kill me.'

'Well, that wouldn't be any fun, would it? I wouldn't get to see you all churned up inside with guilt.' He poked her harder with the knife. 'Pick one.'

Lena's mind was roasting in white-hot adrenaline. She felt distant and not real. But some primitive instinct, deep inside her, lit up fiercely. *Don't let him kill your sister.*

And so there was only one answer to give.

'Sofi,' she gasped.

He smiled, tucked his knife in his waistband and stood, reaching down to help her up. She didn't take his hand, lay on the floor very still. Perhaps there was a way out of this. Her thoughts were trapped inside the hard shell of her skull.

'Sofi it is,' he said. 'Can you get her here?'

Lena's tongue was paralysed, she couldn't respond. Sick guilt suffused her.

He grasped her wrist and pulled her forcibly to her feet. She crashed into him briefly and he straightened her up. 'You stink of alcohol,' he said with a disdainful twist of his mouth. 'Nothing worse than a woman who drinks. Answer my question.'

'I think I can get her here. Just after Christmas.'

'Good. I'll be watching.'

'Please,' she said. 'Do it quickly, don't frighten her.'

Creedy's eyebrows shot up. 'I'm not going to do anything to her.'

Lena was puzzled, but hopeful. 'You're not?'

'No. *You* are,' he said with a laugh. 'You're going to kill Sofi.'

CHAPTER FIFTY-THREE

'Good afternoon, Sofi.'

Sofi started. She sat up, quickly regaining her bearings. St Colette's, Nikita's room. She had fallen asleep in the armchair next to the bed.

Doctor Pelletier was smiling down at her. 'I'm sorry, I didn't mean to startle you. I hadn't realised you were asleep.'

Sofi yawned. 'Is everything all right?'

'Oh, yes, yes. Just doing my rounds.' Her hard mouth turned down at the corners. 'Are you getting enough sleep?'

Sofi had grown very fond of Doctor Pelletier, whose cool exterior hid a warm heart. 'I seem to be sleeping all the time,' she responded. 'Finally catching up.'

The doctor went through her usual series of checks with Nikita. He was having a quiet day today. He had been awake in the morning briefly, staring into space. Sofi had sung to him until he'd drifted off. When she returned from lunch he was still asleep. The quiet days made her anxious, but Doctor Pelletier assured her that when dealing with comatose patients anything was possible; had urged patience.

The doctor slid her pen back in her pocket and turned to Sofi. 'I have seen things today that bear further exploration,' she said.

Sofi leaned forward. 'What things?'

Doctor Pelletier sat on the edge of Nikita's bed. 'You asleep in your armchair with a barely touched cup of coffee on the bedside table. Are you tired, Sofi? Nauseous?'

Sofi was puzzled, then realisation dawned. Her mind raced to do sums, count dates . . . but with all of her energy concentrated on Nikita, her cycles and her sex life were impossible to keep track of.

'One of the nurses is over at the pharmacy now, picking up some supplies. Shall I ask him to bring back a pregnancy test?'

Sofi nodded. 'I think you'd better.'

Half an hour later, Sofi was waiting in Doctor Pelletier's office nervously picking at the hem of her skirt. Her heart couldn't decide if it was terrified or excited: both emotions felt so similar. And so she sat, forcing herself to take deep breaths and refusing to speculate about the future until she knew for sure.

Doctor Pelletier returned brandishing a blue-and-white test strip. 'Congratulations,' she said.

Tears pricked Sofi's eyes. She pressed her hand over her mouth, unable to speak. *A blessing.*

The doctor raised her eyebrows. 'I take it this wasn't planned?'

'How could I have planned anything?' Sofi said. 'Being here for Nikita, trying to keep my business afloat . . .' She stood, sniffing back tears. 'I have to get home to tell Julien.'

'Will he be pleased?'

Sofi tried to smile, but couldn't. 'I don't know. I'm terrified to find out.'

On the drive home she was vague, thoughtless. She nearly ran into the back of a car stopped at lights, had to force herself to focus. She could hear her own heartbeat too loud in her ears. She parked the car badly; her fingers shook as she slid the house key in the lock. Mama greeted her with a choice of meals for dinner, the cat wound around her legs. She gently pushed them both aside, breathlessly promising to return as soon as she had spoken to Julien.

He was in his studio. Since Nikita had started to regain consciousness, he had been painting furiously, as though making up for lost time. She found him standing very still, studying the canvas in front of him, his paintbrush poised halfway across the distance. His brow was furrowed; he hadn't even heard her come in.

She recognised this stance. This was Julien the uninterruptible. Ordinarily she would back out, leave it for another time. And yet, if she didn't speak to him now, the anxiety would flutter in her blood all night. She had experienced enough anxiety for a lifetime already, over Nikita. She hadn't the ability to suffer any more.

'Julien,' she said. 'I'm sorry . . .'

He turned, his eyes still far away. It took him two full seconds to register her presence. 'Sofi? Are you well? You look pale.'

'I'm . . .' She couldn't stop herself from smiling. Or crying. 'I'm pregnant,' she blurted.

His eyebrows rose slowly, a smile teased the corners of his mouth. He dropped his paintbrush and took two steps towards her, seized her and pressed her against him. She buried her face in his shoulder and sobbed with happiness.

Natalya stood under the shower, letting the hot water run through her long hair. The shower glass was steaming up, she was humming softly to herself, when the door to the bathroom opened.

It was Ted, dressed only in his boxer shorts, holding out her mobile phone. 'It's your sister.'

Natalya thought she must have misheard. A month ago, Lena had behaved as though she never wanted to speak to her again. She twisted off the taps. 'Lena?'

'Yes. Lena. She said she's your sister.'

'She is. I just didn't expect her to call.' Natalya stepped out of the shower, reaching for a towel with one hand and the phone with the other.

'Want me to make you some breakfast?' Ted asked.

'Just coffee,' she said, ushering him out. She closed the door behind him, perched on the edge of the basin, among Ted's dozens of shaving and grooming products. Her own place, a serviced apartment at Docklands, was little more than a dumping ground for her clothes and make-up. She didn't want to settle in London yet in case Maxim called her and asked her to come back. Stupid. She knew it.

'Hello?'

'Natalya, I've changed my mind.'

Lena's voice was slurred as though she had been drinking. But it was only nine in the morning.

'What do you mean?' Natalya asked. 'About what?'

'About everything. I've been an idiot. I forgive you. All right? I forgive you.'

'Lena, is everything okay? You sound strange.'

'I need you to call Sofi, I need you to tell her I've forgiven you. I want to have a Winter Gathering this year. Up here, in Briggsby. It's my turn. You can both stay with me. All right? You tell her. You make her come.'

Natalya was taken aback, didn't know how to answer. 'You've forgiven me? Really?'

A deep shuddering breath on the other end of the line. 'Yes. Really. You're my sister, and I can't let . . . anything happen . . . to us.' Lena dissolved into tears.

'Hey, don't cry. Don't cry, Lena. This is the start of something good. I'll call Sofi later. I'll see if I can get her to come, but even if she can't, I'll be there.'

'Don't take no for an answer, Natalya. I need to see her. She has to come.'

'I'll do my best. But she might not want to leave Nikita. Perhaps we should see if she wants us to go over there and –'

'No. It has to be here.' Lena's voice grew shrill, almost panicky. 'It's my turn. It has to be in Briggsby.'

Natalya's unease intensified. 'Are you sure you're okay?'

'I'm just tired,' she mumbled. 'I had a bad night's sleep. Tell her she only has to come for a day or two, not the whole week if she doesn't want to. I really need you both to come and have Winter Gathering again, like we're supposed to. Like we promised each other, okay. A promise is a promise, and I love you, Natalya. I love you.'

'I love you too, Lena.' Natalya fought back tears; so relieved to have her sister's forgiveness that she could almost overlook the demented blur of her words. 'Take care of yourself.'

Ted was pulling on his cashmere overcoat by the door when she emerged, dressed and thoughtful, from the bathroom. 'Your coffee's in the kitchen,' he said. 'I'm late for a meeting. Lock up when you go.'

'I'll leave the key with the doorman.'

'No need. Take it. It's a spare.'

She wouldn't take it. She didn't want to be tied to Ted. For now, he was just a diversion: a pair of warm arms, an appreciative gaze. Ted seemed to want to pin her down. He had hovered around at her photo shoot almost jealously, putting pressure on the stylists and photographer to get every detail perfect. And they had. The pictures wouldn't be published for two more months, and Natalya couldn't wait. She had seen a mock-up of the spread and she looked magnificent. All of those critics who had delighted in noting her fading beauty – not to mention all of those feminists who had held her up as a role model of ageing gracefully – would have to find something else to say about her now.

He strode over, lifted her chin gently. 'Not bad news, I hope? From your sister?'

'No. Good news really.'

'You look upset.'

'She sounded strange. A little crazy. I think she was drunk.'

His eyebrows shot up. 'At this time of the day? Does she have a drinking problem?'

Natalya realised she didn't want to share her intimate family details with him. She kissed his cheek. 'Have a good day.'

Alone in his apartment, she sipped her coffee and replayed the conversation with Lena in her mind. Soon enough she would gather her things and head home to call Sofi; but she started to wonder if she should call Sam as well, just to make sure that somebody close by was looking after Lena. Because she clearly wasn't looking after herself.

Lena didn't come apart completely until the third day, which was Christmas Eve. She rose after another night of sleep in uneven chunks, peppered with half-dreams and thudding palpitations, to find an envelope had been pushed through her mail slot. It lay on the mat, her name written upon it in black. She knew it was from him without opening it.

And yet she opened it. There was no note inside as she had expected, but there were four polaroid photographs. Anna walking back from the shop with a bottle of milk, one foot on the kerb, the other in the gutter. Matthew sitting on Wendy's front fence with two of his friends. Sam and the kids getting in the car. Anna with Izzy, secretly smoking cigarettes at a location Lena didn't recognise.

Terror iced her heart. She clutched the polaroids against her and let out one loud sob, before pulling her emotions back inside. She couldn't let anything happen to them. She had to do as Creedy said.

Lena had frantically thought through a million solutions, but kept coming back to the same place. He was a desperate man, not afraid of anything, determined to elicit the only revenge that would satisfy him before his death. She didn't know how close he was – if he was in the next flat listening to her phone calls, or if he was across the street from Wendy's house with a gun trained on her daughter's head. If she called the police, she couldn't guarantee they would find him before he had followed through on his threats. If she confessed the situation to Sam, she couldn't guarantee that he could remove the children safely from Briggsby before Creedy caught wind of it and went knocking on their door with a knife in his pocket. The thought caused a spike of pain to her heart and she wondered, not for the first time, if this situation might kill her. Her body was brittle, coming unglued at the joints.

The phone rang, jangling through all her nerves. It would be Creedy. She couldn't answer it. But what if not answering it made him angry, made him do something impulsive and awful?

'Hello?' she said on a shaking breath.

'Lena, it's Sam.'

She couldn't speak. Was Creedy listening right now? She strained her ears: was that a click on the line, or just her dripping refrigerator? Were those hurried footsteps in the neighbouring flat, or just the thump of her heart?

Sam continued. 'The kids and I were wondering if you wanted to go down to the High Street with us tonight, to see the Christmas lights.'

Christmas had rushed upon her, forgotten in the midst of her mental chaos, her anxiety that Natalya would convince Sofi to come. God, she was supposed to go over to Wendy's for Christmas lunch the next day. She hadn't even bought presents.

'I can't,' she said quickly. If Creedy saw her with Sam, he'd assume she'd told him. 'I . . . I'm sick. I can't come tomorrow.'

'Sick? What's wrong?'

'I don't know, it's . . .' To her horror, she began to cry.

'Lena, what's wrong?'

Her brain filled with fearful imaginings. Creedy listening in, setting that mean little mouth of his in a hard line. She was giving too much away. She couldn't even tell Sam to be careful of the children, to look after them well, in case that was construed as a warning.

She forced her voice to be even. 'I'm sorry, I've been up all night. I'm sick, I can't come tonight or tomorrow.'

'Do you want me to come over? I can take you to the doctor.'

'I'll be fine.'

'But, Lena –'

'I said I'll be fine. I don't want to see you, don't you dare come over here.'

'All right, all right!' he said. 'But the kids will be so disappointed.'

She didn't answer, too busy forcing breath into her lungs.

'Well,' he said softly, 'if you change your mind, let me know.'

Again, she remained silent.

'Merry Christmas,' he said.

Painfully, she longed for everything to be different, for Christmas lights on the High Street with her family, for her old ordinary misery.

'I have to go,' she said. 'Goodbye.'

Sofi sat with Julien on the soft sofa. The fire crackled, the house had grown silent. It had been a full and rich Christmas Day. Nikita's room at St Colette's had filled with toys, and he had even been awake for six hours to look at them. A purple-and-green toy washing machine had particularly caught his eye, and Sofi had put it on his bedside table and set it running for him over and over again, just to see the spark of engagement in his face. He was improving on an exponential curve now; the periods of consciousness were getting longer and more consistent, not shredding back into darkness the way they used to. He had started physical therapy in his bed, and could now drink by himself from a cup with a straw and eat jelly from a spoon. Doctor Pelletier was convinced he would be home by the end of winter, and the recovery would continue after that. It would be difficult to ever know whether Nikita had permanent brain damage – his autism would always confuse the tests – but now, nearly one year after his accident, Sofi was confident that he was finally coming back to her. Back to the family.

Masha the cat, now getting fat and grizzled with age, stood and stretched, her tail quivering before she curled onto Sofi's lap and purred herself back to sleep. Sofi gazed at the fire, thinking.

Julien stroked her shoulder gently with his thumb. 'I think you should go,' he said. 'I think it would do you the world of good.'

'It's a long time to be apart from Nikita. What if he needs me?'

'He's recovering painfully slowly, Sofi. Nothing dramatic will happen while you're away. If you're really concerned, just go for two or three days, not the whole week.'

'It's such a long way.'

'But imagine the good it will do. Lena has forgiven Natalya; perhaps you can sort out your differences with Lena too.'

Sofi mused on this. The better Nikita became, the less she found she blamed her cousin. Yes, Lena had knowingly taken Nikita out while drunk. But there were so many other random factors in play – the poster that had caught his eye, the car driving on that street at that precise moment – that Sofi had to admit it was truly just an awful accident. Any punishment that she could think of for Lena could never be as great as the guilt Lena had endured for a year. So was it time for the three of them to repair this relationship that had been so precious to them for nearly three decades?

'We were always there for each other,' she said. 'It feels strange being all at odds. Cut adrift in the world somehow.'

'A relationship worth mending, then.'

'All right,' she said, 'I'll go.'

CHAPTER FIFTY-FOUR

The possibility of awkwardness prevented Natalya from phoning Sam at first. But Lena's behaviour grew increasingly disturbing. Her frantic voice on the phone, begging Natalya to make sure Sofi came; then her bubbling sobs of relief when Natalya told her Sofi had agreed. And through it all, the slurred speech, the endless declarations of her love for Natalya, for needing to put things right. Natalya decided that she would try to meet with Sam when she was up in Briggsby, to find out if he knew anything about what was bothering her sister, to make some plans for getting her off the drink.

She ordered a car to come for her early on the day after Boxing Day. She was too important for trains and buses, but could not commit to buying a car in case she left England soon and returned to St Petersburg and Maxim. Of course, there was no evidence at all to suggest that Maxim wanted her back. He hadn't called her, he hadn't even come to the London premiere of the film. He certainly wasn't going to approve of her photo shoot in *Gentlemen's Club*, but that was partly the point of doing it, wasn't it? To show him what he was missing out on.

The driver slid her suitcase into the boot of the car and she climbed in, leaned her head back on the soft leather and took a few deep breaths. Then, when they were on their way, she pulled out her mobile phone to call Sam.

It rang twice, then Anna picked it up. Natalya hesitated, then hung up. Too difficult. Anna would tell Lena that Aunty Nat had called to speak to Sam. *Damn*. She hadn't thought this through properly. Her own fears about awkwardness put aside, she realised that Lena could never know she and Sam had spoken behind her back. Forgiveness could be a fragile thing. She slid out of her seatbelt and leaned forward to hand her mobile to the driver.

'Hit redial,' she said, 'and ask for Sam Tait.'

The driver complied, and in moments she had Sam on the line.

'Sam, I'm sorry, it's Natalya here.'

He was silent for a second, and she thought the line had dropped out. Then he said stiffly, 'Hello.'

'I know this is awkward, Sam, but I'm coming up to Briggsby and –'

'You're coming to Briggsby?'

'Lena didn't tell you? It's Winter Gathering.'

'She doesn't tell me anything,' he replied gruffly.

'Really? She's been acting very strangely . . .'

'I know,' he replied. 'Look, it's hard for me to talk now.'

Of course. The kids would be there, Wendy too, maybe even his hatchet-faced sister.

'Can I meet you?' she said. 'Maybe tomorrow? That little café on the High Street, say about nine o'clock? We need to talk, we need to figure out what to do about her.' She exhaled loudly. 'Sam, I'm so sorry about everything that has happened, it's hard for me not to feel it's my fault.'

'It's not,' he said. 'It's my fault.'

She laughed. 'Perhaps we can argue that one tomorrow.'

'Yes, I'll see you then.'

The line went dead. She snapped her phone shut and stared out the window as the wintry streets sped by.

'Why didn't you wake me?' Julien said sleepily.

'I'm waking you now.' It was still dark, but the car was coming for Sofi in fifteen minutes to take her to the airport.

Julien sat up. His pyjama buttons were fastened out of alignment. 'I could have made you breakfast. I could have driven you up to Paris myself.'

'Not so loud. You'll wake Mama.' She leaned over the bed and kissed his throat, inhaling the warm scent of him. 'I'll be back the day after tomorrow. Make sure you tell Nikita I'll be back soon.'

'Of course I will.' He grasped her around the hips, kissed her belly through her wool skirt. 'Are you going to tell them about the baby?'

'I don't know.' Sofi hadn't even told Mama yet. It was very early in the pregnancy, and she didn't want to arouse hopes and expectations. She wanted the focus to remain on Nikita's recovery. 'Maybe. We'll have plenty of other big things to talk about.'

'Yes, you're right.' He rolled onto his back.

'Will you miss me?' she teased.

'Of course I will,' he said. 'But I won't mind as long as you promise that you and the little passenger come back safely.'

'We will,' she said. 'I promise.'

Sofi's plane was delayed and then cancelled. With no hope of making her connecting flight, she took a cab into the city and waited for the next train to London. Shadows were growing long before she climbed on board a bus to Briggsby. She phoned Natalya's mobile, only to be told to make her way straight to the Briggsby Arms, where she and Lena were ordering dinner. She felt guilty that she had held them up from eating, but annoyed that they couldn't wait long enough for her to drop off her bag. Still, she was probably just cranky from lack of sleep, and from worrying about how Nikita would fare while she was away from him. She caught a cab from the bus station and paid the driver outside the Arms, where uneven strings of Christmas lights blinked rapidly against the night sky. Her stomach rumbled. She had eaten half a cheese sandwich on the Eurostar, and been sucking continuously on barley sugar against the vague nausea since. She was hungry enough to brave a huge serving of battered fish and hot chips.

Inside, a fire was crackling in the fireplace, and the jukebox was playing. Natalya and Lena sat at a corner table. Natalya saw her first, leapt to her feet. Lena followed. Sofi was horrified by her younger cousin's appearance. Lena was pale and bony, her eyes were smudged around with dark shadows. They embraced briefly, then Lena was backing away, not meeting her eyes. Sofi opened her mouth to tell her she looked terrible, but decided against it. This was the toll Lena's guilt had taken on her. For all Sofi knew, she might look just as pale and sick herself from a year of waiting and worrying.

'I'm going to get us a bottle of champagne,' Natalya said. 'Wait here.'

'Could you order me some dinner?' Sofi asked. 'Fish and chips? Something like that?'

'Of course.'

Natalya headed off. Sofi pushed her suitcase behind the table and sat down. Lena was staring at the fire. Sofi reached out her hand to pat Lena's fingers. 'This year has been hard on you.'

Lena took a gulp of her drink. 'Harder on you.'

'Nikita gets better every day. As he recovers, I find I don't really have it in my heart to hold a grudge against you.'

Lena's mouth twisted upside down. Tears leaked out of the corners of her eyes. 'You are a good person, Sofi. You are too good to me.'

'You are a good person too. You forgave Natalya.'

On cue, Natalya returned with a bottle of champagne and three flutes. Sofi didn't want to draw suspicion, so she let Natalya fill her glass. Lena fell silent. Natalya asked a million questions about Nikita. It was clear that she was nervous too, and probably worried about the state Lena appeared to be in. Lena's glass emptied and she refilled it to the brim.

Natalya glanced at Sofi's glass. 'Come on, catch up,' she said.

This was the opportunity to tell them about the baby. But she held off. They weren't as close as they'd once been and, besides, to change the topic to a new baby when they'd just spent twenty minutes discussing her first child – her injured, not-quite-right child – seemed disloyal somehow. As though she thought her worries about Nikita would all disappear when she had a new, normal child to replace him.

So she sipped her champagne very slowly, ate her dinner, and contributed to the tentative conversation. In the middle of Sofi recounting how well her American franchise was doing, Lena suddenly laughed out loud.

'What's so funny?' Sofi asked.

Lena blinked rapidly, as though waking from a dream. 'I wasn't laughing.'

Natalya stared at Lena. Sofi's heart went cold. Something was wrong with Lena. Now she was staring at her hands on the table. Natalya caught Sofi's gaze, shrugged almost imperceptibly. Perhaps Lena had just drunk too much. The time to talk to her about it was tomorrow, when she was sober. Not now. Sofi felt desperately sad for her, and wondered if she should have been in touch sooner, with good news of Nikita, with forgiveness and love.

An old Abba song burst into life on the jukebox and she quickly changed the topic. 'Ah. Do you remember this song?'

Natalya jumped in, and they talked about Papa, about ice-creams in square cones, about how Abba was one of the only foreign bands that the Third Programme, the Soviet pop music channel, was allowed to play, about how they had sung the words in terrible English and never really understood them. Lena seemed to relax a little, and Sofi began to feel very tired, from the long day of travel as much as from her early pregnancy.

At the exit to the Briggsby Arms, as they waited for a cab, Sofi leaned to whisper in Lena's ear. 'Tomorrow, I'd like to have a long chat. There's a lot for us to talk about.'

Lena looked alarmed, lifted her chin almost as though she were fighting for air. 'Yes,' she said. 'Tomorrow. We'll have to get some time alone.'

The cab came, and they all headed back to Lena's for the night.

Natalya was anxious. It had kept her from sleeping. That, and the saggy top bunk. She climbed down from the bed at eight. Sofi was still sleeping. Lena was in the kitchen, looking as though she hadn't slept at all.

'Good morning,' Natalya said brightly. 'Oh, you've already had coffee.'

Lena looked up. 'Didn't sleep so well,' she managed.

Natalya sat next to her, noticed that she stank of alcohol. 'I'm sorry to hear that. Perhaps you can catch up later. I have to go out soon, I hope you don't mind.'

'What? Where?' Lena's eyes were panicked.

The prick to her conscience was painful. Did Lena suspect she was meeting with Sam? Was that why she was so on edge? She immediately saw that she couldn't meet Sam somewhere in public. If a nosy neighbour or family member saw and it got back to Lena...

Natalya remembered she had been asked a question. Her lie was prepared. 'Oh, I promised the local newspaper I'd drop in and say hello next time I was in town. They ran a lovely article about me when the film premiered.'

Lena nodded, her fingers knotting around her coffee cup. Natalya wondered if there was more than just coffee in it.

'And you're going this morning?' Lena asked.

'I said I'd be there at nine.' How was she going to get time alone to call Sam? 'I might just have a quick shower. Could you put another pot of coffee on, perhaps? Sofi will be needing it when she wakes up too.'

In the bathroom, she turned the shower on loud and full and, standing by the basin fully clothed, flipped open her mobile phone. Dialled Sam's number. *Please let him answer.* Not the kids, not Wendy. She was in luck.

'Hello?'

'It's Natalya,' she whispered. 'Change of plans. We should meet somewhere nobody will see us.'

'Ah, yes.'

'The cliff path.'

'Have you seen the weather?'

'All the better. Nobody will be out,' she said. 'Let's meet at the monument up past the playground on the northern end of the path. The one with the engraving of the ship. It's far enough from the road to be hidden.'

'All right. I'll see you there at nine.'

She closed the phone, her heart thudding softly.

Lena waited until Natalya was gone, then she made her way to the kids' bedroom where Sofi was still asleep.

'Sofi?' she said softly.

Her cousin roused, looked up blearily. 'What time is it?'

'Nearly nine.' Lena's hand shook as she turned it over to look at her watch. 'Natalya's gone out. I thought now might be a good time to talk.'

'Of course. Of course.' Sofi sat up. 'I'm just . . . so tired. A long day's travel.'

'I'll make you a coffee.'

'No, don't. I couldn't face it. Just a piece of toast. I'll get dressed.'

'Can we go for a walk?' A surge of adrenaline. 'Down by the cliffs?'

Sofi looked doubtfully towards the window, which was rattling from the wind. 'It might be a little cold.'

'I need the fresh air,' Lena said. 'To clear my head.'

She knew that her head might never be clear again. She had slept fewer than two hours the previous night, jolted awake again and again. Finally, at three o'clock, she had risen and drunk everything in the house. Wine, vodka, cooking sherry. Her stomach was raw with acid, all her nerves were trembling and threatening to come loose, her brain was a fog of weariness and guilt and terror. And dropped into her lap was the golden opportunity: Natalya was gone, Sofi wanted to talk. It was going to happen. *It was really going to happen.*

'Lena, you look like you're going to faint.' Sofi was next to her, trying to guide her to sit on the bed.

'I'm fine,' she said, shrugging Sofi off. 'I'll make you some toast. You get dressed. Put something warm on.'

Lena thought about the long red overcoat Sofi had brought with her. Imagined it splashed against the black rocks. All the air sucked out of her lungs. She turned so Sofi couldn't see her face, left the room and closed the door behind her.

Focusing on practical tasks helped still her nerves. Finding bread, putting it in the toaster. The phone rang, pulling the thread in her heart again. She answered it.

It was him.

'Natalya has left the house,' he said.

Where was he? How did he know? She was speechless.

'You're going to do it now,' he continued. 'This morning.'

'Yes,' she said. 'We're going for a walk to the cliffs.'

'I'll be checking on you.'

The line went dead. Lena hung up the phone.

'Ready,' Sofi said.

Lena turned. Sofi wore a long wool dress, a black leather coat, a grey fur hat. Lena changed the picture in her mind's eye, the body on the rocks now dressed in black and grey.

'Your breakfast,' she squeaked as the toaster popped.

'I'll take it with me.' Sofi peered out the kitchen window at the sky. 'I hope you have two umbrellas. I don't want to get wet.'

Sam was waiting when Natalya arrived, leaning on his elbows on the monument, gazing out over the grey sea. The wind buffeted her body, she pulled her overcoat close around her. He didn't hear her until she was standing right next to him.

'Sam.'

He turned. Smiled weakly. 'Why do I feel so guilty?'

'I'm the same.' She laughed, glad for the release of tension. 'Tell me everything you know.'

So he told her about Lena's increasing reliance on alcohol, how she had lost the kids, had to put the farmhouse up for sale, and then, in the past few weeks, had grown erratic, refused to see him or

Matthew or Anna, was panicked and angry on the telephone. Natalya related her version of events. A few soft raindrops misted down.

'I'm so worried about her,' Sam said. 'You know I still love her?' A gust of wind caught his words and carried them away.

'You do?'

'I never stopped loving her. What we did . . . God, Natalya, we were idiots. I can't believe we did it.'

'Nor can I. But it seemed to make sense at the time. Lots of things make sense at the time and then later, in the cold light of day . . .' Natalya shook her head. 'I know how she must have felt. I didn't at the time, but now I do. Her head would have been full of it all the time. No wonder she couldn't forgive us.'

'She's forgiven you, now,' he said with a shrug. 'Not me.'

'We have to get her help, stop her drinking. Then she'll be able to think straight. If she is willing to love me again, then perhaps she will be willing to love you again too. I think I'll stay with her after Sofi goes home. We'll find somewhere she can do a rehab program. I'll pay for everything.'

'I'd be so grateful,' he said.

'And when she's better, I'll do my best to convince her to repair her marriage.' Natalya stopped herself. 'If that's what you want?'

'It's absolutely what I want,' he said.

'If it means that I have to leave, get out of her life so she never has to worry about trusting us again, then I will do that too.'

'She needs you. Don't do that.'

'Whatever it takes,' Natalya said, feeling hopeful now. 'She's in a very bad place. I'll do whatever it takes to pull her back.'

Lena had already decided the best place to do it was at One Mile Point, so named because it was a mile from town. The path sloped away dramatically, and they would be shielded from view by trees and earth. A lookout protruded from the cliff face. It was one of the only places along the path with a railing, but a recent rockfall had left a gap. The local paper had been reporting on the public outcry about it taking so long to be fixed. She prompted Sofi, who was doubtful, out into the cold wind and cut across the High Street and the back of the school grounds to the southern end of the cliff walk. Drizzle began to fall.

'Maybe we should head back,' Sofi suggested, barely audible over the wind and the crashing of the waves.

'No, no,' Lena said, wondering if Creedy was watching her from somewhere. 'I need to walk. I need the sea air.'

'Lena, you're acting strangely. You haven't slept, you're still drunk. Or drunk again. Is all of this because of Nikita? Because of your guilt?'

Lena kept walking, forcing Sofi to follow.

'Because I forgive you, you know. Nikita is getting well again, and life is very good for me right now. I know I was unkind to you at the start, but I was angry and frightened.'

Lena realised she had to say something, but her mind could barely focus on the conversation. 'You weren't unkind. You did what any mother would have done. The idea of my children being hurt . . .' She trailed off.

Sofi grasped her hand and squeezed it. 'I knew you would understand. Lena, I really can't keep up this pace. Can we stop and rest a moment?' She indicated a park bench, off the path, back towards the road.

'Rest?'

'Just a few minutes.'

What if Creedy was watching, saw them sit down together, assumed she couldn't go through with it? Would he head straight to Wendy's house? Or would he give her a chance? She had no choice: Sofi had walked towards the bench and was about to sit. Lena raced after her, caught her. 'No, we have to keep walking.'

'Lena –'

'Please. Please don't sit down.'

Sofi's eyebrows drew down. Lena's skin prickled. She knew that she was behaving too strangely, that Sofi was growing suspicious.

'Not up here then,' Sofi said. 'Let's head north, back towards home. We'll be stuck a mile up the road otherwise. I haven't the energy for the walk back.'

Lena knew there wouldn't be a walk back for Sofi, but she couldn't tell her that. She had to go along with her or risk arousing more suspicion.

'Sure,' Lena managed. 'Just as long as we keep walking. I feel foggy, I need to clear my mind.'

'It's all right,' Sofi said softly, putting her arm around Lena's waist as they headed away from the bench. 'Don't panic, everything will be okay. I just . . . I need to explain, Lena. I'm tired because I'm pregnant.'

Lena's blood froze.

Sofi laughed softly, spoke so quietly Lena almost couldn't hear. 'There, I'd promised myself I wouldn't tell anyone, but it's come out already.'

And in that moment, Lena made the only decision she could under the circumstances. She had to go over the edge with Sofi. Because she couldn't live afterwards, as the murderer of her cousin and an unborn child.

CHAPTER FIFTY-FIVE

After Sam left, Natalya lingered a while on the cliff top. She leaned on the monument and watched the sea move. The drizzle eased, but the air was moist and salty. She noticed a man standing in the distance, wearing a black baseball cap. He seemed to be staring right at her. She ignored him. She was used to people staring at her. Perhaps he had seen her film. A lot of men in their fifties and beyond had approached her after seeing it, wondering if she really was washed-up enough to date an ageing philosopher. She wasn't. Ted was forty-five, and that was the upper limit for Natalya. She turned to go. The man had moved closer. Was he striding towards her? A prickle of unease. She tensed, ready to run.

'Natalya,' he called.

Too late, she recognised him. Roy Creedy. The scene took on a nightmarish, hyper-real brightness, despite the dim clouds. To see him here, somewhere familiar and safe, unhinged all her nerves. Flashes of memory returned. His overbearing arrogance, his obvious hatred of women, his cruel sense of humour, his taste for pornography and violence . . . Fear overwhelmed her. She froze when she should have been running.

By the time her feet agreed to move, he was on top of her, tackling her.

'My lucky day,' he growled. She fell, slamming her head on the stone monument. Black blurred into her mind, then blurred back out again. Her ears were ringing. She began to scream. On screen, she had screamed many times. But that theatrical performance was nothing like the real thing, which started at the bottom of her lungs and shook through her body, making her throat raw.

He had her hair, was dragging her towards the edge of the cliff. She tried to prise his hands free with her fingernails, all the time screaming for help and hoping her voice wouldn't be lost under the wind and the waves. Surely somebody would come.

'What are you doing?' she shrieked at Creedy, terrified to know the answer.

'Killing two birds with one stone,' he replied.

They were dangerously close to the edge now, and she kicked along the ground desperately. Then, a shout. A male voice bellowing. A shadow. Sam was there.

Everything blurred. Creedy dropped her and tried to run. Sam caught him. A struggle. Natalya saw Sam's feet were too close to the edge. 'Watch out!' she screamed. Sam looked down. Creedy took advantage of his inattention, moved to push him.

Natalya, from the ground, kicked at Creedy's legs. He stumbled, and Sam stepped out of the way, wrestled Creedy's fingers off him. He twisted him away roughly and Creedy overbalanced, fell. His screams were shrill and high, like a woman's, on the way down.

Now that Lena had decided to die with Sofi, she was much calmer. Really, there wasn't much she was leaving behind. Her children of course, but they were better off without her. They would be teenagers soon, they wouldn't need her. Probably, they would come to hate her. At least this way they would remember her fondly. They would inherit the farmhouse, which would be sure to sell quickly now she wasn't standing in the way of every offer. Really, it was very simple. Once she got past the aching fear of the cold unknown beyond death – *just don't think about it* – it made great sense. Her heart rate slowed, acceptance infused her body.

'I'm very happy for you, Sofi,' she said. 'I won't drag you about for much longer. Let's head home, the scenic route.'

She guided Sofi back to the path. Was Roy Creedy watching? They walked a little further, in silence. The clouds had parted and the weak winter sun teased the tops of the trees. They were out in the open now. Traffic passing might even see them. It didn't matter. She no longer had to hide what she did, because there would be no repercussions. Dead women couldn't go to prison. Lena kept her eyes on the edge of the path, a metre of grass and then the drop. She took a deep breath.

'Stop for a moment, Sofi.'

'What is it?'

She encircled Sofi with her arms, felt the killing weight of her own body.

'I love you,' she said.

'I love you too,' Sofi said. Then her body tensed. 'Can you hear sirens?'

Lena stood back. Unmistakably, sirens howling. Befuddled, she wondered if somebody knew what she intended, was on their way to stop her. But then a darker thought occurred to her. *Her children.* Creedy had gone back on his word. He'd gone after her children.

The sirens grew closer. 'They're coming this way,' Sofi said.

As if to prove her point, an ambulance and police car zoomed past along the cliff road. Abruptly, the sirens stopped.

Sofi began to walk swiftly. 'Something's happened,' she said.

Lena dashed after her, aware that her plans were falling apart. 'Wait, Sofi, wait.'

But Sofi was running now, driven by some primitive curiosity that probably rose out of the trauma of Nikita's accident. They rounded the headland, saw the emergency vehicles parked haphazardly on the road's shoulder.

What Lena saw shocked her to her core. Impossibly, Natalya and Sam were there, surrounded by emergency workers. *It must be the children. Matthew, Anna.* Her poor heart, already bursting from the endless anxiety, was raw with fear. She put on a huge dash of panicked speed to catch up to Sofi. Natalya saw them approaching and ran towards them. She caught Lena in one arm, Sofi in the other. 'Oh, thank God. Thank God. You're alive.'

'What happened? The kids?'

'No, no. It was Creedy. Roy Creedy.' Natalya was dirty, bleeding from the forehead, stained with tears. 'He tried to kill me. Sam was there . . . he pushed him over.'

Sofi gasped. 'Creedy?'

Lena's knees began to shake. 'Is he dead?'

Natalya nodded.

Lena's legs gave way. The ground slammed into her. A sharp, hot pain shot through her wrist. A moment later, warm arms were around her. Sam.

'It's all right,' he said in a soothing voice, very close to her ear. 'I've got you, Lena, it's all right.'

The pain in Lena's wrist was monstrous. And yet she felt light and calm.

Creedy was dead. Sofi was alive.

Chaos swirled around her. Police and paramedics, shouting and crying. A slight, blonde paramedic splinted Lena's wrist, which was sitting at a strange angle, and strapped her onto a stretcher. One by one, car doors slammed shut, engines started, vehicles pulled away. Sam went with the police. Natalya, the grazes to her head dressed, insisted on climbing in the back of the ambulance with Lena. Sofi went in the front.

'Does it hurt?' Natalya said, as the doors closed and they moved off.

Lena couldn't answer, she just kept shaking her head.

Natalya slipped off her seatbelt and folded over, hair spilling over her hands. 'How on earth did he find us? Why after all these years?'

'I don't know,' Lena managed. Natalya and Sofi could never, *ever* find out that she knew Creedy was here, that she had put them in the path of so much danger. 'But he's gone now.'

Natalya sat up, nodded, then her face crumpled and she burst into sobs. She threw herself onto Lena. 'I love you, Lena. My baby sister. I love you so much. I thought I was going to die, and I couldn't bear it if we'd never seen each other again.'

Lena raised her good hand to stroke Natalya's hair, speechless.

'You must be wondering why Sam and I were there, but it wasn't to betray you, it was to help you.'

Actually, the fact that Sam and Natalya had been together had barely registered. She'd had more pressing matters on her mind.

'Please, please, nothing's more important in the world than that you say you love me too. That we can go back to being as close as we always were. That you can forgive me and that you'll trust me again. I won't let you down. I promise I won't.'

Lena took a deep breath. 'The slate is clean,' she said. 'Of course I love you.'

There was more to be said, but sobs choked her, so they clung together in the back of the ambulance and trusted that each understood the other.

Sofi sat with Lena and Natalya in the casualty ward of Briggsby hospital, waiting for an X-ray of Lena's broken wrist.

As soon as they had a moment alone, Sofi asked the question that was pressing on her brain. 'Where did Creedy come from?'

'I know nothing,' Lena said quickly.

'Straight from hell,' Natalya offered. 'And now he's gone back.'

Sofi felt a niggle of suspicion towards Lena. Back at the cliff, she hadn't expressed surprise at Natalya's mention of Roy Creedy; she had simply said, 'Is he dead?' before collapsing. Sofi said nothing, though. Lena hadn't been herself; though she seemed much more relaxed now. Perhaps it was the painkillers. Perhaps, when the drama was over and Lena was cleansed of the demon drink that had hold of her, she would ask again. But for now, she was just glad that Natalya hadn't gone off the cliff.

'We're going to have to tell the truth,' Sofi mused. 'To Sam, to the police when they come to talk to us.'

'Let's not mention the robbery,' Natalya said.

'We'll protect you,' Lena said firmly. 'Don't worry.'

Sofi glanced at her cousins, who were caught in each other's loving gazes. Some good had come of this trauma then.

'Well, the past is finally dead,' Natalya said.

'Yes,' Lena replied. 'Here's to the future.'

'Here's to the future,' Sofi said softly. 'Every single precious day of it.'

EPILOGUE
Summer, 2006

Natalya loved her new breasts. A thirty-eighth birthday present from Ted. She especially loved how they looked in a red Emanuel Ungaro gown as she posed for photos against a white roll of paper in *TV Star* magazine's Charing Cross Road studio. Finally, the photographer stopped snapping, the fan was turned off, and she returned to the sidelines to light a cigarette.

The journalist, a love-struck twenty-something who had watched the whole shoot, hurried up to her. He had already conducted a lengthy interview during which she had been at leisure to talk about herself for nearly an hour.

'Great photos,' he said. 'You're going to look so hot.'

Of course she was. She was hot property. The scandal over Roy Creedy's death had attracted international attention. The story was irresistible: three Russian girls orchestrating a Russian bride scam after the collapse of the Soviet Union; going on to huge successes; only to be tracked down years later. Natalya's star rose again quickly. Within a month, she had been offered the role of host on a new reality television show, *Brides to Order*, that followed the lives of foreign brides coming to England. It had been so successful that an American version was in planning. And she was heading to Los Angeles to host it.

It hadn't all been plain sailing. For weeks, she had woken up with nightmares about prison. But the slick defence lawyer Ted had helped her find in Chicago had told her not to worry: as long as she never confessed to stealing the car and jewellery, there was not enough evidence to convict her.

And so, finally, she would become the American princess she had always dreamt of being. More beautiful now than ever, with a wonderful boyfriend who was happy to let her go for three months of filming a year, and a load of money to spend on gowns and accessories to keep the blues at bay while they were apart. Although Sofi often spoke of Roy Creedy's death as though it were a sad event – 'Nobody deserves to die like that, and whether we like to admit it or not, we were ultimately responsible' – Natalya found she had little sympathy. She had nearly been dragged over the edge of a cliff by her hair. The right person had died that day.

She headed to the dressing room to change back into her street clothes and wipe off the heavy make-up. On her way out, the young journalist came up to her again, offering to call a cab.

'It's fine,' she said. 'It's a beautiful day. I'll walk.'

'It was a pleasure,' he said. 'A treat to have you in the office, to have a long chat with you.'

She smiled. 'Oh, no,' she said. 'The pleasure was all mine.'

Mama was waiting for them. They parked the car outside on the cobbled street, fumbled over the clips on the baby seat. New parents again after nearly ten years. Sofi was tired, sore, but in a state of utter bliss.

Mama leapt on her. 'Let me see him. Oh, he's perfect. Perfect.'

Sofi happily let Mama take the child, a little boy named Ivan after her father. Mama fussed while Julien went to the kitchen to make coffee. Finally, Mama handed her precious bundle back.

'Nikita's upstairs, drawing you a card,' she said.

'I'll go up and see him.' Baby Ivan began to cry, and Sofi rocked him gently. 'He'll need to meet his new brother.'

She moved up the stairs to Nikita's room. He had been home for five months now. The accident had set back his therapy and there were many things he had to relearn. But he was slowly improving. Just having him in the house was a blessing; being part of his therapy, part of bringing him into the world, was the ultimate reward. She had scaled back her work commitments again and again, and finally, just before Ivan was born, she had sold the entire business to Jack Merryweather. Now she would only work as a paid designer, for Jack. And for Francette, who had been installed as executive officer of the European division.

With her free hand, she gently knocked on Nikita's bedroom door and pushed it open. Nikita sat on his bed, surrounded by the usual tidy piles of paper and felt pens, all with their lids precisely aligned. He saw her, barely reacted.

'Nikita,' she said. 'Meet your little brother, Ivan.'

'Ivan,' he repeated. Then he offered her a piece of paper, folded carefully in half.

She laid Ivan down on Nikita's bed, between the drawings, so she could look at the card properly. On the front he had written *Welcome home, Mama*. Inside was a picture of a washing machine.

'It's beautiful, darling,' Sofi said, glancing up.

Nikita leaned over his baby brother, touching his soft earlobes with sacred awe.

'What do you think?' she asked him.

'He's very little.'

'He is.'

'And I'm very big.'

'Shall we keep him?' she joked.

Nikita looked up, shrugged. 'Of course.'

Sofi laughed. 'I think so too.'

'For God's sake, you kids. Settle down.' Lena always hated it when she raised her voice at Matthew and Anna, but they were out of control, running madly through the rooms of the farmhouse playing a brutal game of tag that had already seen Matthew stub his toe and Anna graze her knees.

'They're okay,' Sam said from his vantage point at the top of a stepladder. 'They're just bored. Three weekends in a row up here watching us paint. I'd be bored too.'

Lena clapped her hands together hard. 'Come on, you two. Outside. Play until the sun goes down, and then we'd better head home.'

Home, to the flat in Briggsby. Which would only be their home for one more week.

Sam climbed down and came to stand next to her. He had off-white paint in his hair. 'Have I missed anything?' he said.

'Looks fine to me.'

He nuzzled her neck. 'I'm glad. If you're happy then I'm happy.' He straightened, put his paint roller down. 'Next Saturday, after we've moved in . . . shall we have a bottle of champagne? To celebrate?'

Lena shook her head. The nightmarish fear of what she had almost done circled. 'No. Never. It's obviously not good for me, so it's just best if I stay away from it.'

'Your decision,' he said. 'We'll be drunk on love instead.'

'Precisely.'

She considered his familiar face and a pang of regret stabbed her. The years they had been apart. A waste of life. After Roy Creedy, she was determined not to waste another second of it.

He leaned down to her, placed his cheek against her hair. 'I'm looking forward to our lives here, Lena. It's like a dream. Us back together. You forgiving me.' He stood back and gave her a teasing smile. 'Now, that was the biggest miracle of all.'

She laughed cautiously. 'I'm sorry if I was stubborn.'

'I don't blame you,' he said.

She put her arms around him. He smelled like paint and soap and perspiration all at once. Her beautiful Sam. She had almost lost him. The children. Everything. This new life, in the farmhouse that Sofi had paid for them to rebuild and redecorate, was twice as sweet for the contrast with what might have been. She knew for certain that she was the luckiest woman alive.

'We do what we do, and we can't go back,' Lena said, listening to his heart beating. 'But in the end, everyone deserves to be forgiven.'

'Even me?' he said.

'Yes, even you,' she replied. 'Even me.'

Acknowledgements

Thanks are due to so many people who helped me research, develop, write and edit this book. Selwa Anthony, Vanessa Radnidge, Nicola O'Shea, Louise Cusack, Ron Serdiuk and the Queensland Writers Centre provided invaluable advice and support at every stage. Eni Oken helped with details of jewellery-making, and her own beautiful work provided a model for Sofi's pieces; Joanne Sandhu shared her memories of the Soviet Union in the eighties, even the repressed memories; Shannon Breen gave me Roy Creedy's home town; Faye Booth was my contact on the ground in England; Paul Brandon shared his experiences of British television in the nineties; Katherine Howell knew all about accidents; Nicole Ruckels and Howard Copping gave me Richelieu in all its loving detail. My gratitude, particularly, goes to Nicole, who grew up there and let me plunder her fondest memories. All misuses of information are entirely my own. Thanks to Ian Golledge for *Skin Crawlers*, the best title for a B-grade movie that I never thought up. Eternal gratitude and love to Kate Morton for her fantastic cover quote, and for being a true kindred spirit. Thanks to all my writing students, for asking the questions that make me think. Finally, I lovingly acknowledge the time and patience of my family, particularly my mother, my husband and my two magnificent children.

KF, April 2008

www.ingramcontent.com/pod-product-compliance
Ingram Content Group UK Ltd.
Pitfield, Milton Keynes, MK11 3LW, UK
UKHW041300180426
11947UKWH00009B/589